GREATER EVIL

CHAMPIONS OF FATE: BOOK 2

NOEL COUGHLAN

Cover Illustration by MiblArt (https://miblart.com/)

Edited by Proofed to Perfection (http://www.proofedtoperfection.com/)

Proofed by C.B. Moore (https://www.cbmoore-editor.com/home-1)

Published by Photocosmological Press (http://photocosm.org/)

Paperback Edition: ISBN:978-1-910206-21-8

For Padraig & Vanessa.

1

———————

The distant chime of the doorbell made Drinith freeze in the middle of turning a page of the notebook. She reflexively glanced across her study at the bookshelves that hid the secret escape door. The ridiculousness of her reaction made her laugh out her held breath. No assassin would announce his coming in such a fashion. She had become much too paranoid.

She glanced with irritation at the bare walls. When Epmar, her predecessor as Meritocrat Hax, retired to a country estate on the shard of Noster, she had taken everything that had once adorned them with her. The empty hooks mocked Drinith's failure to stamp her presence on the room. She had filled only two hooks in the year since Epmar's departure. Impaled on one was a straw doll, frayed and battered and missing its flower crown, that Quiescat had insisted she must keep. The other bore a large brass map of her home shard, Rhumgad. The kingdom names and boundaries etched on it, from the highlands in the north to the basin of the Wandering Sea in the south, had been swept away by Magian the Infinite's armies around the time of her birth. One day, Drinith would return to wrest Rhumgad from his iron grip and restore her realm, Kaplar. But for now, she must content herself that the blockade of his empire by Gyre and its allies had stymied his greater ambitions.

Smoothing a crackling page, she let her attention return to the notebook.

A great cauldron simmers on a fire. The chunks of wood beneath are shaped like dragons. As the cauldron nears boiling, bubbles disturb its fizzing surface, each warped by a different smiling face. The tops of the bubbles curve like talons. As they sink again, they whisper too softly to understand. More and more bubbles rise until the faces become a froth; their whispers expand into an impossible roar. A shadow is visible in the foam. A hand and forearm, green-black, delicate and feminine, rises out of the spitting churn. The dragons beneath rise and the cauldron overturns, spilling its boiling water across the floor. The draining liquid reveals a gleaming dagger. Its pommel has an amethyst engraved with a dragon's head.

It was one of four prophetic visions of Versifer, the late poet and Oracle of Godsdoor. And friend, though the notion made Drinith queasy given that she had spurned his romantic advances. He had believed the arm in his vision belonged to her. She and Quiescat read the prophesies almost every day, hoping to decipher them. She could recite most of them without recourse to the book, but they remained as enigmatic and sinister as ever.

Before the visions, brief notes, lines of unfinished verse (often scratched out), musings, reminders, and doodles littered the pages— the flitting ramblings of a restless mind. The leaf after the last vision had been ripped out, wounding the book. Versifer must have written the poem he had dedicated to her on it. She should have never asked him to burn it. She longed to remember the words, but she had been too mortified to take them in when he thrust the poem upon her. If she had known what was about to happen to him... After the missing page, the book was blank, untouched by his quill, a painful reminder of a life cut short.

Hearing Fenvar's signature sequence of soft raps on the door, Drinith tucked the book into a drawer and straightened the documents on her desk. "Come in."

The door opened just wide enough for the butler to step across the threshold. Drinith wondered how she maintained such an immaculate appearance. Her snowy bowl crop never had a stray hair. Her teal and black uniform was always crisp and clean, though she worked from before dawn to late into the night. Drinith had been fortunate to keep her services, and Fenvar hadn't followed her former mistress, Epmar, into self-imposed retirement.

"Meritocrats Aretro Falier and Thaxen Savarel have come calling," Fenvar said. "I showed them to the parlor and arranged refreshments."

Aside from a brief introduction at a ducal reception, Drinith had no interaction with Aretro. As Ambassador General, she had negotiated truces with most of Gyre's adversaries in the Short War. But success in Gyre always drew suspicion. Her accomplishments had earned a diverse assortment of detractors among her peers, who damned her as a self-aggrandizing appeaser. Rumors swirled in the dark corridors and alcoves of the Parliament of Merit that she might soon be ousted.

Thaxen was a different matter. The position of the Meritocracy's Intelligencer General was impregnable. She was too useful to Gyre and too dangerous for any potential rival to contemplate moving against her. Thaxen had never made a social call to the Hax Mansion before. Instead, when she had needed to speak to Drinith, Thaxen had simply summoned her with the thinnest veneer of politeness possible. Drinith chafed at Thaxen's overbearing influence over her, but extricating herself from it would make a dangerous enemy.

Something serious must have happened. Gyre's coalition against the tyrant Magian might have unraveled.

"Inform them I shall join them shortly," Drinith said. "Ask Quiescat to meet me outside the parlor." Though she leaned on his counsel, the meritocrats, jealous of their lofty status as oligarchs of the Halcyon Republic, would take offense if he wandered in and plunked himself down beside them uninvited.

Fenvar slipped away with a graceful bow. Drinith lifted her medallion headpiece off its stand. It bore the sigil of the House of

Hax, an alerion taking flight. Resting it on her head, she took a deep breath and headed for the parlor.

Quiescat awaited her by the entrance. Despite his customary white cowl and receding blue hair, the dark eyes the preservators had given him made the lean Rhumgadian lowlander look like a stranger. In a sense, he was. He hadn't yet recovered from the loss of his oracular gift.

"Let's get this over with," he muttered. He pushed open the doors and stepped out of the way for Drinith to enter first.

The parlor always felt to Drinith like a hostile courtroom. While she bristled at the condemnatory stares of her Hax predecessors in their ornately framed portraits, the prospect of banishing Epmar's ancestors to a less frequented corner of the mansion made her uncomfortable.

The two meritocrats sat together on a couch. Aretro's medallion headdress, bearing her emblem, the centicore, peeped out of a burst of whitening red curls. Despite her fiery orange complexion, her large laurel green eyes gave her face disarming sincerity and softness.

Thaxen provided a striking contrast. Dark of hair, her gray face with its chiseled lines made her a forbidding presence at the best of times. Her emblem, the mandrake root, hung proudly on her broad forehead.

"I hope you don't mind," Drinith said as she swept inside and shook their hands. "I invited my steward to join us." She alighted on the couch across from her guests.

Aretro's eyes bulged with surprise. A mirthless grin creased Thaxen's harsh face, but irritation smoldered in her black eyes as she regarded Quiescat. "It's always a delight to meet the Oracle of Godsdoor."

"I'm no longer an oracle," Quiescat said stiffly as he took a seat.

"True, you now lack the prophetic gift associated with the position, but surely there's nobody more qualified to claim the title. Do you harbor no hope of returning to your temple?"

"Its charred ruins, perhaps."

"To business," Thaxen growled, knitting her fingers together and turning her attention to Drinith. "Aretro has a problem that you may be able to help resolve."

Aretro nearly choked as she swallowed the mouthful of cake she had been chewing. "Yes," she croaked. She sipped her tea and locked eyes with Drinith. "We have convinced most of our opponents in the Short War to bring the conflict to a long overdue cessation and join our blockade of Rhumgad. It's in all our interests to check Magian's ambitions."

Thaxen's small mouth tightened. "All except the Shopkeepers."

Aretro directed a sideways frown at her colleague. "Yes, the Ophigeens intend to fight on, distracting us, diverting resources from our campaign."

"But, surely, facing the combined strength of their four rivals, their logical course is to make peace," Quiescat said.

"The other republics, Numenal, Laxur, and Helifer, have entered a truce with us," Aretro said. "But they restrict their cooperation to Rhumgad. They won't coordinate with us in defending against Ophigeen aggression, much less take offensive action against them. Pro-Short War factions remain powerful in all the republics, including our own. Push our coalition too far beyond its stated goals and it will splinter." She took another sip of tea. "To secure the Ophigeens' aid or, at least, the end of their active hostility, we must show them a truce is in their interest." All the while she spoke, her gaze remained fixed on her host, demanding reciprocal attention. Shying from its intensity, Drinith focused on pouring herself some yellow tea.

Thaxen studied the fireplace to conceal a burgeoning smirk. Oblivious, Aretro continued. "The Ophigeens are a vain people, convinced of their moral superiority."

Drinith sipped from her cup before her own smile could slip out. Aretro's description applied equally to many Gyran meritocrats.

"I'm sure they are most moral for slavers," Thaxen quipped.

"They are mistrustful and quick to take offense," Aretro said, still focused on Drinith. "The assurances of Gyre won't convince them to help us. But you might persuade them."

An icy chill raced up Drinith's spine. "What do you mean?"

"You uncovered Magian's plot in Gyre," Thaxen said. "You defeated his assassins. You are the rightful heir to a realm brutally subjugated by him. You understand better than any other meritocrat the threat he poses."

"The Diarchs of Ophigee have formally invited you to visit their court," Aretro said. "They are offering you a chance to convince them that Magian poses a genuine threat."

"Then I must take it," Drinith said, repressing the urge to spring from her seat. "How soon must I depart?"

"A dragon, the *Piquant Buss*, will depart for Ophigee tomorrow morning."

"We'll be ready," Drinith promised.

Thaxen and Aretro exchanged glances. Aretro cleared her throat. "The Ophigeens are prickly at the best of times." She grimaced. "Their invitation extends to you alone. You may take whoever you choose on the journey to Ophigee but the authorities there won't permit them to disembark, not even a personal attendant."

"Apparently, they abide no servants except their own slaves," Thaxen said. "Status based on inheritance is an abomination, or some such nonsense."

Quiescat bolted upright. "No!"

Before two meritocrats' disapproving glares, he faltered, mumbled apologies, and slumped back in his chair. Ignoring the demands implicit in their scowls to reprimand him for his impertinence, Drinith said, "It doesn't sound very safe. Assassins still stalk me."

Quiescat seized upon her point. "Exactly. She's under constant threat from Magian."

Thaxen sneered. "And you'll protect her? You're the oldest courtesar I've ever encountered."

Queasy dismay gripped Drinith. Not only had Thaxen mocked

Quiescat's negligible combat prowess, but, far worse, she had insinuated that he and his adopted daughter might be lovers, an insult sufficient to provoke a lesser man to retaliate. Thaxen wouldn't tolerate any slight, no matter how deserved, and her enmity could be as lethal as any poison. Quiescat folded his arms and fumed in silence. A smile slid onto his face. He must have taken some consolation in his refusal to be goaded.

"The Ophigeens guarantee your safety as long as you remain their guest," Aretro said.

Thaxen smirked. "If Magian kills you while you're under their protection, they'll be honor-bound to join our coalition against him. So your death won't be in vain."

Drinith bristled. Why did Thaxen toss about gibes with such abandon? Did Quiescat's presence really rile her to such petulance? More likely, Thaxen intended her mockery as a reminder she was the Intelligencer General and would brook no challenge from anyone. Drinith would later make clear to Thaxen she wouldn't tolerate casual bullying and humiliation under her roof. But for now, with Quiescat and Aretro present, it was best to keep silent.

"It won't come to that," Aretro promised. "The Ophigeens will ensure your safety from hostile third parties. Our ambassador to their court, Griman Epitan, will guide you during your stay. She's well versed with their customs and will ensure you don't fall foul of their etiquette."

"I will go," Drinith said.

Thaxen stood. "We'll leave you to prepare. Come, Aretro."

With a regretful nod, her companion put aside her half-eaten scone and bowl of tea and plodded toward the door. Drinith and Quiescat rose from their seats.

"Oh yes," Thaxen said. "There's another matter I need to discuss with Drinith. A private matter." She shot a glare at Quiescat.

"Perhaps, Quiescat, you might show Aretro our library." Drinith said. "I understand she is an avid potter. There's a fine collection of tomes on the subject that might interest her." Drinith, being incurious about the craft, didn't know if the works would prove of value to a renowned expert like Aretro, but her guest looked pleased with the prospect. It occasioned her first genuine grin since her arrival.

Drinith kept silent until the door clicked shut. "Some of your comments were in poor taste, Thaxen. In particular when you compared Quiescat to a courtesar."

Thaxen shrugged. "Frankly, I don't care if I offended him. He forgets his place."

"And what about offending me? Am I not a meritocrat like you?"

Thaxen showed Drinith a razor-thin smile. "I'll remember, if you will. I promised Epmar I'd look out for your welfare. Quiescat's former oracular ability doesn't entitle him to special treatment in Gyre. And you were gifted your position by your predecessor. You're an outsider, a foreigner. Your royal ancestry, your claim to the Blood Crown of Kaplar, places you under suspicion in a republic that despises the very concept of monarchy."

"If I'm so mistrusted, why was Epmar permitted to make me a meritocrat?"

"You can use a thing and suspect it at the same time."

"And I'm a thing."

Thaxen pursed her lips. "I'm simply observing the reality of your position. You can't afford to flaunt your exoticism before our colleagues and, dare I say it ..."

"Dare."

"Eccentric weakness. A meritocrat is a leader, not a follower. She is nobody's puppet."

Drinith raised her chin. "You pulled Epmar's strings."

"She could have cut those strings if she chose, but she refused to turn her back on her house, her people, and her state. She is a genuine patriot." Thaxen's eyes narrowed. "I cannot say the same of you yet."

"You question my loyalty, my word!" Drinith fumed.

Thaxen cackled. "You may have committed your head to Gyre, but your heart's fealty perhaps lies elsewhere." She prodded

Drinith's chest. "Don't deny that old dream of reclaiming your lost realm doesn't smolder in there somewhere. You must extinguish it before somebody stamps it out for you. You're a meritocrat now. Like your oracle's temple, Kaplar's dead; another autocracy best forgotten."

Drinith bit back her anger. Best not goad Thaxen too much or she might follow through on her implied threat to Quiescat.

Thaxen's gaze roamed the portraits on the walls, fixed on one. Ambling over to it, she gave the impression of studying it in detail. "This trip will help you. You'll be free of Quiescat's influence while you're in Ophigee. You'll learn to depend on yourself. Then, when you return, you'll be ready to put him aside. Pack Quiescat off to one of your country estates to enjoy a well-deserved retirement. The gossips can sharpen their tongues at someone else's expense."

Perhaps she acted in what she considered to be Drinith's best interest, but her ultimatum was no less stinging. "I'll make my own decisions about my servants, thank you."

"Of course," Thaxen murmured, continuing to scrutinize the portrait. Why should its subject be the focus of her fascination? Drinith didn't even know the woman's name, much less her history.

"That's your right as a meritocrat and the head of your house." Thaxen turned a vexed gaze toward Drinith. "Just make sure your servants serve you and not the other way around." She strolled over to the door. Opening it, she paused at the threshold. Without looking back, she said, "Good luck in Ophigee. I'll collect Aretro. No need to show us out. You've enough to do."

In the instant of Drinith's hesitation, Thaxen sauntered away, leaving her threats to weigh on the air like a coming thunderstorm.

Quiescat was Drinith's father in all but name. She couldn't send him away. He was one of the few people she could trust. She'd be a fool to relinquish his sage counsel. There must be some compromise short of banishment that would sate Thaxen and Quiescat's other shadowy enemies in the Meritocracy. There had to be.

Her cheeks warmed as she remembered her elevation to a meritocrat. Her exultation felt so naive now. No matter how high she climbed, the ground always shifted beneath her, threatening to topple her.

The gods must be punishing her for her sin. The blockade of Rhumgad had been built on a lie. Magian hadn't instigated the attack she foiled at Crevastival, as Gyre believed. No, her former adviser, Gelasin, had been behind the plot.

2

————

"I understand you could glimpse the future," Aretro said to Quiescat as they entered the library. The casualness of her question made it even more painful. His loss, his humiliation, wasn't a topic for idle conversation. Evidently, the meritocrat's reputation overstated her tact.

Tamping down his temper, Quiescat smiled and nodded. He had more than enough enemies among the meritocrats without adding the ambassador general to their ranks. "Alas, that power is lost." He rubbed an eye, felt the fragile ball of tissue beneath the lid. The Tear had always been so hard in comparison.

"I imagine such a power could be as much a bane as a boon," Aretro remarked.

Quiescat grabbed a massive volume at random off the nearest shelf and opened it. "I think you might find this as fascinating as I do," he said, desperate to change the topic. He quickly scanned the page for clues as to the book's subject, but he struggled to make sense of the curious names and colorful language. It was in an archaic pyratic dialect.

Aretro's face lit up with excitement. "I recognize this book! It's *A General History of the Dragon Pyrates*, a particular favorite of mine."

She lifted it from Quiescat's grasp. "I first read this as a young girl. I have since become somewhat of an expert on it, if I do say so." She leafed through the volume. "The text has suffered countless alterations, great and small, through the centuries. My dream is to find a first edition. I wonder how old this copy is." She studied the title page and sighed. "A pity. My earliest copy predates this one by nearly a hundred years. I've spent many happy hours poring over this book. 'The Rise of the Emperor of the Crevast' is my favorite section. Not, of course, that we would ever want to suffer such a tyrant again."

"Of course," Quiescat echoed.

"What's your favorite part?" Aretro asked with earnest enthusiasm.

"The same as you," Quiescat said, bracing for a follow-up question he couldn't answer.

"Aretro, time to go," Thaxen barked from the threshold. Never had Quiescat been so relieved to see the crabby meritocrat.

"Oh?" Aretro closed the book and passed it back to Quiescat. "It's a shame we have to leave so soon." She winked at Quiescat. "Next time, we'll have a long chat about the *General History*, I promise."

"I'll look forward to it," Quiescat said, resolving to find a more recent edition in Gyran pyratic and read it from cover to cover.

"Did you know it had a much more convoluted title originally?" Aretro asked. "*A General History of the Feats and Conquests of the Most Illustrious Dragon Pyrate Captains and Kings from the Cracking of the World to the Silver Age.* Quite a mouthful, isn't it?"

"Aretro, why are you wasting my time by bandying niceties with Drinith's help?" Thaxen growled from the door. "Let us depart and leave this servant to get back to his duties."

Putting the book aside, Quiescat followed the pair at a discreet distance until they exited the mansion. He nodded to Fenvar, who hovered by the shut parlor doors. "Is Drinith inside?"

"She's alone."

Quiescat knocked tentatively.

"Come in," Drinith called from within.

He entered and sat across from her. Fenvar slipped in with the stealth of an assassin and gathered the crockery.

"Fenvar, please ask Jarma to join us," Drinith said.

The butler, balancing a laden silver tray in one hand, nodded and stalked out the door.

Quiescat leaned forward and rubbed the back of his neck. "I don't like this trip to Ophigee. I have heard many odd stories about that strange island in the Halo Sea."

Drinith rose from her seat and stabbed the fire with a poker. "At least I won't be sitting around here, doing nothing. If I can gain Ophigee's cooperation, it'll bring the liberation of Kaplar a step nearer." She threw two fresh logs on the flames, raising a flurry of sparks.

"True," Quiescat conceded. "But you must be careful. You're being sent there because you're..." He couldn't bring himself to finish.

Drinith directed an amused glance over her shoulder at him. "Expendable?"

Quiescat nodded.

The swish of fabric announced Jarma's entry. Dressed in plain black from head to toe, her resemblance to Drinith was remarkable, but Quiescat prided himself on being able to tell them apart. Jarma's nose was slightly smaller, her jaw more pronounced, her eyes a fraction further apart. At one time, her more diffident bearing would have given her away, but since her elevation to Drinith's companion, she had learned to carry herself with a regal dignity her mistress could scarcely match.

Drinith brushed her palms together. "Jarma, please sit." She gestured at the seat she had vacated. "Perhaps, Quiescat, you might fill Jarma in on what happened this morning. I have to get something. I'll return presently."

As Jarma settled in Drinith's seat, Quiescat's surge of irritation took him by surprise. The girl had only acted according to her mistress's instructions. He forced a smile and recounted the meritocrats' visit. He had just finished when Drinith re-entered. She sat down beside Jarma. Drinith held a slim black box that she tapped against her palm.

"We must accompany you to Ophigee, of course," Jarma said. "Obviously, we can't—"

Drinith waved her silent. "Quiescat will accompany me. Woad Glastum will come, too, to protect us on the journey"—the ex-mercenary was an ideal bodyguard and fiercely loyal—"but I need you to stay here." Smiling, she offered the box to Jarma. Quiescat craned his neck to peer at its contents as Jarma opened it. The gold brooch bore the badge of House Hax, an alerion taking flight.

Jarma rested it in her hand and stared at it in disbelief. No, Drinith couldn't have...

"It's yours," she said. "Put it on."

"Only meritorians..." Jarma began.

Rising, Drinith scooped the brooch from Jarma's palm and bent down to fix it to her dress. "I'll file the formal adoption documents with the Office of Merit this very day."

Quiescat couldn't decide what dismayed him more—Jarma's sudden elevation or the lack of warning. Drinith's rueful glance begged him not to make a scene. He managed a brittle smile as Jarma turned toward him, beaming with triumph.

She hopped to her feet and hugged Drinith. "I promise I will prove worthy of this honor."

"I haven't any doubt of it," Drinith said as they parted.

Quiescat rose and offered his hand to Jarma. "Congratulations, Meritorian."

She shook it with enthusiasm. He feared to raise his gaze from their clasped hands. His false bonhomie couldn't hide his anger if their eyes met this close. As soon as her grip loosened, he withdrew far enough to risk looking up again. "I'll leave you two to celebrate. Perhaps, Drinith, you might call on me in the library when you have a chance."

"Of course."

Jarma darted uneasy glances at both of them, evidently picking up on the strain in their voices.

Servants eyed Quiescat with mute apprehension as he swept by them on the way to the library. He slammed the door shut and paced the floor as he attempted to hammer his red-hot temper into a coherent argument.

The opening door halted him mid-step. He whirled to face Drinith.

"I didn't tell you because I knew how you'd take it," she said, preempting his question, "and I haven't time to be arguing. Making Jarma a meritorian protects both of you if anything happens to me."

"It makes me her inferior," he said. There lay the root of his anger. For all his conviction that losing his oracular power had taught him humility, the old vanity remained. He was the same old fool he had always been. His cheeks warmed. "She can barely tolerate me."

"Better her than a stranger handpicked by the Parliament of Merit to inherit my title. Any such appointee might banish you to some backwater on Noster, or even find a pretext to turn you out on the streets. Kaplar would be lost to Magian forever."

I don't care about Kaplar. I only care about you. He could not protect her from whatever danger she faced in Ophigee. It was oddly comforting that not only hurt pride spurred his anger, but also a sense of powerlessness. He wasn't quite as peevish as he imagined. "I suppose you're right."

"You must help Jarma adapt to her new status," Drinith said. "Prepare her in case I don't return."

And who will prepare me? He had lost everything else he cared about. Her death alone in some foreign land was too painful to contemplate. "I will do my best."

Nodding solemnly, she patted his shoulder. "I know you will. If you excuse me, I must make ready for our departure."

As she strolled out of the library, he wrestled in silence with the urge to tell her not to go to Ophigee. Hopefully, the dread twisting his gut wasn't a bad omen.

3

The next morning, Drinith strolled along the pier to the *Piquant Buss*. Quiescat had accompanied her, as had Woad Glastum. Perian, the remaining member of her party, wore a thick black bonnet and several layers over her teal uniform as though the maid expected to march into a blizzard. Quite short, she looked overloaded with the cases she had insisted on carrying. The fevered tinge to her maroon face was no doubt due to this combination of exertion and overdress. Drinith hadn't been eager to bring along an inveterate chatterer like Perian, but Jarma had asserted that it would be unseemly for her to travel without a personal servant, and Perian had proved to be the first and most enthusiastic volunteer from among Drinith's maids. She lumbered beside the stubbornly silent Woad, harassing him with inane babble between grunts.

Perian shrieked and dropped the cases as a shadow loomed over them. Her overreaction irritated Drinith despite her own creeping trepidation as the silhouette of the dragon's long neck split the sky and its head swallowed the sun. How could anyone endure living in that flimsy wooden band around its head, thrown about by the creature's every twitch? It let out a mighty roar and plunged again out of sight.

"I never realized dragons were so big," Perian said as she scrambled to pick up the baggage. "I've seen them from a distance, of course, but I've never been this close. It feels so...monstrous."

Woad fingered the hilt of his sword as he scowled at a pair of passing dockhands. Gold beads adorned the braids of the stocky blue-black lowlander's beard. The Hax alerion had been painted on his breastplate, but the ghost of its former emblem, the snake-hafted double-headed axe, peeped from around its edges.

"Woad, help her," Quiescat urged.

Woad arched an amused eyebrow. "I'm here to guard the meritocrat."

Sighing, Quiescat bent down to aid Perian. He looked surprised and a little alarmed at the weight of the case he picked up.

"Perian, you can go back to the mansion if it's too much for you," Drinith said hopefully.

"I promised to go and I won't let you down, Meritocrat," the maid declared with dignified resolve.

Drinith let the matter rest. Perian was so headstrong, nothing short of an order would send her back to the mansion.

Quiescat's reward for his generosity was to be stuck beside her. Grimacing, he nodded along to her prattle.

Drinith hastened to the gangplank. The sight of the busy saddledeck below drew a melancholic flutter. Memories of her last voyage by dragon haunted her. Of her companions then, only Quiescat and Jarma remained. Epmar was in self-imposed exile. The rest, friend and foe, were dead. Little could Drinith have imagined the cost of that journey.

Cloth-wrapped bales were still being lowered into the cargo hatch as they descended the gangplank. A sweet florid smell with a hint of saltiness wafted on the breeze.

"Smells like brineflowers," Quiescat said, breathing in deeply. "A reminder of home. I always loved the beautiful blooms along the Wandering Sea. They must be destined for Ophigee's perfumeries."

"I doubt they are brineflowers," Woad said, his restless gaze flitting across the deck and back up the gangplank, "given the embargo on trade with Rhumgad."

"Unless some enterprising meritocrat bought a consignment before the blockade began." Drinith grinned, pleased at the shrewdness of her insight.

The crew ignored the strangers on their deck and continued about their business.

Quiescat sniffed and pointed to the windowed compartment on the quarterdeck. "We should try the whereabout. The captain or the saddlemaster must be there."

A tall, thin woman emerged from the whereabout. Her hair was a mess of blonde curls, her skin a deep red. She wore black except for an elaborately embroidered waistcoat, its once-bright images faded like an old tapestry. She bounded down the steps to them. "I'm Grak Byxtin, the saddlemaster. Apologies for my tardiness in greeting you. Captain Gular has already boarded the headstall." She enthusiastically shook everyone's hand in the order of their proximity. "I was reviewing the report from the lighthouse at Themestra. We're in for some rough weather, I'm afraid. A storm is approaching."

"From Rhumgad?" Quiescat asked. "It's surely too early for the rainy season."

"Nothing so fierce. We'll be able to fly through it. But it will last several days, and it may knock us off course a bit. I'm afraid you must stay below deck for its duration."

It was only then that Drinith noticed Perian's silence. The girl's wide-eyed, disbelieving gaze struggled to swallow everything. The scrape of the gangway as it slipped down from the pier drew her wistful glance. This was a new world to her, an utter revelation, and she was adrift in it. As Grak passed her a harness and lanyard, she stared at them with utter incomprehension. Drinith helped her put it on. "You'll be fine," she promised. "I'll look after you."

As the *Piquant Buss* lifted from its perch, Drinith found it hard to believe that a tempest would strike so soon. Even the movement of the Crevast air, normally so vigorous, hardly amounted to a gentle breeze after the dragon had cleared the shelter of the perches.

"Hoist the sails!" Grak yelled. "For what they're worth," she groused, "with the Crevast holding its breath."

Drinith leaned over the bulwark to stare back at the floating archipelago blinking in and out of view to the sweep of the dragon's wings. A cluster of orange edifices—the Ducal Palace, the Dragon Church, the Parliament of Merit: the heart of Gyran power—topped the pink cityscape. Some distance beyond them, the bone-white peak of the Grand Preservatory had turned red as though it wounded the ruddy morning sky. She watched the now familiar buildings shrink and merge into a blur.

Every beat of dragon wings lightened her heart. The land anchored her to her past, ensnared her in others' mazy intrigues. If only she could put them aside for good and be free to wander the Crevast. Grak might let her join the crew of the *Piquant Buss* if she asked. She could live out the rest of her days not as a princess or a meritocrat, but as a draker. It was an idle fantasy. She could never abandon her birthright, however enticing the prospect. At least this journey gave her some respite from her life until she reached Ophigee.

Grak showed Drinith and her companions to a cabin under the quarterdeck.

"I'm sorry more salubrious quarters aren't available," Grak said, blushing. "But you specified you would share one room. The cabin across the way is unused and at your disposal."

Perian looked about with horror, but the room was palatial compared to where Drinith had stayed on the *Surly Bonnacon*. They each had a bunk bed, and the cabin had a large window. "This will be more than sufficient."

Grak nodded gratefully. "I'll leave you to settle in."

That night the tempest struck, tossing Drinith and her companions about in their webbed bunks. The saddle heaved and groaned as if the storm itself rode on the dragon's back. Lightning flashed through the window's shutters. The blurry drumbeat of rain against the hull and the creak of straining webbing couldn't drown out the dragon and the thunder roaring at each other. On it went, an endless tumult battering the senses, tautening Drinith's nerves until she verged on screaming.

An old man with bedraggled gray hair and a shriveled, weather-beaten face swaggered into the cabin with a flickering lampstone in one hand and a swinging bucket in the other. His untroubled grin reassured her, and the storm lost a little of its fierceness. He tied off his lanyard in the middle of the cabin and made hand gestures, the meaning of which eluded her. He offered a small bottle of water and a chunk of bread to each of the passengers. Drinith rubbed a little of her share against her alicorn bracelet to discount the presence of poison. Thankfully, the bracelet didn't heat, so her meal was safe to eat, but her roiling stomach only permitted a sip of the water and she couldn't bring herself to nibble the hard bread.

The storm rampaged through the next day and the day after. Exhaustion numbed her terror enough to let her drift into a fitful and nightmarish sleep.

Magian filled the darkness. He stood before her, a silhouette sometimes of a man, sometimes of a monster.

"Quiescat has betrayed you!" he boomed. "He wanted a more submissive princess, so he has replaced you with Jarma and given you to me!"

"No!" she cried. Quiescat would never betray her. She was his daughter in all but blood.

"Yes! He has put a glamor on Jarma, so she believes she is you! Just as he mesmerized the warrior who stole you from Kaplar at the moment of its destruction."

"I am Drinith of Kaplar!"

"Jarma has become Drinith of Kaplar and you are but her shadow! Because you're weak! Because you trusted! Because you loved! Gelasin warned you, but you ignored him!"

"I defeated the pentaculars."

Magian took on the pentaculars' bland blue-black countenance, the face of her death. "The blind man, the Widow, and the cockerel defeated my assassins! You're the liar who stole their victory!"

"I defeated Gelasin."

"Gelasin defeated himself! He wielded you to cut his own throat!"

"I'll defeat you!"

"You've already lost! You're already mine!"

Tendrils of darkness reached out and wrapped around her, tighter and tighter. Magian roared with triumphant laughter as he loomed over her like a mountain. Black strings bound to her limbs, making her dance according to his whims.

She started as thunder clapped. Disentangling the webbing snarled around her, Drinith could hardly breathe from shock. It was a dream, nothing more. She looked over at Quiescat tossing in his sleep, trapped in his own private nightmare, his groans lost in the storm. Shame weighed on her heart. He had sacrificed everything for her. How could she question his loyalty, even in a dream? If some errant part of Drinith doubted him, the fault lay with her, not Quiescat.

While the heavens raged, she wrestled with this pernicious blot of angst. When the *Piquant Buss* finally passed through the storm, Drinith and her companions emerged from their protective cocoons and climbed on shaky legs up to the saddledeck. Perian had black rings under her bloodshot eyes and a grim expression. Drinith, too, struggled to mimic the jubilant grins of the crew.

Woad pointed starboard. "You can see the Halo Sea of Ophigee." As he helped a somewhat unsteady Perian over to the starboard bulwark to get a better view, Drinith caught Quiescat's arm. "I need to talk to you alone."

His smile waned as he scrutinized her. Glancing about, he drew her to the larboard bulwark. "What's wrong?"

Woad fixed his frowning gaze on them but didn't approach.

"I had a nightmare." Drinith shared every detail she could remember. "I'm sorry. I feel so ashamed, but I had to tell you."

"You can tell me anything," Quiescat said. "You know that. Particularly about dreams. That is my specialty, sifting them for meaning, whether they are glimpses of the future or peeks into an unhappy mind. Thanks to my years of experience, I deduce you doubt yourself more than me. Suspicion is understandable after Gelasin's betrayal. He was as much a father to you as I am."

"You shouldn't put yourself on the same level as that traitor," she chided gently.

"Signal the headstall to take us higher!" Grak yelled up to the whereabout, laughing. "Let's give our guests a better view!"

"Never mind me. We're talking about you," Quiescat said. "Don't be so hard on yourself. Don't take the blame for things beyond your control. You have enough enemies without adding yourself to their ranks."

She nodded, blushing with relief and gratitude.

"Your description of Magian intrigues me," Quiescat said. "According to those who encountered him, he looks as human as you or I. But he never stirs from his palace at Sempiterne, and he sometimes shuns public audiences for years. There are rumors that his appearance changes into something more sinister during these long periods of solitude."

"You never met him?"

His forehead furrowed. "I once interceded with him on behalf of the people of Molkya. In a vision, I had seen their city ablaze, a giant bone tree planted in its ruined palace. I couldn't abandon them to that sorry fate, so I presented myself at Sempiterne like a beggar to plead on their behalf. I never got beyond the flunkies at the gates. I wrote Magian an earnest petition to spare Molkya, but it made no difference. He burned the city anyway. I had appealed to his mercy when no such thing exists. However his appearance might alter during his spans of seclusion, he is, at heart, a monster more inhuman than the worst demon of Empyrosis." Quiescat, noting Drinith's unease, took a lighter tone. "Come, let us forget these grim matters a while and see this wondrous sea I've heard so much about."

They joined Woad and Perian at the starboard bulwark. Peering over the parapet, Drinith gasped at the splendid panorama below. A massive horizontal disk shone a brilliant white. Curved arms of foam swept languidly around its frayed edges. A black knife jutted through its heart, the fabled Isle of Ophigee. As the bright sea drew nearer, its vastness became apparent. The green tinge to the rocky pillar hinted it wasn't as inhospitable as it first appeared.

Quiescat seized Drinith, his fingers digging into her shoulder. She stared aghast at his bulging eyes, trembling mouth. He tottered as if stricken by some dread malady. "What's wrong?" she asked, grabbing his arm to steady his dangerous tilt.

Quiescat's eyebrows arched in disbelief. "Do you not see it? The green-black arm from Versifer's vision."

The Isle of Ophigee looked like an elegant arm rising out of the Halo Sea. The sea itself bore an uncanny resemblance to the surface of a boiling cauldron, its frayed outer edge creating the impression of water spilling over the vessel's lip.

"Versifer had been convinced that it was my arm rising from the cauldron," Drinith whispered.

"No doubt mere speculation on his part that has led our own conjectures astray," Quiescat said. "There's little doubt in my mind that the vision foretells a great danger awaiting you on Ophigee." He pounded a fist against the bulwark. "I am such a blind fool! I have read descriptions of the shardlet I don't know how many times, and only now do I make the connection."

"Don't blame yourself," Drinith said. "There's an enormous difference between reading words and seeing the actual thing."

Quiescat rubbed the back of his neck. "The weaver of these visions always seems to stay a step ahead of us. Though, perhaps, this once I'm being too pessimistic. You haven't even set foot on Ophigee yet. You can return to Gyre, tell the meritocrats you were taken ill—"

"No!" Drinith's outburst attracted the attention of nearby drakers. Leaning close to him, she whispered, "I can't. If I fail this mission, any hope of influencing Gyre's policy regarding Rhumgad is dead. The meritocrats don't reward failure."

Quiescat's lips pressed into a thin line. "You're right," he sighed, nodding. "But we must heed the vision's warning. You must be supremely careful in Ophigee. Your life depends upon it."

Woad snorted. "As if the same didn't apply to Gyre."

Drinith peered at the great green-black arm reaching up as if to seize her and drag her under the water. "The threat in Gyre has passed for now. The danger lies in Ophigee." *Danger follows me wherever I go.*

4

The *Piquant Buss* shuddered as it passed over the edge of the disk. Perian yelped and hugged the bulwark. Drinith gripped it, too, to avoid being thrown about the deck. Her lanyard—it had slipped her mind to tie it off. Twice, jolts made her miss the nearest anchor point. When she clicked the hook onto it, she sighed with relief and patted with a handkerchief the chilling perspiration from her face.

Grinning, Grak strolled over to join them. "The *Piquant Buss* always gets twitchy flying over the Halo Sea. No dragon can stomach flying over land. They love the light of the inner sun against their wings too much."

"They walk on land," Quiescat murmured. "But it's true that they won't fly over it."

"A good thing too," Woad said, "or they'd overrun every shard."

Drinith peered over the side. The sea might have been any other but for the glow of the inner sun coming from beneath its translucent green waters. She pointed out the smooth, black shapes swimming just under the choppy surface. "Are those fish?"

"Those creatures you can see are a pod of leviathans, larger than any dragon," Grak said. "The sea has an abundance of fish life sustained by the tiny plants that thrive in its waters."

The dragon dropped so low that the drafts from its wings patted the waves. Ahead, the isle loomed, mottled with dark greenery and beaded with varicolored buildings. As the *Piquant Buss* neared, these proved to be magnificent palaces. Drinith frowned at their diverse and eclectic styles. Gyran meritocrats would never tolerate such gaudy ostentation.

Perian gasped. "The Ophigeens must be richer than meritocrats to live so extravagantly," she said. Her face reddened with embarrassment.

"Some of them are," Woad muttered darkly. "Others spend their lives as chattel. At least Gyrans don't tolerate slavery."

Grak's smile faded. "I'll leave you to discuss landlubber politics. I must ready *Buss* for landing."

The *Piquant Buss* shuddered again as it settled not on the island itself but on one of several large floating platforms connected by pontoon bridges. Drinith cringed as the perch submerged under the dragon's bulk. She and Woad exchanged nervous glances. Perian squealed. But the dragon and the platform lifted again, sending monstrous waves rippling in all directions.

Drinith shook her head in disbelief. "How could this water support such colossal weight?"

Quiescat shrugged. "It's a manifestation of the same magic that keeps the Halo Sea spinning around Ophigee. Mysteries abound across the Crevast." He brightened with sudden enthusiasm. "Who knows? When we disembark, we might learn—"

"I'm the only one disembarking here, remember." She had forgotten that hard fact until now. Terrible loneliness gripped her.

Quiescat's jaw wavered. He examined his sandals. "Of course." His mouth stretched into an unconvincing grin, his eyes glistened with sadness. "You must tell us all the marvelous things you learn when you return to Gyre."

"Of course."

Drinith turned toward the craned platform being gently lowered onto the deck. Customs officers in light purple livery spilled off it. A black, five-pointed nimbus hat bearing a meritocratic medallion floated above their heads. As they scattered to perform their duties, its wearer became visible—a tall, dark-haired woman with loose, light gray skin and bright orange eyes. A rash of white freckles mottled her cheeks. She had a slight stoop, as if the hat weighed her down. Drinith reached for her medallion, only to remember she had left it in her cabin. Blushing, she waved to attract the meritocrat's attention. The woman's frown turned to a cautious smile as she strode toward Drinith. "I am Griman," she said, offering her hand. "You must be Drinith."

"Yes. The pleasure is all mine, Ambassador."

"Where's your medallion?" Griman asked.

Drinith's cheeks warmed. "I left it below deck for safekeeping."

"Your maid must collect it for you. It makes clear who you are to the Ophigeens and will save us a lot of tedious questions." Before Griman had finished, Perian raced back to their cabin.

Griman leaned into Drinith. "Also, please keep our conversations superficial whenever we're not alone," she whispered. "That includes my servants. Our hosts provided them, and they are all spies. I suppose it's not that dissimilar to home. I miss Gyre, for all its faults," she added with winning candor.

Perian returned, carrying the medallion headpiece with almost religious reverence. Drinith bent her knees so that the maid could rest it on her head.

Griman approved with a nod. "We can leave now that you are ready. Your bags will eventually arrive at my residence after the customs officers have rooted through them. The Ophigeens are drearily methodical in such matters."

Drinith shook Woad's hand. Her embrace of Perian took them both by surprise. Either she had warmed to the maid or Perian had become a momentary proxy for Jarma. Drinith offered her hand to Quiescat, but he threw his arms around her. "You've already survived countless dangers," he said, releasing her. "You'll overcome whatever challenges this place throws at you." Eyeing Griman warily, he gently backed away. "We'll meet again soon."

"I shall look forward to our reunion," Drinith said, affecting reserve.

Griman cleared her throat. "We had better go."

Drinith followed her onto the platform. It trembled as it lifted off the deck and swayed precariously as it slowly swung clear of the dragon. Seeking some distraction from her budding nausea, she studied the Ophigeens working on the docks. "They're all wearing dark green clothing."

"They're thralls. I think it's so they can blend into the background. The ruling elite, the benefactors, can wear any colors they choose except that shade. They call it thrall green."

Drinith spotted a few brightly dressed individuals wandering about and marked them as benefactors. "Where do the thralls come from?"

"Some are foreigners who hope their children will become benefactors. Others failed the Rite of Beneficence or foundered some other way afterward. Some went bankrupt. You'll find they're the most bitter kind. Once you take thrall green, there's no going back." Griman glanced around. "I've heard of benefactors down on their luck who starved to death rather than suffer the humiliation."

The crane gently lowered them down to the network of pontoons. It took them some time to traverse it to the island. As they crossed the last bridge, Drinith called Griman's attention to two thralls, wearing webbed teardrop frames under their shoes, strolling across the water. "How is that possible?" she asked.

"The surface tension of the sea is higher than anywhere else in the Crevast. It resists the weight of objects resting upon it, whether they're the water shoes those thralls are wearing or the dragon that brought you here."

Drinith followed her companion off the bridge onto a stone pier festooned with Ophigeen flags—a black sword girdled with a white halo against a light purple field. "Our embassy is over there." Griman drew her attention to a pink mansion, higher up the rock, that wouldn't have looked out of place in Gyre. "The Ophigeens like to keep their foreign guests near the perches."

A carriage awaited them. The six giant black birds harnessed to it had white beaks and purple casques, not their natural colors. Presumably, the casquars' features had been dyed to match the livery of the carriage. The driver hunched in the box seat wore a heavy thrall green raincoat. A man dressed in rich silks leaned against the cab, arms folded.

Griman's gait stuttered. "What's Niod Humble doing here?"

Niod's lank silver hair swept down to his shoulders. A bright white scar stretched down one side of his long, periwinkle face. His green eyes squinted. "Make haste," he growled. "The Diarchs expect you."

Griman's eyebrows curled into a confused frown. "Pardon me, Niod, but I had not expected the audience to be so soon. My colleague has only just arrived. She's not yet attired for a royal audience."

"The Diarchs don't care how she's dressed. They wish to interrogate her before you've a chance to prepare her."

Unsettled, Drinith looked to Griman for reassurance. Her breezy smile never faltered, but it couldn't hide the hint of alarm lurking in her eyes. "If that is the Diarchs' pleasure..." she said.

Niod smirked. "And it is."

"Then we'll head directly to the Dipalatine."

Niod shook his head. "The Diarchs' instructions didn't mention you."

Griman smiled sweetly. "Then they have no issue with me accompanying Drinith."

Niod snorted. "Suit yourself, Ambassador, but I'll be traveling with you." He opened the door and invited Drinith to enter with a flourish of his hand. As soon as she sat down, he landed beside her, pressing her against the cab wall.

Griman sighed as she sat opposite. The carriage shuddered forward. She flashed a sly grin. "Niod is one of my oldest friends in Ophigee."

"I'm not your friend, heritor," Niod snapped.

Drinith looked to Griman for an explanation of the term.

"Heritor is the worst slur imaginable on Ophigee, so our hosts love to apply it to us at every opportunity," Griman said. "Don't worry. They're not as hostile as they appear. Take Niod. He loves me, really. Why else would he be sitting here with us when he could amass wealth like all the other benefactors? I mean, by the time Niod makes it onto the Council of Affluentors, he'll be an old, old man. That's if he ever does. You must be fantastically rich to become an affluentor. Perhaps he'll be elected an administrant."

Niod straightened and expanded in his seat, pressing Drinith further.

Griman examined her nails. "But even becoming an administrant costs a fortune."

"Nobody hands us our destiny, heritor." Niod thumped his chest. "We must earn our position in society."

Griman grinned. "And your position is in this carriage with us."

Niod snarled and lurched forward. He threw open the door and leapt out.

"Now your position is to walk alongside our carriage," Griman said cheerily.

Niod slammed the door shut.

Griman alighted beside Drinith and leaned close. "We haven't much time. Niod will no doubt rejoin us when his temper cools or his legs tire. He hates Gyre because his brother died in a skirmish with our forces. The Ophigeens regard ambition as their greatest strength, but you can turn it against them. The likes of Niod forever seethe at the frustration of their lofty aspirations."

"Liaison to a foreign ambassador is an inferior position here?"

"Usually, such a post provides certain advantages, but relations between our states are so poor, the Ophigeens would happily assign a thrall as my contact if they could. Niod was chosen because of his implacable detestation for all things Gyran. Even he wouldn't have accepted such a profitless position, but a royal decree made it impossible to refuse."

"But we trade with them." Drinith glanced at the shut door outside of which Niod presumably stalked.

"The Short War is the lifeblood of that commerce. Too many here have a vested interest in keeping it rumbling on," Griman said.

"So my mission is a waste of time," Drinith said.

Griman patted her hand. "Unless you can convince the Ophigeens that the thwarting of Magian outweighs any benefit in continuing the Short War. Tell them about the attack you foiled. If the truth isn't enough for them..." She shrugged.

Drinith smiled despite her sinking heart. "At least that will be easy." She had repeated the lie so often she almost believed it herself.

The creak of the door opening startled her. Niod glowered at them as he clambered into the cabin. Had he overheard anything incriminating? He gave no sign of it as he sat across from them.

"Feeling better after your stroll?" Griman asked, her eyes expanding with a blend of mirth and feigned innocence.

Niod grunted. "Enjoy mocking me while you can, heritor."

Griman leaned back in her seat and taunted him with a wry smile as the carriage wound up the vast column of rock.

"Is the Dipalatine on the summit?" Drinith said, breaking the tense silence.

Niod's guffaw mocked her. "The summit is several days' travel."

"There's a necropolis up there reserved for the royal families, affluentors, and administrants," Griman said. "Affluentors are interred in more fabulous crypts than their diarchs. They can afford such lavishness given they are the wealthiest benefactors."

"They are the eighteen richest benefactors of sound mind," Niod muttered. "Each has earned their place through their own endeavors."

"I understand the members of the original pyrate crews that settled the island are also buried somewhere up there," Griman said, "though I've only visited the tombs of the two captains, Gadia and Typoneur."

"So dragon pyrates founded both Ophigee and Gyre," Drinith observed.

Niod scowled at her. "There, the similarities end. Since the Great Rectification, Ophigee has advanced beyond your backward heritor doctrines. You call yourselves meritocrats or meritorians, but the true merit lies with the dead generations that preceded you. Your wealth is inherited, not earned."

"Drinith didn't inherit her position," Griman said. "She arrived in Gyre as practically a pauper and yet she quickly earned an emblem of merit."

Drinith, shying from Niod's scrutinizing gaze, lifted the window curtain and peered out at the mansions and palaces tucked behind forbidding walls that had seemingly carved up the entire island.

"But she couldn't have done it by herself," Niod said. "A meritocrat must have sponsored her."

"Your new benefactors have mentors to help them," Griman countered.

"And we repay that help with our service. We are all self-made men and women."

"The problem with being self-made is the quality depends on the maker's skill," Griman sneered.

"From thrall to affluentor, we get what we deserve. Can you say the same about Gyre?"

"And you deserve to be my liaison."

"For now," Niod conceded. "But I won't have the pleasure of your company forever."

"That's a pity...for you."

Drinith racked her brains for some innocuous topic to distract her companions from their bickering. They were passing by a cluster of interconnected bone-white towers wedged into a shallow cave in the cliff face. Two familiar hooded statues stood by the entrance. "You have a preservatory on Ophigee, I see."

Niod sniffed. "It isn't merely a preservatory. It is the Great Preservatory."

Drinith couldn't help but grin. She had assumed Gyre's Grand Preservatory to be preeminent, but perhaps all the other preservatories had equally impressive names to flatter the egos of the prickly local rulers on whose patronage and tolerance they relied.

The carriage halted before an enormous palace, or rather two palaces conjoined, jutting over a precipice. One half was a spiraling garland all in white marble, while the other was a boxy structure built of porphyry, with several spearlike towers bunched together at one end. A domed structure stood between them, its white and red struts clasping at the crown to form a petrified flame. It was toward this building that Niod led the two meritocrats.

"The more exotic Flower Palace belongs to the Typoneuran Diarch while his Gadian co-ruler resides in the other," Griman said. "The building in between is where they hold court."

Soldiers, dressed in reddish purple and white, eyed them sourly from sentry alcoves as they entered. The curving, pointed apexes on their helmets filled Drinith with foreboding. She shuddered; the tops of the bubbles in Versifer's vision had curved into talons.

"Your soldiers are impressive," she said to Niod as they proceeded down a long mirrored corridor.

"They are an elite unit dedicated to protecting the Diarchs," Niod said, pleased. "The Talon Guard. Benefactor or thrall can join them provided they can defeat one of their members in single combat."

Above, a painted relief of a golden two-headed dragon glared down. One head was white and the other purple-red. Gilded fire poured from their mouths and spilled down the walls, creating the illusion that the corridor was ablaze.

A young man strutted down it toward them. Clad in shades of bright red from head to foot except for a bright yellow cravat, he could have passed for a courtesar. Even his hair had been cut and dyed into a cerise comb. Several gold chains hung down his chest and a gold spike protruded from his chin like a goatee. Gold studs formed two curves beneath his cheekbones. An oversized earring hung from his left ear. But it was the look of contemptuous superiority on his mint green face that struck Drinith most forcibly. He looked to be the very personification of vanity.

As his gaze fell upon her, the pinching of his lips and the narrowing of his rose eyes accentuated his detestable conceit.

He made a sweeping bow. "Ladies." He sneered at Niod.

"I see you've escaped the executioner's axe for now, Scol," Niod grunted.

"Somebody has to win your wars," Scol said as he swept by. "And spend your money. The Diarchs gave me a raise."

Niod snorted.

"That was the notorious mercenary general, the Tease, wasn't it?" Griman asked.

"Yes," Niod growled. "What of it?"

"I hear he's quite the talent on the battlefield."

Niod sneered. "I doubt Gyre could afford him."

"Our coffers are considerable," Griman said with a hint of irritation.

"So is his appetite for coin." Niod said. "If I were you, I'd worry less about that scoundrel and more about what awaits you in the throne room."

Griman and Drinith exchanged nervous glances.

"What is that supposed to mean?" Griman asked.

"You'll find out soon enough," Niod said with a malevolent grin.

At the far end of the corridor stood a stone door, one leaf of white marble and the other of porphyry. Both bore reliefs of important events—wars, the founding of towns, coronations, military triumphs, the payment of tribute by foreign vassals. Drinith spotted on one battle scene the sunfinch flag of Gyre amongst the fallen standards straddled by a crowned victor. She pointed to another relief where meritocrats groveled before a queen and king.

Griman shook her head. "If that ever happened—"

"And it did," Niod insisted.

"—Gyre would have disowned them."

"Gyre did," Niod said, delighted.

"Open those doors," Griman demanded. "Show Drinith the other sides where your people record your great defeats."

"Unlike you, we don't ignore our failings," Niod said primly, brushing a stray hair from his lapel. "We learn from them."

The doors groaned open, robbing Griman's chance to retort. Niod swaggered ahead, forcing the meritocrats to follow. Drinith shivered with dread the instant before she realized the enormous shadow of a two-headed dragon across the yellow floor was an optical trick created by the marble's shifting colors. Above, a dragon-shaped silhouette against the burnished gold vault added to the illusion.

Beyond, almost unnoticed at first, sat the highest dignitaries in Ophigee. The two Diarchs, female and male, rested on two dragon thrones matching their family colors. The female Diarch sat upright in her seat as she focused intently on Drinith. With her blue-black complexion and thick black hair, she could have passed for a Rhumgadian lowlander. Her co-ruler slouched on his throne, one hand propping up his head, looking bored. His bright rose eyes burned against his charcoal skin and cropped silver-gray hair.

Between them sat the eighteen affluentors on golden chairs, dressed as sumptuously as their monarchs. Most were gray-haired ancients, but the youthfulness of some surprised Drinith. How could they have amassed fortunes worthy of a seat at such a young age? Just below them, three women and two men clad entirely in white snakeskin sat on a black marble bench.

"The ones at the front are the administrants, elected to advise the Diarchs," Griman whispered.

"And who is he?" Drinith nodded at the short man standing beside them. His ivory skull cap bore a stylized relief of a chrysanthemum.

"Nobody to worry about. Unless you lie. He's the court truthscryer."

"And what would happen if you did?" Drinith couldn't help asking.

As their eyes met, Griman's smile slipped. "It would be bad. Very bad."

Drinith sighed. "I thought as much."

5

———

The centermost administrant rose from the bench.

"That's Syascin Brave," Griman murmured to Drinith. "The woman with the winding spire of red-gold hair sitting to his immediate right is his wife, Tharpen Zeal."

A mountain of solid brawn, Syascin looked as though he'd charge at Drinith at any moment. "Come forward to make your case before Their Serene Majesties, the Diarchs Kymalas Gadia and Clacon Typoneur!" he boomed. So many of the surrounding faces burned with hate for her, as though her presence were an insult.

She glanced at the open door behind her, teasing with the false prospect of salvation. Drinith had no sanctuary on Ophigee, no means of escape. As she tentatively stepped onto the dragon's mock shadow, Niod's ugly gash of a mouth mocked her with a triumphant grin. Griman, rubbing her elbow, mirrored Drinith's trepidation. It wouldn't have been a surprise if the ambassador had turned and fled.

Truthscryers weren't infallible. Quiescat had often said that. They could be fooled. All Drinith had to do was pick her words with care.

She glared back at Syascin. "The Diarchs invited me here—"

"You are Meritocrat Drinith Hax?" he asked.

Drinith nodded. "I am." The ensuing silence prodded her to continue. "The previous meritocrat of House Hax adopted me as her successor. I was born on Rhumgad to Juyon, wife to the Emperor of Kaplar, Hemrath—"

"We know your history and why you are here. We summoned you to confirm your account of the foiled attack on Gyre."

"Her word should be sufficient, Syascin," Griman said in disgust.

"In the past, the word of meritocrats proved to be less than reliable," Syascin said. "If your colleague refuses to submit to our truthscryer, then we will conclude she is lying. She will be expelled from our island and your offer of a truce will be dismissed."

"What has she to fear if she speaks the truth?" his wife added.

"True, Tharpen," Syascin said. "She need not be afraid if she speaks honestly."

The Ophigeens offered Drinith a chance to escape, but it was illusory. If she balked now, Griman would report it back and the meritocrats would draw the same conclusion as the Ophigeens.

Mistaking her hesitation for passive assent, the truthscryer stepped forward and produced a glowing white stone chrysanth on a chain. Drinith repressed a flinch as he thrust it at her. "Bow, please," he commanded impatiently, clearly irked that her stature dwarfed his own.

"We should really get a taller truthscryer," quipped an affluentor to his neighbor.

"Perhaps we should get him a box to stand on," deadpanned the other.

Like lowering my head onto a chopping block, Drinith thought as the truthscryer slipped the chain around her neck. She straightened.

"So, you are the Meritocrat Drinith Hax?" he asked.

"Yes."

"You are the daughter of Hemrath of Kaplar?"

Panic stirred in Drinith's breast. If every question required only a yes or no, she'd have no opportunity to dissemble. "Yes."

Ultimately, the culpability for the Crevastival attack lay with

Magian. He drove Gelasin to such extremes. In her mind, Drinith returned to that moment on the canal when she and Gelasin faced each other, but she forced her imagination to replace him with Magian's shifting form.

"You came to Gyre looking for aid to defeat Magian and reclaim your realm?" the truthscryer asked.

"Yes." *Magian, Magian, Magian. Magian planned the Crevastival attack.*

The truthscryer frowned. "Let me ask again."

A tightness in her throat made her touch the chain, but it hung loosely about her neck. The constriction must be in her imagination. *Imagine Magian.*

"You sought Gyre's help against Magian?"

"Is this harangue necessary?" Griman protested. "Drinith already answered. If your truthscryer can't recognize the truth, it's his fault, not hers."

He must have detected ripples of chagrin emanating from the falsehood she had concocted. But Drinith mustn't think of it as a lie. *Magian was behind the conspiracy. Magian, Magian, Magian.*

"This plot you discovered—do you believe the previous Meritocrat Hax had prior knowledge of it?"

"No." But the meritocrat who had freed her from the Ducal Steward's clutches, the mysterious veiled lady, had an inkling.

"You're hiding something."

Drinith smirked. So here lay the reason for this interrogation. The Ophigeens suspected Gyre had fabricated the plot.

"Lying before the Diarchs is a grave matter," Syascin said.

Tharpen leaned forward. "Punishable by death."

"I didn't lie." Drinith stroked her cheeks. Exactly as Gelasin was in the habit of doing. Gelasin was a liar, a traitor, and a murderer. And a father to her. She had never wept for him, not even a tear.

The truthscryer wilted as disapproving frowns from the Diarchs and their counselors piled upon him. "I'm uncertain," he admitted.

What would Gelasin do in her stead? Attack while her opponent was weak. "I wasn't part of the conspiracy."

The truthscryer nodded in agreement.

"Gyre had no hand in the plot either."

The truthscryer's head bobbed again.

"The conspiracy posed a genuine threat."

"She answers honestly," the truthscryer said.

"What more do you want?" Drinith demanded.

"Was Magian actually behind the plot?" Clacon's question rolled through the throne room like thunder.

It transported Drinith back to the canal, but this time, Gelasin refused to let her mask him with her nightmarish vision of Magian. A grin fattened the warrior's ruined cheeks. A traitor to the last. Even his memory betrayed her.

"Yes!" she declared.

The truthscryer beamed with triumph. "She lies!"

"Seize her!" the Diarchs commanded in unison.

As she turned to flee, talon guards swept around her. They grabbed her arms, forcing them behind her back, and pushed her into a stoop. Her emblem of merit slipped from her head and vanished somewhere beneath the encircling press. The medallion made sharp scraping sounds as shuffling boots kicked it about. The truthscryer weaved through the wall of guards, lifted his chain off her, and withdrew to his haunt by the administrants' bench. She envied the relief on his sweaty face.

"There must be some mistake," Griman pleaded.

"The mistake is hers," Syascin said. "She could have stayed silent. Silence would have condemned her as a liar, but she would have escaped punishment."

"She didn't know that."

"Then the fault for her death lies with your incompetence," Kymalas declared to a few approving titters. "We'll return her emblem of merit. She'll soon have no use for it."

Drinith hadn't noticed before the nondescript block of basalt toward which her captors now dragged her. A thrall cradling an axe stepped beside it. His forehead bore a skull, the symbol of an executioner.

She mustn't meekly surrender to her death. Drinith twisted, kicked, threw herself forward to wrench free of the guards' grip. She spat in one grinning face. But the block steadily drew nearer. She howled in frustration.

Griman leapt in front of her, arms outstretched. "This will mean war!"

Laughter echoed through the chamber. Even a guard holding Drinith broke into a giggle.

"We're already at war," Clacon said. "Haven't you noticed?"

"She broke our law," Syascin said. "She must suffer the punishment prescribed for her crime—death."

"Death." The Ophigeens' cries merged into a chant. "Death. Death. Death."

Griman's gaze danced about, desperate for inspiration as Drinith was dragged past her. The thrall executioner practiced a swing of his axe. Countless scar lines from previous executions crisscrossed the top of the block.

"She's sixteen!" Griman cried. What did she think she was doing? Drinith was nearly twenty. A lie had condemned her, and now Griman gambled her own life with another to save her. Did she expect those grinning fools to show clemency? "She claims the right to ascend!"

The court fell silent. Everyone froze and stared at the ambassador.

"You can't claim that for her!" Syascin bellowed.

Spurred by Griman's encouraging nod, Drinith cried, "I claim the right to ascend!" Whatever in Empyr's bowels that meant.

"This is unprecedented," Tharpen groused.

Griman shook her head. "I grant it's unusual, but it's not unprecedented. I've read in your annals of something similar happening before."

"True," Kymalas admitted.

"Foreigners, yes," Syascin said. "But a criminal?" His face curdled in disgust.

"Take her to my dungeon," Kymalas said. "Niod, escort the Gyran ambassador from our sight so we can discuss this matter free of her further meddling."

Everyone stared at Drinith as guards shunted her from the hall. She had eluded death thanks to Griman, but her reprieve might prove temporary. She needed to escape fast.

6

In her tiny cell, Drinith stewed. A day passed, and then another, without confirmation of her fate. Though any of the meals that slid through a flap at the bottom of the metal door might be her last, she couldn't find the appetite to eat. Often, frustration impelled her to pace the cramped chamber. Other times, she lay on the dirty straw mattress that smelled of stale sweat and mold, trying to wring a little sleep from her fatigue. Boredom eventually drove her to examine crude engravings, scars of hope and despair, left by previous prisoners on the porphyry walls. Most of the graffiti was indecipherable, but she could read a line inscribed in Gyran pyratic script.

GYRE SENT ME TO SEEK MY END ON OPHIGEE AND I FOUND IT.

Drinith could have written it. It was impossible to tell how recently it had been etched, but its writer must have been incarcerated a long time to cut so deeply into such unyielding stone.

The rattle of keys jolted her from her musings. Were her executioners coming to finish their task, or had the Ophigeens granted her dispensation to ascend? Whatever that entailed, it had to be better than being trapped here, helpless.

The shriek of the opening door made her cringe. Griman entered, a wan smile on her face. "I won't prolong your agony. You're safe from the headsman's axe."

Drinith exhaled her tension. A sudden weariness weighed on her, and she sat down on the bed. Griman settled beside her, rubbing her hands over each other as if she was shaping an invisible ball. She hesitated to speak.

"Spit it out," Drinith murmured.

Griman stared levelly at her. "You must either accept thralldom or attempt the Ascent."

"There's no choice then. I must ascend."

Griman approved with a nod. "Meritocratic honor and all that."

The reputation of the Gyran meritocracy had nothing to do with it. Drinith preferred death to slavery.

"Oh yes!" Griman wagged a forefinger. "Before I forget, I must ask, why do you think you failed the truthscryer's test?"

"I don't know," Drinith said. "I told the truth." How would she ever escape this haunting lie? Gelasin had forced it on her, but with every repetition, guilt cut deeper into her soul. "The truthscryer didn't like me."

"I hadn't thought of that," Griman said, pouncing on the suggestion. "He didn't. His faltering analysis of your answers embarrassed him before his patrons. That's why we always use truthscryers in pairs in Gyre. I admit your theory fits, though I prefer my own. Someone in the Ophigeen pro-Short War faction bribed him. By discrediting you, they hoped to wreck not only any tentative truce between Ophigee and Gyre but also the coalition we've already built." She gave Drinith's knee a reassuring pat. "I've already sent a dispatch to the Parliament of Merit, informing it of my suspicions."

Drinith bit her lip to stifle a laugh. So a second phantom conspiracy had saved her reputation. The meritocrats eschewed the obvious answer in favor of one more cynical and paranoid. It was a relief to know her colleagues wouldn't turn on her when she returned to Gyre. If she ever got there... "Tell me about this Ascent."

"It's officially called the Rite of Beneficence. It's the initiation ritual into the upper echelon of Ophigeen society. At sixteen, potential candidates are offered an opportunity to take part. If they refuse, they're made thralls. If they succeed, they become benefactors."

"And if they fail?" Drinith asked.

"They're dead or as good as," Griman said. "Think of the Isle of Ophigee as a long pole with the Halo Sea girdling the center. The Ophigeens call the uninhabited part beneath the Halo Sea the Whetstone. A dragon conveys the candidates to its lowest point. From there, they must journey for days through a labyrinth of tunnels back to civilization. Those who cannot do so, for whatever reason, are left down there to die. The Ophigeens are not a sentimental people."

"Do many fail?"

"The weak ones. And the unlucky. You have advantages over the average candidate. For a start, you're more mature than most sixteen-year-olds." Griman grinned, her eyes gleaming with mischief. Plainly, she knew Drinith was older than sixteen. "And you have fought for your life before."

"So it's more than simply a physical challenge," Drinith said.

"All you begin with is a bedroll, a cup, and a knife. The rest is up to you. No laws apply below the Halo Sea. A madness infects some candidates. For example, Niod Humble received his scar during his Ascent."

Griman nervously fingered the chain around her neck. "Your foreignness will be a disadvantage, making it harder for you to find willing allies down there. My advice is to do whatever you must to survive, no matter how unsavory."

The irony tasted so bitter. Griman had distilled Drinith's life in those few words. But Drinith must face this trial alone, without Quiescat and her other friends. They didn't even know she was in danger yet. Quiescat would blame himself for this. Her isolation oppressed her. "Can I ask a favor?"

Griman blinked with surprise. "I will grant you anything within my power."

"I need to write a letter to a friend." Drinith shied from

mentioning Quiescat directly. She couldn't bring herself to dismiss him as a servant, but Griman would be scandalized by any hint of deference toward him. "Two friends, actually."

"I advise against it," Griman said. "Your captors will surely discover coded messages in any correspondence you write, irrespective of their actual presence. The forces who condemned you to this jail would use any letter as another opportunity to vilify you. Tell me whatever messages you wish to pass on and I will ensure they reach their intended recipients."

Start with the easier message first. "Then tell my meritorian Jarma that she is the sister I never had."

Griman's eyebrows climbed a fraction. "Of course."

"And tell Quiescat of Godsdoor, he has been a true father to me."

A blush crept across Griman's cheeks as she glanced about the cell. Most meritocrats knew little about their courtesar fathers. The topic wasn't considered polite.

Drinith stared at the bare stone floor. "Tell him, whatever happens to me on Ophigee isn't his fault."

"Enough morbidness," Griman said. "You can tell him yourself soon enough after you've completed the Ascent."

Drinith didn't bother to contradict her optimism. Her experience might improve her odds, but it didn't guarantee victory. Luck had something to do with it too, and she had been burning through hers for a long time.

7

Zoen took a deep breath and entered the room to face her parents sitting on the opposite side of the dining table. Her mother, Tharpen Zeal, anxiously clasped her hands together, the slight dishevelment of her spiral coif hinting at her distraction. Her father, Syascin Brave, had that thunderous scowl he generally reserved for foreign dignitaries.

"Where's the third?" Zoen asked. Three judges normally officiated a trial.

Mother directed a sideways frown at Father's chuckle. He gestured vaguely at a chair. "Zoen, please sit."

She sat across from them and knitted her hands together. "So…"

"We want to talk to you about your impending Ascent," Father said. "To go or not is your choice." Typical of him—always so fastidious about the law. "We only want to help you come to the best decision."

"I've already made my choice. I'm going." Despite Zoen's best effort, indignation made her voice tremble. Were they really encouraging her to choose a life of slavery?

"Zoen," Mother said, "let's be frank. Your sister, Olen, attempted the Ascent, and she never came back. You're..." She gave Father a pleading look.

"You're not physically strong," he said. "You've poor eyesight, which the gloom of the tunnels will exacerbate."

"So what are you saying?" Zoen demanded. "I'm too weak to survive down there? Olen couldn't for all her athleticism, so what chance have I? I should just accept my fate and live out my life as someone else's property, is that it?"

"Thralls are well treated," Mother insisted.

Zoen snorted. "Not all of them. Not all the time."

"In your case, we'll make sure you're looked after properly." Was there a hint of a blush on Father's cheeks? "We, being your parents, cannot take you into our household, but others, kind people, owe us favors. One of them will take you in. We can guarantee your thralldom will be so light, you won't even notice it."

Zoen clutched the edge of the table with both hands, pressing her pale fingers into the wood until it hurt. What more proof did she need that they had never loved her? But she mustn't lose her temper. No. That would confirm their low opinion of her. "I'd rather die than take thrall green."

"That's exactly the choice you are making," Father said. "Your mother and I both completed the Ascent. We've seen its brutality firsthand. We lived it. Many benefactors refer to it as the Blooding for a reason."

Zoen made a swatting motion with the back of her hand. "I've heard no one call it the Blooding."

"Of course," Mother said primly. "Until now, you've been treated as a child, because you deserved your innocence."

"But you can't afford to be naive any longer," Father said. "You must face reality. Very few people survive the Ascent these days. If you go, you will most certainly die down there."

Zoen shot to her feet. "I suppose you gave the same speech to Olen. You warned her, too."

Guilty silence. They hadn't. They had believed in her.

"Sit down," Father murmured.

"I'd rather stand," Zoen snapped.

Father rubbed a quivering hand over his mouth. "I shouldn't say this. I'm breaking the law by telling you. For several red months, no candidate has reached the Ouroboric Gate. Nobody has completed the Ascent. Understand? At the moment, it's a death sentence."

Did he think a few scare stories would cow her? Zoen slapped the table. "If I am to die, then so be it. I won't tolerate the slow, miserable death of thralldom."

"Excuse me," Mother said as she fled the room, pressing her hands to her face.

"It's easy to talk of death when you know nothing about it." Father spread his hands in a pleading gesture. "Your mother already lost Olen. Don't do this to her."

Zoen folded her arms. "I'm going. There's nothing you can say to change that."

Father's lower lip jutted forward in a pout. "Go to your room."

Zoen maintained her defiant smile until she had retreated to the sanctuary of her bedchamber. She plopped down on her bed, and the facade of strength damming her rage and hurt crumbled. Her squeal turned into a screech. She seized the nearest object, a vase, and flung it against the farthest wall. She pressed her fists against her eyes, but streams of hot tears flowed between the clenched fingers down her cheeks.

The rage passed, but the hurt lingered. Sniffing, she wiped the wetness off her face with her sleeve. Her damp skin stung as if the tears had burned it. She looked at her blurry reflection in the mirror. Red rimmed her eyes and blotched her pinkish-white cheeks. She looked so small and frail, a child, not someone on the cusp of adulthood. Her hair was gray like an old woman's. For all her bravura, deep down she knew her parents were right. She'd never survive the Ascent. Fate had damned her from her birth—poor eyesight, a frail physique, and a sickly paleness. But what else could she do? Live as a slave for the rest of her life?

Exhausted, she threw herself on the bed, closed her eyes, and tried to smother her anguish with sleep.

Some hours later, the creak of a floorboard woke her. Her eyes popped open. The candles had burned out. A wedge of pink moonlight from the twin moons, Neor and Ruis, spilled through the open balcony window, giving shape to the darkness. Something more than the night's chill breath—the murmur of lumbering footsteps on the carpet—made the hair on her neck rise. A thief, perhaps, or something worse. A disgruntled thrall. There might have been thralls in the dining room during her argument with her parents. She couldn't remember for sure. One might have taken offense at her scorn of their lowly status.

Lying on her side, she didn't dare turn to glimpse the intruder. She secretly clutched the pillow, the only weapon she had to hand. How pathetic that her inclination was to fend off an attacker with a bag of feathers. The Ascent would surely kill a weakling like her. If this trespasser didn't murder her first.

The steps drew nearer, plodding and hesitant, as if their maker slowly staggered. A pungent, alcoholic scent impregnated the air. If she had any hope of fighting off the stranger, she must strike now.

She rolled off the bed to her feet and turned, brandishing the pillow. She gasped. Her father stood on the far side, motionless, glassy-eyed, a hammer in his hand.

"You wouldn't listen to reason," he slurred. "You've left me no choice. Dragons, do you imagine you can defend yourself with a pillow?"

"What do you think you are doing?" Zoen took a step away from him.

"I'm going to make sure you're in no fit state to attempt the Ascent. Even living as a crippled thrall is better than dying in the bowels of the Whetstone." The hammer danced up and down, threatening to fly. "Better I endure your hate forever than stand by idly while you get yourself killed." He lurched forward, swinging the hammer.

Flinging the pillow at him, Zoen dashed out onto the balcony. She climbed over the parapet and tried to lower herself as near to the ground two floors below as her arms could stretch, but they couldn't take the strain. She fell.

Branches lacerated her as she landed in a hedge. She fought free of the tangle, afraid to investigate whether the stinging hurt was because of minor bruises and scratches or a greater injury.

On the balcony, still armed with the hammer, loomed her father, washed in pink by the moons. "Come back, Zoen. I promise I won't hurt you."

But she didn't look back. She limped into the night, away from the only home she had ever known.

8

Quiescat rolled the dead Tear between his fingers as he stood in the reception hall. It might be any unsullied ball of glass. As he stared at the mirror on the wall a small boy's eyes gazed back from his haggard face. Quiescat would have dearly liked to make amends to that child. Aside from their brief encounter outside the Grand Preservatory entrance on Shadow Street when the boy's mother spurned his offer of help, all efforts to locate the donor had come to naught. Quiescat wrapped his hand around the crystal sphere, felt its smooth solidity. He had never been more completely human since he first became the Oracle of Godsdoor, and yet he had never felt less complete. The gift was dead, and so was he.

And now this second blow had struck him. Drinith was trapped in Ophigee, condemned by the lie he had encouraged her to adopt. The quick thinking of Gyre's ambassador had won her a reprieve from summary execution, but the prospect of escape the Ascent offered was illusory. For her, it was another death sentence, albeit more subtle. Faced with her certain doom, he had never felt so useless. A vast gulf separated Quiescat from Drinith, and he hadn't the means to cross it. He could only beg for help from meritocrats, most of whom despised him.

He had written to Drinith's predecessor, Epmar, to intervene. She had promised to do everything she could to secure Drinith's release, but, no longer a meritocrat, she had negligible influence over her former colleagues.

Her dismay at Drinith's plight was heartfelt, but the same couldn't be said for Thaxen Savarel. In Quiescat's estimation, she was best positioned to help her protege, but Thaxen had ignored his letters and had turned him away from her door with brittle courtesy. No doubt, Thaxen considered his intervention an act of supreme impudence, a usurpation of meritocratic privilege.

He had called to Aretro Falier, the ambassador general, too. She had welcomed his visit warmly, but her assurances had been far too bland to be genuine.

He had tried Drinith's other meritocratic friends and acquaintances. Even meritorians who might have the ear of their meritocrats. Behind their sympathetic smiles and vague promises lurked an avarice sharper than any knife. If Drinith died and they could annul her designation of Jarma as her successor, her title and property might pass to somebody's surplus daughter or sister. And money and favors could be extracted as a by-product of the negotiation to choose an heir.

So Quiescat had turned to his last and least hope in absolute desperation. Elca Trajar was the consummate politician at the heart of a web of powerful connections within the Parliament of Merit. But if other meritocrats could be accused of cold, perfidious ambition, it was doubly true of her. His skin crawled in anticipation of meeting her again. Her acceptance of his invitation had surprised him, her insistence on calling to Drinith's mansion more so. She probably wanted to check out the property before she engineered its theft. Still, the visit offered a slim hope.

So he waited for his guest to arrive, ready to greet her at the door as a servant might. She was late, but she could afford to be. As Oracle of Godsdoor, he had dismissed tardy monarchs from the threshold of his temple, but he couldn't quibble anymore. Now he was the supplicant.

The bell rang. He nearly dropped the Tear as he fumbled to place it in the pouch hanging from his neck. He opened the door and bowed. "Welcome to the Hax Mansion, Meritocrat."

"Quiescat, how delightful." She swept by him with a simper of superiority, her huge, mesmeric eyes darting about the hall. "You're maintaining this place well in Drinith's absence."

Quiescat seethed behind a stiff smile. That she meant it as a compliment made her observation even more annoying. "The servants have done an excellent job."

Trajar's emblem of merit, the four-horned serpent head, rested on her forehead. She wore her silken black hair in a careless low bun as was her habit on occasion, but her appearance was in all other respects immaculate.

She turned her entrancing gaze on him again. "I've only had the opportunity to admire your new eyes from afar. Mind if I take a closer look?" He flinched as she drew near, but she clutched his cheeks. Her sharp nails pressed into his skin like dagger points as she studied him with unnerving intensity. Did she ever blink? "If I didn't know better, I'd assume they were your natural eyes. The preservators do remarkable work." Her smile broadened as she released her grip.

The impressions made by her nails stung so badly, Quiescat rubbed his cheeks to reassure himself they weren't bleeding. "Fenvar has refreshments ready in the parlor."

Trajar's gaze again swept the hall. "First, show me around the mansion."

"Fenvar would be a better guide," Quiescat said. The last thing he wanted was to wander the building alone with Trajar. She was capable of anything. "She'd be able to tell you some of the history—"

"Nonsense!" Trajar declared, coiling her arm around his and patting his hand. "I already know a good deal about this house. I will give *you* the guided tour. As for the curiosities neither of us recognizes, we can make an educated guess as to their provenance. I like mysteries. The speculation is half the fun."

So she *had* come to survey the property. "How are you familiar with this place?"

"I used to visit Epmar's mother here regularly before her untimely demise."

How old was Trajar? The preservators' arts could extend life or the veneer of youth for some considerable time.

"Let's have a look at the bedrooms first." Before Quiescat could protest, she started dragging him up the stairs.

She paused before one portrait, a sour face peering out of pitch blackness. "Poor Jerlotro. Never was a mother more different from her daughter. She often put Epmar's sentimental nature down to the courtesar who sired her. Jerlotro was fierce and harsh, a born leader. If she had lived, the Halcyon Republic might now shine a little brighter. She would have never tolerated her daughter's romantic adventures. She'd have spent her fortune to put an end to Epmar's lover long before that pentacular did." Her smile slackened to a more pensive expression. "We became estranged near the end, Jerlotro and I. Despite our rivalry driving a wedge between us, the respect remained."

Trajar probably murdered Jerlotro. Try as Quiescat might, the thought proved too compelling to dislodge. It was too easy to imagine Trajar as a killer.

"Speaking of courtesars, my current champion, Muenthax, awaits me outside," Trajar said. "I told him I'd be perfectly safe here, but he worries so much about me."

"I'll have Fenvar bring him a snack," Quiescat said. He hastened to summon her, but Trajar's iron grip held him.

"No point in spoiling him. I just wanted to put your mind at rest that he hadn't a more sinister purpose in accompanying me."

And to warn me that she can call on help nearby if she feels threatened.

Trajar sprinted up the stairs. Quiescat struggled to keep up. She passed two doors, opened the third. "I remember this room. That bed is where poor Jerlotro died." Running a finger along the edge of a dressing table, she halted beside the bed. "This exact spot was where I whispered my last farewell to my friend."

No doubt a final gloat over her victim. The meritocrat's every word, every movement exuded menace.

"I'm curious, Quiescat. Tell me—if you don't mind—are you a virgin?"

Mute shock turned to burning rage, but Quiescat dammed it behind a fake smile, determined not to let her provoke him. "That's a private matter."

"But your order is celibate, is it not?"

While he grappled with an answer, she draped herself across the bed and propped herself up on her elbows. Her bun came apart, spilling her hair onto the bedspread, exposing their snowy tips. For the first time, he found her body as mesmerizing as her lustrous eyes. His gaze mapped out the curvaceous figure beneath her black dress. A slit in the skirt exposed a teasing sliver of a stockinged leg. The low neckline above the three shiny gold buttons revealed an undulating segment of starry cleavage. He had never imagined those white beauty spots peppering her violet complexion could arouse such breathless desire.

"I often slept in this bed when I stayed here. I remember it being very comfortable." She grinned up at him, sinful and inviting. "You haven't answered my question." She patted the bedding. "Come, sit beside me."

An idiotic lust percolated through his horror and confusion. He wanted to run but he couldn't decide which direction, so he stood still, gawping like a fool. How could he politely refuse her advances?

"You have no children. Other than Drinith, that is." Trajar drew a circle on the bed with her finger. "How far would you go to save her?"

"I'd give my life," he croaked.

"I'm sure you would," she said. "I'm sure you'd suffer any trial or humiliation to secure her release."

He swallowed. The sudden dryness of his throat made it hurt.

"Close the door." She spoke lightly, as though the request was a trifle.

The sweat on his palm made the handle greasy. He hesitated.

Shutting the door cut off his only means of an elegant escape. He could pretend he heard Jarma calling him—

"If you want my help, shut the door."

He obeyed.

She sauntered over to him, drew close, too close. The touch of the doorhandle against his back made him shiver. He couldn't look at her. He couldn't look his defeat in the face.

Her open palm slid into his view, proffering a thumb-sized black disk. Tiny, dull white spots drifted across its surface. A lover's nightcap mushroom. "Eat this. It will help you." Her whisper caressed his cheek. Her perfume intoxicated him.

He clung limpid-like to the door, the handle pressing deeper into his back. "Why?" he rasped. "Why would you ever consider me worthy...of your attention?"

"You're a learned man, intelligent. I tire of sharp swords with dull brains. You intrigue me. There's a whiff of the divine about you."

"There's nothing divine about me," Quiescat said. *Particularly now.*

"I'll be the judge of that," she said as she rested the tip of the mushroom against his lower lip. "Open wide."

He jerked his head away. Anger welled within him, rage at himself as much as her. Part of him whispered surrender, a bestial urge his moral squeamishness had long imprisoned. To think he regarded Abecedar's timid romance with Jarma with such disdain, and now he entertained the notion of a tryst with this predator. His temple was gone, as were his powers, his vocation, everything he had earned through his self-mastery and sacrifice. Why rebuff her advances? Why deny himself the pleasure of her body? If she kept her promise to help rescue Drinith...

Using her imprisonment to justify his lust revolted him.

"I can't." He wriggled free of Trajar's enveloping arms.

She gazed at him with bemusement and delight as he fled across the room. "This is refreshing. My lovers aren't generally so shy."

"I'm sorry to disappoint you," he said, skirting around the bed.

Trajar smirked. "You won't. You're wise enough not to disappoint me. You've nowhere to run and you're not the fighting sort." She trailed languidly after him, laughed as he crawled on his knees across the bed to escape her. "The great Oracle of Godsdoor, who once daunted kings and emperors, flits across this bedchamber like a timid bird to escape me."

He dashed for the door. He hesitated to turn the handle. Trajar's promises to help Drinith might be worthless, but if he fled the room, she'd surely block any rescue attempt. He didn't resist as her velvet hand lifted his off the handle. Tugging his cowl, she gently drew him toward the bed.

9

The flap at the bottom of the dented iron door lifted. Sickly green soup slopped about in a battered bowl as it slid through the narrow gap. A lump of black bread resting on the bowl's broad lip fell off. Drinith snatched it off the dusty floor, wiped it with the skirt of her dress, then collected the bowl and sat down on the corner of her bed.

She stared in disgust at the unappetizing yellow slick floating on top. Every meal was the same, morning and evening, the bread getting staler by the day. She'd suffer this insipid fare, but each meal came with danger. Without her confiscated alicorn bracelet to detect poison, any meal might prove her last. Aside from possibly making the food taste better, poison would rid the Ophigeens of their unwanted prisoner.

Still, she had to keep her strength up. Drinith used the bread to fish out the submerged spoon. Shredding the bread into the soup, she forced herself to eat. It was hard to tell what vegetables it contained, but they could hardly be fresh. She feared her teeth would shatter as she chewed the bread's hard-as-granite grains. Hopefully, the soup was more nutritious than it tasted.

Every day, the walls of her cell—so tiny she could pace it off in four strides—shrank a little in her mind. How many days had gone by—nine or ten? After some deliberation, she decided it must have been nine. She needed to record them before she lost track entirely. After she finished eating, she slipped the bowl under the door without the spoon. She listened to the jailer's plodding footfalls approaching the door, the brief scrape of the bowl as he picked it up. His steps faded into distant silence. Either he hadn't noticed the spoon was missing or he didn't care.

She used the handle of her prize to etch a line on a bare patch of wall, but her effort left only a faint scratch. The wooden bed frame would be easier to mark. She lifted off the mattress and gasped. Notches covered every bit of the frame, including the slats. It would have taken years for one person to make them all. Replacing the mattress, she returned to where she had scored the wall. She had all day to deepen her nine marks.

Why hadn't Griman visited again? The Ophigeens might have denied her access. They might have even expelled her. Or perhaps Griman had decided that Drinith had lied. She could have reached that conclusion soon after Drinith's arrest. She might have visited merely to confirm her suspicions. Meritocrats were excellent at concealing their true opinions behind soothing words and disarming smiles.

Quiescat must have learned of her incarceration by now. He and Jarma should be secure as long as hope remained that Drinith could extricate herself from this predicament. But if she failed, what would happen to them? In her will, Drinith had nominated Jarma as her successor and endowed Quiescat with a sizable pension, but would the Parliament of Merit honor her wishes? The meritocrats resented Quiescat, in particular his perceived influence over her. Thaxen despised him. Gyran law was malleable to its makers. They'd find some legal pretext to set aside Drinith's wishes and turn her friends out on the streets.

Drinith sought succor in her imagination. She daydreamed of a peasant's life, ordinary and untroubled, in a mythical land of brine flowers. She created a village where she lived in peace with Quiescat and Jarma. Woad and his wife, Tazran, ran the local inn. She yearned to conjure up her dead friends, but the trespass of fancy on her loss proved too painful. Otherwise, none of the actualities of subsistence living impinged upon her reveries. The idealized life in the village might be trite, but it relieved the grimness of her reality.

A jangle of keys shattered her daydream. She rose to her feet. The jailer must have noticed the missing spoon. She tucked the utensil up her sleeve. It wasn't much of a weapon, but it might come in handy.

A guard in a light purple uniform opened the door of the cell and beckoned to her. As she approached the exit, she glimpsed three, no, four more guards in dark green uniforms lurking in the shadows behind him. Evidently, the Ophigeens had resolved to deny her any opportunity to escape.

The purple guard, presumably a benefactor, led the party through several interconnecting corridors and up a winding staircase to a gray metal door. Opening it, he escorted her inside. A single lampstone in the ceiling illuminated the windowless room. A full bath steamed in one corner. On the table beside it lay a domed tray, some towels, and a cup of water. Two changes of clothes rested on a chair—one thrall green and the other red. A bedroll sat on the latter.

She looked to the benefactor guard for an explanation.

"After you bathe and eat, you have a choice," he said. "You can save yourself the ordeals of the Ascent by taking thrall green. Or you can wear the red."

She bridled at the overt nudge to accept the former. A meritocrat would make a prestigious slave.

"Everyone gets the same offer," the guard said. "If you choose red, you can change your mind up until you disembark the dragon."

"But not if you pick green," Drinith said.

"You are correct. That is a decision made only once." A sly smile played on his lips. "By the way, you won't find any knife. Candidates receive them only after arriving on the Whetstone." He stepped back into the corridor and slammed the door shut.

Drinith tossed the thrall green clothes in a corner. She stripped off her old garments and flung them after them. Too agitated to luxuriate in the bath, she washed quickly, dried, and put on the red clothes. Lifting the cloche, she found an array of delicacies. Drinith did not know if they had some ritual significance, but they tasted nice. She gulped down the water in the little metal cup. She wrapped some biscuits and a lump of hard yellow cheese in a napkin and hid it in the bedroll. She hardly tasted the rest as she methodically ate it.

She tucked away the cup, slung the bedroll across her back and rapped on the door to call the guards. The benefactor blinked with surprise as he opened it. He must have expected her to take longer.

He pointed to a tray held by one of his subordinates. "It is customary to bring some small personal item with you on the Ascent. I took the liberty of bringing the jewelry you were wearing when you were arrested."

Drinith seized the alicorn bracelet. Thank the gods! Slipping it on her wrist felt like donning a shield. She had become so accustomed to its protection, so dependent. She resisted a perverse urge to put it back on the tray. It would be foolish to give it up, when she was already at such a disadvantage. "What will happen to the rest?"

"They'll be kept in the royal treasury until either you complete the Ascent"— he smirked—"or the Gyran ambassador collects them."

Flanked by the thrall guards, she followed the benefactor through another maze of anonymous corridors. As they neared an exit, a monstrous roar echoed around her. Pulsing gusts buffeted them.

"The dragon must have arrived," the benefactor said, picking up his pace.

"We're not going to the floating perches?"

"No. There's a perch outside the palace reserved for the Ascent and visiting dignitaries." Meritocrats apparently didn't qualify, but Drinith was in no position to quibble.

They emerged into a large open area. The dragon, a living mountain, towered above. Drinith had always held the creatures in awe, but viewing one from below, she had to fight against quaking before it. It bore reassuring signs of domestication, like the cinch deck across its belly and the headstall tucked beneath its crest and banding its forehead, but it was hard to believe that such sheer power could ever be truly tamed.

Lost against this daunting backdrop, girls and boys clad in red hooded cloaks formed a line. Immediately behind them stood women and men, their parents perhaps, in couples or alone.

The benefactor pointed to the far end of the line. "Wait over there."

A cordon of thrall guards encircling the group ensured Drinith had nowhere else to go. As she strolled by the candidates, their youthful faces stared back at her with indifference, fascination, fear, and contempt. One boy with a prominent jaw, standing alone, glared at her with a detestation bordering on revulsion as she passed by. He had the typical features of Nosteran heritage—a maroon complexion, pale rose eyes, and cropped dark red hair. The urge to ask him why he despised her slowed her, but she didn't stop.

The girl standing by herself at the very end was shorter and slighter than the rest. She had a sickly pallor and ashen hair. Inspired by their mutual isolation, Drinith acknowledged her with a nod. The girl's bloodshot eyes widened with surprise before she looked away. Drinith aligned herself with the row.

The circle of thrall guards parted for Diarch Kymalas and her retinue, two administrants in their white snakeskin garments and a half-dozen talon guards. She halted and scanned the line, her forceful gaze alighting on the pale girl. "Zoen."

The pale girl stepped forward and bowed. "Your Serene Majesty."

"Your mother begs your permission to join you this day."

"Is she still wed to my father?" the girl asked, anger straining her voice.

The Diarch looked askance at her. "She is, Zoen."

Zoen shrugged insouciantly. "Then I want nothing to do with her."

"Such enmity between a child and her parents saddens me," Kymalas said. "Would you reconsider?"

"It saddens me too, Diarch," Zoen said stiffly. "But I could not bear to be in her presence."

"I have known your mother and father a long time…"

"I thought I knew them but not anymore."

The other candidates and their parents regarded her with a mixture of horror and bewilderment. It must be unheard of for someone, still technically a child, to defy a diarch's will in this way. Such resolve was admirable.

"Then I won't force her presence upon you. I will respect your choice," Kymalas said. She nodded to one of her guards. "Inform Tharpen Zeal." As he stalked away, she studied something in her hand. She offered it to Zoen. "Your mother asked me to give you this."

Zoen gasped, reached for it, hesitated. Finally she took it, wrapping it in her fist.

Kymalas addressed the other candidates. "Today is about choice, your choice. You all have answered the call of adulthood and stand here today ready to shoulder the heavy burden it will place on you. You make the bold choice today, the hero's choice."

A distant wail rose and fell unremarked. "Ours is a just society. In heritor states, privilege isn't based upon merit." She glanced at Drinith, wrinkling her nose in distaste. "It depends not on the capability of the individual but rather the success or otherwise of their ancestors. A parent's resourcefulness elevates foolish and indolent offspring. Men and women capable of marvels are condemned to drudgery by their forbears' failures. This injustice might be delivered with a bludgeon or a veneer of sympathy, but the outcome is always the same. The civilization stagnates, ossifies, and then crumbles to dust."

Drinith's mouth curved into a wry grin. This crumbling must take some time, considering Ophigee was no older than Gyre.

"But not here," the Diarch declared. "Not here." She opened her arms. "Here, your life is yours to shape, the only limits being your potential. Everyone in Ophigee gets what they deserve."

Drinith glanced at the stony faces of the thrall guards. They must die a little inside at every reminder their own failings were to blame for their bondage.

"We reward successful endeavor," the Diarch said. "Those who earn wealth keep it. But each generation must stand or fall through its own effort. Every benefactor starts adulthood the same, with a cup and a knife and a long trek ahead of them. Some of you may not survive the Ascent. And for those who do, the journey doesn't end at the Ouroboric Gate. Perhaps, an exceptional individual among you will become an affluentor or administrant, but whatever your destiny, you'll have the satisfaction that you forged it yourself."

Unless you're dead or a slave.

"I wish you good fortune and leave you in the care of Dieseken Wise. I look forward to your successful return."

Kymalas strode away, her retinue folding into a column behind her. Except one. An administrant, a tall young woman, lingered. Drinith recognized her from the swooping dragon tattoo across her forehead. It clutched the space between her high eyebrows, transforming them into the limbs of a bow.

"Make your farewells," the administrant said. Down the line, candidates embraced their parents.

"I'm not originally from Ophigee," Drinith remarked conversationally to Zoen.

"I know who you are," Zoen said wearily. "Everybody does. You're the criminal from Gyre."

So the other candidates knew she was different to them, a threat, someone untrustworthy. Hope of finding allies among them wilted. "I'm surprised you're talking to me given my ill repute."

"As you may have noticed, I've a reputation of my own. I doubt my obstinacy impressed the Diarch."

Drinith fought the urge to pry deeper into Zoen's personal life lest it kill the conversation.

"It's rumored you're a spy," Zoen said. "But I reckon you can't be if the Diarchs permitted you to accompany us."

Unless they had somehow rigged the game against Drinith and

they knew she wouldn't survive it. She couldn't trust anyone, not even this lonely girl. Drinith must be on her guard.

Zoen added, "They say the Ascent forgives a lot if it forgives at all."

"Enough talk! Time to go!" the administrant barked as she strode along the line. She herded the candidates into a more compact line behind Drinith and marched them toward the waiting dragon.

10

———

Zoen gripped the rail with one hand and shut her eyes as the platform lifted off the ground. The ring stung her other palm as she squeezed it tighter. The sway of the platform in the breeze unnerved her. *This is foolishness. I fell from a second-floor balcony only a week ago and survived.* She forced her eyes open. An impossible distance quickly separated her from the ground, the guards standing below reduced to blurry dark green dots against the crimson yard. There would be no surviving a fall from this height.

Above, the cinchdeck, a belt of interconnected compartments curving across the dragon's belly, drew nearer.

"Are you all right, Zoen?" asked a spiky-haired Nosteran-type beside her. It took her a moment to recognize her former schoolmate, Oristan, shorn of his usual brashness. The perpetual sardonic slant of his mouth failed to distract from his sweaty fear.

"Are you?" she asked.

With a testy mutter, he turned toward the plump lad with typical Nosteran features behind him. Govren had his eyes squeezed so tightly shut, it must have hurt. A girl with enormous cornflower blue eyes and a light amber complexion patted Govren's hand. Fisken changed her hairstyle with such jarring frequency Zoen had often wondered if she wore wigs. Today, copper coils peeped from beneath her red hood.

So, two of Oristan's most fervent hangers-on had accompanied him. It was surprising that more of his clique hadn't volunteered to follow their leader to the Whetstone. They were all about the appropriate age. If they didn't ascend soon, they'd have to take the green. Counting the foreigner, there were only nine candidates present, two short of the usual complement, leaving plenty of room for more of Oristan's cohorts. He mustn't have been as popular as everyone supposed.

The platform jolted to an abrupt stop beside a small open hatch. The administrant, Dieseken Wise, clamped the platform to the cinchdeck and stepped across the narrow gap into the hatch. As the candidates clumped to follow her, a kerfuffle at the front prevented their boarding. Oristan pleaded with a stubborn Govren to enter.

"Dragons, let him take the green," a lantern-jawed boy jeered. Zoen didn't know him. He must have hailed from one of Ophigee's colonies on Noster.

"Mind your own business!" Oristan growled. He shoved Govren toward the hatch until tattooed arms reached through it and hauled him inside. With sighs of relief, the other candidates shuffled forward again.

As Zoen took her turn, drakers helped her across the gap. "She's a light one," one of them said, much to her disgust. She found herself in a curved tubular corridor. The dragon's sulfuric scent, soft in the open air, took on a burning pungency as though soaked into the walls. The structure shuddered to the lumbering thump of the beast's heart.

Govren sobbed quietly in a quivering ball on the floor. Dieseken stood over him, arms akimbo, her body trembling with indignation.

Oristan slipped between them, hands raised. "He'll be fine. He has a thing about heights, that's all. I'll sort him out."

"Make sure you do," Dieseken said, "or it's thrall green for him." She stabbed Oristan's chest with her finger. "Understand?"

Wary deference quickly displaced the spasm of outrage on

Oristan's face. "Of course, Administrant. He won't cause any more trouble. I promise."

"Make sure of it," Dieseken grunted. She sneered at Drinith as she stepped inside. The administrant craned her head as she counted the candidates, her lips moving along to her tally. At her nod, the drakers undid the clamp and shut the hatch, blinding Zoen until her eyes adjusted to the gloom. "Follow me."

Dieseken led the candidates down the corridor to a barrel-shaped, windowless room. The flat floor and the stacked bunks tilted at a slight angle. Knotty webs of rope covered the bunks and a low wall flush with the curved shell opposite the door. A single lampstone in the ceiling offered anemic illumination. "Make yourselves comfortable. It'll take a while for us to reach the disembarkation point at Stepstone." After they filed inside past her, she shut the door.

Zoen settled on the nearest bunk, wrapped her arms around her knees, and rested her head on them. The lantern-jawed boy leaned against the opposite bunk's post nearest the door.

In her peripheral vision Zoen watched as Drinith climbed up to the top bunk across from her and looked down upon the other candidates with raptorial interest. With black olive skin, large black eyes, and neat rows of braids across her scalp, her exotic and regal appearance gave credence to the rumors Zoen had heard about her unusual ancestry. Foreign monarchs were the worst type of heritor. It was hard to believe even the hated Gyran meritocrats would adopt someone with her background into their ranks. Her manner didn't strike Zoen as pretentious. Of course, meritocrats had a reputation for deceit. Zoen would have to be careful dealing with her.

She opened her palm and studied the ring, a duplicate of the one her parents had given Olen on the day she set off to the Whetstone. The amethyst had left an impression of a dragon's head on her palm. She slipped it on her finger.

Oristan and Fisken sat against the low wall opposite the door, wedging the trembling Govren between them.

"Why didn't you take that concoction your doctor gave you?" Oristan asked, his voice sharp with irritation.

Govren covered his face with his hands and breathed deeply. "I thought I could manage without it."

"Well, you were obviously wrong." Spurred by Fisken's indignant glare, Oristan patted Govren's shoulder and added, "You'll be fine. We'll look after you." His expression showed no trace of the confidence in his voice. Zoen, too, was doubtful. Boarding the dragon had proved to be an almost insurmountable trial for Govren. Disembarking would be an even more daunting prospect.

Oristan beckoned Zoen, but she pretended not to notice and looked away. He had never taken much interest in her before. She had no intention of joining his little clique now.

Two girls settled on the lower bunk across from her. Both wore their hair in plaited buns. The sturdier of the pair had typical Nosteran features, aside from her button nose and broad, friendly face. Coral pink mottled the carmine complexion of her wiry companion. Dark, thoughtful eyes softened her angular, pointed face. Her nod of acknowledgment surprised Zoen, who reflexively responded in kind.

Another girl plopped onto Zoen's bunk. The fieriest rose eyes Zoen had ever seen were set in her lavender face. She looked much older than sixteen, perhaps because of the acne scars that roughened her cheeks. Her greasy hair, yellow streaked with blue, was tied back in a messy ponytail, revealing the dozen gold studs in her ears.

"I'm Kaliop from the colony of Tyngor," the girl announced. Zoen shook the calloused hand she offered.

The girls on the opposite bunk perked up. "We're from Tyngor, too," the wiry girl said. "I'm Toskar, and my friend beside me is Nezon. You're obviously not the same Kaliop we knew back home."

"I confess I never actually spent much time on Tyngor," Kaliop said. "My parents traveled on business a lot. They used to take me with them."

"You look like the other Kaliop," Nezon said. "I mean, your coloring is remarkably similar."

"That's an interesting coincidence," Kaliop said, looking intrigued. "On my brief visits home, I've been mistaken for her. I had assumed it was down to us having the same name. I hadn't realized we were so physically similar."

"I doubt anybody would fail to tell the two of you apart," Nezon said. "The other Kaliop has a slighter frame..." She blushed.

Kaliop rubbed her cheek. "I'm sure she's quite the delicate flower compared to me."

"I didn't mean any offense," Nezon blurted. "Sometimes I trip over my tongue."

"No offense taken, I assure you." Leaning back on the bunk, Kaliop propped herself up on her elbows, oblivious to the appraising gaze Toskar had fixed upon her. "I'm sure by the time we reach the Ouroboric gate, we'll all be firm friends." She sat up and nodded to the lantern-jawed boy. "And what's your name?"

"Siga," he grunted.

"Are you from a colony, too, or from Ophigee?"

"Ophigee."

"A local lad, eh?"

He folded his arms and stared at the floor.

Kaliop shrugged and lay down again. "Not the talkative type, I suppose."

So this was the extent of Zoen's band of companions. She hadn't before given much thought to who would accompany her to the Whetstone. She'd need to find allies among them if she was to survive the arduous journey to the Ouroboric Gate. Though Toskar and Nezon seemed pleasant, Zoen didn't know them well enough to be sure she could depend on them. Drinith was an enigma, but Zoen trusted her more than Kaliop, despite the latter's amiability. It was hard to identify a solid reason for the vague unease Kaliop inspired. Perhaps it was merely an echo of Toskar's clear skepticism of her story, but Zoen couldn't shake off her suspicion. Siga seemed determined to prove to everyone that he was worthy only of their hatred. That left Oristan and his two comrades, the only familiar faces in the group. It would be safer to be part of his clique than to stand alone. The next time he invited Zoen to join them, she'd accept.

Eyeing Govren, Siga wrinkled his nose in disgust. "How can anyone who spent their life on Ophigee be so frightened of heights? The island is a precipice in every direction. Did he never leave his house?"

"Mind your own business!" Oristan snapped.

As the entire structure jolted, Zoen gripped the side of her bunk. Siga hugged the post he had been leaning against to halt his lurch forward. The floor and everything affixed to it—the bunks and the low wall—tilted to and fro.

Govren whimpered. As Fisken fastened webbing around the three of them, Oristan clamped a hand on Govren's shoulder. "The dragon is shifting, that's all. Nothing to worry about."

Everyone else secured themselves, even Siga, who climbed up onto the bunk above Zoen's.

When the dragon's roar vibrated throughout the room, Govren wasn't the only one to yelp. Kaliop tutted and shook her head in bemusement. "Have none of you ever been on a dragon before?"

"Of course," Toskar said. "How else would we come from Tyngor?"

Kaliop smirked. "I bet it's the first time you've traveled across the belly though." She chuckled. "Well, you're in for quite a treat."

The structure violently shuddered, squealing and groaning as if it might break asunder. Zoen stifled a cry as the floor shifted to remain horizontal inside the cabin. The door climbed up the wall, revealing a curved ladder embedded beneath it.

"We're lifting off," Kaliop said. "Nothing to worry about."

Zoen's panic waned as the shuddering gentled to a languid rocking. The floor gently returned to its original position in relation to the entrance.

"The floor moves so we're not thrown about as the dragon lifts off. The cinchdeck expands and contracts to the sweep of the dragon's wings," Kaliop said. "All perfectly natural."

Of course. Zoen *knew* that. She had studied the mechanics of dragon flight, the principles of drakership, but this was the first time she had experienced the physical reality of life on board a dragon. "Does the saddledeck tremble like this?"

Kaliop shook her head.

"I can't believe anyone would choose to work down here."

Kaliop sniffed. "The headstall shakes worse. Up there, a jerk of the dragon's head can send you bouncing off the walls. A friend of mine was flung out a hatch to his death by one such sudden movement. And there's more work to be done on the saddledeck, sails to trim and the like. The cinchdeck is not so bad once you get used to it."

"You certainly must have a lot of experience with dragons," Toskar observed pointedly.

Kaliop grinned irritably. "Like I said, my parents traveled a lot."

Govren shrieked, his eyes bulging with terror. He ripped off his webbing, slipped free of his companions' clutches, dashed for the door. "Let me out!"

Oristan leapt up and flung his arms around him. "Stop!" But Govren's momentum carried them both onward. Govren slapped both of his hands against the door and squealed all the louder. As Oristan wrenched him away, Siga slipped down from his bunk and punched Govren's jaw. Dumbfounded, Oristan broke his embrace, letting his stunned friend drop to the floor.

"There was no need for that!" Oristan said to his would-be helper with savage indignation.

Shaking off his daze, Govren crawled to his feet and rushed again for the exit. Oristan threw himself in his way, hugged his waist, and slammed him against the door. With a desperate wail, Govren let fly a flurry of slaps. One strike to the face stung Oristan to rage. He punched Govren hard. Govren raised his arms and whimpered, but Oristan's fist continued to pound him until he sank to the floor. Siga joined in the rain of blows with relish.

"Stop!" Fisken cried as she attempted to peel Oristan off their friend. "You'll kill him!"

"Dragons, shut up!" he growled, pushing her away.

A vicious kick from Siga silenced Govren's whimpers. Before he could deliver a second, Oristan dragged him away. "Enough!" He looked shocked by his own brutality, but Siga beamed with delight, accentuating his prominent jaw.

"You didn't need to be so rough," Oristan muttered.

"You thumped him harder," Siga observed with amusement.

"You're both shameful," Fisken said. "You wouldn't treat an impudent thrall like that."

Siga sneered. "If he was a thrall, he'd think it a mercy."

"Govren is supposedly your friend," Fisken said to Oristan.

"He wouldn't listen to reason," he pleaded. "He'd have taken the green if I hadn't stopped him."

"That's right," Siga said smugly. "We did him a favor."

Fisken glowered at him. "Who are you? You claim to be from Ophigee, but I don't know you."

Oristan sneered. "You wouldn't. The children of thralls don't move in our circles."

Siga's massive jaw clenched. His fists tightened. His entire body tensed as if readying to leap upon Oristan at the next hint of provocation. "I've as much right to be here as any of you."

"How did you know he's thrallborn?" Fisken asked.

"You can see it in his eyes—the smolder of resentment." Oristan smirked. "How else could we have never come across him on Ophigee before?"

Govren's plaintive moan drew Siga's scowl. "Shut up, or I'll break your jaw!" he barked, his whole body quivering with rage.

"I guess that's why we're not given our knives until we disembark," Kaliop said.

"I heard they stopped issuing them with the last meal because somebody tried to stab a benefactor," Fisken said.

"I heard they tried to kill Diarch Clacon," Nezon whispered, looking at the door.

"Maybe they tried to knife their parents," Siga said, shooting a sour glance toward Zoen. Who was he to mock her? Refusing to be baited, she kept a dignified silence.

"We'll need those knives when we get to Stepstone," Oristan said as he pressed a cloth to his bloody knuckles.

Siga snickered and pointed at Drinith. "To protect us from Thrall Green?" he sneered, coining the most offensive epithet imaginable for the foreigner.

"I'm not a thrall," Drinith said firmly.

"But your skin is thrall green," Siga said, raising a few nervous chuckles. "It must be terrible being unable to take off your clothes in case you're mistaken for a thrall."

"You'd know all about it," she said, "being the son of one."

Siga's hands balled into fists, his eyes gleamed with murderous rage. He muttered under his breath as he stormed from the room. Govren emitted a pained groan as the edge of the door clipped the back of his head.

"You hit a sore point, it seems," Oristan said to Drinith. "Thrallborns are always so touchy."

"Do you know many thrallborns?" Nezon asked, ignoring Toskar's gesture to be quiet.

Oristan gave a languid shrug. "A few. Do you?"

"Our past makes no difference," Toskar said. "We all have to prove ourselves on the Ascent whether we are the children of an affluentor or the lowest thrall."

"Of course." Oristan settled back down against the low wall. Fisken knelt down beside Govren and rubbed his back.

"What did you mean by we'll need our knives?" Kaliop asked, knitting her heavy eyebrows.

Oristan stared at her with incredulity. "You haven't heard the stories?" Everyone focused on him.

Kaliop glanced at the ceiling. "No."

"Nobody has completed the Ascent in several red months," Oristan said.

"I heard the same rumor." A ripening blush warmed Zoen's cheeks. "My father told me. I assumed he said it to put me off the Ascent."

"He wasn't lying," Oristan said. "Nobody has passed through the

Ouroboric Gate for three red months. That's the likely reason we number only nine. Prospective candidates are putting off their Ascent for as long as possible. I'm only going now because I'll be overage soon. I assume most of you are in the same predicament."

"If the Ascent is so impossible, why are they letting us attempt it?" Kaliop demanded savagely.

"Similar droughts have happened before. The Ascent is sacrosanct."

"Great," Kaliop muttered, rolling her eyes. "So you're telling me we're as good as dead."

"We are if we don't work together," Oristan said. "It's not as if we have to compete against each other. Cooperation offers our best hope of survival."

"The previous groups who failed before us might have thought the same," Kaliop said.

Oristan shrugged.

"I suppose you intend to lead us," Toskar said.

He grinned. "I hadn't given it much thought, but if you're offering, I'll be happy to be leader. Unless there's anyone else who wants to challenge me."

Nezon inhaled to say something, but Toskar's wagging finger silenced her.

"What about her?" Fisken nodded at Drinith.

Oristan gave a bemused frown. "For leader?"

Fisken dismissively batted the notion with the back of her hand. "Is Thrall Green part of our group? She's not even Ophigeen."

"Does she want to?" Oristan turned toward Drinith.

"I don't understand why I am singled out for exclusion," she said.

"Because you're a spy," Fisken said.

Oristan stroked his chin. "Can we trust you? That's the question."

"The Diarchs trust her enough to let her take part," Zoen said.

"According to you all, nobody has finished the Ascent for ages," Kaliop said glumly. "In such circumstances, sending her to the Whetstone might as well be a death sentence."

Drinith stroked her cheeks. "It's in all our interest to complete the

Ascent. And you need every bit of help to reach the Ouroboric Gate. I'm not a spy, but I am a warrior. I've fought for my life against tougher foes than any we might face on this Ascent, and I survived."

No no no. You're talking yourself up too much. Oristan will see you as a potential threat to his nascent leadership.

Perhaps wary of the hint of brittleness in Oristan's smile, Drinith added: "I'm an outsider. My knowledge of your ways is superficial. I must defer to your better judgment. Nonetheless, I'm certain I can be of help."

"The Diarchs ruled that she could attempt the Ascent," Zoen said. "Who are we to question their judgment? We don't know what dangers await us in the Whetstone. We'd be fools to spurn her help."

Oristan was about to speak when Siga stumbled back into the room. "What's going on?" he demanded.

Fisken pointed at Drinith. "We're deciding whether to include her in our group."

"So we're a group now, are we?" Siga asked as he leaned against the door. Zoen nodded along with Nezon and Toskar. "She's not one of us," he said. "Let her make her own way up the Whetstone."

"What's your name, Thrall Green?" Oristan asked.

The girl hesitated, pursing her lips as though reluctant to answer to that epithet. "Drinith."

"Drinith, welcome to the group."

"She's in?" Siga glared at him. "What gives you the right to decide that?" His fist danced in front of him. "Who chose you to be leader?"

A smile spread across Oristan's face. His finger did a vague circle of the room. "Everyone except you."

"What?"

Oristan grinned. "If you're unhappy, you can ascend by yourself. Perhaps you'd prefer it. You strike me as the sort who doesn't like to depend on others."

Siga bowed his head, his fists hanging by his sides. "No. I want to travel with the rest of you."

"Then, you too are welcome," Oristan said with sneering magnanimity. He had established his leadership with impressive efficiency. Time would tell if his abilities extended to keeping them all alive in the Whetstone.

Dismay quickly fractured Zoen's relief that Drinith had secured her place among them. Zoen knew nothing of her beyond a few rumors and the little she had shared with the group. What had impelled Zoen to speak up for the foreigner? Was it simply down to her recognition of a fellow outsider? Or had Drinith manipulated her in some subtle way? Hopefully, Zoen wouldn't come to regret her generosity.

11

———————

Trajar drew a breathless Quiescat step by step toward the bed.

A rap on the door transfixed them both.

"Quiescat?" Jarma said, entering. She blinked with surprise. "Oh, Meritocrat Trajar, I didn't realize you were still here. I heard you had called, but I assumed as you weren't in the parlor, you had left."

In a panic, Quiescat swatted where Trajar's hand had held his cowl. It was already gone, though the ghost of its touch lingered.

Trajar shrugged. "I'm afraid I cajoled Quiescat into giving me a tour." Her hair still hung loosely down to her shoulders. Thank the gods, nobody else in the mansion had seen it tied up in a bun on her arrival.

Jarma raised an eyebrow. "I must apologize for the unkempt state of this room. It's not one we use regularly. I will have the servants tidy it."

Quiescat burned with embarrassment as he followed her gaze to the tousled blankets. He'd have to explain later how he'd mussed them as he crawled on his knees across the bed to escape Trajar.

"I assume this isn't strictly a social visit, Meritocrat," Jarma added. "You have some word of Drinith?"

"I'm afraid not. I called to see how you both are coping in Drinith's absence. By the by, Jarma, there's no need to address me with such formality. You're a meritorian now. Call me Elca."

"That's gracious of you, Elca," Jarma said. "Let's have some refreshment. I'll have Fenvar show you the rest of the mansion later. I can tell you from personal experience, she is a most knowledgeable and entertaining guide."

They strolled down to the parlor, Quiescat keeping a wary distance from Trajar.

The witness to his shame shared a couch with his humbler while he sat alone across from them. Jarma checked the teapot, pressed a hand to it. "It's cool. I'll have a fresh one made. I'll be back momentarily." She strode out of the room, leaving the door ajar.

"You promised to help Drinith," Quiescat said, vexed at the plaintive whine in his voice.

"Best keep what happened in the bedroom to ourselves," Trajar said. "Courtesars can be violently jealous. Muenthax wouldn't be the only one to take offense. And if Drinith survives Ophigee, she might misunderstand. She might reject my friendship, which wouldn't be wise in the current political climate. I'm a better friend than an enemy."

"You promised to help her," he repeated, sensing the hint of panic in her threats. He needed to glean some benefit from the humiliation she had inflicted on him, tangible proof that his embarrassment hadn't been for nothing.

Her tight smile hinted annoyance. "My advice is this. Gyre cannot help you. Our republic is already at war with Ophigee, so the threat of war is no threat at all. The Parliament of Merit cannot escalate the conflict without weakening our blockade of Rhumgad. So forget petitioning the parliament. Go to Ophigee yourself and rescue her. I understand the Rite of Beneficence takes place in the island's underside, the so-called Whetstone. Take a dragon there. I know a captain ideal for such an enterprise, expensive but discreet—Lawster Forte of the *Parched Tongue*. When perched at Gyre, he frequents an inn called the Dragon's Spit. If you mention my name, I'm sure he'd help you for two hundred thousand ducats."

"I could buy a dragon for that amount," Quiescat groused.

"Perhaps," Trajar admitted. "But could you crew it? Such work takes a special breed of draker, a risk-taker as close to a pyrate as makes no difference but who won't draw the attention of the law. Captain Forte is just such a person. He's well respected...in certain circles."

She bit her lip. "One other thing. You need to be careful amassing the money for such an enterprise. Thaxen has made it her business to watch you. If you try to use Drinith's property as collateral for a loan in any bank in Gyre, she'll find out. She'd relish an opportunity to have you arrested for embezzlement."

"But my only purpose would be to save Drinith's life."

Trajar shook her head sadly at his naivety. "That doesn't matter. A meritocratic title is more important than its bearer, particularly one who has no blood ties to the rest of the Meritocracy. Drinith's greatest imperative, after protecting the Halcyon Republic, is to preserve the Hax fortune for her successors. Penury is an unforgivable sin for a meritocrat. And you're not a meritocrat, but the servant of one. You'd face more than disgrace and banishment. You'd end up walking the Plank."

Quiescat was fastidious about avoiding Crimson Plaza on execution days. Mention of the Plank sent a shiver down his spine. He dreaded being shunted off that slender tongue of rock to plummet into the inner sun. "How, then, am I supposed to get the money?"

"Carefully. Many foreign diplomats and merchants live in the city. There are cults, too, from distant shards desperate to build temples here. There was one from Phule..." She twirled her finger in a circle as she looked for inspiration on the ceiling. "They pestered everyone, begging for a site for their temple."

"The Dudgeon of Hissimir," Quiescat said gloomily.

"That's them. Their High Dudgeon would pay any price for a site. You have access to the deeds of Drinith's properties. Offer him one. After you rescue Drinith, she can smooth any ruffled meritocratic feathers with my help, provided you restrict your endeavors to those silly foreigners. Many meritocrats would admire your initiative as long as they weren't its victims."

"You make it sound like a jolly adventure." Quiescat scowled to emphasize his sarcasm.

"What's the worst that can happen?" Trajar asked with a languid shrug. "You might be condemned as a criminal and executed. But you've already lived longer than Fate decreed."

How did she know about that? She must have a spy within the household.

"No blame can be attached to Drinith for your crimes," Trajar assured him. "Or am I wrong about you—that, despite your declarations to the contrary, you value your life more than hers?"

Quiescat pressed his mouth shut so hard his jaw hurt. Despite his anger, he couldn't afford to vex her.

Trajar glanced at the door. "And keep Jarma out of your schemes."

"To protect her?"

"To protect yourself. She may have been a loyal servant, but she's a servant no longer. She has everything to gain from Drinith's death and your ruin."

How dare that viper impugn Jarma's loyalty! Trajar's transparent attempt to divide them would not work. This very day, Jarma had pried him from her clutches and preserved the dregs of his dignity.

"I can see you're skeptical, but don't be so quick to dismiss my advice," Trajar said.

Panic gripped Quiescat. Could Jarma be listening through the open door? No, she wasn't so underhanded. She and Quiescat may not have always been on amicable terms, but she had never given him any reason to doubt her trustworthiness.

"Watch her and decide for yourself," Trajar said. "In the meantime, be careful what you tell her."

Quiescat was about to inform Trajar exactly what he thought of her distasteful counsel when Jarma returned, accompanied by a maid carrying a fresh pot of tea.

"I'm sorry for the delay," Jarma said as she seated herself and the servant poured yellow tea into bowls.

"Dear Jarma, now that you are a meritorian, you must learn not to apologize for such inconsequential matters," Trajar said.

Jarma's eyes narrowed. "And what about meritocrats? Do they never apologize?"

"Meritocrats leave expressions of regret to their servants."

Quiescat suffered through the ensuing conversation in pained silence. It dealt with trivialities, mostly gossip about various meritocratic families. The interminable chatter about serenades, trysts, and courtesar duels oppressed him. Jarma asked too many questions. She should have let the conversation die, so Trajar might take the hint and leave.

"Have many courtesars tempted you onto your balcony yet?" Trajar asked her.

Jarma shook her head, her smile softening. "Drinith usually gets all the attention, and frankly, I'm glad of it. I lost someone dear not so long ago. I'm not quite ready for another romance yet."

Trajar leaned close and touched her hand. "How tragic! I hadn't realized you lost a courtesar already. I don't know how that escaped my attention, given I currently hold the position of Arbiter of Courtesars."

Jarma glanced at Quiescat. "Abecedar wasn't a courtesar. He was briefly Oracle of Godsdoor before he died."

Quiescat rose to his feet. He could hardly breathe. "If you excuse me, I'm feeling unwell." He forced a smile and fled. Retreating to the sanctuary of his bedchamber, he collapsed onto the bed and wished he had died on the *Surly Bonnacon*, as Fate promised. Shame weighed on his chest. To think, he had condemned Abecedar and Jarma for their earnest and relatively timid romance. Quiescat came so close to yielding to his lust and fear. If Jarma hadn't interrupted, he would have been fallen prey to Trajar's seduction.

A tentative knock on the door. He held his breath and hoped whoever it was would go away.

"Quiescat?"

He sat up. "Come in, Jarma."

She entered, her arms folded below a frown. "What was going on in that bedroom?"

"I don't want to talk about it," he pleaded. "I can't." Choking on his embarrassment, he shook his head.

"Why did Elca call?"

"I asked her. I hoped she might help free Drinith."

"Why didn't you tell me?"

"I thought..." He hadn't thought of her at all.

"I'm not some maid to be ignored. I'm a meritorian, and I'm in charge until Drinith returns, not you! Who else have you asked to help?"

He listed Thaxen Savarel and the rest, as many as he could remember.

She rolled her eyes. "Did you ever consider that those pleas might be received with more sympathy if they came from me?"

She was right. "I'm sorry," he murmured.

"I'm sorry, too!" she roared, making sweeping gestures with her arms as if conducting her anger. "I'm sorry for my friend trapped in Ophigee. I'm sorry you squandered numerous opportunities to help her because of your blind pride."

"You're right," he said. "I should have involved you from the start." *Be careful what you tell Jarma.* Trajar's warning came unbidden. "You could contact them now."

She shook her head. "Too late. Any intervention I might attempt now will be viewed as made at *your* behest. I'll be regarded as *your* puppet."

The doorbell rang. Jarma cursed under her breath. "That insufferable woman must have forgotten something."

Shoes padded up the carpeted hall. Fenvar peered into the room. "Meritorian." She acknowledged Quiescat with a nod. "Meritocrat Savarel awaits you in the parlor."

Jarma smoothed her dress. "I'll meet her. You can stay here if you wish, Quiescat."

"I'll come with you," he said. "She might have some news of Drinith."

Thaxen scowled as they entered the parlor. "I wish to speak to the meritorian alone."

"Is there any news of Drinith?" Quiescat asked.

Thaxen looked away.

"You had better go," Jarma murmured to him.

With a growl, he stomped out of the parlor. As he glanced backward, he caught a glimpse of Thaxen's malicious grin through the shutting doors. He refused to be defeated so easily. He needed to know what news of Drinith Thaxen brought. Nobody else was about, so he crouched by the keyhole and listened.

"What chance has Drinith of surviving the Rite of Beneficence?" Jarma asked anxiously.

"If our spies are correct, none," Thaxen said. There it was, the pronouncement Quiescat most feared. "You need to prepare to take her place."

"But I'm... I was a servant until recently. I..."

"Drinith obviously thought you could be more. You have been exceptionally diligent in your studies, I understand."

Jarma cleared her throat. "I do my best to honor Drinith's faith in me."

"Our Arbiter of Merit, Tival Ronad, can help you adjust."

"And I'll have Quiescat to advise me."

Thaxen snorted. "You must rid yourself of him the moment the parliament declares Drinith dead. He'll only ever see you as a menial. Many meritocrats were already suspicious of Drinith because of the influence he exerted over her, and she had the advantage of saving the city from Magian's attack. If he stays in your household, they'll dismiss you as his puppet."

Gods, Quiescat had proved Thaxen's point by his own actions. *What a blundering fool I have been!*

"He saved my life," Jarma said.

Quiescat nodded in appreciation.

"I thought it was Halyard who slew the pentacular hunting you."

"Quiescat helped me to climb onto a balcony and escape. He encouraged me to go."

"And what was his reaction when Drinith elevated you to a meritorian?"

A hesitant silence. "It surprised him. She did it without his counsel."

"And why would she do that if she thought he would support her decision?"

Jarma didn't answer.

"Why am I getting letters from him?" Thaxen asked. "Why is he calling to my door? Why did Elca Trajar visit him specifically this very day? Do you know?"

Silence again.

"You should. You're entitled to know. You're the meritorian here. You should make the decisions for your household in your meritocrat's absence. He's usurping your role. However well-intentioned his actions might be, he's undermining you. He'd never do that to Drinith, but your title is merely an inconvenience to him. His devotion to his princess is unquestionable, but would he display the same loyalty to an ex-servant who, in his eyes, has climbed above her station?"

Gods damn Savarel! Her lies were more venomous than any snakebite. It took Quiescat great effort to control his temper listening to this slander.

"He might have been considered a sage back on Rhumgad," Thaxen continued, "but when it comes to the subtleties of meritocratic politics, he's a witless fool. Quiescat is blind to his limitations. He denies his lowly standing. It must chafe him that here he is inferior to a former servant."

Her claims contained an undeniable kernel of truth. Quiescat's elevated status had evaporated with his oracular ability, and he was still a novice in the nuances of Gyran politics. His encounter with Elca Trajar had laid bare the weakness of his position and his naivety in dealing with these cunning oligarchs.

"You must be rid of him as soon as possible," Thaxen said. "In the meantime, you must prevent him from undermining you. Keep a close eye on everything he does. Remind him of his place. Chasten him. Wrest control of the Hax finances from him. They aren't his to fritter away. That money belongs to you." She paused. "You look troubled."

"Drinith wouldn't approve."

"Drinith's not coming back. Jarma, you're a meritorian and soon you'll be a meritocrat. You need to follow your own good sense."

"You're right." With two words, Jarma sealed her betrayal.

A cough alerted Quiescat to a shadow over him. He turned to find Fenvar behind him. The butler arched a quizzical eyebrow as Quiescat offered a strained smile.

"I dropped something," he said lamely. How long had she been watching him?

"Would you like me to help you look for it?" she asked smoothly.

He patted his cassock, located the bunch of keys in one of his pockets. He pulled it out and waved it at the butler. "There it is! I don't know how I missed it. I was certain I dropped it."

The butler nodded sympathetically, but Quiescat was sure she didn't believe him. She'd report what she had seen to Jarma at the first opportunity. Quiescat needed to get out of here.

Mumbling farewell, he fled the reception hall and hastened to Drinith's study. Every step of the way, a small part of him screamed that he was overreacting, but he had no choice. He had heard Jarma's treachery firsthand.

He had the key to the study ready by the time he reached the door. Locking it behind him didn't make him feel any safer. He opened the secret door behind the bookshelves and pressed two hidden levers just inside the passage. The concealed trapdoor on the threshold clicked open a fraction. Quiescat lifted it to reveal the strongbox underneath. He worked through the combination on the dial and unlocked it with the key, but the lid wouldn't rise. He must have fumbled the combination. Jarma couldn't have changed it already. He needed to calm down. He dialed the safe again, more carefully. This time it opened when he tested the handle.

Rifling through the contents, he took a bag of coins and Drinith's letter granting him authority to enter into financial contracts in her absence. He scanned the deeds carved on sheets of dragon scale and picked out the least valuable of the properties, a vacant building on Salt House Lane. The handful of dragon scale promissory notes from Trustworth Bank sorely tempted him but they were too traceable for this illicit enterprise.

He relocked the strongbox and closed the trapdoor.

The handle of the study door jerked up and down. A fist pounded the door. "Quiescat, are you in there?" Jarma's voice.

He hesitated to answer. "Just a moment!" His gaze shifted from the flapping handle to the secret passage.

"Quiescat, let us in!"

So she wasn't alone. How many were with her? Had she come to arrest him?

Fleeing would be an admission of guilt. He'd be condemning himself.

The scrape of metal on metal preceded the key dropping from the lock. As the door opened, he dashed into the secret passage. He slammed the bookshelf door shut and jammed the opening mechanism with a stick. It wouldn't take Jarma long to figure out how to open it. She'd dispatch servants to catch him as he exited. He raced down the passage.

He reached the nearest exit, opened the door.

"Quiescat!" Jarma's cry echoed down the tunnel after him. He closed the door, raced down the lane, and plunged into the crowds milling along the street at the far end. He was on his own now and, for all he knew, the whole city was against him. Thaxen had won.

12

____

Drinith shied from Siga's glower as he settled across from her on the other top bunk. If she had gained a somewhat ambivalent ally in the group's new leader, she had also cemented the thrallborn's enmity. He wouldn't forget the humiliation Oristan had meted out to him on her account. She, in the group's eyes a foreigner and a criminal, must be the only one here considered lower status than the son of a thrall. And status mattered to him, mattered to them all. For all Toskar's talk of starting out as equals, the essence of their former lives clung to them, shaping their attitudes.

Fisken steered Govren back to the low wall, and Oristan helped her wrap the three of them in netting. A morose silence settled over the cabin that dampened even Oristan's lopsided grin. The candidates' subdued demeanor was painfully out of step with the Diarch's heroic depiction of them. The uncertain nature of the danger they faced in the Whetstone made it even more threatening. Drinith lay down on her bunk and stared at the ceiling to avoid looking at them. She had enough misgivings without adopting theirs.

What judgment would Oristan have pronounced on her if Siga hadn't blundered into the cabin at that particular moment? It irked her to have to depend on these mistrustful strangers, but she had no choice. She'd likely not survive the Ascent without their help.

A sudden jolt woke her. She must have drifted off to sleep. The cinchdeck shuddered. It squealed and groaned as if in agony. The floor and the bunks swayed back and forth. She looked for reassurance to the other candidates, only to find her panic mirrored in their faces. Kaliop was the only exception, but her bemused smirk irritated as much as it comforted.

The quake ceased as abruptly as it started.

"What you think caused that?" Fisken blurted.

Yawning, Kaliop slipped off her webbing, climbed off the bunk, and luxuriated in a stretch. "We've landed."

The door opened and Dieseken Wise peeped inside. "Time to go."

"When do we get our knives?" Siga asked.

"Soon. You must disembark first." A chilly gust of wind howled into the compartment and tousled Dieseken's dark hair. "Follow me."

Two drakers waited beside the open hatch. A rope dangled through it from a winch in the ceiling. Drinith peered down. The line reached a sooty outcrop jutting from the body of the island. A blackened stone dragon head adorned the opening in the cliff face, its worn tongue merging with the promontory.

"This is your last chance to take the green," the administrant said. "After you climb through this hatch, you're on your own. Nobody will come to help you." She waited for a moment. Nobody took her offer. "Who's first?"

"Her." Siga cocked a thumb at Drinith.

She didn't bother to argue. She eased herself onto the narrow sill outside the hatch, expecting to be buffeted by the wind, but the air hardly moved, as though the Crevast held its breath. Seizing the line with both hands, she weaved it between her feet, forming a clamp the way Gelasin had taught her. Someone snickered as she descended. She moved slowly, pushing away from the ledge until she cleared it. She slid down to the bare rock. A smattering of applause greeted her safe landing.

Zoen descended next. Wrapping the rope around one leg, she

dropped slowly and deliberately. The slightness of her frame belied her physical strength. She grinned as she touched the ground.

The others descended gracefully, more or less, using the same technique. It must have been a standard skill taught on Ophigee. Kaliop proved to be the exception, employing a technique similar to Drinith's.

Govren or Oristan should have followed her, but neither emerged. Drinith stared up at the hatch with the rest, straining to discern the reason for their delay.

"What's keeping them?" Fisken muttered.

Oristan finally climbed out. He looked down, wobbled, seized the upper lip of the hatch with both hands. He dared a timid glance downward and flinched. Terror had transfixed him, but Dieseken wouldn't permit him to cling on for long. Either she'd have him shoved from the hatchway or she'd drag him back inside and force him to take the green.

Siga grinned up in triumph. "He's afraid. He's afraid." He cupped his mouth with his hands. "Jump!"

"Shut up!" Fisken snapped.

Snickering, Siga pointed to the rope. "If you want to help him, be my guest."

Fisken's gaze followed the rope up to the paralyzed Oristan. Pursing her lips, she shook her head and stepped back.

If Oristan took the green, Siga might succeed him as leader. Drinith couldn't afford that to happen. Grasping the rope, she started up it.

"Be careful!" Zoen yelled.

Had the dragon remained perfectly still, it would have been easier for Drinith to pretend she was climbing toward a rocky ceiling, but its scaly belly expanded and contracted with each hissing breath. Its massive columnar legs shifted, sending the panicked candidates scurrying toward the mouth of the tunnel. Any moment, the dragon might lie down, flinging Drinith against the rock below, crushing her beneath its massive weight. No, the whisperers in the headstall would never permit that to happen. She had to believe that. She kept climbing.

She drew alongside the ledge and stepped onto the sliver Oristan's frozen form didn't take up. The drakers watched with a mixture of surprise and admiration, but Dieseken glowered at her. Govren knelt on the floor behind them, facing the wall, shivering with sobs.

"This is most irregular," the administrant declared. "Step across the threshold, either of you, and it will be tantamount to taking the green."

Oristan, jammed across the hatchway, didn't offer Drinith the slightest acknowledgment. Fear blinded him to her presence. She needed to be careful. Startling him might get them both killed.

"Oristan," she said. He didn't react. Perhaps she had spoken too softly for him to hear. She bit her lip. "Oristan," she said louder, "we need you."

He turned toward her and shook his head. "I can't."

"Then take thrall green," Dieseken muttered. "We'll be lifting away soon regardless of whether you are off." One of the drakers scurried down the corridor at her signal.

"I was fine until Govren took thrall green," Oristan said. "He couldn't even face climbing out here."

"But you did," Drinith said. "You did the hard part. Just a little further to go. We need you down there."

"I doubt Siga would agree."

"Siga's a fool. You know how to abseil?"

"Yes," he said, "but I've never descended so far."

"It's not as far as you think," Drinith lied. "You could jump it safely from here, though the rope would make it easier."

He guffawed. "I think it's a little further than that."

"I'm surprised you're not holding onto the rope. You'd be less likely to fall." Clinging on to the edge of the hatch, she pushed the line toward him.

He lurched for the rope, grabbed it, wrapped his legs and arms around it, exactly as she hoped. She shoved him off the ledge. He cried in terror as he slid down.

"I'm coming down!" she yelled as he slowed his drop. "Keep going or I'll knock you off." He flew down too fast and hit the ground with enough force to hurt himself, but he staggered clear of the line, apparently uninjured. She grabbed the rope and slid down.

As she landed, Oristan brushed a hand across his sweaty face. "Thanks for your help," he murmured. "I don't like heights." He glanced guiltily at Siga.

Siga sneered. "So our perfect leader's not so perfect after all."

Oristan's lopsided grin lacked conviction. "At least I've faced my worst fear and bested it. Can you say the same?"

Siga snorted. "Thrall Green bested it, not you."

"What happened to Govren?" Fisken demanded.

Oristan shied from her anxious gaze. "He took the green."

"Why didn't you stop him?" she shrieked. "You're supposed to be his friend. You're so damn selfish, abandoning him like that."

He glared at her. "But for the witch, I'd have been forced to take the green myself. You did little to help Govren or me down here."

Fisken's jaw dropped. "I couldn't…"

"Climb up and bring Govren down since you think it is so easy. Go on!" he growled, but the rope had already slithered back up to the cinchdeck.

"Where are our knives?" Siga yelled up through cupped hands. "You promised us our knives!"

A head peeped out from the hatch. "Look out below!"

As the candidates retreated, a rain of knives fell from the hatch, glittering as they dispersed before clattering against the slick black stone. A rebounding blade just missed Drinith's foot. She snatched at it as two gusts from opposite directions crashed around her. It did a teasing dance beyond her chasing grasp until it dropped off the promontory.

Everyone else scrabbled after knives bouncing and skittering across the rock to the quickening beat of the dragon's wings. Nezon had to grab Toskar before she followed one into the void.

The wind, surging to frightful intensity, halted the pursuit as candidates clung to the rock to avoid being swept away. Drinith's clothes billowed and flapped as competing icy blasts threatened to tear her from the rocky burr she hugged. The rising beast engulfed the sky. Its shadow shrank and slid away, taking the wind with it. The group leapt off the ground and chased the remaining weapons. Siga wrenched a knife from Fisken's hand. She stared in horror at the clean red line across her palm.

"Give that back to her," Zoen said.

"It's mine," Siga insisted, waving the knife at her.

"It belongs to the group." Oristan extended his palm, flexed his fingers impatiently. "Hand it over."

Siga's nostrils flared. "You just want it for yourself."

Oristan pressed his hands against his sides. "Keep that blade and ascend by yourself or hand it over and prove your value to the group."

Disgust twisted Fisken's face. "You can't let him walk off with a knife."

Oristan sneered. "He won't."

Siga tossed the blade at Oristan's feet.

Keeping a wary eye on him, Oristan retrieved it. "Who else caught a knife?" Kaliop, Zoen, and Nezon raised their hands. That left four of the group unarmed, including Drinith. Oristan offered her the blade. "I have one already."

Fisken's eyes bulged with indignant disbelief. "You can't! The thrallborn stole that knife from me!" She displayed her injured palm. "He cut me taking it too!"

Drinith reached for it, hesitated. Taking the knife would make another firm enemy.

"That's right," Oristan said. "And now Siga has no knife, either. We don't know for certain what dangers we must face here, but our weapons must go to those best capable of wielding them. Take it, Drinith."

Fisken didn't like her anyway and, without a knife, Drinith would be even more dependent on the group. With a nod of thanks, Drinith took it. The black-handled weapon with a round handguard was double-edged like a dagger.

"Traitor!" Fisken yelled, her voice trembling with rage. "First, Govren, now me. Is there anyone you won't betray?"

"The group's survival must come before other considerations," Oristan said haughtily. "If that's not to your liking, make your own way to the Ouroboric Gate."

Fisken's indignation wilted. She shook her head; her blue eyes, naturally huge, swelled bizarrely with fear. "I'll stay."

"What about her?" Siga pointed at Zoen. "You can't seriously consider that weakling more fit than me to carry a knife."

Oristan regarded him coolly. "That weakling caught one."

"You're some hypocrite." Siga jerked a thumb at Drinith. "You'd be wearing thrall green now if she hadn't rescued you."

"Come on, try to take my knife," Zoen growled, brandishing her weapon. "If I don't kill you, you can pick it out of your chest."

Oristan did a double take and burst out laughing. "Are you going to take up her kind offer?"

Siga scowled. "Turning on each other won't help us. We're already down to eight."

Oristan sneered. "Agreed."

Fisken struggled to tie a handkerchief around her wounded hand. Drinith approached to help, but Fisken waved her away. "Don't touch me, Thrall Green!"

Siga watched her continue to struggle. His face squirmed with guilt and indecisiveness until, with a grimace, he turned away. Toskar sauntered up to her and, with a sympathetic murmur, took the handkerchief and bandaged the wound.

Zoen's gasp drew Drinith's attention skyward. The bright disk of the Halo Sea swirled far above them. A mountainous lance pierced its heart, the very column on which the group stood. Conifers protruded downward from the underside of ledges. The vista inspired a terrible vertigo in Drinith, as if she dangled upside down and might plunge into the sea at any moment. She focused on her feet until the sensation passed. Others tottered as they gaped at the spectacle above them. Zoen fell to her knees as though inspired to worship before this wondrous vista.

A gull flapped by, oblivious to the spectacle above.

"They say no birds lived below the sea before Giada and Typoneur settled on Ophigee," Zoen said. "None could endure an ocean whirling above them. That gull hatched down here, so it knows no different."

"We had better go," Oristan said, pointing to the open jaws of the stone dragon head.

"Agreed," Kaliop said, hugging herself. "The sooner I don't have to look upon that freakish sky, the better."

Zoen kept her gaze fixed on the ground as Drinith helped her to her feet. "Part of me longs to look up again, but I doubt I could do it without toppling over."

Oristan strode into the tunnel. Toskar, Nezon, and Fisken entered together. Kaliop followed close behind, her efforts at engaging them in conversation meeting stony silence. Siga lingered to pick through the loose rocks scattered around the entrance until he found a palm-sized stone to his liking. Reluctant to have him walking behind her, Drinith waited for him to enter. Zoen, too, loitered, perhaps inspired by similar distrust of his intentions. Siga coveted her knife. Glancing at each of them, Siga smirked and strode into the dragon's mouth. Side by side, Drinith and Zoen followed him into the maw of ominous darkness.

13

———

It took some time for Zoen's eyes to adjust to the darkness. The dragon's gullet proved to be an arched brick tunnel. Lampstones lit its length at regular intervals, but several were missing or damaged.

"What is this place?" Drinith asked her.

"Before the Great Rectification, it was a lampstone mining settlement and an occasional sanctuary during times of war. It's named Stepstone now, but in its heyday, it was called Luckslap."

"And what is the Great Rectification?" Drinith asked.

Zoen stared at her with bemusement, verging on alarm. "You know nothing of Cysgulur Prescriber? He created most of our traditions, including the Ascent."

Zoen's heart sank as she caught sight of Kaliop drifting back to them.

"Mind if I join you?" Kaliop asked.

"I thought we were all one group already," Zoen blurted with unintended sharpness.

Kaliop snorted. "The three girls ahead of us don't seem to think so," she murmured conspiratorially. "Our leader is a target of their ire, it seems. As are the three of us."

Zoen fought the urge to push her away. The group was divided enough without her stoking dissension. "Idle chatter, best ignored."

"Still, it's good to know your friends down here, don't you think?"

Zoen didn't reply.

"Hmm, not talking to me... I wonder what I've done wrong to upset everybody..." Kaliop looked to her fellow outsider, but Drinith shied from her imploring gaze, perhaps wary of the hint of fabrication in her expression of hurt innocence. "I don't understand why I'm being treated as an outcast. I've done nothing wrong."

Zoen stubbornly maintained her silence until it drove off Kaliop. With a wistful backward glance, she skirted by Siga and disappeared. Zoen breathed a sigh of relief.

"You don't like Kaliop much," Drinith whispered.

"She makes even less sense here than you. She's not who she claims to be. Everything about her is off." Drinith's troubled expression made her add, "You did a good thing back there, rescuing Oristan."

"It was nothing. Anyone might have done it."

"But only you did."

"I'm only sorry that I couldn't help Govren, but it was already too late by the time I reached the hatch."

"That's where you and Kaliop differ. I can't imagine her being so altruistic." Of course, self-interest could have easily driven Drinith's intervention. If Oristan had taken the green, his successor mightn't have treated her presence with such tolerance.

"You knew Oristan already, didn't you?" Drinith asked.

"We went to the same red school. He has always played the future affluentor. Govren and Fisken grew up in the shadow of his greatness." *And basked in it. Basked in a shadow. Never a clever thing to do.* "Fisken especially. She has always wallowed in being his appendage. The only time she exhibits a spine is when some other girl catches his eye. Oristan favoring you over her has made Fisken your implacable enemy."

"I gathered that, but I had only a superficial understanding of the rage his snub might provoke in her. I hadn't realized she loved him."

Drinith's naivety took Zoen by surprise. Fisken's infatuation with Oristan should have been self-evident even to the most casual observer.

"I advise you to watch your step around her. Fisken never resorted to physical violence in the past. She always employed social embarrassment to crush her rivals, but, down here, where no law applies, who knows what she is capable of?" *To think I envied her,* Zoen thought. *No, not Fisken, not really. I coveted Oristan's exalted standing. I wanted to be at the center of his clique and not some inconsequential outsider adrift on its periphery, only acknowledged because of who my parents and sister were.* Zoen glanced at the ring on her hand, the duplicate of Olen's. Aside from their parentage, it was one of the few things they had in common.

"I'll be careful," Drinith said. "Thanks for the warning. I appreciate it."

As they traveled deeper, the sulfurous breath of the Crevast gave way to a damp, loamy scent. The lampstones petered out, forcing the group to rely on glowing roots dangling through pitted mortar joints for illumination. In places, roots as thick as an arm had punched holes in the masonry. Black stains beneath these wounds marked water bleeds. Elsewhere, the roots descended in great gnarled curtains, obscuring the path ahead. The group compressed as it passed through them.

"I don't like this," Toskar said. "Anything might lurk behind these roots."

"Everyone, have your knives at the ready, just in case," Oristan said.

"Easy for you to say," Siga grumbled. "You have one."

They encountered a section where the roof had caved in. Roots reached out along its jagged rim like demonic fingers. Buttery dust sprinkled Zoen's face as she peered into yawning darkness above them. It was impossible to guess how far it extended. A whispery flutter somewhere in the blackness drew a few panicked gasps.

"It's just a bat," Oristan said. "No need to panic. I'm sure we'll encounter a lot more of them." They quickly picked their way across the litter of crumbled bricks back under an intact ceiling.

They reached a junction. The roots here showed signs of having been cut back. Rubble blocked the route ahead, leaving them with a choice of branches to the left and right.

"Look!" Siga pointed to an arrow hewn into the rock. "It's pointing left."

"So we follow it?" Kaliop asked.

"We shouldn't discount the right tunnel," Toskar said. "The arrow might be a trick."

"Or it might mean nothing. We don't know how long ago this was made," Oristan said.

Toskar pointed to above the right tunnel mouth. "There's a circle carved up there." Stacking a few loose bricks to make a pedestal, she strained to get a better look at it. "It's a serpent eating its tail, an ouroborus."

"It's the old emblem of Ophigee," Zoen whispered to Drinith. "It would have been white originally to represent a ghostwhip, a venomous snake native to the Whetstone."

"The same symbol marks the other tunnel," Siga said. Drinith sliced through a large root and ran it along the wall revealing other notches and etchings of varying refinement and age. The arrow to the left stood out, almost as if it had a ghostly shine.

Siga smirked. "So, leader, time to lead. Left or right?"

Oristan stroked his chin. "We'll scout both directions. Kaliop and I will check the left route. Drinith and Nezon can explore the other."

"I'm staying here," Nezon said.

Oristan pursed his lips. "Fine, Siga can go."

"Give me a weapon and I'll go. Otherwise..." Siga shrugged.

Oristan looked around, fixed his gaze on Zoen. "You'll have to go instead."

Zoen's heart skipped a beat, but she nodded.

"Don't stray too far and get lost," Oristan said. "Just get a flavor of what lies ahead. Nezon, you're in charge here until I get back."

"Toskar would make a better deputy than me," Nezon said.

As Oristan glared at her, Zoen tensed. Fortunately, he mustn't have noticed Siga's triumphant sneer. Otherwise, he might have exploded in rage and anything might have happened.

"Very well," Oristan spat. He stalked down the tunnel. "Come on, Kaliop."

Knives at the ready, Zoen and Drinith set off in the opposite direction. The sound of bickering followed them for some distance down the tunnel. It was a relief to escape the rest of the group and their incessant rancor.

As she and Drinith rounded the bend, the latter whispered, "If this group's behavior is typical of previous recent candidates, no wonder none of them reached the Ouroboric Gate. Can they not grasp that we must work together?"

"Everyone wants to be in charge," Zoen said, though it wasn't true. Aside from Oristan, only Toskar and Siga harbored leadership ambitions. The thrallborn had no hope, but Toskar had a good chance of displacing Oristan. Having lost Govren and alienated Fisken, his authority looked precarious. "But dissension in previous parties by itself surely couldn't have led to their total failure. Some external force must be responsible."

"True," Drinith conceded. Whatever it was, hopefully they weren't about to blunder into it as they crept down the winding tunnel.

Rubble blocked several branches they encountered. Others opened into rooms, ransacked long ago, containing only a few fragments of rotting timber or broken masonry. The tunnel itself came to a dead end. A sloping wall of piled masonry blocked it, except for a shadowed crevice at the very top.

Drinith climbed up to examine it. "There's a soft breeze blowing through it."

"Be careful," Zoen said as Drinith peered into the darkness. "Anything might lurk in there—creeping hands or even a ghostwhip."

Drinith backed away from the hole, looked askance at her. "What's a creeping hand?"

"It's a long-legged centipede. Its bite is painful enough to cripple you for several days."

Drinith cut a length of glowing root and shoved it into the opening. She leaned into the gap. "There's nothing creeping about inside." She pulled out the dulling root and tossed it behind her. "There's a sizable space beyond it. I'll wriggle through to get a better look." She disappeared hip-deep into the cavity, then up her knees.

"Don't go too far," Zoen urged. "What can you see?"

"The tunnel continues on, branching in several directions. This barrier isn't accidental. Dead roots have been deliberately woven across the far side to reinforce it. Somebody has gone to a great deal of effort to prevent us from going any further."

An arm reached around Zoen. As she gasped in terror, a sharp point pressed against her throat.

"Drop your knife," her attacker murmured, his sour breath caressing her cheek. Having no choice but to obey, she let it spill from her hand.

14

___

I t wouldn't take Gyre's constabulary, the cordents, long to hunt Quiescat down if he continued to wear his familiar cowl. He headed to a pawnshop to buy a change of clothes. As he entered, the pawnbroker, a bald man with a long, three-pronged blue beard, gave him a hard stare but said nothing. The shop was stuffed with a hotchpotch of furniture, antiques, paintings, musical instruments—Quiescat admired a golden harp whose frame was a dragon's coiling body, its crown a snarling mouth—most of it showing signs of wear. An abundance of gaudy trinkets looked out from dusty glass cabinets. The nicer items must have been castoffs from meritocratic families and other well-to-do households.

"Have you any garments for sale?" Quiescat asked.

The pawnbroker pointed to several large bins. An ill-dressed woman muttered curses as she rooted through them. Quiescat joined her and began to pick through one. Many of the garments were the wrong size or soiled or damaged. His face burned with embarrassment as he dug ever deeper. He wasn't used to thinking about what to wear.

Eventually, he chose a bright navy-blue knee-length tunic and a black velvet hat. However, his greatest prize was a heavy red coat that must have originally belonged to a rich merchant. Aside from a small black stain on one sleeve, it looked brand-new. As he held it up to admire it, the woman attempted to wrench it from his hands.

"I thought Gadflies like you wouldn't be allowed in here," she said as they tugged it back and forth. Quiescat gritted his teeth. Her casual utterance of that heinous epithet for Rhumgadian exiles made him determined to win.

"If you rip it, both of you will end up paying for it," the pawnbroker barked from behind his counter.

This squabble was getting out of hand. Any moment, the pawnbroker might summon cordents. Quiescat didn't need this aggravation. He let go. The woman stumbled backward. Her surprise quickly turned to indignation. "You did that deliberately." She waved the coat at the pawnbroker. "How much is this?"

"Two silver finches."

"Two silvers?" She peered into her money pouch. "I'll give you seven copper dragons."

The pawnbroker rubbed his chin as he considered her offer.

She gave Quiescat a venomous glance. "It's hardly worth that much after this Gadfly soiled it."

"I'll pay the two silver finches," Quiescat blurted, snatching it from her. "I'll be happy to pay the full price. I'll take this hat and tunic as well."

"You can't do that!" the woman cried, grabbing the coat back.

"Are you going to pay the two silver finches?" the pawnbroker asked her.

"No."

The pawnbroker shrugged.

The woman huffed, threw the robe on the floor, and stormed out of the shop.

"How much do I owe you?" Quiescat asked as he picked up the garment. No doubt, he had overpaid for the robe already.

The pawnbroker's eyes narrowed. "Four silver finches."

Quiescat opened his money pouch, picked out a gold ducat, and placed it on the counter.

The pawnbroker's eyes boggled. He licked his lips as he picked up the coin and examined it. "I don't see birds of that bright plumage in here that often. How did you get it?"

Panic gripped Quiescat. What should he say?

"Never mind," the pawnbroker said. "None of my business." He dug around in his cash box, rooting out coins.

"You can keep the change if you forget I was here," Quiescat said quietly. "I also need somewhere to change my clothes."

"I only ever remember the money." The pawnbroker pointed to a narrow hall almost lost in the stacked bric-a-brac. "You'll have a bit of privacy down there."

Quiescat thanked him, squeezed into the passage and changed, careful not to knock against anything. On the way out, he dumped his cowl in a clothes bin. He kept checking behind him as he strode away from the shop in case the pawnbroker dispatched some thugs to relieve him of the rest of his ducats.

He hurried to the Blue Quarter, silently cursing Jarma all the way. Raising the coin for a dragon was too much for Quiescat alone. He needed Woad and Tazran's help, but he had to reach them before Jarma turned them against him.

Black mold mottled the once-elegant buildings of the slum like a permanent shadow, its musty scent heavy in the air. Hard stares appraised him. The fancy clothes he wore, which he had regarded as a stroke of luck, drew too much interest from the Rhumgadian exiles who dwelt here. He pulled his coat tighter around him to hide his money pouch. Its weight tapped against his hip as he walked. He had been a fool to bring it here. Such a proclamation of wealth drew the eye of every scoundrel he passed. Yet, stashing it in some corner of the city held its own risks.

Wariness overcame his haste as he neared the Gad Moon Inn. He could be walking into a trap. He lingered across the street to observe the patrons' comings and goings before entering. This was eerily reminiscent of his first visit to the inn. The last pentacular hunting Drinith, the one who slew Halyard, could have surveilled the inn from this same spot. Jarma had been on Quiescat's side back then.

They had had a fractious relationship over Abecedar, but Quiescat had never imagined that it could degenerate to the point she posed a threat to his efforts to save Drinith.

He yelped as a sharp point prodded the small of his back. His whole body tingled with fright.

"Don't move."

Quiescat strained to glimpse his assailant.

"Don't move, I said." A hand patted him down.

Quiescat should have heeded his instincts. Now he'd lose his money and with it, any chance to rescue Drinith. The sharp pressure in his back eased as the thief drew back one side of his coat. A queasiness gripped Quiescat's stomach as, from the corner of his eye, he glimpsed a dagger cutting off the pouch. He swung round and punched at his astonished mugger. The blow struck the boy's throat. As he stumbled backward, the coins spilled from the pouch and scattered across the cobbles. Squealing for help, Quiescat raced for the door of the inn. A hand gripped his arm, swung him around. The boy stabbed his chest, but the dragon scale deed concealed under his tunic stopped the blade.

The boy, ignoring Quiescat's flailing fists, stabbed him a second time in the same spot. The knife stuck in scale. Quiescat's robe billowed as the boy tried in vain to pull his weapon free.

A meaty fist struck the boy in the jaw. Woad's blow flattened him. The boy curled into a ball and tried to shield himself with his hands as he squirmed to the ex-mercenary's kicks.

"That's enough," Quiescat said, alarmed at Woad's ferocity, but his protest emerged as a murmur.

Woad relented, wiped his brow. "Crawl away while you can."

The boy raised trembling hands. He looked so young, barely out of childhood. "I didn't know he was a friend of yours, Woad."

Woad's eyes narrowed. "I suggest, from now on, you assume any Rhumgadian hanging around here is my friend unless I tell you different, Sujad."

"I will, I promise." The boy struggled to his feet. As he limped away, he kept glancing warily over his shoulder.

"What in Empyr's blazing bowels made you come down here dressed like that?" Woad asked.

"I'm in disguise," Quiescat said, scrambling to pick up the coins, slippery from the wet cobbles.

"As an idiot maybe." Woad helped, scooping up the money much faster.

Quiescat surveyed the bare cobbles. "I think that's all of them."

Woad shook his head. Grabbing Quiescat's shoulder, he yanked Sujad's blade free. "You were begging to be robbed wearing that expensive garb down here. You're lucky that boy was green. For the coin you're carrying, a more hardened thief would have dragged you to some secluded spot, slit your throat, and picked your carcass clean at his leisure."

"Have you heard anything from Jarma?" Quiescat asked nervously.

Woad's eyebrows knitted. "No. Should I have?"

"I need your help."

"So I gathered," Woad said wearily. "You wouldn't be down here by yourself otherwise."

Quiescat followed Woad into the inn. The common room was empty aside from Tazran glaring at him from behind the counter. Her first three husbands had predeceased her, earning her the sobriquet, the Widow. Tazran's severe face always made her look on the verge of rage. Or perhaps it was Quiescat's imagination.

"Look who I found." Woad sat down, facing the bar.

Tazran squinted. "Quiescat? You're hardly recognizable in those clothes. Sit down. I'll get you a drink."

Quiescat slumped into the seat across from Woad. "A drink would be good. This morning's events have left me parched." Relief brought an oppressive weariness. He could have happily laid his head on the table and fallen asleep.

A sharp tickle at the back of his neck made him forget his tiredness.

"Remember when you pressed a knife to the back of my neck?" Tazran said, her voice hard and menacing. "How do *you* like it?"

Quiescat was too shocked to answer. What in the bowels of Empyrosis brought this on?

Woad sat forward and folded his hands on the table. "Jarma sent word you ran away after rifling Drinith's safe this morning. Would you care to explain why?"

Quiescat leveled with them, recounted the whole sordid business, including Elca Trajar's attempt to seduce him. Sometimes, he lost track of his account thanks to Tazran's unwavering blade. Quiescat had to fight the urge to rub the back of his neck.

"That's the entire story," he finished.

At Woad's nod, Tazran withdrew her knife and sat down beside him. "I guess we're even now."

Quiescat massaged away the lingering tickle of her blade. "So you believe me?"

Woad nodded. "Even taking into account the illicit nature of your trip to Ophigee, you could hire ten dragons for what Trajar suggested you should pay."

"I wouldn't know," Quiescat admitted.

"Trajar and Savarel might be in cahoots," Woad said.

"But it's well known in meritocratic circles that they're bitter enemies." Nonetheless, Quiescat should have considered the possibility before he fled the mansion.

"They might despise you and Jarma more than each other," Woad added. "They clearly detest your influence over Drinith. Jarma's elevation might equally vex them given her humble origins. They mightn't like monarchs, but I'm sure they don't appreciate uppity servants either. These interventions by Trajar and Savarel might well be coordinated to discredit both of you."

Quiescat shook his head and sighed. "If so, I've played into their hands."

"You need to explain to Jarma what happened," Woad said. "You two need to work together. We'll help."

"You're right," Quiescat said. A small part of him squirmed at having to throw himself on Jarma's mercy. "Would one of you take a message to her?"

"I will," Tazran said.

Woad led him upstairs to their bedroom, which doubled as their office. Quiescat wrote a letter begging Jarma to forgive him and inviting her to meet him at the inn. He kept everything vague, avoiding mention of his flight from the Hax mansion. The letter might be used against both of them if it fell into their enemies' hands. It was safer that Tazran explained verbally.

After Quiescat handed the letter over to her, Woad offered him a vacant room to rest in. Quiescat was so tired, he quickly drifted to sleep.

He dreamt again of Godsdoor burning at the foot of the massive obsidian frame that gave the temple its name. The lumbering dragons' gleeful roars belittled the thousand years of tradition, learning, and wisdom their fires gutted. Cradling the baby Drinith in his arms, he could do nothing but bear witness to this cataclysm. Godsdoor would be avenged sometime, somehow. Yes, Magian would pay for the destruction he had wrought. But not today. Today, survival was the nearest thing to vengeance he might achieve. In the distance, black smoke rose, draping across the great doorway like a death shroud...

Waking, he blinked away the tears blurring his vision. He sat up and rubbed the tickly droplets off his cheek, the chill dew across the bridge of his nose and below his left temple. He couldn't escape his failure even in sleep. He had already lost Godsdoor, the gift to which it had been dedicated, the child for whom it had been sacrificed. Trajar had swooped down and picked his carcass clean of any vestige of self-respect. Survival had felt a victory of sorts in the immediate aftermath of Godsdoor's fall. Now, it weighed on him like a curse.

He walked over to the window, flung the shutters open on Gyre's twilight cityscape. Drinith's rescue seemed as impossible as reaching the stars dimly visible against the ocher glow of the Crevast.

Woad burst into the room. "We have to go."

"Where?" Quiescat asked, slipping on his sandals and hastening to follow Woad to his room.

The battering of the front door carried through the inn. "Cordents! Let us in!"

"Away from here," Woad muttered. He slid open the secret panel in the back wall, and they entered the stairwell. He passed a lampstone to Quiescat. "Hold that." As Woad slid the panel back into position, the sound of splintering wood came from downstairs. "We had better hurry. They'll find this exit fast enough."

"What do you think happened?" Quiescat asked as he puffed up the stairs behind him.

"Either Jarma has set cordents on us or she, too, has been arrested." They emerged from the stairwell onto the canal. Woad shut the metal door behind them and jammed the handle with a stick. "Either way, we have to assume we're on our own." He stepped onto his punt. Quiescat took his hand and climbed on board. He yelped as the boat wobbled beneath him.

"Which direction do we head?" Woad asked.

"The network of sympathetic Rhumgadian exiles you've been putting together on Drinith's behalf—could they help us?"

Woad shook his head. "Without Drinith, there is no network. Her reputation holds it together."

If Quiescat didn't save Drinith soon, he never would. "Then head for the Temple District."

"What's your plan?" Woad asked as he punted down the canal. "Pray for divine intervention?"

"In a way," Quiescat said. "A cult from Phule petitioned Drinith for help to establish a temple to honor their god Hissimir in Gyre. They have a cramped little room in a tenement temple, and they are desperate for something more impressive. In a city filled with grand temples, a poky little shrine doesn't attract many adherents. I'm going to sell them one of Drinith's properties."

Woad looked as if Quiescat had slapped him in the face. "That's the sort of thing that will earn you a stroll off the Plank."

"Only saving Drinith matters," Quiescat said. If throwing himself into the Crevast would achieve that, he'd gladly do it.

15

———————

At Zoen's panicked yelp, Drinith crawled back out of the crevice. Drawing her knife, she turned to whoever or whatever assailed Zoen, but it was already too late.

"There's no need to be afraid," the youth said, but he kept his knife against Zoen's throat. A typical rose-eyed Nosteran, he was a good two feet taller than his hostage. He must have been a candidate, judging from his worn red garments. A translucent red stubble covered his recently shorn pate and his jaw. He regarded Drinith not with anger or fear but a weary sadness, as if this whole matter was beneath him.

"I didn't hear him sneak up on me," Zoen rasped, rigid with terror within his one-armed grasp, her head tilted as far as it could go from the point of his blade. "I'm sorry."

They must have passed him somewhere in the tunnel. How had they missed him? "If you're no threat, prove it. Let her go," Drinith said.

"Drop your weapon first," he said. "Then we can talk."

"Don't!" Zoen blurted.

Drinith sheathed her knife and slowly raised her hands level with her shoulders. "That's as much as I'm prepared to do."

The boy bit his lip. Glancing down at Zoen, he gasped. "Where did you get that ring with the amethyst engraved with a dragon's head?"

A shudder of recognition passed through Drinith. Versifer's second vision had included a similar gem, but it had been the pommel of a dagger. Could Zoen be connected to the prophecy?

"It's mine," Zoen said.

The boy's face hardened. "That's funny. A friend of mine has one just like it."

"Olen!" Zoen cried. "You must know my sister Olen! She has a ring just like this one. Where is she?"

"I know her. We came to the Whetstone in the same party of candidates. She's a good friend of mine. She often mentioned you fondly—you're Zoen, yes? My name is Lesym." Withdrawing his blade, he removed his arm from around her and stepped back. His tunic bore a crude painting of the emblem of Ophigee in black, but the blade of the haloed sword pointed upward. Judging from the tracks of dirt down the garment's front, he must have crawled through the gap earlier. Perhaps he had made it himself. That would explain the loose rocks at its base and the streaks of dust around the mouth of the gap.

Zoen turned to him. "Please, is Olen alive? Where is she?"

He glanced over his shoulder. "I'm not sure. Part of the reason I traveled to this region of the Whetstone was to search for her. So far, I've found nary a trace." Keeping his gaze fixed on the girls, he picked Zoen's knife off the ground and, delicately holding the flat of the blade, gave it to her.

"Apologies for any distress my crude method of introduction caused." Lesym sheathed his knife. Drinith lowered her arms. "Being trapped down here for three red months has taught me caution. I assume you belong to a new batch of candidates."

"Yes," Zoen said. "There are eight of us, newly arrived."

"Not a full complement, then?"

"There had been nine originally, but one boy took the green rather than leave the dragon."

Lesym's bleak smile accented his haunted expression. "Many trapped in the Whetstone would envy his foresight. A band of vicious cutthroats dominates this area. They call themselves Stedfasters. In the past, my friends and I came down here to rescue new candidates from their clutches, but the Stedfasters recently blocked the routes out of their territory, imprisoning me in their domain. Alone, I'm able to hide from them, but a group of your size won't evade them for long.

"When they find you, they'll claim all sorts of noble intentions. They'll offer you comfort and safety. They'll warn you that my people are terrible monsters. But the Stedfasters are the real threat. Their self-styled queen, Nykostar, only wants to build a little empire down here. She uses those she captures as soldiers and..." He winced.

"And?" Drinith asked.

Lesym looked back down the tunnel. "The Stedfasters' territory lacks the tubers common higher in the Whetstone. Animals are rare here, too, thanks to their overhunting. Yet Nykostar comfortably sustains a band of three dozen or more. Need I say more?"

Drinith's skin crawled. "You're implying they're cannibals." Tales of marooned drakers eating their dead to survive were common, but she found it hard to believe that anyone could resort to such barbarity this close to civilization.

Lesym nodded. "Sounds preposterous, I know, but it's the truth."

Zoen looked as though his revelation had physically struck her. Disbelief quickly turned to terror. She clutched his arm. "Did they... my sister?" she whispered.

Lesym patted her shoulder. "Don't give up on her yet. If I have avoided the Stedfasters, so can Olen—she's a clever and athletic girl. She could well be lurking somewhere around here. Or she may have returned to our friends higher in the Whetstone."

"You claim hiding from the Stedfasters would be impossible for us," Drinith said.

"For a group of your size, yes."

"What do you expect us to do, then? Fight them?"

A grim smile played on Lesym's lips. "No, my advice is to surrender."

Zoen gasped.

Drinith emitted a mirthless chuckle. "You can't be serious."

"You can't hide from them for very long and you can't outfight them," Lesym said. "Your best chance, your only chance, is to get to my people. They'll look after you. But to do that, you need to find a route out of Nykostar's realm. There must be one. The Stedfasters would never cut themselves off entirely from the rest of the Whetstone. Ingratiate yourselves with them, find that exit, and use it to get away. ... Neither of you looks convinced."

"You're saying we should put ourselves at the mercy of cannibals," Drinith said.

"If you run, if you try to fight them, they'll hunt you down anyway. If you agree to join them, they'll take a little time to determine which of you will fit into their group and which will be...you know... livestock." He opened his hands and shrugged. "If there was any other way..."

"What about you?" Drinith asked. "You could pretend to be part of our group." *And share the risk you're pushing on us.*

"Several of them know me already," Lesym said. "If they spotted me with you, not only would my life be forfeit, but yours as well. They'd slaughter the lot of you without hesitation. I'll cling on here as long as I can. If you can reach my people, they might open one of the blocked exits and I, too, can escape."

"If you show us where one is, we might be able to open it," Drinith said.

"The blockages are likely extensive and the Stedfasters patrol their locations regularly. The obstructions must be cleared from the far side to have any hope of success. I've had some time to mull over this. The course I offer you might be"—he pulled a face —"unpalatable, but it's the best I can come up with. You should hurry back to your friends and warn them before the Stedfasters reach out to them." He patted Zoen's shoulder. "And don't lose heart about your sister. I'm sure she'll turn up. As I say, she's very resourceful."

He skirted around the girls, scrambled up the obstruction, and slid feet first into the gap at the top. "Good luck," he said as the darkness swallowed him.

"I find his story hard to accept," Zoen confided. "I can't believe Ophigeens could stoop to such depravity."

"He's an Ophigeen too, isn't he?" Drinith countered. "Desperation can make people do terrible things." Gelasin's pitted grin came to her unbidden. "They've been stranded down here for red months."

"Do you think they...hurt my sister?"

"Lesym is certain they haven't." If only Drinith shared his optimism. The dragon head amethyst suggested either Zoen or her sister must hold some importance for Drinith's future. Quiescat might have been able to glean some deeper insight into what that might be, but Drinith hadn't his counsel to lean upon. Only one amethyst had appeared in Versifer's vision, not two. That might be an ill omen for the missing Olen. Or perhaps Drinith read too deeply into a coincidence. "We had better get back to the others."

As they raced along the tunnel, Zoen kept falling behind, forcing Drinith to wait for her to catch up. On the third occasion, Zoen pressed a hand to her chest. "I just need a moment to get my breath back," she rasped.

"We can't delay long," Drinith said, hiding her irritation behind a smile. "We need to reach the others before the Stedfasters." Was she and Zoen already too late? What had Oristan discovered down the left tunnel?

Bending over and resting her hands on her thighs, Zoen nodded. "We need to talk to Oristan before the others. I don't trust Kaliop. She'd betray us in a heartbeat. And we can't rely on Siga either—he's a hothead, and he detests us all."

"And what about me?" Drinith couldn't help asking.

Heaving a laborious breath, Zoen straightened. "Believe me, you scotched any lingering doubt I might have had after our encounter with Lesym. You could have abandoned me back there."

"It's not in my nature to forsake anyone in danger," Drinith said, disconcerted. "Would you not do the same for me?"

Zoen's head jerked back a fraction. "Of course, but..." She blushed. "I'm just saying that I trust you, that's all. We had better get going." They set off again at a slower pace than before.

Oristan stood alone at the junction where they had left the others. Where had everyone else disappeared to? Silhouettes sprouted around him from where they had been crouching or sitting. The dim root light revealed the familiar faces of the other candidates.

Drawing Drinith to a stop some distance from the group, Zoen beckoned Oristan, saying, "We must talk to you in private."

He looked jittery as he stalked over to them. The aplomb he had shown in taking charge of the group was gone. Had his moment of weakness descending from the dragon proved a fatal blow to his confidence, or had it waned for some other reason?

"Keeping secrets, are we?"

Siga's jeer drew an exasperated wince from Oristan, but he offered no retort. He leaned close to Zoen. "So, what do you have to say?"

As she gave a quick summary of their encounter with Lesym, his face contorted with horror and disbelief. If Drinith had reported back by herself, he would never have accepted her account.

Beyond their little huddle, the other candidates had formed their own. Their distance prevented Drinith from making out exactly what they were saying, but the sneery tone of their conversation grated.

"So this Lesym wants us to surrender to a bunch of cannibals?" Oristan asked after Zoen finished.

"He says it's our only option," she said firmly.

Oristan glanced back at the other candidates. "You were right to tell me this first. To be honest, I don't know how some of the others will react when they find out. Particularly the thrallborn. If we follow your friend's advice, Siga might very well betray us."

"I would think Kaliop is a greater threat," Zoen said.

"Kaliop? No. I've gotten to know her a bit. She's sound. The groundless hate her two fellow colonists directed at her has left her bewildered and afraid."

Zoen arched an eyebrow. "And why do you think they should take such a dislike to her?"

"Toskar's a schemer. Who knows how her mind works? She has been cozying up to Fisken, trying her best to turn her against me. She won't succeed, of course. Though I'm not exactly popular with Fisken at present, her anger will pass. She and I have been friends since we were toddlers."

Drinith dammed surging anger behind compressed lips. Oristan viewed everything through the lens of his authority. They hadn't time for this petty politicking. "So what do we do?"

Oristan threw up his hands. "This Lesym character may be lying. He might be in league with these Stedfasters. This could be a clever ruse to secure our meek surrender."

"He knew my sister," Zoen said.

"That doesn't mean we can trust him," Oristan said. "His story doesn't make sense. Why haven't his friends finished the Ascent? Why linger on this side of the Ouroboric Gate? The more I think about it, the more I'm convinced this is some sort of trap. He's in league with these Stedfasters and he's engineering our capitulation. Dragons, we don't know if these Stedfasters even exist. They might be a figment of a fevered imagination."

"But what if Lesym is telling the truth?" Zoen asked.

"That doesn't mean we should take his advice."

The others, now silent, watched intently, no doubt straining to listen in. They must have caught intriguing snatches of conversation already, thanks to Oristan's loudness.

"Speak softer, please. The others might overhear," Drinith said, herself whispering. "This rampant speculation is getting us nowhere. We need to come to a decision. The Stedfasters might arrive at any moment."

"Let me think," Oristan pleaded, massaging his forehead.

They needed a decision fast. It frustrated Drinith she couldn't take charge, but the likes of Fisken or Siga would never accept her as leader. She needed to guide Oristan to the right answer. "Do we follow Lesym's advice or do we try to avoid the Stedfasters until we have a clearer idea of what is going on here?"

"Caution sounds like the prudent course to me," Zoen said.

"I've had enough of this," Siga declared, striding toward them.

Oristan swung around and brandished his knife at him. "Stay where you are! Don't come a step closer!" Had he gone mad? Drinith readied to pounce on him at the first hint he might make good on his threat.

Siga wilted, raised his hands, stepped back.

Oristan stared at his knife as if struggling to comprehend why it was in his hand. Unlike the knives that spilled from the dragon, it had a steel crossguard and diamond-shaped pommel. The leather grip was red, not black. He had brought this weapon with him. What else had he smuggled to the Whetstone?

Sheathing his blade, Oristan rubbed a hand down his sweaty face. "We'll avoid the Stedfasters for now. You said your tunnel was partially blocked?"

"Deliberately barricaded, but there's a gap at the top," Drinith said. "Lesym climbed through it as we left so it must go somewhere."

"Then that's the route we should take, the one the Stedfasters obviously don't want us to." Oristan turned to the others and pointed down the tunnel. "We're going this way."

The others hesitated, doubtless spooked by his earlier outburst.

"We'll explain when we can, but for now you'll have to trust us," Drinith said, feeling foolish. Most of them distrusted her already.

The distant echo of pounding of feet sent a shiver through the candidates.

"Come on!" Zoen urged. "Move it!"

"Shouldn't we talk to them, whoever they are?" Fisken pleaded, but she ran with the rest, carried on the same momentum of fear.

Drinith kept pace with Zoen, steadying her when she wobbled and dragging her along when she flagged. By the time they reached the barrier, Fisken had already crawled into the gap. Toskar and Siga waited behind her, looking embarrassed and guilty, while Nezon, Kaliop, and

Oristan readied their knives to face the oncoming Stedfasters. Drinith drew her blade and fell in beside them. Zoen doubled over and gasped for breath. She was certainly in no state to fight.

"Give me your knife," Siga pleaded. "I'll fight in your stead."

"Give it to me," Toskar urged behind him.

"Toskar, get through that gap now," Nezon growled.

Toskar shook her head defiantly. "Not without you."

Zoen thrust the weapon into Siga's hands. "Take it," she rasped.

Siga gave an appreciative nod.

Almost drowned out by Zoen's labored gasps, the Stedfasters' rapid footfalls eased to a leisurely amble. A sonorous female voice bellowed, "Why did you run away? We're no threat to you! There's no need to fear us! We're friends!"

"Hurry up," Oristan hissed. "They're taking their time because they assume we have nowhere to run."

Pushed by Nezon, Toskar grudgingly climbed through the hole. Zoen struggled to follow until Siga helped her up.

"I'm coming unarmed to talk to you," the Stedfaster said. The sound of footsteps drew closer.

"Nezon, come on," Toskar whispered from the far side of the barrier. Nezon moved toward the barrier, but Kaliop pushed ahead of her and climbed through first. With a murderous scowl, Nezon followed.

"Drinith, your turn." Oristan's whisper drew a sneer from Siga.

As Drinith wriggled through the breach, hands reached from the far side and dragged her through.

"They've knocked a hole in the barricade!" the Stedfaster roared. "Quick! Get them!" Brisk footfalls rumbled down the tunnel.

Drinith's helpers deposited her on the ground. She rolled clear to leave space for the next one through.

"What are they arguing about now?" Toskar muttered, throwing up her arms.

Barking curses, Siga scrambled through the gap. The group yanked him out of the way to make room for Oristan. Nezon and Kaliop reached into the hole to help him through. As the top of

Oristan's head peeped out, everyone reached to grab him. Drinith scrabbled to latch onto any fragment of him, a limb, a piece of clothing. She gripped a ball of his tunic.

He disappeared back into the hole.

"Help!" he wailed. "They've got me!"

"Pull!" Nezon roared. "Pull!" As the candidates tugged to the rhythm of her cries, Oristan shunted forward. His head emerged again from the darkness, his face racked with pain. He roared as he slid back into the breach. Nezon released him as a crude spear was thrust at her through the gap. Siga grabbed the shaft of another, aimed at him, with both hands and wrenched it from its wielder's grasp. The cloth Drinith held ripped away as Oristan slid back into the darkness.

"There's nowhere for you to run!" The Stedfaster was barely audible over Oristan's screeches. "Shut him up!" The shrieks ended in a meaty thump.

"Pull down the barrier!" the Stedfaster cried to her comrades. "Hurry!"

As shifting stones clattered on the far side of the wall of stone, the candidates raced down the tunnel.

16

Zoen struggled to keep up with Drinith as the rest of the group slipped away from them. They had no idea where they were heading as they plunged pell-mell down crumbling, root-veined tunnels. They had no leader, no plan, and no time to come up with one. Their pursuers might catch up with them at any moment.

The regular brick-lined tubes and hand-hewn chambers gave way to natural tunnels that constricted and expanded with unnerving randomness as they wound through the rocky core of the island. As roots grew scarce, Drinith cut pieces to illuminate their way through dark sections. Unfortunately, her harvest of these fragments provided little time for Zoen to recuperate properly from her exertion.

"Keep moving," Drinith said. "You're doing great. Not long now before we can take a break."

Zoen hadn't the breath to tell her to shut up. Her legs hurt, her chest burned with every wheezy inhalation. Anger—at her feebleness, at her stupidity in surrendering her knife to Siga—powered her movement. She had acted out of blind panic. Zoen hadn't possessed the strength to wield the blade at the barrier, and he had been the nearest candidate in need of a weapon. She should have known he'd run off with it without giving her a second thought. He only cared about himself. Thank dragons, Drinith hadn't forsaken her like the rest.

Zoen strained in vain to discern any movement in the subterranean gloom ahead. "Can you see the others?"

"There's not been any sign of them for some time," Drinith admitted with a hint of disquiet. "Hopefully, we're not too far behind them."

Even if Zoen had the breath to call to them, she daren't risk alerting nearby Stedfasters. Hopefully, the other candidates hadn't abandoned them.

Sudden sharp pain in the arch of her left foot made her limp.

"Did you pull something?" Drinith's voice jangled with alarm.

"Old injury. Bothers me on and off. I fell out of a window."

Drinith emitted an incredulous chuckle. "How...?"

"I don't want to talk about it." Would the desperation in her father's drunken eyes that night ever cease to haunt her? "Run ahead and see if you can find the others."

"We have to stick together," Drinith said fiercely.

Tell that to Oristan. The memory of his desperate screeches as the Stedfasters tore him from her grasp made Zoen shiver. Her eyes burned with the urge to cry. She, the weakest of the bunch, would inevitably be next to die. Her parents had been right. "There's really no need to stay with me. I'll be fine by myself."

"If you give up now, you'll never learn what happened to your sister."

Zoen bristled at mention of Olen, but Drinith was right. More than anything, Zoen craved to know her sister's fate. Wincing with every painful step, she quickened her pace.

The stringy light Drinith held vanished in an instant as if swallowed by the darkness. Zoen gasped as Drinith shoved her against a wall and pressed against her. An urgent shush cut off Zoen's protest. A blurry silhouette appeared at the far end of the tunnel. The boy hastening toward them carried a stumpy spear. Drinith exhaled and lifted off Zoen. "It's Siga."

"There you are! I feared we had lost you two," he said with surprising warmth. "Here, this is yours." Zoen took the knife he offered.

"Thanks for lending it to me. I've my own weapon now," he said, flourishing his spear. A knife blade acted as its head and its crooked wooden shaft was thick enough to be wielded as a club. It was the work of an enthusiastic amateur, not a skilled artisan, but Siga looked lovingly upon it as though it were the finest weapon ever fashioned.

Tearing his gaze from it, he said, "I came back to make sure you hadn't gotten lost. The others aren't too far ahead. Follow me." He bounded down the tunnel. Zoen blushed as she limped after him. She was a burden, nothing more.

After some time, they reached a spot where the tunnel ceiling had collapsed, leaving a sandy incline up to a large natural cavern. Fresh footprints ran up the slope. A narrow channel wound down it on one side like the track of a snake.

"The others are waiting up there." The speaker, springing apparition-like from the shadows, made Zoen reach for her knife, but it was only Nezon. She led them up the slope. "Our group isn't the first to pass through here, it seems." Scattered around the fresh footprints were countless older, faded tracks. The pain in Zoen's foot redoubled as she hobbled up the incline after the others.

Great tresses of shining bone-white roots dangled down from the shadowy ceiling in every direction, their density forming a thicket impenetrable to the eye. The roots directly over the incline had been hacked back. Elsewhere, others been bundled and tied back to create several triangular pathways through this bizarre forest. Countless footprints pocked the soft ground. A splash against Zoen's face alerted her to random drops of water falling from above.

Nezon pointed to a series of low boulders peeping from the root forest's edge. "The others are in there, but we need to be careful to leave no tracks directly to our hiding place. Remove your boots and walk sideways to the rocks, stepping into existing prints where possible."

It took some time for Zoen to reach the boulders. Her sore foot made her movements dangerously awkward, and she almost fell over twice. She greeted the hands helping her onto the boulders with relief.

After they descended on the far side, Nezon took a moment to brush away any mud their feet had left on the wet stone. They pushed their way through the dangling roots. Some that reached the floor had anchored in the soft mud, forcing Zoen to pull them free or step around them. They found Toskar and Kaliop cutting down roots to expand a small clearing. Fisken sat on a small boulder, her legs curled against her chest, her hands pressed to her face as she quietly sobbed.

"You covered your tracks, Nez?" Toskar asked. Kaliop took her stopping work as a cue to do the same.

"Of course, Tosk."

"Good. We should be safe here for now. Everyone, sit down and rest yourselves."

Zoen eased herself onto the nearest rock, grateful to take the pressure off her foot. She massaged it in the forlorn hope it might relieve her ache.

Toskar loomed over her, arms akimbo. "You were limping."

"Old injury," Zoen said. "It comes and goes."

Toskar crouched in front of her. She offered a small jar and a roll of clean white bandage. "Rub some of this salve where it hurts. It will relieve the pain. Wrap the foot in the bandage. Use the ointment sparingly, though. I haven't any more."

Zoen pried the cork off with difficulty. She recognized the emerald green color of the balm and its sweet, oily scent—symphyre. It wouldn't cure her foot, but it would relieve the symptoms. Toskar had smuggled it and the bandage to the Whetstone, but it would be churlish to condemn her cheating given Zoen benefited from it. She nodded her gratitude and applied the salve. As its warmth turned to a burn, the pain in her foot subsided.

While she wound the bandage around it, Toskar settled on a stone across from her. "Now, can you two maybe tell us what in the bowels of Empyrosis happened before we ran for the barrier?"

Zoen jumped in before Drinith could speak. The story would be better received coming from an Ophigeen. As Zoen summarized their encounter with Lesym, Siga gazed upon a worn scrap of red cloth he clutched, Fisken continued to weep, and Kaliop's mouth shifted as though she sucked on something bitter. Toskar's gaze never wavered from Zoen while Nezon kept glancing at her friend.

"We certainly are not surrendering to a bunch of cannibals!" Toskar declared when Zoen finished. "I've never heard anything so ludicrous in my life."

Nezon gave an emphatic nod. Most of the others, including Zoen, murmured their agreement.

Siga tucked away the cloth. "But we do need a plan—something better than running around here until these murderers catch us."

"In time, we'll come up with one," Toskar said. "But let's eat first."

Zoen's tummy rumbled in agreement.

"Eat what?" Siga asked, his eyebrows lifting with bewilderment.

Toskar carefully unfurled her bedroll, revealing a collection of pouches, tools, and other oddments. She picked out a small leather bag and tossed it in the middle of the circle. Nezon enthusiastically dropped two small parcels beside it. Wiping her eyes, Fisken added another package. Kaliop shrugged and contributed a lump of cheese. Even Drinith donated tidbits kept from her last meal, crushed and unappetizing but still edible. Siga and Zoen looked at each other, aghast.

"How did you all know to smuggle supplies?" Siga demanded. "Who told you to do it?"

"It just seemed the sensible thing to do," Nezon said with a mischievous grin.

"I've heard rumors of worse," Fisken croaked. "Much worse. Candidates with maps of the tunnels. Benefactors smuggling supplies down here for their children."

"If somebody has a map, this would be a great opportunity to share it with the rest of us," Kaliop quipped, but nobody laughed. Expectant gazes swept the group.

"Cheats!" Siga snapped.

"You're just embarrassed you didn't think of it yourself," Fisken said.

Zoen's cheeks and ears burned. Being the daughter of two administrants, she should have known that the Ascent would be as open to manipulation as everything else in Ophigee. Had Olen brought secret provisions with her? Possibly, she hadn't felt she'd need them.

No. Family and friends must have encouraged the other candidates to flout the rules, though none of them dared admit it. Zoen's parents would have done the same with Olen.

"I had considered it," Siga grudgingly admitted. "But I wanted to succeed without cheating."

Kaliop smirked. "Gods, I didn't take you for such an idealist."

"I didn't realize I was one until now," Siga said ruefully.

Toskar snatched up the nearest parcel and tore it open. "Let's eat." She pulled a square gray sausage from it and passed the parcel along. It moved around the group until it reached Zoen. Her nose crinkled as she took a sausage. She bit down on the cold, grisly meat and chewed on it, though it threatened to turn her stomach. She offered the packet to Siga, but he passed it on to Kaliop.

"There's no shame in eating this even if it is contraband," Zoen said to him.

"That's right," Kaliop said, taking two sausages and offering the packet back to Siga. "Principle won't fill your belly. Eat. Remember, those hunting us don't care about our morals."

Siga waved it away, but moments later, he picked up a couple of crackers from another parcel. He stared at them for some time before eating one.

"Kaliop, I've never met an Ophigeen before who swore by gods instead of dragons," Toskar observed icily.

"Like I told you, my parents traveled a good deal. It's a bad habit I picked up. That's all."

"Who are you really?" Toskar asked.

Nezon's hand slipped onto the hilt of her knife.

Kaliop rubbed her lower lip. "I'm a thrallborn."

Siga scowled at her. "You kept quiet when Oristan humiliated me. Dragons damn you!"

Toskar shook her head. "She's lying. She's no thrallborn."

"I'm not from your colony," Kaliop said. "I'm from another."

"You're not from any colony. You're a foreigner and a liar."

Zoen tensed as Kaliop and Toskar glared at each other.

"You're right," said Kaliop, smiling bitterly. "The real Kaliop's parents tricked me into coming here. They considered their daughter much too delicate to survive the Ascent." The echo of her own circumstances made Zoen blush. "They hired me to take her place. They figured nobody on Ophigee would recognize her. I wasn't supposed to be in this party with you, but both of our groups were merged because of their small numbers."

"And after you ascended, she'd swap back," Toskar said.

"But they don't look that much alike," Nezon observed. "Except for their coloring."

"Many new benefactors head to the Great Preservatory as soon as they can afford its treatments to fix any deficiencies in health or appearance," Toskar said. "After the preservators had finished with the real Kaliop, who would know what she looked like beforehand? Who would care?"

Siga lifted his eyes. "So, the real Kaliop would become a benefactor without ever putting a foot on the Whetstone."

Kaliop smirked. "That was *their* plan. It wasn't *mine*. I'd have taken all the risk. Why should I give up the reward to some weak coward? I'd come clean after the Ouroboric Gate. Kaliop and her parents would be punished for their crime while I'd enjoy all the advantages of being a benefactor."

"Outrageous," Siga blurted.

"The Ascent forgives all sin, remember," Kaliop said. "Passing through the Ouroboric Gate would absolve me of my crimes. I'd be a benefactor according to Cysgulur's law." She tore off a lump of the yellow cheese. "It's no different than all of you smuggling food here. It's against the law, but everyone in the know does it. The Ascent may have many rules but only one really matters—survival. My transgression is on a larger scale admittedly, but the principle is the same." She swallowed the cheese. "I may be a foreigner, but my spirit is more Ophigeen than any of you. My past is inconsequential. Pay no heed to how I ended up here. It's unimportant. Focus on the actual threats that face us. We need a better hiding place. We need more food and water. And we need to find a way out of the Stedfasters' territory before they catch us."

"We need a leader," Siga said.

"We have one—Toskar," Nezon said as if it was self-evident.

"Of course you think she should lead," Siga snarled. "You're used to following her orders, being her pet thrallborn. Don't deny it. I sussed what you were when I first met you."

Toskar grinned. "You've got it the wrong way around. I'm the thrallborn, not Nezon."

Fisken's eyes opened painfully wide.

Siga eyed Toskar suspiciously, as if she were some sort of trap. "I don't believe you."

Toskar shrugged. "Why would anyone claim to be a thrallborn?" She slid a snide glance at Kaliop.

"You kept your mouth shut when Oristan mocked me," Siga grumbled.

"That's the difference between you and me," Toskar said with a wry smile. "You don't know when to shut yours. Anyway, it makes no difference here whether you are the child of a thrall or an administrant."

Siga smirked. "It wasn't supposed to make a difference before we arrived here either."

"True," Toskar conceded. "I am well aware that I was lucky to be adopted by Nezon's parents. But we're all equal here and now. We all face the same danger. I'm willing to take charge if you'll have me. Siga no doubt thinks he should be leader." She glanced at Drinith. "Anyone else want to put themselves forward?"

Drinith ignored Zoen's elbow nudge, so Zoen spoke for her. "I nominate my friend here. She saved my life. She rescued Oristan from being forced to take the green." She realized the awkwardness of her point given his tragic fate, but she persisted. "At all times, she has—"

"I can't believe you would throw your support behind that criminal!" Fisken said.

"Kaliop said it best. The only law down here is survival."

Toskar crinkled her nose. She obviously didn't appreciate Zoen praising someone she regarded as an interloper.

"If it's a choice between Toskar and the witch, I'll pick the witch," Siga declared, much to everyone's surprise.

"And I choose Toskar," Fisken said.

Toskar pursed her lips. "That's, of course, if there is a contest. Drinith hasn't actually said she wants to be leader."

Drinith's scowl filled Zoen with trepidation. Drinith hadn't sought the position. Zoen had thrust it on her.

"If the majority chooses me to lead, then so be it," Drinith said finally.

Kaliop laced her fingers over her head, yawned and stretched. "That, of course, leaves me with the deciding vote."

Toskar turned to Siga. "I thought you hated the witch."

Siga smirked. "I found somebody I hate more. Some advice for the future: you won't win over anyone by belittling them. You knew you might need my vote and yet you couldn't help mocking me. You assumed you could buy her"—he pointed at Zoen—"with a little ointment. Your parents may have been thralls, but you're no thrallborn. You think you're above me and probably everyone else here too."

"You know nothing about me!" Toskar snapped. "Nothing at all. My parents chose to send me to Nezon's family so I'd have a better life."

Siga's eyes narrowed. "Is that what they told you? Thralls don't choose. They have decisions made for them. Nezon's parents didn't need the permission of thralls to take you in to be a playmate for their daughter."

"They are good people," Toskar insisted. "They'd never—"

"Have you ever met your real mother and father?"

"Don't let him rile you," Nezon pleaded.

"You haven't, have you?" Siga asked. "You've never even sought them out. Too embarrassing for you." He shrugged. "You might have passed your parents every day as they went about their drudgery, and you never knew. You didn't want to know."

"Dragons burn you," Toskar hissed under her breath. "You know nothing."

"This is all very entertaining"—Kaliop formed a steeple with her fingers—"but it doesn't help me to choose between two such capable candidates. Hmm. I think it's in the best interests of the group that Toskar leads for now."

Toskar blinked with surprise. "Then it appears I am leader." Nezon patted her shoulder.

"We'll see how long you last," Siga growled. "Our previous leader didn't survive very long."

Fisken bolted over to him. He seized her hand as she swung to strike him, but she slapped him with the other and kicked at him. He grabbed her and pulled her to the ground, but she continued to rain blows.

"Stop this instant!" Toskar hissed. "Do you two want to get us killed, like Oristan? Any passing Stedfaster might hear you."

Siga pinned Fisken's arms and legs, but she didn't give up, trying furiously to head-butt him. Her enormous eyes smoldered with hatred.

"I'm sorry," Siga said breathlessly, over and over.

"For the last time, stop this," Toskar said. "Nezon, Drinith, pull them apart."

Siga rolled off Fisken. She crawled after him, but Drinith dragged her back.

"Get off me, witch!" Fisken yelled, squirming to free herself from Drinith's grip. "Let go!"

Nezon stepped between them and Siga, but he raised his hands as he sat up. "She attacked me, remember. I'll behave."

"Shut Fisken up or we're all dead," Toskar warned.

Nezon helped Drinith pinion Fisken. They stuffed a handkerchief in her mouth until she regained some semblance of composure. They let her go, ready to seize her again at the slightest hint of trouble, but she lay where she was, quietly sobbing.

"I'm sorry," Siga murmured.

Nezon helped Fisken off the ground and sat her away from Siga. He leapt up and stormed into the roots.

"Where's he going?" Nezon asked.

Toskar rolled her eyes. "Dragons know."

The impulse to follow Siga and try to calm him made Zoen rise and test her foot. The pain remained but it was much duller. She could certainly walk on it. As she hobbled toward the root curtain, Toskar approached Drinith and they shook hands with grim formality.

A bloodcurdling roar filled the cavern. "We got one of them!"

17

———

Quiescat and Woad weaved through the milling crowds in the Temple District. Hawkers of holy trinkets vied with preachers for the attention of passersby.

"It's funny people call Gyre the Godless City when the place is overrun with deities," Woad muttered.

"No gods are native to Gyre," Quiescat said. "Some say the archipelago is too small to be worth a god's attention. The city's founders worshiped dragons. Religions from Noster and beyond settled here and set up shrines and temples over the centuries. Even Rhumgad's pantheon had a large temple here until their adherents' money ran out. The meritocrats welcome all these peddlers of the divine as long as they cause no trouble in the city and can afford to pay a hefty annual tax."

The little pouch containing the Tear of Fate tapped urgently against his throat. He usually left it at Drinith's mansion. It didn't feel safe to carry it about.

Ahead stood the local dreamery, a transparent crystal sphere where the physical manifestation of Fate, the Fate Healer, resided. Even after passing it without incident on previous occasions,

Quiescat's skin crawled at its proximity. He hastily slipped the crystal sphere from its pouch and squeezed his hand around it.

"There's a dreamery on every shardlet in the archipelago," Woad said. "Perhaps Fate is the true god here."

"Fate is superior to all the gods," Quiescat muttered.

"And you worship Fate, so does that make you better than their priests?"

"No." They loved their gods. Quiescat lived in fear of Fate. The Tear of Fate pressed against his fist, pulled toward the dreamery by the attractive force it exerted.

The majority of the crowd stood a respectful distance around the sphere. Inside this circle, an odd array of men and women stood, young and old, some in shabby, stained cowls, others in vestments worthy of royalty. They murmured to themselves in a variety of prayerful poses. One rose from his genuflection, marched up to the orb and pressed his body against its curved surface. The crowd gasped as he rubbed himself against it. He collapsed on the ground, shaking and frothing at the mouth. Some of the other priests and holy men broke from their prayers to stare at him. Others droned on as if the spectacle was beneath their interest.

"The Fate Healer has granted me a vision!" the man declared, thrusting his arms skyward in triumph. The cheering crowd flooded around him, lifted him up, and carried him away on their shoulders.

"Is that how you used to get your visions?" Woad asked.

"No," Quiescat said. "These are charlatans. Every last one of them. If they understood the force they toyed with, they'd run away screaming and throw themselves into the Crevast." He could feel a fraction of that force in his hand. Afraid he might let the Tear slip from his sweaty palm, he wrapped his other hand around it. "I can't go any nearer the dreamery. We'll have to approach the Dudgeon's tenement temple by another route."

Yes, he could feel the power of Fate in his hand, but his intimacy with it wasn't much deeper than these frauds and madmen. The first Oracle of Godsdoor, Agebor the Larcener, had come face to face with the Fate Healer, but he had revealed little about their encounter. His successors were forced to study the dreameries and their custodian from afar for fear she'd steal back the Tear and punish them for his crime.

Woad mumbled a string of curses under his breath. "Every moment we delay—"

"I mustn't lose the Tear." The words sounded hollow. Quiescat might physically possess it, but he had lost its oracular gift. He had tried to reawaken it many times, weeping over it like a spurned lover in hopes his tears might make it sufficiently malleable for him to reinsert it into his ocular cavities, to make it part of him again, but it remained a hard, dead shell.

"Very well," Woad sighed. They reversed and worked their way through back streets. It took them some time to reach the far end of the Temple District, but Quiescat didn't feel in a position to complain. He tucked the Tear back into its pouch.

"If you had to give the Tear up to save Drinith, would you?"

Woad's question took Quiescat by surprise. "Yes. Absolutely." What use was the bauble aside from its pull toward dreameries? Any dragon's attracton had the same capability at a much greater distance. Those instruments had a function. They simplified navigation of the Crevast. The Tear only served to remind Quiescat of everything he had lost and taunt him with its impenetrable mystery. And yet while he possessed it, a chance remained that he might regain the gift he had lost, that his order might yet return to Godsdoor.

They quickly found the tenement temple containing the shrine to Hissimir. From the outside, it looked as grand as any other edifice along the street, if bare of specific symbols. The interior was divided into tiers. At the bottom, all around a narrow apse, were a number of large side temples, barred to prevent the trespass of non-adherents. The cult of a bizarre chimera, a wolf-headed scorpion covered with screaming mouths, held the prime position at the end of the aisle.

Curiosity drew Quiescat toward it. As the Oracle of Godsdoor, he had learned the names and attributes of nine thousand, nine hundred and ninety-nine deities, but he had forgotten most of them, and countless others existed whose names had yet to reach this part of the Crevast. The god's name came to him—Modegaw, the Lanscarian god of righteous vengeance.

"I hope that's not the deity whose cult we intend to mess with," Woad muttered.

"No," Quiescat said. "They're somewhere upstairs."

"And will this god we're looking for take offense on behalf of his followers?"

Quiescat winced. They shouldn't be discussing this here. "Why should he? They'll gain a temple."

"And the enmity of the entire Meritocracy."

"That's not my fault," Quiescat said lamely.

"I just want you to be sure of what you are doing. No backing out at the last moment. No pangs of conscience. No regret."

My whole life is regret. Not entirely true, but very near it. If he failed Drinith... "I'll do what I must. Have no fear."

The first level of balconies gave access to smaller chambers devoted to poorer religions. On the second level balconies, the rooms were so small, they were little more than cells. The shadowy top level, devoted to the cults too poor to afford even that much space, contained only niches for statues. Some were empty or contained doll-sized figures. They could only be accessed by narrow ledges jutting from the walls.

A few discreet inquiries revealed that the Dudgeon of Hissimir had secured a chamber on the second level balconies. Quiescat and Woad found their chief priest, the High Dudgeon, crammed into a poky chamber with two acolytes and a statue of his scowling god. Dusty tapestries draped the walls. Worn and faded, they recorded various calamities the great Hissimir had wrought.

The High Dudgeon was a corpulent man, pink-faced. The silver lightning bolts over his eyes gave him a permanent frown. He hadn't struck Quiescat in their earlier meeting as particularly learned or wise. His mulish devotion to his god was possibly his major qualification for his position, aside from his habit of mentioning Hissimir in practically every other sentence.

"We meet again, High Dudgeon," Quiescat said. "How goes your proselytizing?"

The High Dudgeon puffed out his cheeks and shook his head. "His Inclemency inspires fear and awe on Phule, but in Gyre, his miracles are hardly noted, much less exalted. We are failing him, lost in this babble of myriad religions and cults. On his home shard, Hissimir is a member of a pantheon of twenty-seven. In Gyre, he must compete with thousands of gods. The climate of the archipelago is too gentle for its populace to appreciate Hissimir's power."

Guilt gnawed at Quiescat's resolve. What right had he to add to this man's misfortunes?

The High Dudgeon sighed. "If only Hissimir would send some meteorological calamity to shake them from their complacency." His face contorted with rage. "If he drowned this city in vinegar, its denizens would soon beg for his forgiveness."

The violence of his demeanor dulled Quiescat's sympathy.

The High Dudgeon rubbed his eyes and pinched the bridge of his nose. "Yesterday, I invited a merchant to serve His Inclemency. She laughed in my face and informed me she only joined fashionable religions. Hissimir, that's the problem here in a nutshell. People take fashion more seriously than religion."

He looked forlornly at his god's statue. Daggers of lightning protruded from its thunderhead bouffant. Quiescat shied from its murderous glower.

He cleared his throat. "I come bearing good news. I have a property for sale on behalf of my meritocrat which would make an excellent temple."

The High Dudgeon clapped his huge hands together, his eyes gleaming with wonder. "Hissimir be praised! Can it be true?"

Quiescat, looking around to assure nobody was watching, drew the deed from beneath his cloak and proffered it. "It's not quite in the Temple District, but it is a fine building. Ideal for a temple for an important god like Hissimir."

The High Dudgeon's massive frame spilled through the doorway toward him. "So long have we suffered here in this temple of everything and nothing. Every day, our failure rings in our ears as larger congregations than ours fill the whole building with prayers to their *accursed gods*." He whispered the words. "We're condemned to this poky nook, because no chambers are available on the lower floors. How much would this building cost?"

Quiescat cringed, as if expecting a blow. "Eighty thousand ducats." Woad frowned. It was too much. But the High Dudgeon would surely try to barter him down.

"Done!" The High Dudgeon cried, offering his hand.

"Do you not want to view it first?" Quiescat asked. Woad's glower deepened. He must have thought Quiescat mad to quibble.

The High Dudgeon grabbed Quiescat's hand and shook it. "Of course not! The Oracle of Godsdoor wouldn't lie to me, would he?" The two scowling acolytes peeped out from behind him.

Quiescat rubbed the back of his neck. "No." He wasn't lying, but he wasn't telling the whole truth, either.

"Praise Hissimir!" The High Dudgeon's cry echoed with little enthusiasm on the lips of his acolytes. His whispered instructions to the two young men sent them racing along the balcony.

"Where are they going?" Woad asked.

The High Dudgeon lumbered out of his shrine. "To summon our lawyer and inform the faithful that Hissimir has worked another miracle this day."

"We want the money up front," Woad said.

The High Dudgeon swelled with indignation. "Are you implying that we are not good for it?" he bellowed.

Quiescat raised a placatory hand. "Of course not. We would never question your integrity. Hissimir would surely strike us down for such an insult." Cold fear shivered through him. Hopefully, Hissimir wouldn't take too much offense at this sordid enterprise. His vengeance couldn't reach them all the way from distant Phule.

Forgive me, Hissimir. I made sacrifices to your pantheon at Godsdoor and asked for nothing in return. If by some miracle I return there, I will offer more, greater in value.

Quiescat was a swindler, no matter how he looked at it. He was either scamming this poor priest or the Meritocracy. Neither would take kindly to his deception.

A flustered acolyte returned leading a woman primly dressed in dark clothes, her hands clasped behind her back. Her rose eyes stood out against her light purple face. Gold rings pierced both her lips. Her hair was tucked under a round hat. She looked vaguely familiar, but Quiescat couldn't place her.

"Why couldn't this business be conducted in my office?" she asked sourly. She touched the gold brooch on her lapel. It bore the leontophone of House Pitero. Quiescat's heart sank. The lawyer was a meritorian.

"I wanted Hissimir to witness this momentous event," the High Dudgeon said. "My friend here, Quiescat, represents the seller, Meritocrat Hax."

The lawyer's eyes narrowed. "Quiescat of Godsdoor. I recognize you. Though we've never been formally introduced, you've been pointed out to me on several occasions. I'm Gafyso Pitero, the younger sister of the meritocrat, Tomyr."

Tomyr Pitero's sister! Gafyso must know about Drinith's arrest in Ophigee. She would surely guess Quiescat hadn't permission to sell her property.

The woman smiled at his quiet consternation. "I might be a meritorian but I am also a lawyer and bound by confidentiality." She lifted her hat and revealed the tattoo of a closed mouth on her forehead. "You can discuss anything, anything at all, confident that I won't abuse your trust. If my word isn't enough, I have this." She produced a black vial. "On my client's instruction, I can forget several hours. Obviously, that comes with a hefty fee."

"I thought drug-induced amnesia was illegal," Quiescat said. Only the meritorian knew the true contents of her vial.

"Not to lawyers."

The High Dudgeon flourished a hand toward the shrine. "Please enter, Gafyso. You, too, Oracle."

Gafyso sat by the far wall. The High Dudgeon took the next stool, partially eclipsing her in his shadow. Quiescat sat nearest the door.

Hissimir's menacing glare loomed over them all. Woad and the acolytes observed from just beyond the threshold.

"Is that not a little disrespectful, conducting our business beside your god's sacred altar?" Quiescat asked.

"Our business honors Hissimir," the High Dudgeon said. "How could he find offense in it?"

Gafyso put on round glasses with thick black rims. "May I inspect the deed?"

"In Hissimir's name, place it there," the High Dudgeon said, indicating the slim black marble shelf below the statue.

Quiescat's eyes narrowed. "You're not trying to trick me into offering the deed to Hissimir, are you?"

The High Dudgeon pressed a hand to his chest. "I don't understand what you mean."

"If I laid the deed on the altar, under Gyran law, I would be offering it to your god."

The High Dudgeon looked to Gafyso with feigned astonishment. "Is this true?"

"It is," she said with stony disapproval.

"It's lucky you knew of this peculiar law," the High Dudgeon said, grinning nervously at Quiescat.

"Yes." *Lucky for me.*

Gafyso's eyebrows arched as if such skullduggery was beneath her. She reached across the High Dudgeon and gestured for the deed. Quiescat lifted from his stool just far enough to hand it to her. He followed the slow movement of her gaze down the document. She scrutinized every detail slowly and methodically. "It has notches embedded in it as though it has been stabbed." The deed had saved Quiescat from Sujad's knife, but now its damage might thwart his scheme.

"Does the damage mean…?" the High Dudgeon asked reluctantly.

Gafyso shrugged. "It's fine." Quiescat shied from her intense, scrutinizing gaze. "If it's a forgery, it's a convincing one. Obviously, I must confirm its stub at the Hall of Records to be sure. The question for me is, do you have the right to sell it?"

"My meritocrat granted me full authority to act on her behalf while she is away." Quiescat showed her the letter to that effect Drinith had left with him.

"Drinith is in some bother in Ophigee, I understand," Gafyso said amid her languid perusal.

The High Dudgeon's eyes bulged. He struggled to twist around to look at her, but Gafyso's attention remained fixed on the letter.

"We are in bother here too," Quiescat said. "We have some liquidity issues that the sale of this small building will resolve."

"They must be serious issues to require a transaction of this magnitude." She pursed her lips. "It's possible the meritocrat may seek to annul the sale on the grounds that her steward"—she leveled an accusatory glance at Quiescat—"overstepped his remit."

"If she were to win, would we be entitled to get our money back?" the High Dudgeon asked.

"There lies the problem. You're giving the money to Quiescat, not her. If she disowns him, or if she fails to return and her successor similarly cuts him off, he may not have the means to pay you back should he spend this money."

The Tear of Fate hung heavy around Quiescat's neck. He could offer it as collateral. The High Dudgeon would surely recognize its incalculable value. But how could Quiescat prove its authenticity? "But what of the letter? Surely it proves I am entitled to sell her properties as necessary."

Gafyso raised a hand to quiet him, and she continued to study the letter. "It looks...comprehensive. But we need to keep it in case of any litigation in the future."

"What do you say, Oracle?" the High Dudgeon asked.

It was the only slim defense Quiescat had. He sighed. "If you must, then take it."

Gafyso's eyes narrowed, but she tucked away the letter. "I'll check the stub just to make absolutely sure. If you'll excuse me."

The High Dudgeon rose and squeezed his massive frame against the wall to let her by. Gafyso's face crinkled with disgust as she stepped over his stool, passing through the narrow gap between

Hissimir and his chief priest. Quiescat stepped out of the shrine to let her by, forcing Woad and the acolytes to retreat from the door. She acknowledged him with a curt nod and hurried away, her echoey footsteps stabbing the silence.

The High Dudgeon beamed as he mumbled a prayer to his god. "I'm sure that will be a formality," he said, exiting the shrine. "In the meantime, I will arrange a promissory note for the sum we agreed upon."

A promissory note would be far too traceable. It could only be converted to coin at the Trustworth Bank. "I would rather have the payment in a more convenient form," Quiescat blurted. He should have discussed this detail with Woad beforehand.

The High Dudgeon's forehead crumpled above his theatrical frown. "What do you mean? Eighty thousand ducats in coins would be prohibitively cumbersome to lug around this city."

"We'll take payment in diamonds," Woad said.

"And who might you be?" the High Dudgeon asked.

"I'm the Oracle's...attendant."

The High Dudgeon's scowl turned thoughtful. "Very well. I shall leave one of my acolytes here while I get your diamonds."

"I'll go with you," Woad said.

"You don't trust me?"

Woad shrugged. "If I don't go, we'll have to get the value of the diamonds verified. Everything will drag out longer."

"You're right," the High Dudgeon conceded with a sigh.

Quiescat waited in the shrine for them to return. The remaining acolyte batted away his efforts to draw him into conversation with single-word answers.

Shouts and screams and curses alerted them to a fracas breaking out between two rival cults on the ground floor. Even the acolyte was tempted from the shrine to look down on the melee. After a while, he slapped the banister with both hands and grunted. "These squabbles happen all the time. People turn up at the wrong hour to worship. The followers of Efemer are particularly prone to it, which is ironic given she's supposedly a goddess of time." He shook his head as he strolled back into the shrine.

Downstairs, cool heads on both sides pulled the battling worshipers apart. One group and then the other trickled out of the temple.

Gafyso looked fierce as she emerged from the stairwell. Quiescat's mouth parched as she stalked along the balcony toward the shrine, a slim black case swinging in one hand. She came to a crisp halt before him. "The deed matches its stub. I've brought the documentation necessary to complete the transfer. I assume the High Dudgeon has gone to organize the payment."

Quiescat nodded and peered over the balcony to avoid her dissecting gaze. Below, a small knot of adherents gathered around another shrine. They murmured their prayers too softly for him to hear properly. Two women entered another shrine and began to keen, their yowls reverberating throughout the temple. A family entered, carrying bunches of flowers. One child halted and stared at the wailers' shrine, but his mother dragged him after her. As the family delivered their offering, the lamentation ceased, and the temple fell silent except for the patter of feet.

"How can anyone believe in this nonsense?" Gafyso asked.

"Don't let the High Dudgeon hear you," Quiescat said. *Or the gods you so glibly disparage.*

Gafyso smirked. "I assure you he is well aware of my views."

"You don't believe in gods?"

"I worship dragons like my forbears. I understand that Fate is your god."

"I worship all gods. I prayed to many of the deities in this temple in the past. Fate is...was the source of my prescience." He touched the pouch hanging around his neck, felt the hard, round sphere it contained. Fate was more akin to a demon than a god, something to be not loved but feared.

"All gods? You must be a busy man."

He'd dedicate himself to any god who could save Drinith. Even Fate. Yes, he'd sacrifice himself to Fate if it deigned to save her.

The High Dudgeon lumbered toward them, flanked by six nervous, armed acolytes. Woad trailed after them, looking about, one hand resting on his dagger.

"I have your payment here." The High Dudgeon opened a small pouch and showed it to Quiescat. A cluster of diamonds glittered at the bottom under the radiance of the temple lampstones. "Your associate is content they're genuine."

"I had them verified by an independent diamond merchant," Woad said with a smirk, "to make sure the High Dudgeon wasn't cheated."

Shooing the acolyte from the shrine, Gafyso turned her briefcase sideways. With a flick of her wrists, four legs sprang from the bottom to form a table. The forelegs, being slightly closer than those at the back, gave the impression of an animal about to pounce. Quiescat and the High Dudgeon stood at the doorway, while she slipped a stack of parchments from the case. "This is a standard transfer contract, but you should both take the time to read it to confirm you're happy with the details."

The High Dudgeon dismissed the suggestion with a wave of his hand. "I trust your good judgment, Gafyso."

I wish I could say the same. Quiescat slid past the High Dudgeon and picked up the contract. The legalese quickly left him baffled, but he made sure that the property he offered was the only thing being transferred and the price was correct.

He signed and imprinted the Hax emblem on one of the molten blobs of wax Gafyso put at the bottom, then stepped out of the way to let the High Dudgeon complete the contract.

"It's done," Gafyso said.

A triumphant grin fattened the High Dudgeon's face as he tossed the pouch of diamonds to Quiescat. Taken by surprise, he almost dropped them.

"Don't spill them," the High Dudgeon warned with a chuckle. "They're yours now. If you lose them, they're your loss."

"Let's go," Woad growled. "We have people to see."

"Wait," Quiescat said. "How many diamonds were there?"

"Sixteen," Woad said. "Each worth five thousand ducats."

"You don't trust me," the High Dudgeon muttered.

"After your stunt with the altar, no, I don't," Quiescat said.

Gafyso leaned back, folded her arms, and regarded him with a cool stare. He counted out the sixteen diamonds in the pouch. He counted them a second time to be sure. "Ready."

As he and Woad hastened along the balcony, a half-dozen cordents entered the temple.

"There was a fight here earlier," Quiescat said. "They might have come about that."

The cordents stopped the first person who happened to pass them—a woman dressed in orange priestly vestments. She pointed to Hissimir's shrine.

Woad clutched Quiescat's arm. "We need to find another way out fast."

18

Drinith plunged into the root forest toward the roar, knife at the ready for oncoming Stedfasters. At least she wouldn't face them alone. Toskar, Nezon, Kaliop, and Fisken pushed their way through drapes of roots not far behind her. Siga must have given himself aw—

No, Siga stood before her, his finger pressed to his lips. He pointed to a chink in the stringy curtain. Drinith bent down and peered through it.

Two squalid youths held Lesym in a stoop, his hands pinned behind his back. Their unkempt hair and loose, shabby garments emphasized their emaciation. Despite the spears and slings they carried, and the viciousness in their hollow faces, Drinith fancied her chances against them in a fight. But they weren't alone. She didn't dare shift the roots to see the owner of the booted foot just in view, in case the movement gave her away.

An immaculately dressed woman with bright rose eyes strode into view. A live white snake hung languidly around her neck like a stole, its white scales looking as though they were braided. She wore her pink hair neatly plaited in a dragon tail style. Her round, burgundy face showed no hint of the hunger that ravaged her compatriots. She had two or more rings on every plump finger. Four daggers hung from her belt. This must be Nykostar, the Stedfasters' leader.

Three more Stedfasters stepped forward around her, including the owner of the foot. They were better fed than the two holding Lesym.

Nykostar stroked her snake. "Where did you find him?"

"We were hunting for the new candidates like everyone else," one of Lesym's captors said. "We happened on him as he was climbing up the High Wall. You should have seen his dismay when we pounced on him."

A hand tugged Drinith's shoulder. "Let me see," Toskar whispered.

Drinith brushed her hand away.

"Good work," Nykostar said. "So, Lesym, we meet again. How is your beloved Prystian?"

"You don't have to live like this," Lesym said, his gaze fixing on each Stedfaster in turn. "This isn't the life you dreamed of when you came to the Whetstone. The Diarchy has abandoned you to slowly die in filth and depravity. Put aside the fears that trap you here and join us."

"Become Prystian's slave like you, you mean," Nykostar said. "No thanks. Nobody else will be joining your little revolution. We've blocked every route upward except for the one in our village. Starved of recruits, your cult will wither while we can only strengthen. In time, when we have swelled to a sufficient number, we'll purge the Whetstone of your friends and finally pass through the Ouroboric Gate."

Lesym sneered. "I wonder how many people you will have eaten by then."

"You won't be around to count them," Nykostar said. She turned to the young man nearest her. "Clespro, any sign of the new candidates?"

"They came here, but from the tracks, they appear to have doubled back. My best guess is they're heading toward the Sisters. The lake levels are low at the moment. The first doesn't reach the roof of the chamber. A good swimmer could cross the second on a single breath. The third, of course, is impassable. If they hide there, either hunger or rising water will drive them out eventually, and we'll be waiting for them."

"Take a detachment to check if they're down there. I'll head back to the village with our guest. Everyone else can keep looking in case your hunch proves wrong. I don't want them wandering free, causing mischief. The Whetstone is new to them. They're at their most disoriented and disorganized now."

"Are we going to try to make friends?" Clespro asked.

Nykostar shook her head. "Our encounter at the barricade put paid to that. They have every reason not to trust us now. We need to treat them as hostiles until we've broken them."

The Stedfasters parted in opposite directions. The sound of their soft steps faded into the distance.

"What do you make of that?" Siga whispered.

"We must rescue Lesym," Drinith said. "Or at least try."

"Nearly half of us are unarmed," Toskar said.

"All the more reason to do it," Siga said. "We need more weapons. You heard their leader. We'll end up on a butcher's block like Oristan if they catch us. This is war."

"I'm in charge, and I say we don't risk it," Toskar insisted.

"I didn't elect you," Siga growled.

"We had a vote," Nezon said.

"Every moment we dither," Drinith said, "brings Lesym a step closer to certain death. I'll be back as soon as I can." She pushed through the curtain and leapt from the stone into the clearing.

"I'm coming too," Siga said, following her.

"You're not!" Toskar hissed. "I'm in charge!"

"Not anymore," Kaliop said, joining Drinith and Siga. "I've changed my vote."

"You can't do that," Nezon blurted as the three of them raced off.

Drinith took the lead as they followed the freshest set of prints down a path through the root forest. Nykostar's party could not have gotten far dragging Lesym along.

She spotted the Stedfasters in the distance. Lesym, still bowed, was sandwiched between his two guards, while Nykostar strode ahead of them.

Drinith had almost closed the gap before the Stedfasters noticed her. As Lesym's guards drew their weapons, he jostled them, knocking over one and distracting the other long enough for Drinith to stab him.

"Mercy!" his comrade cried, raising his hands.

Drinith leapt by him. Siga and Kaliop could deal with him. Capturing Nykostar would surely end this nightmare here and now.

Nykostar drew her knife and ran. "Stedfasters, to me!" she cried.

Drinith gained steadily on her, but could she catch Nykostar before her people arrived?

Nykostar kept glancing over her shoulder. Snatching the snake from around her neck, she flung it at Drinith, then plunged into the root forest. Dodging the hissing serpent, Drinith moved to follow her, hesitated. Nykostar could be waiting for her just behind the veil of roots. Someone grabbed her shoulder. Siga leapt back as Drinith turned her knife on him. She opened her free hand in a placatory gesture. She had been so focused on chasing Nykostar she hadn't noticed him following her.

He made a thrusting motion with his spear, then gestured for her to be ready to leap into the forest. As he drove the spear through the curtain, Nykostar yelped. Drinith dashed into the roots. Nykostar stared wide-eyed as Drinith easily avoided her knife thrust and stabbed the weapon from her hand. Nykostar fumbled for another knife from her belt, but Drinith's punch sent her sprawling backward. Snapping roots cushioned her fall, but before Nykostar could wrest another dagger free, Siga's spear against her throat stilled her.

"Not another move or I'll kill you!" Siga growled.

"You wouldn't dare," Nykostar hissed, anger rekindling her courage.

"The Ouroboric Gate forgives all sins, remember."

"You need me alive."

Siga smirked. "But not necessarily in one piece."

Drinith plucked Nykostar's three remaining knives from their sheaths, grabbed a coil of cord from the girl's belt, and bound her hands. As a precaution, Drinith also gagged her. She and Siga dragged Nykostar back onto the path.

"Her hand is bleeding," Drinith said. "We should bandage it."

Kaliop raced up to them. "Lesym wants to talk to you, Drinith." She grabbed Nykostar by the collar. "I can manage this one."

Lesym shook his head gravely as Drinith drew up beside him. "Gambling your lives to save mine was a foolish thing to do."

"You could thank us," Siga groused behind her, "instead of whining."

"Thank you," Lesym grunted. "Just don't blame me for what your generosity may cost you. The Stedfasters won't forgive you for this." He gestured to the dead boy at his feet. "They'll show no mercy when they catch you."

"We have their leader," Drinith said. "They'll surely grant us safe passage out of their territory to get her back."

"But if they don't, what then?"

Drinith glanced at the bound Stedfaster, staring wild-eyed up at her from beside the corpse of the one she had slain. What indeed? She could never condone torture, but the Stedfasters didn't know that. "Whatever it takes to change their minds."

"Whatever cruelty you think you're capable of, be in no doubt the Stedfasters' capacity exceeds it. Nykostar's value as a prisoner may not be as great as you believe. They may simply replace her as leader." He glanced back down the path, gasped. "They're gone."

Nykostar and Kaliop had disappeared.

"Did the Stedfaster overpower her?" Siga asked in bewilderment.

"Kaliop betrayed us," Drinith said. "She made a deal with Nykostar to save her worthless hide. We had better get out of here."

The prisoner cringed as Siga reached for him, but Drinith pulled him back. "Leave him. He'll only slow us down."

The ground shook. The roots danced about as grinding filled the darkness.

"Earthquake!" Siga yelled. Drinith couldn't hear the rest of what he said over the thunderous crack of stone.

19

Zoen sighed as Toskar and Nezon bickered. She did her best to ignore their prattle.

"This is my fault," Toskar admitted finally.

Fisken leapt to her feet and thrust a finger at Zoen. "No, it's hers! She's the one who encouraged the Gyran witch to challenge you. Now she's run off with half the group and most of the weapons and we're left stranded here." She threw her arms up in disgust. "And it's your fault too, Nezon, groveling to a thrallborn instead of standing on your own two feet and taking charge."

Nezon marched up to Fisken and leaned so close they could have felt each other's breaths. Fisken shied from her glare and moved to back away, but Nezon's grip on her arm held her firm.

"I'll tell you why you didn't take charge," Nezon snarled. "You're nothing but a follower. Toskar's worth a dozen of you. She didn't have to come here yet. She had another year's grace. But she chose not to abandon me. You followed your beloved Oristan here and now he's gone, you're desperate to latch on to someone else. Toskar's parents may have been thralls, but you're lower than any thrall."

Fisken's cracking slap made Nezon stagger back a step. Fisken's anger wilted, but a malicious grin peeped from behind Nezon's hand as she rubbed her cheek.

"Enough!" Toskar said. "Fighting among ourselves won't improve our situation."

"Tosk, you are the smartest person here," Nezon said, "but being smart isn't enough. You need to stamp your authority on this group or it will fall apart."

"Kaliop has dismissed me in favor of Drinith, remember. All the while Drinith and I sought to be leader, Kaliop quietly took control."

"Well, you need to take it back."

"You're right," Toskar sighed.

Nezon offered Toskar her knife.

"I can't take that," Toskar said.

"You have to," Nezon insisted. "You'll get no respect from the likes of Kaliop and Siga otherwise. Your authority can't depend on me. You taking charge of this group will protect us better than any blade."

Toskar waved it away. "You're the better fighter. Keep it. It's more important that you apologize to Fisken."

"I don't want any apology from *her*," Fisken huffed.

"You paid back any wrong she did you tenfold with that slap. These circumstances are making us all...testy. We need to make allowances for the stress everyone is under. All I am asking is for you to put aside your enmity for the good of the group and forgive Nezon."

"Very well," Fisken said. She stood, her mouth pressing into a narrow line as she offered her hand.

As Nezon shook it, Toskar turned to Zoen. "The group is in danger while Kaliop holds the balance of power. It would be better if Drinith and I could come to some form of agree—"

The cavern shuddered and growled. The frightening tremble of the soft ground forced the four girls to clamber onto a rock as dangling roots whipped about them. Zoen instinctively covered her head with her arms in the event the roof collapsed. Even the air shivered.

The quake ceased as abruptly as it started. They stepped warily onto the soil, now still again.

"Are earthquakes common on Ophigee?" Toskar asked.

"I don't remember there ever having been one before," Fisken said uncertainly.

"Neither do I," Zoen admitted.

Hisses came from every direction. Something white slid down a root beside Zoen. The ghostwhip lifted its head to look at her, its tongue flicking. She froze, mesmerized by the gaze of its large pink eyes with their sinister black ellipses. Nezon screeched behind her. Fisken yanked Zoen back before the ghostwhip struck. It hit the ground, still anchored to the root by its tail. As it coiled back onto the root, Zoen's attention turned to the other snakes slithering out of the forest, winding down roots, dropping from the darkness above.

"We have to get out of here now or we never will!" Toskar blurted, dragging Nezon behind her as she dashed into the veil of roots.

Fisken chased after them. Zoen followed so close behind that she almost slammed into Fisken when she came to a sudden halt.

"Our provisions!" Fisken cried, lunging toward the litter of forgotten leather parcels and bedrolls.

Following, Zoen scooped up what she could into her arms. A snake dropped at her foot, but before it could twist about to strike she had already rushed for the root curtain.

Her skin crawled, her heart lurched as the roots lashed her and slithered across her face. All about, snakes maintained a dreadful hissing chorus, as if the root forest itself cursed her. She slashed at the grasping tendrils with her knife, squirming free with muttered curses.

She stumbled into the open, almost falling over a boulder, as breathless as if she had been drowning in the forest. She brushed her head and reached behind her to confirm the sensation of something creeping up her back was her imagination.

Toskar grabbed her, looked her over, turned her around. "Were you bit anywhere?"

"I don't think so," Zoen said, but already Toskar and Nezon had turned their attention to the root forest. "Where's Fisken?"

"Behind me," Zoen said between gulps of air, her heart still thumping.

"Dragons," Nezon gasped. "I'll go in after her."

"It's too dangerous," Toskar said. "You're likely to get bitten."

"We can't just abandon her," Nezon said.

A figure wrapped in a blanket burst out of the forest. Bundled blankets dropped from beneath her arms, spilling pouches, parcels, and tools. Fisken cast aside her makeshift shawl and exhaled through puffed cheeks.

"What possessed you to delay? You could have been bitten," Toskar said as she and Nezon checked her for telltale punctures.

Fisken grinned. "We need our supplies, such as they are. My only regret is I couldn't grab more."

Zoen looked down at the pile of pouches and bedrolls at her feet. Her haul was a pittance compared to Fisken's.

"I was wrong about you, Fisken," Nezon said.

Fisken shrugged. "Perhaps I did rely too much on Oristan. It never entered my head to put myself forward to lead the group." She blushed. "Not that I want to do that now. It's just I never even considered the possibility. It's not very Ophigeen."

The four girls gathered the items scattered on the ground. Zoen had no idea what was in the parcels she had tucked inside her tunic. A ghostwhip slithered near her booted foot. She kicked it as far as she could. With a deafening hiss, it coiled into a knot and struck out at her, but she had already backed beyond the reach of its curved fangs.

"We need to leave," Toskar said. "The ghostwhips aren't the only danger here. Stedfasters might come upon us at any moment."

"But what about the others?" Zoen asked. "They'll never find us if we leave."

Pounding footsteps came from somewhere in the forest. Zoen tensed. She and Nezon drew their knives, but Fisken and Toskar were unarmed.

"It might be the others," Fisken said.

"Be ready to run," Toskar murmured.

Two figures armed with spears raced toward them.

"Run!" Toskar cried as she turned to flee.

"Wait," Nezon said. "One of them's Siga."

Toskar gave her a skeptical look as though that was little comfort, but they lingered.

Zoen gasped as she recognized Lesym running alongside Siga. Drinith, also carrying a spear, kept glancing over her shoulder as she followed not far behind them.

"Where's Kaliop?" Toskar asked.

"Gone," Drinith said. "She betrayed us and fled with the Stedfasters' leader."

"No loss," Siga said as he passed knives to Nezon and Fisken.

"We must go," Lesym said. "Nykostar will be in pursuit as soon as she has mustered enough of her people. I know a place we can hide. Follow me." He dashed down the slope. Zoen rushed to follow him like everyone else.

They pounded down a bewildering succession of tunnels. Zoen quickly drifted to the back of the group. Her foot hurt, but not bad enough to throw off her gait. She simply wasn't as fast as the others.

Zoen greeted Drinith and Siga, waiting for her at a junction, with relief.

"Keep going," Drinith said, pointing down one tunnel. "The others are that way."

Too breathless to speak, Zoen nodded as she passed them. Fat drops of water dripped from the ceiling. She splashed across a stream, little more than a crude shallow channel worn in the floor. The tunnel twisted upward, then down. Drinith and Siga jogged just behind her. The roots illuminating their way petered out, and they were forced to negotiate the narrowing path in darkness. Stone struck Zoen's forehead. It took her a moment to shake off the dazing pain. She kept herself hunched after that. The tip-tap of water from the ceiling turned to a persistent shower and then a deluge. Panic gripped Zoen, wading blind through ice-cold water up to her knees. Did Lesym really know where he was going? Might they drown down here? She could hear nothing beyond the incessant splash of water.

The tunnel sloped upward. The downpour waned, and the water receded. Zoen's heart jumped at the sight of a distant light flickering through the knot of shifting silhouettes ahead of her. The tunnel opened into a large chamber. A circular body of water occupied most of the floor. Except for the sheer cliff face on the far side of this pool, bright roots, some as thick as Zoen's arm, webbed the walls. A dark layer topped the roots and collected on ledges like black snow. The air stank of must and stale urine. Somewhere high above, lost in the darkness, bats flapped, their chattery clicks barely audible against the distant thrash of water.

"We must climb up there." Lesym pointed to the darkness at the top of the bare cliff.

Siga shook water off like a dog. "Do we swim across it?" he asked, pointing to the dark pool.

Lesym picked up a loose rock and flung it into the pool. It made a loud echoey plop as it disappeared under the water. Daggers of white streaked from the black depths to crisscross just below the surface. "Not unless you want to be shocked to death by those levin eels." He pointed to the ledges and folds in the encircling curtain of rock. "We'll have to skirt around the sides."

"We'll go first," Toskar said as she scrambled along the haphazard mesh of roots woven across the rugged curtain of rock. Nezon and Fisken followed. Toskar's foot slipped, but she clung on thanks to Nezon's steadying grasp. She wiped her forehead with the back of her hand. "Be careful. The roots are wet and the bat droppings make everything slippery."

As Toskar started to climb the cliff, Drinith shouted to her to wait, then turned to Zoen. "You had better cross next. Toskar, Nezon, and Fisken can help you up the cliff. Siga, Lesym, and I will follow."

"At the top, there's a river," Lesym said. "Follow it upstream to a waterfall. There's a cave behind it. We'll meet you there if we get split up."

As Zoen carefully picked her way along the wall, she did her best not to touch the black beads of bat guano that filled every ledge and crevice. She didn't slip like Toskar but the deliberation of her every movement slowed her.

"Hurry up!" Toskar snapped, making a circular motion with her arm. "The Stedfasters will be on us before you're across at this rate."

Zoen hastened, her foot slipped, and she stumbled, dangling both feet above the pool. Her shoulders and arms hurt as she scrabbled for purchase with her feet. A pouch dropped from under her tunic and struck the pool with a dull plash, sending a dark ripple across its black surface. It bobbed under the water a few times, then white flashed beneath it, and it disappeared. Zoen managed to locate a foothold and climbed up.

"Hang on." Fisken nimbly made her way back along the wall to help her. Meanwhile, Lesym, Drinith, and Siga began their crossing. Toskar and Nezon, apparently losing patience, started up the cliff.

Three figures appeared at its summit. Slings spun over their heads and lashed out like striking snakes. The shots cracked against the wall around Drinith. Everyone reversed course.

The Stedfasters reloaded, the whir of their slings ending in snaps. A stone struck just above Zoen, clattered down the wall and landed in the pool.

"If you don't move fast, we're both going to die," Fisken warned her. "I'll keep a good grip on you. I won't let you fall." Toskar and Nezon closed fast. Drinith, Lesym, and Siga leapt clear of the wall on the far side of the pool. As though they'd gone mad, they yelled and brandished their spears to attract the slingers' missiles. The snap of slings sent them scurrying for cover before the stones could struck them.

Toskar and Nezon had already reached Fisken. Zoen blocked the three of them. They were going to die because of her.

A broad ledge lay ahead. If Zoen pressed against the wall there, the others could slip by her. But, as she paused, Fisken shunted her onward.

"Keep moving, keep moving..." Fisken chanted. Zoen pushed forward. She was nearly there.

The whirring from the cliff grew louder. Zoen looked up. Two new Stedfasters had joined the assault. The slings snapped. Shots rattled around her.

She leapt off the wall, falling onto the rough ground beyond the pool. A rock struck her ribs. Another scraped her elbow. She crawled behind a boulder while Fisken and Toskar raced for cover.

Toskar half-turned, froze. Horror contorted her face. "Nezon!" she screamed. Fisken grabbed her and, with Lesym's help, dragged her behind a boulder.

Nezon wobbled onward, hunched to one side, wincing with pain; one arm hung limp, the other lurched from one hold to the next.

The Stedfasters reloaded their slings.

Drinith dashed toward Nezon and stretched out her spear so she could grab on to it. It was barely a foot beyond Nezon's reach.

Siga yanked Drinith back. Two shots zinged past where she had been.

Nezon screamed as she struck the water with a splash. Shaking free of Siga, Drinith scrabbled across the wall and again stretched out the spear, but Nezon had floated beyond its reach. Lightning flashes sped through the water.

"Drinith, come back!" Lesym cried. "It's too late! The levin eels have her."

A shimmery white ball of the whiplike eels engulfed Nezon, dragging her down. Siga tugged Drinith away from the pool as predators and prey vanished into the inky depths.

Toskar's pained screech as Fisken and Lesym dragged her back toward the tunnel couldn't drown out the menacing whir of the Stedfasters' slings. Everyone plunged into the darkness, heedless of where they were going.

20

Quiescat looked around for inspiration. A nearby shrine belonged to Murcos, the Nemon goddess of doorways and passages. He dashed toward it. "If there's a way out, it'll be in there."

"Welcome," the ancient priest said as he struggled to stand. Behind him stood a gilded statue of his deity. The series of open archways that formed her mouth extended through her head. A door protruded above her mop of wormy hair. Her eyes were shiny gems set at the bottom of screw-like depressions. A circular knocker pierced her nostrils and rested on the tear-shaped groove under her nose. Her skirt comprised a series of doors.

"We seek a miracle from Murcos," Quiescat said.

"What?" The priest clutched his necklace of keys.

"We come with an offering for the Queen of Ways," Quiescat said, thrusting a diamond at the ancient.

The priest's eyes opened wide with surprise. Woad gasped. Quiescat was offering the priest a fortune, but it would be well spent if it secured their escape.

"We need a way out of here," Quiescat said. "Murcos never has an entrance without an exit."

"You know Murcos well." The priest nodded and plucked the gem from Quiescat's hand.

The priest opened the central door in the statue's skirt to reveal a wedge of blue sky. Wind whistled through the hole.

"What magic is this?" Woad asked.

"The sort you can wield with a sledgehammer," the priest said.

Woad chuckled appreciatively. "I'll go first," he said as cordents raced by the shrine. It wouldn't take long for the High Dudgeon and Gafyso to direct them here. The ex-mercenary crawled through the little passage and disappeared. Quiescat quickly followed. Cordents tramped into the shrine moments before the door slammed shut behind him.

"You can't come in here!" the priest protested. "This is a hallowed sanctuary!" Quiescat couldn't make sense of the muffled conversation that followed other than it was acrimonious.

He could see nothing beyond the end of the tunnel but blue sky until he peered over its lip. A ladder hung down to the tiled roof below. Woad stood at its foot, beckoning him.

Quiescat shut his eyes a moment to quell his dizziness. He awkwardly twisted around and eased himself down onto the ladder. He descended very slowly, one rung at a time. It was reassuring to face the little tunnel and then the wall.

Woad steadied him as he reached the bottom and pointed down to the edge of the roof. "There's another ladder over there." He moved with unnerving speed across the brown tiles. "Hurry."

With a forlorn glance at the crude hole through which he had exited the temple, Quiescat followed. He took a deep breath to steady his nerves as tiles rattled beneath his feet. He descended the slope backward in a stoop, clinging onto the tiles he passed.

"I didn't know you were so scared of heights," Woad said with a hint of vexation.

"I'm not, normally," Quiescat said. It was the precarious nakedness of being up here that he found so intimidating, buffeted by the breeze with nothing between him and a steep drop.

Straightening, he faced the top of the ladder peeping above the edge of the roof. "Is it far down?"

"No distance at all," his footsure friend assured him. Woad gave Quiescat's shoulder a companionable slap that sent him toppling forward. Woad latched on to his coat just in time.

"Whoa! I know you were slow on the roof, but jumping down to the street isn't the answer. We need to hur—" Woad cursed; Quiescat trained his gaze to where he pointed. Figures rose above the ridge—cordents. Either they forced their way through the tunnel in the shrine or they had found some other route onto the roof.

"Go on," Woad urged. "It's not that far down."

"You go first," Quiescat said. "I'm too slow."

Woad didn't argue. He started down the ladder. As Quiescat moved to follow, he glimpsed the dirty lane a long way down. Woad had already descended a third of the ladder. How could he move so fast?

"You told me it we weren't far from the ground," Quiescat bleated.

"It won't be when you're at the bottom of the ladder!" Woad growled. "Now, move it!"

Quiescat awkwardly climbed onto the ladder and started downward. The slipperiness of the mucky rungs forced him to cling to the side rails, exacerbating his clumsiness. He had traveled halfway down when the first cordent reached the top of the ladder.

"Stop!" he cried, but Quiescat kept moving.

Woad beckoned him at the bottom. "Hurry up!"

Quiescat's grip slipped. He scrabbled for the ladder, clutched a side rail, hugged himself to it. The cordent descended the ladder while a second peered down.

Quiescat couldn't possibly escape them. Woad had the contacts to get to Ophigee. He had the skills to rescue Drinith. Quiescat wasn't equipped for such a venture. "Run!" he yelled. He dropped the diamond pouch.

Woad caught it, but waited. "Not without you."

The fool! The blind fool! He was throwing away any chance of saving Drinith out of misplaced loyalty. Indignation at Woad's pigheadedness spurred Quiescat to renewed vigor.

The first cordent closed fast. By the time Quiescat neared the bottom, the cordent's boots were only two rungs above him. Quiescat squealed in fright as Woad ripped him off the ladder. "Take the pouch," Woad growled, pushing it into his hands. Quiescat lost his footing, fell. His elbow banged against the cobbles, but his arm cushioned his head. Still clutching the pouch, he scrambled to his feet.

"Run!" Woad cried as he punched the first cordent. The second cordent slid down the ladder, threw himself at Woad. Three more cordents raced down the lane toward them, baying for Quiescat to halt.

Stuffing the pouch into an inside pocket in his coat, Quiescat fled in the opposite direction.

As he reached the end of the lane, he glimpsed three cordents beating Woad down with batons. Two chased Quiescat. He couldn't outrun them for long. He needed somewhere to hide.

He turned the corner. An elderly man in a nightdress, rubbing his bleary eyes, filled the threshold of an open doorway. "What's happening?"

Quiescat pushed his way into the house, forcing the man back inside, and slammed the door shut.

"I'm being pursued by cordents. I'll make it worth your while to hide me."

The man stared at him in shock and horror as he raised his hands. "Please don't hurt me and my family."

"Put your mind at ease," Quiescat said. "I won't hurt you, I promise."

"Oh, thank all dragons!" the man gasped. Resting his hands on the back of a chair, he took several deep breaths. "He's in here!" he roared. Quiescat fled deeper into the house in search of a back door.

He found it in the next room, a small kitchen. The stiff latch refused to budge so he pulled on the handle of barrel with both hands and leaned back. The barrel slid across with a loud snap and the door swung open, sending him staggering backward. He recovered his balance and dashed outside as the cordents rushed through the front door.

A canal stretched ahead. Quiescat jumped onto a punt, cut its mooring, and pushed it away from the bank with a pole. If he could make it to the far side...

A cordent, her face grim with resolve, leapt off the canal bank. Quiescat cringed and closed his eyes as the woman flew toward him.

His eyes popped open at a large splash. Landing short, the cordent thrashed in the canal water. Gliding to the far side, Quiescat hopped off the boat and fled. Reaching a busy street, he slowed, hoping to melt into the crowd. He spotted a beggar and convinced him to sell his mangey cloak for a ducat.

The diamond pouch—had Quiescat dropped it? He patted his clothes until he found it. The fifteen diamonds lay nestled at the bottom.

They hardly compensated for the loss of Woad. His draker contacts were gone, too. Quiescat should have asked their names. Now, his only lead was the captain Elca Trajar had suggested, Lawster Forte, no doubt an untrustworthy scoundrel.

Quiescat headed for the perches. The captain of the *Parched Tongue* was his best chance, his only chance, to save Drinith and sort out this mess.

21

———

Toskar's every quiet sob tightened the knot of guilt in Zoen's chest, but she kept silent. Nothing she could say would deliver absolution for her part in Nezon's death.

The group had crammed into a tight crevice. This wasn't a suitable long-term refuge, but at least they could get a break from running. Although a mesh of roots hid the entrance, Drinith and Siga kept guard in case Stedfasters stumbled across them.

Toskar covered her face with her hands as if trying to hide from their grim reality. Fisken nestled beside her and laid an arm across her hunched shoulders.

"She said nothing," Toskar whimpered. "I heard her gasp as the shot hit her but I never imagined... I didn't realize... She knew I'd never leave her, so she kept quiet. If she had said... If she had told me... I came here to protect her and I ended up killing her."

"It was my fault," Zoen blurted. "If I had been quicker..."

Fisken shook her head. "If you had been quicker, we'd have been halfway up the cliff when the Stedfasters attacked, and we'd be all dead now."

Zoen acknowledged Fisken's crumb of solace with a grateful nod, but it didn't alleviate her guilt. Weakness was the worst sin in Ophigee, and she was frailty personified. She was the very sort of weakling the Ascent was intended to weed out.

"Anybody hungry?" Fisken asked. Nobody bothered to answer. Nobody had an appetite.

"After we get to this famous refuge, what then?" Siga asked. "We hide there until the Diarchy decides to clean up this mess? That might take a long time."

"Another dragon arrives in a few days," Fisken said. "Some friends of mine are on it. We might be able to raise the alarm. If the Diarchy understood what is happening down here..."

"The Ascent is sacrosanct," Lesym said. "If the Diarchs dispatch an expedition to restore order to the Whetstone, it'll be for their benefit, not ours. They might force us to take the green, or they might even kill us to prevent this travesty becoming common knowledge and undermining their authority."

He scratched his jaw. "Nykostar let slip that there's a route out of the Stedfasters' territory in their village. We have to gain access to it somehow."

Siga grimaced. "The *somehow* is the problem. There's only sev— six of us against dozens of them."

"You should surrender," Lesym said. "I doubt Nykostar would show me mercy. Or Drinith either for that matter, after humiliating her. But the rest of you are different."

"I doubt that applies for me," Siga said. "I was a member of the party that freed you, remember. I'm not that forgettable. The others... The others might have a chance."

Not Zoen. The Stedfasters would smell out her feebleness.

Toskar looked up from her hands, her tear-stained face livid with hate. "Do you think I could politely surrender to Nezon's murderers? Do you imagine I could debase myself by fawning over their leader?"

"Keep your voice down, please," Lesym said. "Your best hope to avenge your friend is to reach my people."

"And who are they?" Toskar asked. "Why is the sword drawn on your tunic pointed the wrong direction?"

Zoen craned her neck to glimpse the front of Lesym's tunic. The haloed blade indeed pointed upward, a shocking blasphemy.

"My people, the Uprisers, been taught the same lesson as you," Lesym said. "We, too, have lost friends to this cursed place. We've survived its hardships and horrors. We want this nightmare to end not just for us, but also for all the generations who follow us.

"Put aside a lifetime of indoctrination and open your eyes! See the squalor and depravity around you for what it is—a natural consequence of the system that condemned all of us to this deathtrap!"

"You speak treason," Toskar said.

"Before you condemn us, talk to our leader, Prystian," Lesym said. "I lack his insight and eloquence. If he can't convince you of the righteousness of our cause, then so be it. The Ouroboric Gate forgives all sins. First, you must escape the Stedfasters."

Toskar shook her head. "I'll not surrender to them. No way."

"There's no point in throwing your life away in some vainglorious gesture. I understand your anger. I share it. My blood seethes at the prospect of your meek surrender, but it offers your only chance to escape. Survival is your best revenge."

"What about you, Fisken?" Toskar asked. "Would you meekly submit to Oristan's killers?"

"No."

"Zoen?"

"No," she lied. If doing so would save the others, she would. She was probably doomed anyway.

Toskar folded her arms. "So, there you have it. Nobody's for your plan."

Lesym sighed and rubbed a hand over his stubbly pate. "So your plan is what, exactly? Hide and hope for the best?"

Toskar's face contorted with rage. "Do to the Stedfasters what they've done to us—pick them off one by one until they're afraid to stir from their village."

"Either they'll have hunted us down or we'll have starved to death before that can happen."

"There's another possibility," Drinith said. "It's somewhat of a long shot, but when the next dragon comes, the arrival of a new batch of candidates might prove a sufficient distraction for us to sneak into the Stedfasters' village and escape."

Lesym's eyebrows rose. "That's a risky plan. It might work, with a lot of luck."

"It's hardly moral to abandon a new group of candidates to the Stedfasters," Toskar said.

Drinith's mouth tightened.

"I'll stay behind to warn them," Lesym said. "The rest of you can make your escape."

"Of course, we have to survive until the dragon arrives," Zoen said. They had already lost over a third of the group in a day, if even that. It was impossible to measure time properly in this perpetual subterranean gloom. It felt a lot longer. A lifetime.

"We had better get going," Drinith said.

Siga shushed her and signaled that someone was coming. Zoen listened. The footsteps were hard to distinguish at first from random drips, but they grew steadily louder until the tunnel outside echoed with them. From the sound, three or more Stedfasters crept toward them.

Everyone readied their weapons. A pebble clattered inside their crevice. Heads swiveled in search of the culprit. Zoen met Fisken's condemnatory scowl with a shrug. She had nothing to do with it. Nobody owned up.

"Did you hear that?" a Stedfaster blurted.

Silence. Not even a footfall. Tingling fear crept up Zoen's spine.

Furtive movement whispered in the tunnel—the delicate rustle of loose roots, the sporadic scuff of leather, the shift of a pebble, the soft slosh of water. Wood scraped against stone. The rhythmic tap of a water drip missed a beat and then another. Perfectly still, Zoen listened to the breathless silence, straining to make sense of what was happening outside. Did the Stedfasters realize they were in here?

Drinith and Siga stood still in crouching positions immediately behind the drape of roots, spears at the ready, primed to attack.

Shadows shifted beyond the root mesh. A hand holding the shaft of a spear shone through a gap. The web shifted.

Drinith sprang forward. Siga followed a fraction of a moment later and screams filled the tunnels.

22

Shock flashed on the boy's face as Drinith rammed her spear into his chest. Siga struck another Stedfaster in the stomach, pinning him to the ground. The second boy screamed and writhed, his arms desperately flailing. A third Stedfaster to Drinith's left thrust a spear at her. She deflected it with one hand, wrenched her spear free with the other and struck him in the chin with its butt. He staggered backward and fell on top of the Stedfaster behind him. Drinith spun her spear around, ready to skewer them both, but they already crawled away.

Siga yanked his spear free, drove it down on his wounded opponent. This time it cracked through the Stedfaster's ribcage. Siga staggered backward and retched to one side. Stedfasters scuttled into the distant gloom like startled rats.

"You let them get away," Toskar whined behind her.

Drinith didn't dare look at her, not even a glance, in case she lost control of her temper. The boy's face. No hate, no anger, only surprise. Eyes wide with incredulity, mouth hanging open. She threw her bloody spear aside and picked up one that the Stedfasters had discarded.

She had killed before, but never by ambush. The knowledge

that he would have slain her and her companions if she hadn't struck first couldn't cleanse her of nagging shame. This place had turned the Stedfasters into monsters, and now it was doing the same to her.

Lesym pushed by Drinith and stepped over the Stedfaster Siga had killed. "We had better get moving before they regroup." Most of the others had passed her by the time Siga tugged her from her daze.

"I never killed anyone before," Siga croaked. "Maybe I should have let him live."

"Killing him was a mercy," Drinith said. "He wouldn't have survived that stomach wound. He'd have suffered a long, agonizing death."

Siga made no reply. His haunted eyes spoke for him.

They were all children here, even the Stedfasters. Children playing the Diarchy's cruel game. The regime on Ophigee was as brutal as anything Magian inflicted on Rhumgad. It needed to be rooted out, destroyed. If Drinith survived this, she'd do her best to help Lesym's people, the Uprisers, bring an end to this travesty. The understanding that the Stedfasters weren't the true villains here added to her frustration. For now, she just had to stay alive.

They raced down the tunnel until it intersected with another, barely wide enough for them to walk along. Its low, arched roof forced Drinith into a slight stoop. Her sudden realization that its surface had been carved to look like snakeskin filled her with foreboding.

"What is this place?" she asked, her voice echoing around her.

"It provides access to a catacomb," Lesym said. "It circles it in fact. Part of this tunnel has collapsed but we should be able to pass through the catacomb to reach the far side."

They entered through a broken door, the rotten boards covered in bright orange mushrooms. Human skulls adorned the circular frame. Several were missing mandibles. A few had lost their facial bones, leaving only hollow brainpans. It reminded Drinith of a mouth full of rotten teeth. Inside, broken bones, pottery shards, and bits of masonry littered the floor. Over each empty rectangular alcove, a name had been carved. Somebody had ransacked the place, taking whatever grave goods might be useful.

"They say that the first thing a miner did on coming here was to dig his own grave," Zoen said as the candidates shuffled through a series of interconnecting chambers. "I don't remember hearing of any invading force ever penetrating Luckslap."

"This was done by candidates long ago," Lesym said. "Perhaps not all at once, just the gradual erosion by desperate generations."

"I can't believe any Ophigeen worth the name would desecrate an ancestor's grave," Zoen said.

"And yet the proof lies all around you. Ophigeens did this. The perpetrators may even have earned an eventual resting place in the necropolis on Ophigee's summit."

A fly brushed Drinith's cheek. She swatted at it with her hand, missed. More flies flew by. The stench of putrefaction assaulted her long before the candidates entered the last chamber. Drinith hardly dared to breathe the insufferable stink. The floors in the chamber were clean. Thankfully, the corpses in the alcoves had been wrapped in patchwork red shrouds, but the black stains on the cloth hinted at the rotting flesh beneath.

"The Stedfasters must bury their dead here," Siga said, crinkling his nose. "At least, the ones they haven't eaten."

That handsome, youthful face, that frozen gasp of surprise, came unbidden to Drinith's mind. She knew it was seared into her memory forever. *He'd have killed me in a heartbeat,* she reminded herself. She needed to move on.

"They may come here soon enough to inter their newly fallen comrades," Lesym said. "We had better keep moving." As if anyone might choose to linger in this place of death and carnal decay.

An ouroborous framed the cracked doorway on the far side. The door itself was completely missing. They entered the outer ring tunnel, took the next branch off it. They followed Lesym through winding natural caves again, ever alert for any hint of Stedfasters nearby. Veins of lampstone sporadically illuminated their way, but they often traveled in blind darkness. The narrowing of the tunnel forced them to stoop and then crawl.

"Lesym, are you sure you know where you're going?" Siga groused.

Lesym emitted an aggravated sigh. "Yes."

The tunnel constricted so tightly around them, Drinith could barely wriggle through it. In this oppressive darkness, it was being like a worm burrowing through the earth. She became wedged in a pincer of rock. Panic gripped her. Lesym, Toskar, and the others had already slipped through. She wriggled and squirmed until she freed herself. A boot slapped her in the face.

"Sorry," Toskar said.

Drinith crawled on, wary of the feet moving somewhere in front of her. Every breath tasted of dust and staleness. How much longer must they endure this black terror? Another quake might crush them, entombing them in this darkness forever.

Light flickered ahead. Toskar disappeared and the light spilled inside. Lesym offered Drinith his hands as she reached the exit and dragged her clear. As she patted dust off her tunic, she looked around. They were encircled by sheer cliffs except for a slope of jagged rubble up one side. "Have we to climb up that?"

Lesym blinked as he looked at it. "The last time I passed through here, that was a cliff face. An earthquake must have shaken it apart. We're lucky the tunnel wasn't blocked or the river above hasn't spilled down here."

The gradient upward may have been gentle, but negotiating the massive boulders was a slow, wearisome process. Between them lurked shadowed gaps, sometimes concealed by loose gravel, posing a threat to any unwary foot. Siga scurried ahead, apparently heedless of the risk. Everyone else climbed with more deliberation, but Zoen struggled to keep up and dropped behind some distance.

Drinith swallowed growing irritation. "I had better go back down to her," she said to Lesym.

"We're close to the refuge. At the top of the slope, head down the tunnel to your right. It should lead you to a river. Follow it upstream to the waterfall."

"Leave me," Zoen wheezed as Drinith neared her. "I'll catch up."

"Take a moment to gather your breath," Drinith said. "Then, we'll go again."

"I don't want anyone throwing their lives away for me," Zoen said irritably.

"Then stop feeling sorry for yourself and move," Drinith snapped. "That boy I slew back at the crevice—his face is haunting me."

"You had no choice." Zoen climbed again.

"I have had to kill before. I already took the life of a Stedfaster while rescuing Lesym. But I never struck first without warning before."

"I doubt he would have given killing you a second thought. They killed Oristan and Nezon, remember."

"It's... It's just I always hoped I was a better person than that."

"If you hadn't struck first, neither of us might be alive to have this conversation. It's this place. It is steeped in evil."

Lesym, about three-quarters up the slope, kept nervously checking their progress. Siga waved his spear from the top and disappeared.

A yell echoed through the cavern. Everyone took cover behind boulders. Drinith glanced upward. Siga raced by the slope, pursued by two reedy Stedfasters. As they closed, he swung round and drove his spear into the belly of the one immediately behind him, shoving him backward. As the second Stedfaster stumbled clear of his wounded companion, Siga, wielding his spear as a club, struck him on the head.

Cupping his hands, Siga yelled to some point beyond the pit. "Hoy, Stedfasters!" He spat, as if the name left a bad taste. "Cowardly scum!"

As he raced away, the wounded Stedfasters picked themselves up and staggered after him. A half-dozen more joined the chase. Siga was leading them away, giving the rest of the group time to escape.

At Lesym's signal, the candidates crept up the slope again.

"Do you think they'll catch Siga?" Zoen whispered.

"Hopefully, he'll give them the slip." *If he doesn't get himself trapped in a dead end.* Drinith would look for him after Zoen safely reached the waterfall. She owed him that for saving them. "No more talk. Save your breath for the climb."

Apprehension gripped Drinith as Lesym, Toskar, and Fisken reached the summit and disappeared. She and Zoen were on their own now. Silent except for Zoen's labored breaths, they worked their way up the slope, sticking as best they could to the shadows nestling between the boulders.

After what seemed an eternity, they neared the top.

Drinith halted Zoen. "Rest up a bit. We won't get another opportunity until we reach the waterfall." Zoen nodded gratefully and passed her a lump of cheese. It was warm and soft and tasted a bit off, but Drinith ate it anyway.

She waited until Zoen's rasping breaths softened to gentle whispers. "Is your foot hurting you again?"

"A little."

"We need to reach the waterfall as fast as we can. We can't stop no matter how tired you are or how much your foot hurts."

Zoen scowled. "I won't delay you."

Following Lesym's instructions, they quickly entered a large cavern lit by slashes of lampstone across its ceiling. A black river snaked languidly through its scree-littered floor. Judging from the rocks jutting from the water, the river was not that deep, but it must have filled the chamber on occasion. They scrambled upstream along its bank until they neared the waterfall. The absence of a welcome from their comrades made Drinith uneasy. They should already be here, watching out for the pair.

"Wait here," she said to Zoen. "I'll check it out first."

She raced over to the waterfall. Behind the curtain of spilling water was a dark cave. Why did the others not greet her? Perhaps they mistook her for a Stedfaster.

"It's me." She tightened her grip on her spear and stepped inside.

"Drinith!" Fisken's voice. "Ru—!" A loud slap cut her off. Hands ripped Drinith's spear from her grasp, reached for her. She drew her knife as she rolled away from them. She splashed through the waterfall before dropping into the river, the venom of its icy touch momentarily paralyzing her. Too late, she crawled from the dark figures encircling her. Laughter thundered above her before a foot forced her head under water. She struggled to hold what little breath remained as the numb cold seeped through her skull. The foot lifted and so did she, but only to her hands and knees. A brutal kick to her side knocked her over. She landed faceup, gasping for breath as a circle of scrawny faces grinned down at her.

Drinith flinched as Nykostar swung the point of a spear down on her. It settled right under her chin.

"So, we meet again," she said. "This time, our situations are reversed, it seems. You won't escape me as easily as I did from you. Did you really think you'd find somewhere to hide from us? This is our domain. We know every nook and cranny."

Behind her, Kaliop grinned.

Drinith thrashed the water with her fists. "Traitor!"

Nykostar laughed. The other Stedfasters hesitantly joined in. The point of the spearhead stung Drinith's throat. "Bind her."

Claw-like hands fell upon Drinith, dragged her from the water and pinned her to the rugged floor. A bag covered her head, its stench of rotten meat roiling her stomach. She breathed slowly and shallowly to inhale the fetor as little as possible. She wriggled as the Stedfasters twisted her arms behind her back and bound her wrists with cord. They lifted her, forced her onto her feet. Panic gripped her as another cord constricted around her neck. Did Nykostar intend to strangle her here and now? The cord tugged Drinith forward, and she had no choice but to stumble on across the loose stones according to its whim.

23

———

The instant Quiescat entered the tavern, the smokiness of the air set his eyes watering. His cough made several of its patrons look up from their tankards to glare at him. Walking around looking like a beggar might have protected his anonymity, but here his shabbiness drew unwelcome attention.

The Dragon's Spit—that explains the muck on the floor, Quiescat mused with disgust. *Apt name.*

"What do you want, Gadfly?" the barkeep snarled, his nose curling possibly at the damp, sweaty scent of the cloak.

Quiescat opened it to reveal the finer clothes beneath. He planted a gold ducat on the counter. "Water, please."

"We don't get many requests for that in here," the barkeep muttered. He picked up the ducat, weighed it in his palm. "Sit down. I'll give you your change at the end of the night."

Quiescat leaned over the bar. "I'm looking for someone," he whispered. "A captain by the name of Lawster Forte."

The barkeep arched one shaggy eyebrow. "If you're carrying around any more of those pretty coins, he'll sniff you out."

Quiescat took a small, empty table. He mumbled thanks as a serving girl dropped a mug before him. Wrapping his hands around it, he stared at his water, which had an unwholesome oily residue. It was safer than making eye contact with the other patrons. He couldn't afford to get in a fight with any of these ruffians. A careless glance might be enough to draw their ire.

The squeal of a shifting chair made him look up. A man approached the table with a gait alternating between a swagger and a stagger. Red ribbons peppered his silver beard. Dark stains marred his white blouse and his blue jacket trimmed with green. A half-dozen or more belts crisscrossed his waist. A black felt hat with a rounded crown and broad rim rested atop tossed silver curls. His rose eyes shone against his violet complexion. The barkeep watched him expectantly from behind his counter.

The stranger sat across from Quiescat and grinned, revealing two lines of gemstone-studded teeth. "I hear you're looking for me. I'm Lawster Forte, captain of the *Parched Tongue*. And who might you be?"

"My name is unimportant. I'm simply someone who needs to get to Ophigee and back. The part under the Halo Sea. A friend of mine there needs rescuing."

The serving girl planted two frothy beers before Lawster. He held her arm. "Wait." Never taking his lecherous eyes off her, he downed one tankard and passed it to her with a triumphant grin. He watched her leave, belched, and licked his purple lips with his black tongue. "So you want to go to the Whetstone without an invitation." He lifted his hat and, scratching his greasy hair, gave a whistle, low and skeptical. "That won't be easy, and it won't be cheap." He took a long quaff from his tankard. "A hundred thousand ducats."

Though half the price that Trajar had suggested, it was still more than Quiescat possessed. His dry mouth begged for water. He took a sip of his water, wincing at the oiliness. He should have offered less to the priest of Murcos. Lawster's stare demanded an answer. "I can pay seventy-five thousand."

"I don't haggle," Lawster said, picking up his beer while pressing his free hand against the edge of the table as if to rise. "I offer my best price."

"Best for you," Quiescat said. "You could retire with that sort of money. My offer is way over the going rate for such an enterprise."

Lawster looked right and left. He gave an impish grin. "There are plenty around here who'd ask for more. The Shopkeepers don't take kindly to foreign dragons trespassing in their territory. The Whetstone is kind of special to them. I give us a half chance at best of making it away from there alive. If I'm going to risk my life and the lives of my crew, I need to be well compensated."

"Seventy-five thousand is all I can afford for now," Quiescat said. "I'll pay another twenty-five thousand on completion of the mission."

Lawster let go of the table and thoughtfully sipped his beer. "You'll pay another fifty thousand."

"Thirty-five thousand." Capitulate too easily and he'd only ask for more. "That's ten thousand over your original price."

Lawster snickered.

"A hundred and ten thousand ducats is a lot of money for a few days' work," Quiescat said.

"And you'll pay seventy-five thousand upfront?"

That had been a mistake. Quiescat should have promised much less, but it was too late to say anything else. "That's right."

The captain beckoned the serving girl. "Bring us two of the house specials, Mulny."

She arched an eyebrow. "You're obviously in the money."

He nodded at Quiescat. "No, but he is."

Mulny snorted, then blew out the candle on the table. Catching Quiescat's quizzical gaze, she said, "The house special is explosive in more ways than one."

After intense discussion with the barkeep, she returned with two pewter thimbles, depositing them with alarming care before Lawster and Quiescat. The common room fell silent. Expectant gazes focused on the table. From the clear liquid in the thimbles emanated the vilest stench Quiescat had ever experienced. It burned his nostrils. "What in Empyr's name is this?" he spluttered.

Lawster winked. "Fermented dragon spit. To seal the deal."

The barmaid drew Quiescat's attention with a cough. "You must pay up front."

"I already left money up at the bar."

"Not enough."

He took out another gold ducat. Lawster's intense stare discomfited him as he handed it to her. "Will this cover it?"

She nodded. "Don't break the table this time," she said to Lawster.

"If you don't want me breaking a table, don't give me a defective one in the first place."

"I've never drunk fermented dragon spit before," Quiescat admitted. "Is it genuine?"

Lawster shrugged. "The price is. I've never drunk it anywhere else." He picked up his thimble and admired it. He actually savored the scent, while it was all Quiescat could do to keep from keeling over. "It's an acquired taste." He nodded at Quiescat's cup. "Best to drink it up before it eats through the pewter."

Quiescat picked it up. Would Lawster be offended if he demurred? "Perhaps you'd rather drink this one too?"

Lawster shook his head. "And deny you the pleasure? Never. Down the hatch." He gulped down the dragon spit, flung his cup over his shoulder as he hissed and slapped the table. The candle wobbled but stayed upright.

Quiescat lifted his drink and nodded. *For Drinith.* Quiescat spat out the spirit the moment its fire touched his tongue. His mouth burned so much it had to be blistering. He gulped down his water, then grabbed the next nearest substantial drink, a tankard of beer from a neighboring table, and chugged it down, much to the disgust of its owner. Some of it spilled down Quiescat's chin and throat and soaked his tunic, but he didn't care. The sour draft couldn't heal the raw hurt of the spirit.

"Are you trying to kill me?" Quiescat lisped. Every word stung.

Lawster just rolled on his chair, laughing. "It has a bit of a kick to be sure."

The entire room erupted in laughter. A monstrous arm slammed across Quiescat's shoulders. The ugly, grinning face of the draker whose drink he had stolen leaned close and roared, "Get this man a proper drink before his tongue shrivels to nothing! Milk for my friend!"

Quiescat dipped his head into the bucket of milk a smirking Mulny plopped before him and gulped it down. As the scalding pain cooled to an aching rawness, he glanced up at Lawster's gemmy smile.

"Get my friends a round of drinks," Lawster said. The entire tavern clapped and cheered as he tipped back Quiescat's cup of dragon spit with a defiant hiss. Quiescat could have sworn plumes of steam shot from his mouth.

"Call to the *Parched Tongue* early tomorrow morning," Lawster said, sliding from his chair and sauntering back to his crewmates at another table. "Bring the money." They left soon afterward.

The barkeep appeared beside Quiescat. "Buying for the house has cost you another two gold ducats."

It had been Lawster, not Quiescat, who called that, but Quiescat sighed and handed over the money. "Have you anywhere I could sleep for the night?"

"There's room in the cellar. It's free of charge given how much you spent here tonight," the barkeep said. "Be careful of that pyrate, Lawster. He's not to be trusted."

And yet, Quiescat had no choice. Lawster was his only hope to save Drinith.

24

———

Drinith's head slapped against stone, dazing her. As she lurched about in pain, her captors guffawed.

"Oops," a male Stedfaster said. "I guess I misjudged how low that ceiling was."

A growl from Nykostar cut short the laughter. "If you knock her out, you'll have to carry her back to the village."

"I don't see why we need bags over their heads..." opined a nervy voice.

"They'll wear them because I say so," Nykostar snapped. "That a good enough reason for you?"

"Of course, Nykostar. Of course." Evidently, the Stedfasters' leader was determined to deny her prisoners any opportunity to escape or otherwise cause mischief.

Hands shoved and punched Drinith forward, steering her, forcing her head to dip at random times. As the journey dragged on, Drinith's terror gradually waned. Even her captors lost their vicious exuberance and their handling of her gradually gentled.

It took her by surprise when they snipped her bonds. They forced her to sit against a wooden pole and retied her wrists behind it. Then, they left her in black silence.

Drinith held her breath as feet padded across a stone floor. The bag lifted to reveal Nykostar crouched before her. Drinith was tied to one of the stakes that encircled them. *I must be in some type of pen.*

Drinith jerked toward Nykostar, straining against the cords holding her, but the Stedfaster's mocking grin never wavered as she rose to her full height. "In different circumstances, I would have gladly recruited you. There aren't many who can get the better of me, even briefly." She studied her wounded hand, now bandaged in red cloth. Drinith's alicorn bracelet hung around her wrist. "I could have even forgiven you for the loss of my pet snake. Unfortunately, the embarrassment you caused me cannot go unpunished. You understand?"

"I understand that you and your gang are nothing more than a bunch of dirty cannibals. I suppose you intend to eat me."

"Eventually," Nykostar conceded. The regret on her face mocked Drinith's plight all the more because of its apparent sincerity. "It's hard to keep meat fresh down here. We don't kill until we have to. We'll execute Zoen first while there's still a little meat on her bones."

Drinith's stomach turned somersaults. "She did nothing to you."

Nykostar shrugged. "She's the sister of one of Prystian's most enthusiastic followers, and she's feeble. She's exactly the sort of weakling the Ascent is meant to eliminate. I promise we'll execute her with merciful quickness."

As if that's any consolation. "And what of the others?"

"Lesym will die after you. We haven't captured Siga yet, but it's only a matter of time."

While he's at large, there's a chance he might be able to help us escape.

Nykostar smirked. "Toskar and Fisken will be offered an opportunity to join us."

"They would never stoop to such depravity."

"I'm sure you thought the same of Kaliop. It's eat or be eaten down here. In time, your friends will come to the right decision. Particularly Fisken." Her eyes opened a fraction before she burst out laughing. She nodded toward the open gateway. A silhouette hidden by the stakes shifted slightly. Nykostar pressed her knuckles to her sides, her face stiffening with impatience. "Come in. No need to be shy."

Drinith shuddered as a sheepish Oristan entered. In an instant, shock turned to rage. "Coward! Traitor! Grinning snake! Worthless forager of dung! May your name be forever a curse!"

Oristan looked away and blushed. His head bowed, he murmured something to Nykostar. She dismissed him from her presence with a languid wave of her hand. "Fisken has already consented to join us, it appears."

As Oristan fled outside, his silhouette flitting behind the wooden poles, Drinith's jeers chased him. "That's right—run, you pathetic coward! You can't even face me with my hands tied behind my back! May a thousand demons feast on you! May Empyrosis swallow you and defecate you into the Crevast! May—" Nykostar's vicious slap across her face stunned her into silence.

"You're giving me a headache," the Stedfaster murmured.

Drinith attempted to massage her stinging cheek with her shoulder. "I'm sorry to inconvenience you." The salty taste of her own blood spurred her to spit at the cannibal. "There's an appetizer."

Nykostar rubbed the dripping pink smear off her dress. "Do you really think a little blood bothers me? You think you're so superior. When I first arrived here, there were others like you. I stared into their dull, hollow eyes as they realized the futility of their squeamishness, sometimes too late to save their lives. The only law down here is the imperative to survive...and my word, of course."

"You don't have to live like this. Prystian—"

"Prystian is a liar. He has his followers convinced they're going to topple five hundred years of tradition and law."

"At least the Uprisers have a higher purpose than living like ignoble animals."

"Prystian used to dispatch smiling fools down here, offering false promises of salvation. He knew we'd kill them, but their lives were inconsequential to him. When he realized his deceit could not buy us, he tried to circumvent us and recruit new arrivals directly. We blocked all the routes out of our territory but one—the Upgate."

She turned toward a sheer cliff visible through the gateway behind her. A stone ladder had been carved into it up to another cave. About two thirds of the way up it, a large horizontal crack split it into disjointed sections. A boy emerged from the cave's darkness and descended the ladder, deftly negotiating the break. A second Stedfaster climbed upward past him. Observed from this distance, they looked like two flies crawling on a wall.

"Only two days ago, the Uprisers tried to storm it, but our guards easily rebuffed them," Nykostar said. "Compare their inability to deal with us to their lofty talk of taking on the might of Diarchy. Pathetic. Very soon, our numbers will be sufficient to crush them. A red month or two at most."

"And you expect the Diarchy to greet you as a hero and forget the atrocities you committed?"

"The Ouroboric Gate forgives the worst sin. It would even forgive you if you reached it. Of course, you won't."

"But what you've done here can never be forgotten. Whispers of your barbarity will haunt you to the grave and beyond."

Drinith flinched in expectation of another slap as Nykostar moved her hand, but she only tucked a stray hair behind her ear. "Plenty of dignitaries interred in the Summit Necropolis did much worse. One of my ancestors butchered a mock emperor and his family over a lost pendant. Another starved a city into submission, only to poison most of its famished denizens simply because he did not trust them to honor the terms of their surrender once their hunger was sated. Nobody remembers or cares. Nobody sees beyond the magnificence of their crypts. My transgressions are minor in comparison, and I only do what I must to survive. It's no different from the Stedfasters you killed. Where were your precious scruples when you butchered them, eh?"

The surprised face of the boy Drinith slew leapt unbidden from her memory. She would have preferred to be struck. "I acted in self-defense." But Nykostar already strolled toward the gateway, tittering to herself, clearly delighted that her gibe had struck home.

As her laughter faded into the distance, Drinith tested her bonds again, to no avail. She looked around, caught sight between the stakes of columns of smoke rising from the rectangular houses behind her. Swatches of red fabric, relatively new, patched their wooden roofs, but the structures themselves looked old and decrepit. They could have stood here for a hundred years or five hundred. The ruins of several other houses lay scattered around them, their fallen walls slumped and sprawled across the ground.

Two snickering Stedfasters dragged another prisoner through the gateway and tied him to a stake on the far side of the pen. The upside-down haloed sword on his tunic confirmed it was Lesym, but even after the bag had been removed, the bruises and cuts on his face made him unrecognizable. His head hung limply. His eyes were so painfully swollen, it was hard to be certain if they were open or shut.

"Lesym?"

No reaction. He must have passed out.

"Lesym? Are you awake?"

The battered head lifted. "Yes."

"Have you seen Zoen?"

"She's tied up in another pen. I overheard Stedfasters say they must break her before…"

Horror shuddered through Drinith. "What does this breaking entail?"

He dropped his head and shook it ruefully. "I'm sure we'll find out when they're finished with her."

"No," Drinith said. "We have to save her. We must escape. Siga is still free. He may be able to help us."

"What can he do against dozens of Stedfasters? What can any of us do, trussed and penned here, waiting to be butchered?"

No, there had to be a way to escape. Whatever it was, Drinith needed to find it before the Stedfasters murdered Zoen.

25

The Stedfasters lashed Zoen to a pole. Fat flies buzzed about her. She shifted about as much as her binds allowed to dislodge those that settled on her exposed skin. The stench of stale gore made her stomach clench. On the far side of the pen stood a stained frame. How long would it be before they hung her upon it? How much longer had she to live?

The monotony of her wait slowly drained her horror. It might have been a day. It might have been two. Time dragged in this gloomy land. The distant trickle of water taunted the dryness of her mouth. Her hunger made even the scent of rotting flesh appetizing.

The Stedfaster's leader, Nykostar, entered the pen, carrying two battered metal cups. She raised one of them to Zoen's mouth. "Drink." Zoen shied away, but the cup pressed against her lips. "It's only water. It won't harm you."

Relenting, Zoen exulted as the sweet water washed over her parched mouth. She drank it all down. She tried to lick the last bead of moisture clinging to the cup's rim, but Nykostar took it away. The water, though welcome, failed to slake Zoen's thirst.

A wicked smile slipped onto Nykostar's face. "Hungry?" She moved the second cup near enough for Zoen to smell the sweet scent of cooked flesh it contained. The sudden watering of her mouth horrified her. She spat out the saliva as if it was poison.

"It's just meat."

The diced cubes of flesh in the cup could have been from any animal, but... As the cup drew closer, Zoen clamped her mouth shut and vehemently shook her head.

Nykostar laughed. "Don't worry. It belongs to nobody you know." She withdrew to the open gateway of the pen. "I'll be back tomorrow to check on you," she said, as a visiting doctor might say to a patient. She shut the gate as she left.

Zoen's relief at her departure quickly faded. Time dragged with nothing to mark its passing except the occasional Stedfaster going about their business outside the ring of stakes. Everything beyond it was a blur.

The gate opened and Nykostar entered with the same infernal grin, carrying two cups as before. She crouched in front of Zoen. "You know you're not strong. I wonder how long a puny girl like you can last without eating. You must know a point will come when you won't be able to eat even if you want to."

The Stedfaster again offered the cup of roasted meat. When Zoen refused, Nykostar ate chunks of it with relish, savoring every bite, licking her fingers. Revolted, Zoen turned away, but she couldn't block out the sounds of munching and the sucking of greasy fingers.

"Enjoy your disgust," Nykostar said cheerily. "It might stave off your hunger for a while, but in the end, you'll come to understand it's as empty as your stomach." She drank from the cup. "You thirsty?"

Zoen gave a hesitant nod, wary of the girl's sly smile. Nykostar must be planning some cruel trick, she guessed, like perhaps spilling the cup at the last moment.

Nykostar rubbed her lips and ran her fingers around the rim of the cup to smear it with grease from the meat.

Zoen turned away as the Stedfaster thrust the cup at her. "I don't want it."

Nykostar persisted, shoving the cup at Zoen's mouth as she

twisted her head one direction and then the other to avoid it. "Come on. A little sip. It's only water. Nothing more."

"Thank all dragons," Zoen whispered as the cup withdrew.

Nykostar looked at her with mock sympathy. "There's no need to suffer like this. All I ate was dead flesh. Anything that made it human is gone. You persist in your misery, wallowing in your meaningless morality, screaming your superiority to a deaf, uncaring world, for nothing. When you put aside this meaningless taboo, when you finally accept the reality of your situation, you'll look back and wonder why you had put yourself through this torment."

"I hope you burn in Empyrosis!" Zoen growled.

"Why? I'm not a demon." The girl leaned in, so close Zoen could smell the meat on her breath. "I'm human like you. But I won't sacrifice my life on the altar of misplaced morality. I want to live. Do you not want to? Have you given up? No?" She stood and gulped down the water. "Eat or die—the choice is yours. But don't delay too long or you won't have the strength to make it."

Again and again, she returned to tease Zoen, but the temptation ached the worst in the hollow silence between Nykostar's visits. It merged with the bleary ache in Zoen's head and the sucking emptiness in her stomach. The shapelessness of time in this subterranean world exacerbated her agony. How much time had passed between the Stedfaster's visits? Each succeeding interval seemed to stretch longer.

She drifted in and out of consciousness, sometimes awakened by the sharp prod of Nykostar's finger. Zoen refused the food each time, but little by little her willpower weakened, withering from the inside like the heart of a dying tree, until only the grim facade remained, a brittle mask ready to shatter.

Finally, her resolve collapsed. The next time Nykostar came, Zoen would eat because she had no choice, because she wasn't ready to die yet. She had fought to the brink of death. Nobody could condemn her for succumbing to the hopelessness of her plight.

The memory of Nykostar's soft voice echoed in her mind, repeating her soothing arguments, encouraging her surrender. Zoen should have despised the intrusion, but she could only muster dull irritation.

"You don't look well," Nykostar said when she finally appeared. "I doubt you'll last much longer." She laid the cups on the floor.

Zoen shivered as she drew one of her knives. Nykostar smiled, evidently relishing Zoen's panic. She stabbed a chunk of meat and brought it within kissing distance of Zoen's mouth.

"You don't even have to eat it. Just lick it and I'll get you something to eat more to your liking. You'll be free."

Zoen's lips tingled with temptation. She licked them. No, she mustn't. Better to die.

Nykostar picked the meat off the tip of her blade with her mouth and chewed thoughtfully. "You know Fisken and Toskar have joined us."

No, Toskar hated the Stedfasters. Nykostar must be lying.

Nykostar's grin broadened as she stabbed another chunk. "And Drinith too, of course. You're the only holdout now." She thrust the meat close to Zoen's nose, its warm sweet scent wafting under her nostrils. "Just give it a little kiss," Nykostar whispered.

"No," Zoen pleaded. She could just as easily have said yes.

Nykostar snorted. "You're stubborn, I give you that." She picked up the cups and left.

ZOEN STARTED AWAKE. She must have passed out. Oristan stood over her, a knife in his hand. Two cups lay at his feet. What fresh horror was this? Did he intend to torture her until she ate? She wouldn't give that traitor the pleasure of breaking her.

"Dragons, you're in a worse state than I feared." He crouched down and reached behind her. Something tugged on her bonds and her wrists separated. Why had she not noticed the aches in her shoulders before?

She lamely tried to fight off the cup he pressed to her lips. "It's only water, I promise." Zoen gulped it down, uncaring, almost choking on its coldness. He offered the second cup. It contained what looked like thick porridge. "It's root mash. Eat slowly or you'll get sick. I'll be back as soon as I can with the others. We're getting out of here while most of the Stedfasters are away, preparing to ambush the next party of candidates."

The relief coursing through her was so strong it hurt. "I nearly ate," Zoen whimpered. "I nearly became one of them."

"If you had eaten, Nykostar would have had your throat slit. She considered you too weak to be anything other than meat. The Stedfasters despise martyrs. Your resistance embarrassed them. It called into question their conviction that they had no other choice."

Horror shivered up her spine. She had been so close to condemning herself to slaughter. As Oristan raced out the gate, she held the cup with trembling hands, scooped up gobs of sticky mash in her dirty fingers, and stuffed them into her mouth. She had won, she had survived, but her victory tasted as bitter as the doughy glop she chewed upon.

26

Quiescat found the *Parched Tongue* easily enough. It was clear from the multiple scorch marks on its saddledeck that the dragon had recently seen a lot of fighting.

As he descended the gangplank, a grizzled draker snarled at him. "What do you want?" His begrimed red bandanna covered one eye. A bright, jagged scar peeped below it.

"I'm here to see your captain," Quiescat explained with ill-concealed ire. "He's expecting me."

The one-eyed draker sneered, exposing his broken teeth. He beckoned a scowling woman over. "Keep an eye on the landlubber. I'll go tell Lawster his guest has arrived."

Quiescat waited with the second draker. The woman's leery stare never wavered, no matter how broadly he smiled.

The first draker returned. "He's in his cabin. I'll show you to him."

At first, Quiescat didn't recognize the princely figure sitting behind the desk in the captain's cabin. Lawster had traded his stained garments for fine clothes dripping with jewels. His pearl bib necklace was particularly striking.

"It seems you've dressed up for our meeting," Quiescat observed.

Lawster bared his gemmy grin and peered behind Quiescat. "I don't see any chests of gold."

Quiescat placed the diamond pouch on the table. Lawster spilled out its contents. He stroked his beard as he gazed at them, his eyes sparkling with avarice and admiration.

Quiescat cleared his throat. "You're free to get a jeweler to verify them if you so choose. I mislaid the jeweler's certificates of authenticity."

"I don't put much store in certificates. I prefer the gems themselves to tell me if they're true." Lawster placed a slim wooden case on the table, reverently removed the brass scales and weights from inside it. He arranged the diamonds in a line. Having weighed them, he examined each one with a loupe.

His lingering scrutiny of one vexed Quiescat. "They're all real, I assure you."

"I have no doubt of it," Lawster said. "They're so pretty." He carefully returned the diamond to the line. "They're much prettier than the reward that the cordent generals have offered for information on your whereabouts."

Quiescat tensed. He fought the urge to dash for the door. It was too late to run.

"Yes, I know all about you, Quiescat of Godsdoor. I don't do business with just anyone. I investigated your character thoroughly." Lawster drummed his fingers on the desk. "I could hand you over to the authorities for the reward and keep the diamonds."

"You'd never be able to return here."

"Who's going to tell the cordents about the diamonds? You? They didn't specify you had to be alive."

"They know about them already," Quiescat said. "There's no way you can keep the diamonds and take the bounty. And it will be a pittance in comparison to the reward Meritocrat Hax will give you if you help me to rescue her."

Lawster played with his pearls as he cogitated. "The thing is, the journey to the Whetstone is awfully tricky. Success isn't guaranteed. What's to stop me from throwing you into the Crevast and keeping the lovely diamonds? Your mission is a coin toss between vast wealth and a terrible death. And you've no coin to flip."

Quiescat opened the pouch around his neck and placed the Tear of Fate on his palm.

Lawster leaned forward, frowned. "You thought I'd be impressed by that glass bauble? Hah!"

"It's the most sacred relic of the Oracles of Godsdoor. This gem has caused empires to rise and fall, brought down conquerors, and elevated beggars to kings. It is the petrified tear of the Fate Healer, and it's unique in the Crevast. Its monetary worth is limited only by imagination. And I'm offering this to you along with the other wealth I promised, though all the treasure in Gyre is a pittance compared to its value."

Lawster reached for it, but Quiescat pulled back his hand. "The Tear is bound to its owner. It can only be willingly yielded. Fate will curse anyone who attempts to take it by force. It gouged out the eyes of the last man who tried to steal it. Why do you think I carry it about my person as if it was a trifle? If you don't believe me, get a truthscryer and test me."

The captain rose from his chair. He continued to play with his pearls as he stared out the window. He looked over his shoulder at Quiescat. "You would really surrender this jewel to me?"

"Yes," Quiescat said with conviction. It was dead anyway. Its monetary value didn't matter now that its oracular power was gone. If anything, it was a burden, a reminder of what he had lost, a wound that would not heal.

Lawster sucked in a deep breath. "I guess you have your coin, after all. I'll do it. I'll help you save your princess." He scooped up the diamonds and poured them into the pouch. "If anyone asks," he added, winking, "the price we agreed was fifty thousand. Wait for me outside."

Quiescat stood in the little corridor until Lawster emerged from the cabin. "Follow me!" he thundered.

They climbed the steps on the outside of the quarterdeck. "Ready to fly!" Lawster bellowed at the rotund saddlemaster on the deck. He popped his head into whereabout. "Call down the headstall! We're boarding! Ready for Ophigee!"

"Would it not be better if I stayed on the saddledeck?" Quiescat asked.

"You're going wherever I go," Lawster said, "and I'm going to the headstall."

As they reached the springboard, a massive shadow spread over them. The silhouette of the head and neck of the dragon blocked out the morning sun. Quiescat couldn't stop shaking as the neck curled and the underside of the frill drew near like a yawning mouth. In its shadow, the headstall hung like a little wooden fortress. It halted a fraction above the plank jutting from the deck. A hatch opened and two men reached out.

"Come on," Lawster said. He raced across the plank and let the two drakers help him on board.

Quiescat took a deep breath and followed. The board trembled beneath his feet. One misstep would send him falling to his death.

"Hurry up!" Lawster roared. "We haven't all day!"

As Quiescat reached the end, the yawning gap between the springboard and the headstall made him hesitate.

"Back!" Lawster roared. The headstall swung back so fast, Quiescat cringed in the expectation of its impact, but hands seized him and lifted him inside. The hatch slammed shut. Quiescat panted to catch his breath. The overpowering odor of dragon wax and stale sweat made him queasy. Lawster's heavy slap across his shoulders didn't help.

"You survived," he observed with a mocking wink. "We'll make a draker of you yet."

His underlings chortled in appreciation as they ascended the ladder. Quiescat glanced around the chamber. Webbed shelves lined the walls up to the next level. Most contained casks, but a few at the bottom had been kitted out as bunks. A snoring man in one used a leather drawstring bag as a pillow. In another, a sleeping woman hugged an identical bag.

"They're two of our whisperers," Lawster said as he grabbed a rung and hoisted himself upward. "The other two are earwigging our lady. I don't know how anyone could choose to spend their lives stuck down a dragon's earhole. I wouldn't do it for all the dragon wax in the Crevast. Each to their own, I suppose."

Quiescat puffed up the ladder after him. He clung to it in terror as the whole structure shifted sideways. Lawster looked down at him and guffawed. "You had better get used to that. The head's never steady. It can be like living in the bowels of an earthquake at times."

It certainly smells like someone's bowels, Quiescat thought bitterly.

At the top, two drakers stood by a window. One stared at the saddledeck with binoculars. The other rested her hands on brass levers. Quiescat followed Lawster down one of the curving passageways that hugged the dragon's head at an upward angle. Large windows and hatches punctuated the right side at regular intervals. Quiescat shrank from getting too close to them. Brass tubes and guide rails for lanyards ran below them. The webbed shelves on the opposite side were packed with casks, sacks, and bundles. The erratic motion of the dragon's head forced Quiescat to grab on to webbing to avoid falling.

The acrid smell of dragon wax worsened to the point it stung his nose as they passed a well. Lawster crouched down beside it. "How's it going, Vergard?"

Sounds of a greasy slither came from inside the dragon's earhole. The slick, glistening head of a whisperer peeped out of it. He removed his goggles, revealing two circles of clean skin around his eyes. "She's raring to go! She's hungry for the sun! I hear we're going to Ophigee!" Every word hurt Quiescat's ears.

Lawster flashed a grin. "That's right. We're going to rescue a princess."

"Makes a change!" Vergard bellowed. "Generally, we're the ones putting people in need of rescue!"

Quiescat's heart skipped a beat.

Lawster gave him a nervous glance. "That's right. We'll talk later." As they moved along the passageway, he whispered, "Have to keep on the good side of the whisperers."

"Remember, you won't get the Tear of Fate until Drinith is returned safely to Gyre."

"How do I know you won't trick me?" Lawster asked.

"You have my word"—Quiescat's eyes narrowed—"just as I have yours." Panic gripped him. Had his reply been too adversarial? No, it was better to make clear to Lawster he wouldn't be a pushover.

Lawster laughed as if Quiescat had made a hilarious joke.

The passage opened into the pineye, the compartment in the headstall from which a captain commanded his dragon. It took Quiescat a moment to realize the hole gaping before him was an enormous window. Thankfully, all he could see ahead was blue sky. The seven drakers sitting before it regarded him with sullen contempt.

"I've never been in a pineye before," Quiescat admitted. "I had imagined it much smaller."

A rotund draker was ensconced on the ornate chair in the center of the room. A swirling floral pattern covering his face merged seamlessly into his wavy beard. He hopped off the seat with a deferential nod to his captain. "We've been cleared to fly."

Lawster slid onto the seat and stretched. "Very good, Marclan. We had better get out of here before they change their minds." He pointed to a spare seat at the window. "Better strap in, Oracle, before you end up bouncing about the pineye."

Before Quiescat could close the clasps on his belt, the whole structure shuddered. The dragon's roar reverberated through him. The sky fell away, and the city rose to meet him with such frightening speed, he shut his eyes to escape the dizzying view.

"Don't you dare get sick on me," his neighbor warned to the accompaniment of his crewmates' snickers, "or I'll send you out the dump box one piece at a time."

The dragon's violent movements threw Quiescat about in his chair. The headstall creaked and groaned, frightening him out of his self-imposed blindness. The bored expressions of the drakers reassured him. A string of jagged stars necklaced the bare sky. He picked out Rhumgad by the bright speck hovering above it—the crystal moon, Bawror—before the shard slipped from view. A cankerous mountain of cloud swallowed the sky ahead, lightning flashes whitening patches of its leadenness.

"This morning's report from Fort Themestra didn't mention foul weather," Marclan said. "It's as if it came out of nowhere."

Hissimir's vengeance loomed before them. Quiescat gripped the arms of his seat. "Can we fly around it?"

"We'll try," Lawster said without his usual confidence. He leaned forward and stroked his beard. "It looks to be moving fast though."

Quiescat daren't give Lawster any hint that his crew faced divine retribution thanks to him. They'd attempt to appease the storm god by chucking him overboard. Yes, Quiescat might well have damned them all.

27

Movement on the cliff through the ribs of her cage caught Drinith's eye. A flailing youth dropped from the cave mouth, his scream thinned by distance to a buzz. Another figure climbed jerkily down the ladder. Drinith followed their descent until they disappeared from view. What was happening? Could Lesym's people be storming the Upgate?

Her every muscle tensed as Kaliop strode into the pen, carrying a bloody knife.

"So they sent you to kill us," Drinith said. She'd make it as difficult as possible for Kaliop to cut her throat.

"Nykostar and the rest of her crew are off ambushing the next batch of candidates," Kaliop said. "It's our best chance to get out of here. I've dispatched the guards at the Upgate already. You may have seen one of them flying down the cliff."

Kaliop—always the traitor. First, she betrayed her fellow candidates, now Nykostar. "Why?"

"Because they'd stop us from escaping. There was no other way."

"No, I mean why have you chosen to help us?"

Kaliop smirked, shrugged her shoulders. "I thought the plan was to ingratiate ourselves with the Stedfasters so we could escape." She turned to Lesym. "That was your advice, wasn't it?"

"You betrayed us," Drinith said. "You cut a deal with Nykostar."

Kaliop's grin mocked her. "Lucky for you, I won her trust. Otherwise, you'd both end up cooking on a spit. I already saved Oristan—"

"That worthless coward!"

"As we speak, that worthless coward is freeing Toskar and Fisken. And Zoen, if she's still alive. They'll meet us at the bottom of the ladder to the Upgate. A little gratitude would be nice, though I neither need your admiration nor approval. Just keep your temper in check until we're safely through the Upgate. You can whine all you want afterward."

Rage was too gentle a word for the violent emotion coursing through Drinith. She'd have happily beaten Kaliop to a bloody pulp, but she throttled back her anger for the sake of the group. "Free me," she murmured.

Kneeling, Kaliop reached behind Drinith and snipped her bonds. "Oristan and I could have easily headed through the Upgate by ourselves and left you here to die, but we're not the scoundrels you think we are."

Drinith massaged the painful furrows cut in the back of her wrists by the cord as Kaliop turned her attention to freeing Lesym. Oristan rushed inside. "Toskar and Fisken are climbing up to the Upgate," he said, warily eyeing Drinith. "Zoen's too weak to make it up the ladder by herself. We'll have to hoist her up."

Kaliop inhaled, but Oristan cut her off before she could speak. "No! We're not leaving her here to die."

She rolled her eyes. "I'd never suggest that."

"Then what were you going to say?"

A brief moment of hesitation betrayed Kaliop's mental rummage for a reply. "Have the two girls got a rope?"

"Of course."

Drinith rose and stretched her spine to relieve the ache in her back. Oristan handed her and Lesym knives, and the four of them headed for the Upgate.

"I risk my life to save you, and what thanks do I get?" Kaliop groused.

"To be fair," Oristan said, "we couldn't do this without you. I couldn't have done what you did at the Upgate. And Nykostar didn't trust me even after...you know."

Kaliop smirked. "You became a cannibal."

Oristan scowled. "You ate, too."

Kaliop shook her head no.

"You must have."

"I ate a lump of stale bread," Kaliop said. "I dumped the meat the Stedfasters gave me when they weren't looking. Sleight of hand is a useful skill. You should learn it."

Zoen sat propped against the foot of the cliff, looking dazed. Clutching the wall, she started to stand, but quickly collapsed again.

"She has already eaten some root mash. She'll be fine in a few hours." Oristan's soothing words, said mostly for Zoen's benefit, sounded hollow. Drinith's stomach growled jealously. She couldn't remember the last time she'd eaten. If a creeping hand should crawl by, she'd have been tempted to swallow the centipede whole. She'd rather risk poisoning herself than suffering this gnawing hunger.

The rope slapped the wall as it uncoiled down to the ground. Kaliop started up the ladder while the other three tied the rope around Zoen's waist.

"You need to hold on to the rope with both hands," Oristan warned her. "I'll stay down here with Zoen." He turned to Drinith and Lesym. "You two, climb up and help the others lift her."

Dizziness gripped Drinith as she climbed up the ladder. She clung on until it passed, then continued upward. As she scrabbled into the cave with the help of Toskar and Kaliop, Lesym slipped. He groaned as he clung on by his fingers. He kicked until his feet landed on a rung.

"Take your time," Drinith said, squeezing the desperation from her voice. He, too, must be suffering from the debilitating aftereffects of their captivity.

He halted. "I need a break."

"No time for breaks!" Drinith insisted. "Every moment you delay puts us all in jeopardy. You need to keep moving."

Lesym climbed again, faster than before. He slowed near the end, prolonging Drinith's agony. Drinith sighed with relief as she and Toskar hauled him into the cave. Lesym wiped the sweat off his face. "That was hard."

Fisken had already tied the rope around her, so the other four took hold of it, Drinith at the front. She peered down at Oristan. "We're ready!"

"Ready here, too!" Oristan roared. To the rhythm of Drinith's chanting, they pulled. As Zoen rose into the air, Oristan held on to her, but as soon as she traveled beyond his steadying touch, she spun. She had to use her hands and feet to keep herself from bumping against the cliff or snagging on the ladder. Drinith hooked her with both hands as she reached the top and rolled her clear of the cliff. Zoen made a feeble effort to rise, gave up. Drinith cut her free of the rope. "She's fine," she assured the others. At least Zoen appeared no worse for wear than she had been. "Oristan, you can come up!" No answer came. "Oristan?" Drinith peered down the cliff face again. He had vanished.

"Where's he gone?" To find Siga? Surely Oristan understood the impossibility of locating him in this immense maze.

"We need to get out of here," Lesym urged. "Before the Stedfasters return."

"Oristan must have gone to warn the dragon," Kaliop said. "I thought I had convinced him not to."

"We have friends on that dragon, remember," Fisken said, hugging herself.

Drinith climbed onto the ladder. "I am going to get him."

"Don't be a fool," Kaliop said. "There's no point getting yourself killed along with him. You don't even know where's he gone."

True, but Oristan had risked his life to save them. "You must have an idea. Tell me where you think he's gone. I'll do the rest."

28

───────

Quiescat lay in his bunk, but it could not shelter him from the tempest's ferocity. Rain battered the hull like a thousand angry fists as lightning flashed and thunder reverberated through the headstall. Everything swayed from side to side and back and forth as if Hissimir himself shook the structure. But for the webbing across his bunk, Quiescat would have been thrown into passage. His mouth tasted of vomit. He retched sporadically, but his clenching stomach had nothing left to expel. This storm, a hundred times worse than the one that struck his first voyage to Ophigee, went on and on. He should have known better than to trifle with a sour god like Hissimir.

Lawster held on to the guide rails on both sides of the passageway as he tramped down it. "It's foul out there." The hint of worry in his voice deepened Quiescat's anxiety. Drakers generally went about their business with reassuring nonchalance. For an experienced captain to be troubled, the storm must be fierce indeed.

Holding the rail over Quiescat's bunk with both hands, Lawster bent down and peered inside. "You look worried," he said as he rocked to the storm's rhythm. He removed a metal canteen, pulled the cap off with his glittering teeth. Quiescat refused its sloshing contents with a wave of his hand.

Lawster shrugged. He gulped down some drink and hissed. "It's as if some storm god poured the contents of his thunder mug down on us."

Quiescat shivered.

"Would your bauble have any sway over the weather?"

"If it had, I would have used it already."

"We lost a mast," Lawster said. "I'd be surprised if we don't lose a second. Maybe all three. The only good news is the Ophigeens will keep their dragons perched for the duration." He grinned. "They're not brave enough to venture out in this dread tempest."

The headstall quaked.

"What now?" Lawster grumbled as he climbed back up the passage.

So Quiescat waited alone again for the storm to abate or destroy them. Perhaps he should pray to Hissimir, offer some sacrifice in penance. He fingered the pouch around his neck as he tried in vain to come up with a modest offering to appease the angry deity. He closed his eyes and wished this nightmare would end.

He woke to an icy wind buffeting his face. He opened bleary eyes to stare into the naked storm. A hole gaped where the hatch opposite him had been, like an open mouth ready to swallow him. The headstall tilted, sliding him against the webbing across his bunk. The mesh emitted a menacing creak as his weight pressed against it. A rope snapped with a sharp twang. Casks toppled into the storm. He couldn't hear his own cries for help. He might be the only one left alive in the headstall. He'd die here, chewed up by the storm or worse, suffer a slow death in his own private hell of torment and starvation.

He hung his head. "You win, Hissimir," he muttered. It was too late to beg for clemency. He had been wrong to toy with a god. Did he never learn? Didn't the history of his order, and his personal experience, teach him the dangers of dabbling with the divine. But the tragedy of most mortals was they made the same foolish mistakes over and over, their whole lives through, and he was no exception. The cold, wet wind sank its bite into Quiescat's flesh and he slowly numbed to the weather, the danger, life itself.

A dull but insistent tug at the back of his neck roused him. He struggled to make sense of the black silhouette looming above him. The pouch containing the Tear patted Quiescat's chest as Lawster withdrew his hand. "I had begun to fear the storm had killed you." The broken hatch had been boarded up and an eerie quietness had descended over the headstall. The *Parched Tongue* must have cleared the storm. Quiescat mumbled something. Even he couldn't make sense of what fluttered from his numb lips.

"Wax him before the cold takes him," Lawster said to the two drakers behind him. "Don't remove the pouch from around his neck. Its contents are cursed." A dangerous ambivalence warped his face as though he doubted his passenger's survival was in his best interests.

Quiescat floated out of the bunk. As he drifted down to the floor, two orange-tinted faces looked down upon him. He shivered to the air's touch as his wet clothes were peeled away. Heat brushed across his body, leaving an aching burn. The two whisperers turned him facedown and applied the same hot substance to his back. Turned over again, Quiescat's head was tilted forward and flame poured into his mouth. A hand clamped his jaw shut before he could spit it out.

"Swallow it if you want to live." Lawster said.

Quiescat struggled not to gag as the wax scalded the back of his throat. Its molten pain gentled and diffused through his chest. His whole body tingled with warmth. "What did you do to me?" He managed only a hoarse whisper.

"You've been waxed inside and out to drive the cold from your body before it kills you." Lawster stood, arms akimbo, grinning down at him. "Dragon wax is not the most pleasant medicine to take, I admit." That explained the awful slimy sensation in Quiescat's mouth.

The whisperers stepped back and Quiescat rose unsteadily to his feet. The brush of air against his skin reminded him of his nakedness. He snatched up his sodden garments to protect his modesty.

"Forget them. I'll get you some proper clothes," Lawster said with a clap of Quiescat's shoulder. "Clothes fit for a draker." He wandered down the corridor, examining the shelves. He picked a bundle of clothes from one and a pair of boots from another and dropped them at Quiescat's feet. "Pick out what you need and put the rest away."

The clothes were a hodgepodge of sizes, but Quiescat picked out a mismatched ensemble he could wear comfortably. He needed two pairs of socks to make the boots fit.

He joined Lawster in the pineye. Through the main window, the bright ring of the Halo Sea floated high in the sky, the black dagger of the island pointing downward through its heart.

Lawster grimaced. "I had hoped we'd be nearer, particularly given the damage to our masts. If we meet any patrols, we won't be able to outrun them."

If he got cold feet now and turned away, Quiescat might never get another opportunity. "At least we're approaching from below. That's good, isn't it?"

"As long as no patrol spots us. I had planned to pretend we were heading to Ophigee for trade and dip below the disk at the last moment. Approaching Ophigee from this angle will draw the attention of any nearby patrol dragon. When the Ophigeens discover our current state of disrepair, they'll insist on escorting us to the perches." Lawster stroked his beard. "Perhaps we should head there anyway, make our repairs, and then slip under the sea on the trip out."

Quiescat winced. "How long would that take?"

"Four days, maybe more."

Four days was too long. Drinith might be dead by then, if she wasn't already. In any case, Lawster was lying. Similar damage had perched the *Surly Bonnacon* for a red month. Quiescat beckoned Lawster into the passageway. "There must be some other way."

"I could kill you and take my chances with the Tear."

Quiescat dismissed the threat with a mirthless laugh. "I thought you drakers were brave."

"Brave, yes. But foolish? That's a different matter. The perches are the best I can do. Maybe you can find some way to the Whetstone from there. Ophigeens love bribes." Lawster squinted. "But don't get any ideas about giving that gem to someone else. You promised it to me. You gave me your word, which must mean something given you're holy and all that."

"If you helped me rescue Drinith," Quiescat said.

"No, if I helped you get to the Whetstone." Lawster shook his head. "I didn't specify the route. The Ouroboric Gate that provides access to it is only a short distance from the perches. The Tear is mine."

The Tear belonged truly to she who wept it, but now was not the time to quibble. "I know our deal and that isn't it."

Lawster folded his arms. "You know, tossing you into the Crevast is getting mighty appealing."

Quiescat stamped on the floor. "Then do it before your insufferable jabber bores me to death. But have no doubt that you'll be throwing the Tear in with me. It cannot be taken against my will." They locked stares.

"Dragon, ahoy!" yelled a spotter. Lawster and Quiescat hurried back into the pineye. The spotter pointed to a lumpy star moving on the virtual horizon.

With a glower at Quiescat, Lawster stomped over to the window and trained his spyglass on it. "It's an Ophigeen drake-o'-war heading this direction. I guess that settles matters. You'll have to take your chances at the perches."

Unless Lawster makes good on his threat before the dragon arrives and attempts to steal the Tear. "Then it appears Drinith will have to wait to be rescued. How long did you say it will take to repair your saddledeck?" Quiescat would try to gain access to the Ouroboric Gate in the meantime. If only he hadn't promised the Tear to Lawster...but Quiescat had to keep his word. It was all he had left, aside from the useless bauble hanging from his neck.

A crafty smile crept onto Lawster's face. "It could take a red month, maybe more. I can't do a proper survey of the damage from here."

Quiescat's heart lurched. That was a long time for Lawster to wait for the Tear.

"I'm a man of my word," Quiescat declared.

Lawster winked. "You might very well love your honor. But you loved that bauble too, and yet you promised it to me. I wonder what else you'd be willing to sacrifice for your princess. She must be quite a woman."

"She's my daughter," Quiescat muttered, turning away before Lawster's lecherous grin drove him to violence. As he wrestled with his anger, he pretended to watch the approaching dragon, though he couldn't focus on it.

Lawster might have a point about his desperation. Quiescat hadn't dishonored himself yet, but the escapade with the Dudgeon of Hissimir had come dangerously close. As for the captain, was it dishonorable to cheat the ignoble rogue? He wouldn't have given a second thought to swindling Quiescat. This very moment, he must be mulling over how to procure the Tear without having to keep his part of the bargain.

Quiescat must strike first. But how? His naivety dismayed him. How could he best a man who'd spent a lifetime practicing the arts of deceit and betrayal? Would Quiescat even recognize an opportunity to do so if one came? Lawster's greed and fear had gotten Quiescat this far, but already the balance trembled to tilt the other way. Quiescat was Lawster's captive until he surrendered the damn jewel.

The drake-o'-war, a hulking black monster with massive wings like claws of shadow, drew alongside the *Parched Tongue*. The flags and sails on its three masts bore the haloed sword of Ophigee. Open gunports pocked the side of the saddledeck like squinting eyes. However impressive these man-made appendages might be, they were minuscule compared to the beast that carried them. The interlocked rows of triangular teeth in its enormous mouth gave it a menacing leer.

"She's a fine beast," Lawster said. He watched intently as a light blinked from its headstall. "Her name is the *Cauldron Grin*. Signal the Ophigeens back with our tale of woe!"

Quiescat held his breath as the *Cauldron Grin* replied. A sudden tremor reminded him to tie off.

"They're going to escort us in," Lawster said.

Helpless, Quiescat watched as the underside of the Halo Sea slipped from view and Ophigee drew ever nearer. He had come so, so close. A second drake-o'-war joined the two dragons as they drew flat with the disk, its frothy edges turning gradually before them. The two Ophigeen dragons exchanged signals across the *Parched Tongue.* Suddenly, they banked away in opposite directions.

"What happened?" Quiescat asked.

"The storm scattered a large convoy from Laxur," Lawster said. "The *Cauldron Grin* and her friend have gone to aid the search."

"Yes!" Quiescat cried. "This is our chance. While the Ophigeen dragons are distracted, we can slip below the Halo Sea unnoticed." Lawster's hesitant gaze killed his exuberance. So, the captain was a coward, after all.

Lawster shied from his glare. "It's too dangerous. I'm sorry. Maybe when we're leaving..."

"You gave your word," Quiescat fumed. "Liar."

Lawster nodded to two of his crew. "Get this old fool out of my sight. Tie him to a bunk. For his safety."

As the drakers closed, Quiescat grabbed the handle of the hatch behind him. "I warned you." He released the catch, and the door flew open, throwing him into the abyss.

29

The echo of fighting ahead stalled Drinith's headlong rush down the tunnel.

"You traitor!" Siga's familiar growl. Dashing onward, Drinith bumped into a careering Oristan. He fell at her feet, clutching his shoulder.

"What are you doing with that traitor?" Siga demanded, waving his bloody knife at Oristan.

"I told you," Oristan said. "We're all on the same side."

"I saw you." Siga pointed the tip of his blade at him. "Yes, I saw you and Kaliop wandering about the cannibals' camp, chatting to them, exchanging pleasantries."

"I'm sure you noticed too that Drinith was bound to a pole, waiting to be slaughtered, but—"

Siga took no heed as he charged, knife at the ready, his face twisted by hate. Drinith stepped by Oristan, her gaze fixed on the sweep of Siga's blade. Catching his wrist, she pulled him toward her and threw him. He slammed against the cave floor, his knife skittering away from him. She pressed her foot against his chest before he could rise. "He's not your enemy."

"Listen to her," Oristan urged.

"How can you take his side?" Siga demanded.

"He freed us," Drinith said.

"I told you." Oristan winced as he rose, pressing a rag to his wound. "We're all on the same side."

"You've never been on my side!" Siga raged. "You still don't recognize me, do you?"

"I know who you are," Oristan murmured. "I saw you with your parents just before the embarking ceremony. I didn't know until then they had a son."

"You didn't bother to acknowledge them as you passed by."

Oristan blushed. "I didn't want to intrude."

"It was the first time I met them since I was packed off to green school, nine long years since I left your parents' household." Siga bucked, pounding the ground and kicking his legs in frustration, but Drinith kept her foot firmly pressed down. "I came here so that I'd never be controlled by your like again, and here you are, still playing games with my life."

"Put that aside for now or we're all going to die down here," Drinith urged.

"I can't."

"If you throw away your life here in a fit of pique, you'll never know what it means to be free of his shadow. Freedom awaits beyond the Ouroboric Gate. There's a route out of the Stedfasters' territory in their village, the Upgate. The others are waiting for us there."

Siga raised his hands. "You win. I'll behave." Drinith released him, and he warily clambered to his feet. Drinith tensed every time he flicked a glance at her as he sauntered over to his knife and picked it up. She didn't trust the relief surging through her. He might still turn on her at the slightest provocation.

She looked around. Oristan had gone. "Where's he disappeared to now?"

"Probably switched sides again," Siga muttered.

"No, he must still intend to seek aid from the dragon that's about to arrive, or, at least, warn the new party of candidates it carries," Drinith said. "He's going to get himself killed."

"Pardon me if I don't—"

"Enough!" Drinith snapped. "We have to find him now!" She hastened down the tunnel. Siga followed belatedly. Slowed by his wound, Oristan couldn't have gotten far.

Something stirred in the gloom ahead. They paused. It could be Stedfasters. The sound of labored breathing reached them down the tunnel.

"Oristan, wait!" Drinith cried, but Oristan's listing silhouette kept staggering forward.

"Help!" Oristan roared. "They're after me!" Beyond him, feet clattered down the tunnel. Black shapes poured past him, merging into a torrent of movement.

A hand clutched Drinith's shoulder. "I warned you," Siga snarled. "Run!"

He led, choosing each branch without hesitation. Did he know where he was going? It couldn't be long before their luck ran out, and they hit a dead end. But what choice had they with the Stedfasters bearing down on them?

Panic gripped Drinith as they turned a corner to face a dead end, but Siga charged on, spurring her to follow. A hidden exit opened to the left. She dashed through it. Where was—?

A hand slapped across her mouth, an arm encircled her waist. "It's me," Siga whispered, as if that should comfort her, as he dragged Drinith into a sliver of darkness. The narrow space jammed their bodies together. Siga's sweaty odor filled her nostrils. The clammy breaths buffeting her cheek ceased. She, too, held her breath as the Stedfasters raced by.

As their clamor faded into the distance, the pair exhaled in unison.

Siga slid out of the crevice. "The tunnel splits ahead in several directions, which should keep them distracted for now. I probably know their territory better than they do after having to avoid their hunting parties for days. As much as it galls me to let Oristan get away with his treachery, we need to get back to the village before his friends return there and block the Upgate."

Drinith knew from bitter experience the complicated nature of betrayal, but Siga's smug sneer irritated her. "Oristan risked his life to save me and the others. Why would he choose to betray me again? He could have yelled to warn us and not the Stedfasters."

"Or cowardice could have got the better of him. Again."

"Does a coward run toward an enemy while wounded?"

Siga folded his arms. "What do you want us to do? Take on all the Stedfasters by ourselves?"

"I just... I just can't abandon him. If he manages to warn the new arrivals, if he convinces the dragon's crew to help, then leaving the Stedfasters' domain would be putting ourselves in greater danger." She couldn't bring herself to entirely trust Lesym's enthusiasm for his charismatic leader. She struck the cave wall with her fist. "I wish there was some way to know for sure."

"There might be..."

Siga's hesitancy infuriated her. "Spit it out!"

"No need to shout." Siga glanced about. "I found an opening with a view of the perch. We'll be able to see the dragon."

The narrow, whistling crack that formed the entrance stretched sideways like a crooked mouth. Drinith forced herself through it after Siga. The chill wind blew against her like an incessant wheezy breath. As she dragged herself between the crevice's jagged surfaces, jabbing spurs scraped and bruised her. If the Whetstone shuddered now, she'd die here, chewed to death in this dreadful maw. She took the hand Siga offered and let him pull her out while she used her free hand to negotiate the last few toothy obstructions.

Emerging into the stinging light, she shielded her weeping eyes with her hand. Siga's hands on her arms anchored her, lessened her nervousness. Slowly the smarting passed, and Drinith took in her location. The tops of sailed masts scarred the wall of empty sky beyond the slim ledge. She didn't dare look upward at the sea lest vertigo should strike. Siga, crouched beside her, gestured for her to peer over the edge. A massive black dragon sat on the charred perch where Drinith's party had disembarked. Three candidates stood before it. Surely they couldn't represent the total complement.

Another candidate slid like a descending spider down a bright cord to join them. Three more emerged from the fanged cave mouth. One staggered forward from between his companions, clutching his shoulder.

"Well, Empyrosis curse me—Oristan," Siga murmured. "Guess I was wrong."

The six candidates encircled Oristan as a seventh, eighth, and ninth descended. Drinith strained to listen to their conversation, but she could hear nothing beyond the whisper of the wind. Would Oristan be believed?

The circle dissolved and rushed toward the dragon, hands raised, begging for help, but their desperate cries reached Drinith as a wavering buzz. Oristan lurched after them, adding his voice. Two candidates began to climb the rope while the others gathered around, waiting their turn.

With a roar, the dragon spread its wings and flapped, the resultant gusts flooring the cluster of candidates beneath it. Their dangling compatriots screamed as they jounced on the dancing rope. It snapped and dropped, a streak of white carrying the two climbers into the void. The dragon rose off the perch, hovered above it.

Drinith slammed both fists against the ledge. "Run!" But the dragon's roar swallowed her cry. A blazing spout poured from its yawning jaws and spilled across the perch, engulfing the fleeing candidates, pouring over the sides. The conflagration danced to the beat of the dragon's wings. Oristan and the candidates were gone, washed away by flame.

"There's nothing we can do here," Siga murmured. "We had better go before the cannibals return to the village."

Drinith's shock turned to rage. She twisted round to vent her fury at Siga, but the utter despair on his face muted her. She nodded.

The dragon swept away the lingering remnants of the fire as it landed again. It squeezed its head into the cave mouth. Clouds of black smoke billowed out as it poured flame down Stepstone's throat.

Anyone within reach of its incandescent phlegm would be incinerated.

Siga tugged Drinith's arm. "Let's go."

She tore her gaze from the spectacle and followed him back through the crevice.

Reaching the edge of the village, they crept toward the ladder to the Upgate. The corpse at its foot had been removed. Drinith blocked Siga with her arm. His brow furrowed in confusion.

"Someone returned ahead of us," Drinith whispered.

"You reckon they're waiting for us up there?" Siga whispered back.

She nodded. If the Upgate was guarded, their only chance of escape was gone unless... She signaled Siga to wait, then ran to the main dwelling. A fire burned brightly in its hearth. Picking up two brands, she used them to pull the fire apart and scatter flaming roots across the floor. She hastened back to Siga and gave him one of the brands. They moved from hut to hut, setting anything combustible alight, then retreated to wait for the fires to spread.

Siga's irritating jitteriness infected Drinith. It was hard to be patient given that more Stedfasters might arrive at any moment.

The gray smoke rising from an increasing number of dwellings drew no reaction from the Upgate. Perhaps it was unguarded. Flames spread across the cloth roofs of some huts.

A yell. A Stedfaster scrambled down the ladder, followed by two more. They hastened to the nearby rivulet and, filling pathetically tiny vessels with water, rushed toward the nearest burning hut.

Drinith and Siga could wait no longer. They dashed for the ladder and started climbing.

The drum of countless footfalls cut through the billowy roar of the fire. It had to be the main contingent of cannibals returning. Successfully negotiating the fissure, Drinith drew close to the cave mouth. A stone cracked against the rock face. Another clattered down the ladder, lightly tapping her shoulder as it passed. More missiles followed as a growing knot of Stedfasters slung stones. A scrawny face leered down at her, ugly with triumph. The haggard youth pointed a spear toward her. If she could grab it as he thrust it toward her…

Blood misted down. The Stedfaster fell forward and toppled down the cliff, the spear clattering by his side. His comrades groaned and howled, their onslaught momentarily paused by their dismay. They had hit their own man.

Drinith hauled herself over the ledge, rolled clear, and waved her knife about in case another Stedfaster awaited her. Confirming she was alone, she scurried back to help Siga, but he had already crawled into the cave. They lay on its floor, staring at the ceiling, panting.

"Your friend Oristan is dead!" Nykostar roared up from the bottom of the cliff with spiteful glee. "The dragon burned him to a cinder. I warned him that the Diarchy would rather see us dead than break its precious traditions. He wouldn't listen. He thought himself a hero. As if we hadn't tried." Resentment soured her triumphalism. "Early on, some of us had approached a dragon to beg for help, only to be burned alive. Do you think we love this squalid life? We have no other choice. Now you've destroyed what little we had. I hope you're proud of yourselves"

"I am, you cannibal!" Drinith roared back. "Don't look for sympathy from me. You'd have happily gnawed on my bones!"

A soft scraping sound sent a tingle down her spine. Nykostar's taunts must have been intended as a distraction for Stedfasters creeping up the ladder.

"I hope your moral superiority sates your stomachs!" Nykostar exclaimed. "I hope it protects you when you fall into Prystian's clutches! We've seen the corpses floating down the streams!"

The scuffing drew nearer. Drinith and Siga readied their daggers.

"If your climbers rise over the top of the ladder, there'll be more corpses!" Drinith yelled. The scraping stopped. As far as the Stedfasters knew, all of Drinith's companions could be here with her. Drinith tensed as the scraping started again, but it quickly waned as the climbers descended the ladder. Metal jangled brightly as a knife dropped by one of them danced down the cliff.

"You can't wait up there forever!" Nykostar sneered, but Drinith and Siga were already slipping away.

"I hope that this is the last we hear from her," Siga whispered.

"The others can't be too far ahead," Drinith said.

They followed the tunnel to the first junction where the others should have been waiting. "Lesym, you there?" Drinith waited for an answer that never came.

30

———————

Quiescat laughed at Lawster's gaping face staring down at him from the hatch as he held his knife to the slender lanyard that attached him to the dragon.

"You mad old fool!" Lawster roared.

"You were right," Quiescat said as the icy wind spun him and rocked him back and forth like the corpse of a hanged man. "To save Drinith, I'd sacrifice my life and this gem you covet so much. Death holds no terror for me. I've already lived beyond my allotted time."

Lawster sighed. "Very well. If we must go to the Whetstone, so be it. Let us haul you up."

"No!" Quiescat yelled. "Touch that lanyard and I'll slice through it."

"But you're a landlubber! You'll freeze to death down there before we ever reach the Whetstone!" Lawster exclaimed.

Quiescat smirked. "The dragon wax will keep me insulated from the wind's chill." He glanced at the ragged wall of churning water directly ahead. "Now, keep your promise or I'll slash this cord and feed the Tear to the inner sun." Should he fray the umbilical to underline his threat? But it might snap...

Above, such violent spite contorted Lawster's face, he might have cut the lanyard himself. He barked orders into the headstall. The *Parched Tongue* tilted downward.

The raging waters drew nearer, expanding before Quiescat until it filled his vision. Silent terror seized him. Had the descent begun too late? His mouth dried as the *Parched Tongue*'s downward angle steepened into a nosedive. The sudden plummet sent him dancing on the end of the lanyard, slapping him hard against the dragon's cheek and the headstall until he managed to grab on to a dragon scale. Far below, twisty pillars of cloud reached up like waiting arms from the inner sun's sepia veil. The Halo Sea drew ever closer, a millstone of seething water ready to grind the dragon into nothing. The spray it spat washed over Quiescat like rain.

The wall gradually curved above him. Thank the gods, they were going to make it.

One of the dragon's wings clipped the ocean. Through the punctured surface, a vast column of water poured down. Quiescat clung tight to the scale as the deluge struck. The terrible weight of the water pressed down on him, forcing the air from his lungs, ripping him from his handhold. And then, mercifully, the *Parched Tongue* cleared the torrent. Gasping painfully for breath as he dangled at the end of his precious lanyard, he glanced back at the vast waterfall. In moments, it had slowed to a trickle. Whatever mysterious force held the Halo Sea together had healed the wound.

His left arm and shoulder hurt from striking the dragon. They weren't broken, or he'd have lost the use of them, but the bruises must be epic.

As the ocean filled the sky, his whole body screamed that he must be upside down. Beholding the Halo Sea from below induced a terror he had never imagined.

A choking sound drew his attention to the *Parched Tongue*. An enormous fish tail flopped from the side of the dragon's mouth. With a mighty gulp, the dragon swallowed it.

Clapping and a loud guffaw came from the saddledeck. "I guess she's fed herself for this trip," Lawster said. "You survived, I see.

Enough of this nonsense. Let us haul you up before the *Parched Tongue* mistakes you for another fish."

Quiescat touched the pouch dangling from his neck, felt the hard sphere within. "I'm staying here until we perch."

Lawster rolled his eyes. "You really are the most obstinate, mistrustful man I've ever had the misfortune to encounter. Suit yourself."

Ahead, the black rod of the island protruded downward from the center of the sea. They'd land there in a few hours. Quiescat had struggled so hard to reach it, but what would he discover when he arrived? Did Drinith still live? He daren't think otherwise.

As they drew near the pocked pillar with its innumerable potential perches, Lawster peeped through the hatch again. "Any idea where we should settle?"

"The bottom, maybe."

"You don't sound so sure."

"I'm not, but the site where the candidates are dropped must be down there." Drinith already had plenty of time to travel a good distance from her disembarkation point. She could be anywhere in the column.

Lawster shrugged. As the *Parched Tongue* moved in a downward spiral around the column, Quiescat scanned the passing cliff face for any sign of Drinith or other candidates. Tresses of waterfalls poured down, disappearing into the clouds below. The rocks weren't as bare as they first appeared. Dark green forests furred them. Their species changed the further down the dragon traveled. Some trees even grew upside down, reaching for the inner sun instead of the outer one. Here and there in the forests' midst peeped signs of settlement long abandoned—weed-clogged villages, overgrown terraces of fields, the eroded threads of roads, the scattered bones of forsaken temples.

At this very moment, Drinith could be watching the dragon from somewhere in this verdant sprawl. He opened his mouth to bawl her name, only to be struck dumb by the foolishness of the impulse. The chances of her hearing him were minute.

Something flashed below. Too long and too golden to be

lightning. Perhaps a glimpse of the inner sun through a chink in the cloud or—

"Dragon ahoy!"

A monstrous brute, bigger than the *Cauldron Grin*, rounded the island below them. The *Parched Tongue*'s fire poured down on it, splashing flame across its saddledeck. The blazing masts prodded through the trailing column of black smoke rising from the dragon's back.

Lawster shushed his cheering crew. "Enough! We didn't douse the head, so we still face an angry dragon. Keep the *Parched Tongue* above her."

The tarry blot turned as the dragon within it emitted a defiant roar.

"Up! Up!" Lawster roared. The bent landscape of the island sped by as the *Parched Tongue* flew upward, but the Ophigeen dragon gained on it fast. Only its yawning jaws protruded from the pursuing black plumes. In moments, it would snap on the *Parched Tongue*'s whipping tail.

"Drop!" Lawster cried and the *Parched Tongue* plunged. Everything spun in an instant—the Crevast, the island, the sea, the jaws reaching from the smoke. Its fall ceased in a massive shudder. The *Parched Tongue* rose as its opponent tumbled. The smoke dissipated enough to see the Ophigeen dragon desperately flapping its wings to stabilize its plummet. One struck jutting rock with a mighty crack. Quiescat watched with bated breath as it shrank and disappeared into the sepia cloud.

This time, Lawster didn't hush the crew's cheers. Quiescat trembled with relief, but he couldn't bring himself to join their rowdy celebration. Sending the Ophigeen dragon and its crew to the inner sun wasn't something to take pleasure in. As the *Parched Tongue* returned to its descending spiral, Quiescat mouthed a prayer for its victims. The whiff of smoke on the breeze was all that remained of its foe.

They found a charred ledge at the very bottom. A cave mouth in the shape of a dragon's jaws opened onto it. This had to be the place.

The *Parched Tongue* flapped its wings to hover over the perch. Quiescat tensed for a violent landing, but it alighted with remarkable gentleness.

Its head craned upward, slapping Quiescat against the headstall. It roared.

"Dragon ahoy!"

Impossible. The *Parched Tongue* had already consigned its foe to the inner sun.

"Lift!" Lawster roared, but the new dragon already filled the sky. Puffs of smoke blossomed along the drake-o'-war's cinchdeck as its cannons fired. Sharp crunches followed as their volley of projectiles punched through the *Parched Tongue*'s saddledeck. "Abandon dragon! Abandon dragon!"

Lawster's crew glided down ropes onto the *Parched Tongue*'s back, and then to the ground. A few even jumped with sailcloth parachutes. As the *Parched Tongue*'s head lowered, Quiescat began to cut through his lanyard. His feverish sawing only nibbled through the cord, while the Ophigeen dragon's shadow spread ever wider and the blasts from its wings buffeted him. Ropes dangled down from it like a descending web. Black beads sped down them—a boarding party.

Lawster peered down from the hatch and shook his head. "I should have known you'd never have the strength to cut that rope." He raised his sword. "You had better give me that gem."

With two blows, he hacked through the cord and Quiescat fell, his dagger spilling from his hand. He slid down the *Parched Tongue*'s wing, dropped again, this time landing on something soft and wet. He rolled off the dead draker that had broken his fall and scrambled to his feet. Lawster slid down a rope and landed gracefully by his side. "I hope that jewel of yours is all it's cracked up to be, because it's already cost me a dragon."

They fled into the cave's charred mouth. "What about the rest of your crew?" Quiescat asked breathlessly.

"What about them? They've already scattered in here somewhere. They forgot me the instant their feet touched the ground."

"And how do you propose we escape?"

Lawster scratched his bearded jaw. "We're at the start of the Ascent, so I suggest we climb and the Ophigeens might take us in as their own. And your pretty gem will buy me a new dragon, maybe more—a whole conflagration of them. I probably have enough gems in my mouth worth to see me comfortable until I can hock the Tear."

Quiescat met every part of Lawster's plan with a cringe. Part of him wished he had fled like the *Parched Tongue*'s crew. But if he was to rescue Drinith, he needed Lawster's help.

From somewhere deeper in the tunnels echoed a scream. "It's a bit too early for my crew to start killing each other," Lawster muttered.

A dragon roar resounded around them as if in answer. A hot gust howled through the tunnel. "Oh, no," Lawster whispered, his eyes bulging.

"What—?" The aureate radiance filling the tunnel dazzled Quiescat mid-sentence. He saw the deluge of fire too late to run.

31

___

To Zoen, it seemed they traveled through the same tunnel over and over as she drifted in and out of consciousness. Who were these unfamiliar smiling faces who carried her? Before she could ask, she passed out again.

She awoke with a start, tried to rise, but Toskar's hand gently pressed against her shoulder.

"No need to be frightened. You're safe." Beyond Toskar, Kaliop and Fisken sat in a circle with a half-dozen strangers. Zoen was startled to realize one of them was Lesym. She hadn't recognized him immediately because of the bruises on his face.

"Some of Lesym's people met us near to the Upgate," Toskar said. "I reckon we've been traveling upward for about two days. It's hard to track time here."

"Any sign of Drinith?" Zoen asked as Toskar propped her up with a pile of blankets.

Toskar shook her head. "No sign of either her or Oristan, I'm afraid."

"That traitor, Oristan?" Zoen asked, aghast.

Toskar gave her a sympathetic smile. "He rescued us from the Stedfasters. Do you not remember?"

Even as Zoen shook her head, a familiar fear stirred, followed by the memory that spawned it—Oristan carried a knife as he loomed over her. But he hadn't hurt her. No, he had freed her. "What happened to him?"

"He ran off to warn the dragon that was arriving, we think. We're not entirely sure. Drinith went to stop him before he got himself killed."

"And you just abandoned them?"

"I would have stayed, but the others outvoted me," Toskar said. "Lesym and Kaliop were determined to put distance between us and the Upgate and Fisken went along with them. Lesym has promised to send a search party for them after we've safely reached the Uprisers' camp."

If Zoen had been conscious, the matter might have been decided differently. Her frailty might have cost Drinith her life.

Toskar pressed a spoonful of hot root mash to her mouth. Zoen gently pried the spoon from her hand and ate it. It tasted sweeter than the last time Oristan had fed her. She remembered the others hoisting her up to the Upgate, but everything after she reached it remained stubbornly blank.

"I'm surprised you've recovered this well already after the Stedfasters starved you," Toskar said.

Her compliment washed over Zoen, broken on the rock of her self-disgust. "They sensed my fragility." Like a predator stalking an easy kill.

"You proved them wrong though," Toskar said, blushing. She glanced over at the others. "I wish I had your strength." She passed Zoen the battered metal cup containing the mash and rose. "I'll leave you to eat in peace." Looking embarrassed, she joined the circle.

Zoen had almost finished her meal when Lesym approached her. "You're much recovered, I see, but we'll carry you as much as we can for now."

"I can walk," Zoen said.

"There'll be sections we must climb and obstacles to negotiate. Save your strength for them."

"Any word of Olen?"

"There's been no sign of her, according to the others. Maybe she has found an alternate route out of the Stedfasters' territory and awaits us at our camp."

Zoen nodded in appreciation of his optimism, but such a miracle could never happen in this bleak place. She rubbed the finger where her ring should have been, but it was gone. "Dragons damn the Stedfasters! They stole my ring!"

"Nykostar probably took it," Lesym said with manifest distaste. "She has a partiality for her victims' jewelry."

Zoen shook her head ruefully. "I didn't even realize it had been taken until now."

"Olen would have been very proud of you, you know," Lesym said.

"I'd be long dead but for everyone's help." *Olen should be here, not me.*

As she convulsed into tears, Lesym threw his arms around her. But for his embrace, she might have shaken apart as grief and anger and shame coursed through her. "We had a fight the morning she left for Stepstone. The last thing I ever said to her was that I hated her."

"Those were the words of a child," Lesym whispered. "You didn't even know their meaning. You're an adult now. Put aside such childish guilt and live for Olen. Live for your sister."

Lesym was right. Zoen needed to pull herself together. The warmth of his body, the reassuring strength of his arms, soothed her. Her weeping petered out to sobs like the last fat drops of a storm. This wasn't the place or the time for wallowing in grief. Rubbing the wetness off her face, she gently pushed free of Lesym's embrace without verbal acknowledgment of his support. Giving words to her anguish might strip away her brittle composure. She needed to be strong. It was what her sister would have wanted.

In the days that followed, she gradually recovered her strength. She walked as much as she could, partly to relieve her carriers but also to establish her independence. Olen would never have accepted the humiliation of being a burden. Zoen's foot hurt on and off, but she ignored the pain. Sometimes, she had no option but to climb. At first, Lesym insisted she had to wear a rope in case she fell, but thereafter she consented only in the severest circumstances, as it was too akin to being tethered like an animal.

Lesym's friends were amiable enough companions, but she couldn't warm to them. Their fixed grins and unwavering optimism jarred her. They all worshiped their leader, Prystian. Their uncritical devotion infected Zoen's comrades. Fisken praised Prystian at every opportunity despite having never met him. Toskar was a little more circumspect, but she, too, began to slip under the same spell. Kaliop certainly praised the Uprisers and their leader, but it could have been mere lip service. Part of Zoen wished Kaliop would admit to the same lingering uneasiness about their new allies. Another part of her lived in horror of it. Zoen's paranoia discomfited her. The Uprisers had saved her, after all. She owed them.

Lesym was the exception. She trusted him. She sought his company when possible, but he never seemed to be on his own, making a private conversation with him impossible. He smiled when he met her glances, but a wariness lurked in his dark rose eyes, and he often turned pensive. Perhaps he feared to intrude on her sorrow, or her earlier outburst had embarrassed him. She wanted to confront him, talk it out, apologize, but the opportunity to do so eluded her. She began to suspect he deliberately engineered this lack of availability. Whatever the truth of the matter, she had no choice but to quietly suffer her chagrin.

On the fourth night—"night" being a subjective term in this eternally dark realm—of their journey, a pained yell woke everyone from their slumber. The leader of the Upriser patrol, Sulgara, winced as he pressed both of his hands to the back of his head. "She jumped me and knocked me out with a stone."

Zoen instinctively knew who *she* was. Kaliop and her bedroll had vanished.

While the other Uprisers treated Sulgara, Lesym opened the bags that contained the group's provisions. "At least she left us just enough to avoid starvation until we reach the camp."

"She can't have gotten far," Toskar said. "We should go find her."

"No," Lesym said firmly. "Forget her. Our priority is to reach the camp."

"But if she gets to the Ouroboric Gate, she could tell the Diarchy about your people, Prystian, everything."

"The only route there is through our camp," Lesym said. "The best thing we can do is beat her there and warn my friends about her."

They pushed on, with greater urgency than before. Respites from walking were rare and brief. Zoen found herself drifting to the tail end of the group. Lesym sent one or the other of his friends to check on her every so often, though he never came himself. When she came across the others huddled together just ahead, she redoubled her efforts to reach them.

"Dragons damn it," Lesym muttered at the front of the group. Zoen weaved through the others to his side. "What's wrong?"

"That." Lesym pointed at the shimmering darkness at the far end of the tunnel. "That's what's wrong. The dreamery has expanded and blocked the tunnel. We'll have to take an alternate route."

"Dreamery?" Zoen frowned. "But there are no dreameries on Ophigee."

"So the Diarchy has always claimed, but as in so many things, they're wrong." He waved a hand at it. "There's one in front of you now. It was only slightly bigger than a head when we first found it. We tried to move it, but it refused to budge. It has grown massively since then. Each time it swells, the Whetstone shudders. It wouldn't surprise me if it breaks off the bottom of the island, eventually."

Somewhere behind that black pearl of time, a witch weaved the fates of others. Zoen shivered.

"There's nothing to fear. Aside from its expansion, it's quite inert." Lesym strode over to the glassy surface and knocked on it. "Hello, Fate Healer. Are you in there? My friend wants to meet you."

"No." Zoen rushed to him, pulled his hand away. "Don't, please."

"Don't what? Tempt Fate?" She felt a thrill as he took her hand. "I promise you, it's safe to touch. Whoever or whatever dwells within, the shell is inert." He gently pressed his warm hand over hers on the cold, smooth surface. "Our people have never believed in Fate. Why should we start now?"

She blushed and smiled at him. He recoiled, snatched back his hand. Rubbing it as if it had been stung, he cleared his throat. "There's an alternate route we can take. We had better get going."

Burning with embarrassment, Zoen followed him back down the tunnel.

32

———————

"Lesym!" Drinith yelled through cupped hands. Burdened with Zoen, he and the others couldn't have traveled fast, but the echoes of her cry faded without an answer.

"Could the Stedfasters have captured them?" Siga asked.

"We'd have never gotten through the Upgate if that was the case."

"I'm sorry. I was unfair to you at the start. I... I resented that the others looked down on me more than you."

Drinith couldn't resist a smile. "If they did, it was only by a fraction."

"Throw a morsel to two hungry dogs and they'll scrap over it no matter its size. I couldn't help seeing everyone in the group as enemies, particularly Oristan and his little clique. I always thought of him as a worthless fop, but he proved me wrong."

They discovered an abandoned campsite in a branching cave. A sift through the ash revealed fresh embers. The fire must have been recent, though Drinith could only guess exactly how long it had been left untended. A few red threads and dollops of cooked mash littered the ground.

"This has to belong to some Uprisers," Drinith said. "Lesym and the others must have met up with them. They're probably on their way to their main camp. They can't be far ahead of us."

Siga scratched his stubbly jaw. "They know where they're going. We have to guess our way."

His words proved prophetic. Again and again, they met with dead ends, often tunnels choked with rubble, forcing them to double back. Of Lesym's party or the Uprisers, they saw no trace. It was as if the rocks had swallowed them.

To sustain themselves, they gathered whatever small tubers they could find. Eating them raw was about as palatable as chewing wood, but it was better than starving. One kept watch while the other slept. Siga often took out his little patch of red cloth and brooded over it. Eventually, Drinith mustered the courage to ask about its significance.

"My mother gave it to me the day I was sent to green school," he said, his gaze lingering on it. "That's where they send thrallborns supposedly to learn not to become their parents, though it breaks more than it builds. Her gift was supposed to remind me that thrall green wasn't the only color I might wear. I held this in my fist going to sleep every night. And I promised myself that when I ascended I'd buy my parents' freedom."

He squeezed the cloth into a ball in his fist. "I had been dreaming of meeting them for nine years, but their presence at the Dipalatine overwhelmed me with rage. They were so weak and subservient, not at all how I remembered them. They were too afraid to accompany me to the embarkation ceremony. Made their excuses and fled. Why must life always teach me shame?"

Drinith embraced him as he wept, but he broke free and ran away. She didn't chase after him. He clearly resented sympathy. For him, it was too close to charity.

He was gone so long, she feared he had abandoned her. At last he came running up with a wild grin and beckoned her. "Come quick. You won't believe what I've found."

He led her down a series of tunnels. She halted as she turned a corner to face a concave, vertical pool, black and glistening, like a giant spider's eye. She gasped as she realized that both she and Siga were missing from the reflection of the tunnel on its surface, as if they didn't exist. "It must be a dreamery. They don't reflect living beings."

"Everything we've been taught is a lie," Siga said. "Here's more proof. It was drummed into us at green school that there was no dreamery to be found on Ophigee."

"Maybe your teachers didn't lie. Perhaps they didn't know of its existence." Drinith couldn't avert her gaze from its mesmerizing blackness. She had never been this close to a dreamery before. Quiescat's dread of them had infected her, but the delicacy of its curved surface drew her to touch it. It felt impossibly soft against her palm, as smooth as a bubble of air.

Her hand sank through it. Her arm wrenched her shoulder as it was sucked into the spherical abyss. Siga locked his arms around her midriff and pulled, but they both slid into the dreamery, screaming.

They spilled onto the floor of another cave. Behind them, the dreamery stood as enigmatic it had been before it swallowed them.

"What just happened?" Siga asked as they untangled themselves from each other.

"I don't know."

The trip through the dreamery had appeared instantaneous, but how could they be sure? In there, a thousand years might have passed in a heartbeat. Drinith's friends might be long dead, and the domains that had shaped her existence toppled and forgotten. Loneliness shivered through her at the prospect of being stripped of her time.

"Where do you think we are?" Siga asked.

Drinith could barely breathe. "I know no more than you do." She forced herself to walk away from the dreamery. Siga plodded behind her.

They followed the winding tunnel until they reached the foot of a large cascade—a dozen waterfalls or more, disappearing into the darkness above.

"I guess we must climb that," Drinith said.

Something floated in the pool separating the two nearest falls. Drinith climbed up, stretched out across its black water, grabbed a fistful of sodden clothing, and dragged the mound ashore. She turned the corpse's face toward her. The girl's pale eyes stared up at her with frozen horror. Y-shaped lesions pocked her face. The jawless mouth revealed a larger Y-shape cut in her shriveled tongue.

Siga waded across the pool to another half-submerged mound on the far side. He pulled it onto land and flopped it over. "Another girl. Mutilated in the same manner." He crouched by the body. "Dragons! Quick, come over here."

Drinith's trepidation spiked as she crossed the pool to join him. He pointed to the ring on the corpse's hand.

"That's Zoen's ring," Drinith said in a small voice.

"It can't be her," Siga said. "This girl is too tall to be Zoen and her hair color is much darker."

Relieved, Drinith nodded. "It must be Zoen's sister." *So Nykostar had been telling the truth,* she mused, *at least in part.* Something foul was happening in the upper tunnels, as sinister as the Stedfasters' predation of their fellow candidates. The ring came easily off the girl's finger. Drinith would give it to Zoen if they met again.

Reluctant to leave the two corpses to slowly rot in the pool, she and Siga pushed them over the fall. Hopefully, the river would eventually carry them to the inner sun.

Tightening her fist around Olen's ring, Drinith stared up at the cascades. "We need to climb these. The answer lies somewhere above them." *Somewhere up there, Olen's murderer awaits us.*

They climbed against the spilling water, up one cataract and then the next, but the icy rush raging down the third sheer drop drove them back. They scrambled back down to where they had started, shivering and exhausted.

With their backs to each other, they stripped off their clothes and wrung them out. As she redressed, Drinith caught a glimpse of the scar lines across Siga's back. It was hard not to feel sympathy for him. Once fully clothed, he turned around and regarded Drinith with something other than his usual contempt. Drinith, realizing her damp clothes hugging her figure left little to the imagination, felt supremely self-conscious. But if Siga found this accentuation in any way provocative, he masked his feelings well. His momentary curiosity faded, and he held his lantern jaw at its customary imperious tilt.

"We'll have to find another way up," he said.

Drinith nodded as she tried to quiet her chattering teeth. "We'll retrace our steps back to the dreamery. We might have missed some other exit."

They soon found themselves back at the dreamery. Its perfect black, glistening curve eyed them.

"What do we do now?" Siga asked. "We can't climb the cascade and there's no other way out." He licked his lips. "Unless we pass through the dreamery again."

If it lets us... "Whatever happens, it will happen to both of us."

Siga squeezed the hand Drinith offered. A tense silence settled over them as she reached out to the dreamery. Her hand hovered above its smooth surface. This tunnel would be their grave if the dreamery didn't take them away from here.

She pressed her hand against the dreamery...

And tumbled into a cave. Siga laughed at her side. "I guess it worked." They scrambled to their feet and dusted themselves off. Drinith's clothes were dry. The water's biting chill had left her body. Had the change been instantaneous, or did it mark the passage of time?

Siga's gaze swept the cave. "I don't recognize this place."

Drinith stared into the darkness ahead. "Hopefully, it won't prove a dead end like the last one."

The tunnel eventually branched in several directions. They chose the first one that appeared to be heading upward. The tunnel split again and again. When they met a dead end, they doubled back to the last junction and tried another route. Drinith's frustration at this labyrinth mounted. They couldn't be sure if they were progressing up the Whetstone or traveling in circles. At every turn, she feared they might face the dreamery again.

Armed men and women emerged from the shadows as if by magic. Before Drinith could draw her knife, they seized her and wrestled her to the floor. She freed a hand and clutched for her knife, but the sheath was already empty. She writhed as both of her arms were tied behind her back. She glimpsed a symbol on their worn tunics, an upside-down haloed sword—the same Lesym had worn.

"Lesym sent us!" she cried as the scrum constricted around her.

A boot pressed down on her cheek. She strained her eye to glimpse its owner. A tall woman glared down at her. "Then where is he?"

The coarse gravel scraped Drinith's other cheek as she spoke. "I don't know." The boot pressed down, digging the stones deeper into the other side of her face. She screamed.

"Leave her alone!" Siga yelled.

"You had better hope Lesym shows up soon," the woman said, her voice dripping scorn. "Until he confirms otherwise, you two will be held as Stedfaster spies."

33

L awster leapt upon Quiescat, slamming him against the wall. The draker's calloused hand pressed over his eyes. Quiescat screamed as searing heat threatened to roast him like a pig on a spit, and tongues of flame singed his tunic. How long would this blaze take to kill him? Too long.

"Stop screaming, you silly landlubber," Lawster hissed. "You're louder than any dragon."

The fire subsided, but Quiescat's exposed skin still burned. Scrabbling off him, Lawster threw away his burning hat and battered his coat off the ground until it ceased to smolder. Quiescat checked his hands and arms. They were clear of blisters, at least for now. He massaged the back of his hand to ease its smarting, but Lawster yanked away his arm. "You'll rub through the wax and then you really will burn if more fire touches you."

The draker captain dragged him through a bewildering network of tunnels beyond the char of the dragon's breath. "We'll find some of my crew. Safety in numbers."

As he turned a corner, a cutlass flashed. Quiescat reached for his knife only to find its sheath empty.

The cutlass halted a hair's breadth from Lawster's stomach. "I almost ran you through there, Captain," Marclan said. Three other crewmen appeared behind him, looking sheepish. One of them was the surly, one-eyed pyrate Quiescat had met when he boarded the *Parched Tongue.*

"Lucky for you, you didn't scratch me, Marclan," Lawster declared. "I'd have flayed you alive and used your skin for a bandage. Now, let's get out of here before the Ophigeens come looking for us."

"You really think they'll bother?" Marclan asked.

Lawster sneered. "Might as well ask, would they let a lot of foreigners trample on their sacred ground and maybe earn the right to become part of their society?"

"You might have a point, Captain," Marclan admitted.

Lawster peered around him and frowned. "Who're the corpses?"

Marclan shrugged. "Some locals who tried to jump us."

Quiescat desperately pushed his way through the drakers. Three dead children lay sprawled in a pool of blood. None of them were Drinith, thank the gods. The matted hair, the shabby clothes, the unhealthy thinness pointed to desperate squalor. Marclan and his three friends, little better than pyrates, had merrily butchered these unfortunates as if they were livestock. Shame formed a hard lump in the pit of Quiescat's stomach.

I'm going to die here, Quiescat thought morosely, *and I deserve no better for associating with these criminals.* "I'll lead the way." He couldn't take the risk that Drinith might attack them next. His companions' bemused chuckles wilted before his forbidding scowl.

Lawster's eyebrows shot skyward. "You can't be serious. Supposing you're attacked—"

"I'm sure I can rely on you to save me." *And the fortune hanging around my neck.* Quiescat waved dismissively as he trod ahead. "Keep watch for my princess. She's Rhumgadian with green-black skin." He paused and stared back at the dumbfounded drakers. "I thought you were in a rush to get going."

With a growl, Lawster stamped after him. The others followed.

Quiescat bounded forward, powered by nervous strain. Drinith had to be alive. He couldn't have come all this way for nothing. He chose randomly at each junction he encountered, sometimes left, sometimes right.

"Have you any idea where you're going?" Lawster muttered.

"Have you?"

A loud voice reverberated down the tunnel as though the rock itself spoke. "Surrender and take the green, or die!"

"Pay no heed. Taking the green is worse than death." Lawster grimaced, exposing his bejeweled teeth, and ran a dirty finger lovingly across them. "I'm certainly not about to surrender. The buggers would rip my choppers out!"

Quiescat reflexively clutched the Tear.

"That may be, Captain," Marclan said, "but how do you propose to get out of here without a dragon?"

"We complete the Ascent. Then we're as much Ophigeen as anyone can be. Granted, we'd start out as poor as dirt, but we're resourceful chaps. We'd soon get another dragon if we worked together." He winked. "One way or another."

Despite his crewmen's avaricious glances, nobody mentioned the fortune in gems decorating Lawster's smile or the pearls hanging from his neck. Although assassinating him for the booty must have crossed some of their minds, everyone's first priority was survival.

As they passed a half-dozen bodies of drakers and children, a boy scurried from their midst on all fours. Lawster, laughing, bounded after him. The boy rose to his feet, but the draker punched him in the back, knocking him to the floor.

"You move fast for a corpse," Lawster said, pressing a boot on the boy's back. The captain leaned over, putting more of his weight on his captive. "And what would your name be?"

"You'll break my back," the boy pleaded.

"You had better hurry up and answer then," Lawster said.

"C-Cl-Clespro," the boy stuttered.

"An honor to meet you, Clespro. Would you be good enough to show us the way to the Ouroboric Gate?"

Quiescat rolled his eyes. If the poor boy knew the route back to civilization, he would surely have taken it.

Clespro yowled as Lawster twisted the heel of his boot from side to side.

"Lawster, don't..." Quiescat begged.

An ugly grin spread across Lawster's face as he looked him up and down. "Or you'll do what? Don't worry. I won't cripple him. He's even more valuable than you until we get out of here. I can be a good friend to those who are friendly to me. If he helps us, he'll be rewarded." Lifting his foot off, he turned Clespro over with the toe of his boot. He leaned down. "So, what have you to say?"

"I... I can lead you to the Upgate. It's the only way out of our territory."

Wolfish howls rose up. "Good, though from the sounds of it, this territory won't be yours much longer," Lawster said. "The guards have brought hounds, it seems."

"Crag wolves," the one-eyed draker corrected. "I recognize their cries. They'll catch up with us fast on this rocky terrain. Make no mistake."

"And their masters no doubt close behind, Tinmar," Lawster said, bending down. Clespro, his face a mask of terror, crawled backward on his elbows, but Lawster seized his tunic. "You had better play fair with us or I'll feed you to them. Understand?"

Clespro gave an emphatic nod. Lawster slipped off one of his belts.

"You know why I wear so many belts?" he asked Clespro.

"No," Clespro murmured breathlessly.

Lawster winked at the boy. "They're trophies from the men I killed who were worth killing."

Clespro squealed as Lawster wrapped one belt around his throat and used it to drag his prisoner to his feet. "Lead the way. Remember, if you try any tricks, you'll wish the crag wolves had torn you apart."

They raced through the subterranean maze, Clespro choosing every turn without hesitation, but the howls grew louder. Quiescat, exhausted and breathless, struggled to keep up.

"Wait," Lawster said, stopping so suddenly he almost choked Clespro. "Give the holy man a chance to recover his breath."

Ignoring his crewmen's scowls, he sauntered over to Quiescat. "Perhaps you should give me the Tear now," he whispered. "It's probably slowing you down."

Quiescat emitted a wheezy laugh. *And give up the only reason you haven't forsaken me?* "No."

"I swear, sometimes I think you'd be happier feeding it to the wolves than honoring your promise and giving it to me."

"I'll keep my promise," Quiescat said between painful gasps, "when you've delivered on yours. No sooner."

Lawster's hand lurched forward as if to seize the pouch. Quiescat cringed in expectation of a struggle, but the draker shook his head and turned away. "Enough rest. Move it."

Smoke wafted in the air, growing more intense the farther they traveled. Lawster yanked Clespro's makeshift collar. "You wouldn't be leading us up a dragon's nostril by any chance?"

"No no no. It's our village. It's on fire."

Lawster squinted. "How did that happen?"

"A prisoner escaped and set it alight. A foreigner from Gyre."

Quiescat stalked up to him and seized a fistful of his tunic. "Was the foreigner's name Drinith?"

"Yes. Yes, it was."

Lawster snickered. "Looks like your princess isn't dead yet."

Quiescat released Clespro and staggered back, shocked by the violence of his grasp. "Sorry," he said, rubbing his hands against his tunic, smiling as joy percolated through his astonishment. Nothing could dim the wonder of this miracle. Drinith still lived!

"Looks like we might both get what we want on this journey," Lawster said. "I guess you're not as mad as you appear."

The other drakers smiled, too, but with bewilderment. How soon would that puzzlement turn to curiosity? How long before they looked for their cut?

Quiescat needed to be careful. If they came to covet the Tear, they would not be so easily dissuaded from taking it by force. Worse, he was leading these scoundrels to Drinith. His stomach turned at what they might do if she fell into their clutches. And chasing them, the

Ophigeens and their murderous beasts. Anything might happen. If only he could glimpse the future again. It might yet prove a blessing that he had lost the gift. At least, while uncertainty remained, hope could mingle with the fear.

They coughed as the smoke thickened. Every hot breath irritated Quiescat's nose and the back of his throat. They entered an enormous cavern. Fires lit up the thick haze. Movement in the pall halted Quiescat, but it was only the flicker of flames through the char-black ribs of the huts they burned.

Clespro paused. "The Upgate lies on the far side."

"Then why are we waiting here?" Lawster growled, flicking Clespro's lead like a rein. He glanced at the other drakers. "Keep your eyes open for any of this lad's friends lurking around here. This looks like a nice place for an ambush."

Clespro shook his head. "They're gone. They're not fools."

"If I want your advice, I'll ask for it. Now, giddyap." A glancing blow of his boot against Clespro's backside sent him stumbling forward.

As the group weaved through the burning village, Quiescat's eyes strained through the smoke for someone, anyone, waiting to pounce, but the writhing shadows confounded him. Terror shuddered through him at a loud creak coming from a circle of burning poles. One of them toppled against its neighbor, knocking over the pole next to it and so on until the entire structure collapsed inward like a closing hand, hurling a massive swarm of sparks as far as the cavern's ceiling. The sooner they got out of here the—

Ragged shadows swooped around them from all sides. Clespro grabbed at the belt around his throat as Lawster yanked him to the ground. An attacker fell, then another. Two leapt on one of Marclan's friends and stabbed him to the ground. As they rose, Marclan beheaded one and, after kicking the other in the stomach, grabbed him by the hair and smashed his head against a boulder.

"Marclan, watch out!" Quiescat cried, too late. As the draker stepped away from his handiwork, a girl ran him through with a thick spear. She lurched backward to clear the sweep of Lawster's blade, slipped on shifting rocks and landed on her behind, her eyes round with surprise. Lawster growled as he thrust his sword at her chest, but Clespro threw himself in front of the point of the blade. As it sank deep into his chest, with both hands he wrenched the hilt from Lawster's grip, and tumbled to the ground, dead.

"I always carry a spare," Lawster muttered as he drew his second sword from its scabbard. He addressed the girl: "What's so special about you that my 'dear friend', Clespro, would give his life to save you? Was the poor lad sweet on you, maybe?" He answered her haughty glare with a roguish grin. "You're better dressed than the rest of these ragamuffins. And armed with more daggers, I see. Lots of pretty rings, too. I reckon we have here what passes for a leader in these parts."

As she drew a knife, Quiescat caught sight of the amethyst ring on one of her fingers. The stone bore an engraving of a dragon's head, exactly as Versifer had described in his second vision. Quiescat dashed forward, vainly reaching out to stop Lawster. "Don't! We need her!"

Lawster drove his sword at her head. With an eek, she tried to shield her face with her hands. The sword knocked away the dagger she clutched. "If you move, you die." He turned to his surviving crewmate, the one-eyed draker. "Tinmar, collect the rest of those knives she's wearing. Then get my belt from Clespro."

"Quiescat," Marclan whispered. Quiescat knelt beside him. The spear still jutted awkwardly out of his belly. Marclan seized his hand, desperately squeezed it. "Quiescat!"

"Yes?"

"Thanks for the warning." His face slackened, his eyes glazed over. His lifeless hand slipped from Quiescat's.

Quiescat stood and surveyed the scene. He hadn't seen how the fourth draker, or three more of their foes, had died. The mayhem whirling around him had left Quiescat unscathed, as though he had stood in the eye of a storm of death.

The girl glared at Lawster as Tinmar tightened the belt around her throat.

"You did the right thing sparing her," Quiescat said.

Lawster nodded. "She'll show us to the Upgate if she wants to keep breathing. What's your name?"

She bowed her head. "Nykostar."

"Don't hurt her," Quiescat pleaded.

Lawster sneered. "Who's going to stop me? You? The only reason you're not dead is these fools were too busy fighting real threats to notice you." He chuckled. "You don't even have a knife." He picked a dagger off the ground. "Open your hand."

Quiescat obeyed with some hesitation. The blood greasing the hilt Lawster laid in his palm was still warm.

"Sorry about this, Marclan." Pressing his foot against the dead man's chest, Lawster ripped the spear free. He strode over to Nykostar and, taking the tip of the belt around her neck from Tinmar, yanked her to her feet. "The Upgate, please."

They soon came to a daunting cliff. A fracture crossed the ladder carved into it. Lawster craned his back and stared up at the cave at the top. "We have your leader down here! Attack us and I'll slit her throat! Tinmar, you go up first."

Looking dubious, Tinmar started up the ladder. Reaching the top, he disappeared into the cave. Quiescat didn't dare breathe until the draker cried, "All clear!"

Dropping his makeshift lead, Lawster started up the ladder. "Move it, Quiescat."

Wolfish howls filled the cavern. "What about the girl?" Quiescat asked.

Lawster chuckled. "She's clever enough to know she has only two directions to go, one of which land her in wolves' jaws."

Nodding at Nykostar, Quiescat gestured at the ladder. "Go up first. I'll follow."

She stared at him with surprise and puzzled calculation, as though she struggled to work out the trap concealed in his offer.

"Hurry!" he pleaded. "Before the crag wolves are upon us."

As she reached for a rung, Quiescat spotted an alicorn bracelet on her wrist. It looked exactly like...

"That's Drinith's bracelet!" he cried, snatching it off her. Nykostar scowled murderously at him but started up the ladder.

"Now all you have to do is find the rest of her," Lawster quipped. "If the crag wolves don't get you first. Move it!"

Nykostar grunted every time she heaved himself upward, wobbling from side to side. Quiescat climbed as soon as enough space opened beneath her.

"Quiescat, you ass!" Lawster screeched. "Your misplaced gallantry is going to get you killed. I'm sure that 'lady' is more than capable of fending for herself. Girl, move out of the way! Let Quiescat through!"

Nykostar kept climbing, one rung at a time. Quiescat followed her in the same stepwise fashion, just below her trailing foot, every part of him willing her more speed.

He glimpsed the spear being brandished above her. "If you don't get out of his way, I'll push you off with the pointy end of this!"

"If you harm her in any way, I'll step off the ladder," Quiescat declared.

"You'll break your neck!" Lawster sounded as though he would be happy to snap it himself.

"I know." They couldn't be far from the top now—another couple of rungs, perhaps.

Lawster sputtered on his rage. "It's always the same with you. Your answer to every problem is to threaten to jump off something. Fine, I promise I won't harm her but—"

A bestial howl silenced him. Its ferocity made Quiescat shudder. The crag wolf must be close. His heart thundered in his chest, aping the rhythm of a fast-approaching gallop. Having reached the cave's mouth, Nykostar clambered out of his way—Lawster and Tinmar must have lifted her up. Quiescat climbed, but the crag wolf bounded faster up the cliff until it paused just above him on a slender ledge, defying gravity. It was like no wolf he had ever seen. Spiky hair covered its body like myriad black lances. A profusion of twisted horns crowned its head. Razor-sharp teeth filled its massive mouth. He cringed as it leaped. It stretched above him, jaws yawning wide.

It fell by him, tumbling downward, Lawster's spear lodged in its side spinning round and round, shattering against the cliff face.

"Don't gawp at it like a fool!" Lawster roared. "Keep moving."

Quiescat scurried up the last rungs. The drakers hauled him clear of the ladder. He panted as he glanced over the edge of the precipice. Below, four crag wolves feasted on the broken, bloody carcass of Quiescat's attacker.

"Amazing animals," Tinmar said.

Lawster shook his head and emitted a rueful sigh. "I hope you think they're so wonderful when they're chomping on your innards. That meal won't keep them distracted for long. Their handlers will see to that. We need to move fast."

On trembling legs, Quiescat hastened after Lawster and the others. He kept glancing back, expecting a crag wolf to attack him. Where could Drinith be? Would he live long enough to find her?

34

———————

The first warrior emerged from the tunnel wall as if by magic. Nezon yelped in surprise. Toskar whipped out her knife. Zoen drew hers. Her blade trembled as more warriors emerged from crevices and nooks around the group.

"They're friends, fellow Uprisers. Everyone relax," Lesym said as the tunnel filled with the excited babel of greetings. Feeling foolish, Zoen awkwardly sheathed her knife. A lean, athletic girl with radiant red hair hugged Lesym. The palpable relief on her beautiful face drove Zoen to look away. This girl must be the reason for his aloofness. He could have said as much. Zoen would have understood.

"Thank all dragons, Lesym, you're alive," the girl said. "Those bruises must be sore. The Stedfasters certainly gave you quite a beating. I feared they had killed you."

"They very nearly did, Redanaxan," he said. "But for the help of my new friends, I would have died down there."

Zoen shied from Redanaxan's grateful smile. Drinith and Oristan had rescued Lesym. Zoen couldn't even save herself.

"Zoen, come here." Lesym beckoned her to his side.

She repressed her instinctive resistance and stepped forward. Better not to create a scene.

The touch of Lesym's hand against hers thrilled her as he drew her before Redanaxan. "Has Olen made it back? This is her sister, Zoen."

Redanaxan's grin faded. "There's been no sign since Prystian sent her below."

"I should report to him," Lesym said, letting go of Zoen's hand.

"Of course. Your new friends must be also eager to meet him."

Lesym glanced at Zoen. "They need a little rest and food first."

Zoen's stomach growled impatiently.

With a parting nod, Lesym plunged into the knot of chatting Uprisers and disappeared.

Redanaxan called for everyone's attention. "I'll accompany Sulgara's patrol and our guests to the kitchen. Axalisan, you're in charge here until I get back. Everyone back to your posts."

Every step strained tired muscles. Zoen stretched her back to dislodge the ache between her shoulder blades. Weariness weighed on her.

Smoke stung her eyes as she entered a large cavern. A fire burned in a crude hearth near a steaming pool. The fire's attendant poked a stone from the fire. The pool hissed and steamed as the stone plopped into it.

The trestle benches provided a jarring intrusion of civilization in otherwise primitive surroundings until Zoen sat on one of them and grasped their crude construction. The wonky planks of rough-hewn wood were still a marvel, however uncomfortable they were to sit upon. It must have taken a red month to fashion even this basic furniture.

Redanaxan filled cups with root mash and passed them out. Despite its slight bitterness, Zoen had grown to like it. It reminded her of home for some reason, though she had never tasted it before she came to Stepstone. The smell—that was it. It used to waft from the thralls' quarters, but only sometimes, on feast days and other special occasions. Having enjoyed spices all her life, she might, in more hospitable circumstances, dismiss such a simple dish as tasteless, but now she savored every sustaining mouthful.

She guiltily eyed the others as she licked the cup clean.

"You want more?" Redanaxan asked with a knowing smile.

Zoen and her companions gave enthusiastic nods. Collecting the cups, Redanaxan sauntered over to the steaming pool near the fire. She prodded four tubers from the water, sliced them open and scooped out the flesh. Crushing them with a stone, she deposited the fresh mash into their cups. Zoen ate her second portion with even more gusto, as if the taste of food had given her body permission to admit hunger again.

"You won't get fat on root mash, but at least you won't go hungry," Redanaxan said.

Zoen leaned back from the cup, satisfied. A pain stirred in her bloated stomach. Her sudden, prolonged belch set everyone laughing. Blushing, Zoen joined in the hilarity herself.

"Prystian will see you now," Lesym said, appearing behind her as if from nowhere. Zoen was much too full and too happy to puzzle over his somber demeanor. After making their farewells to Sulgara's patrol, she, Toskar, and Fisken followed him through twisting tunnels daubed with the Uprisers' now familiar symbol. As they approached a large wooden door, built in the same rough fashion as the benches, the pair of guards leaning against the wall on either side of it snapped to attention. One acknowledged Lesym with a deferential nod. Zoen's scalp tingled as Lesym knocked formally on the door. "I've returned with the new candidates we rescued."

Zoen grinned at his inversion of what really happened. Lesym must be desperate to impress his leader.

"I will see them one at a time." The leaden voice didn't sound particularly charismatic.

Lesym swung open the door and nodded to Fisken. She hesitantly entered. He disappeared inside with her for a few moments, then returned, closing the door behind him. Lesym invited Zoen and Toskar to sit on a bench beside the door, but he didn't join them. He leaned against the wall, arms folded. Under his cool gaze, Zoen waited for her turn. In the silence, time dragged. What was taking so long?

The door opened, and Fisken strode out. Her cheeks glistened, her eyes were red, but her grin proclaimed the tears to be joyful.

"I'll take you back to the kitchen in a moment," Lesym said. "Zoen, it's your turn."

He led her through an anteroom into a larger chamber. Her first glimpse of Prystian standing with his back to her in front of a window left her disappointed and nonplussed. How could this unprepossessing youth with unkempt red hair inspire such ecstatic devotion?

The crystal cyan water beyond the window had to be Halo Sea, so at least the Ouroboric Gate must be nearby.

As Prystian turned toward her, Zoen fell immediately into the gravity of his stare. She could see nothing beyond those lustrous black eyes as if they filled her horizon. Even Lesym faded from her sight. Prystian outshone him as the outer sun surpassed the moons. She hardly heard Lesym's introduction.

Prystian opened his arms. "Welcome, Zoen. Sit, please."

She sat before him and basked in his beatific smile.

"Why are you here?" he asked.

"Lesym brought me." She glanced around, looking for him, but Lesym was gone. She hadn't noticed his departure.

Prystian nodded. "Why are you here?" he repeated.

The question perplexed her. What did he want her to say?

"Go deeper," he said, his voice resonating with authority.

"We volunteered to complete the Ascent," Zoen ventured.

"Excellent. But now go deeper. Why are you here?"

Zoen frowned as she grappled with the question. Why was she here? To punish her parents. Because she despised her dead sister. Shame twisted her gut. She had never hated Olen, not really. Sibling rivalry, maybe? No, because Zoen had never come close to being Olen's equal. Jealousy—the only word that fitted what she felt— stupid, pointless jealousy. If only her parents hadn't made her feel so pathetic all the time. They had tolerated her but never loved her. No, that wasn't true. The night she fled her home, their worry for her had been genuine. They had humiliated themselves by arranging thralldom for their own daughter to protect her. Even her father's attack had been an act of utter desperation. It would have ruined him if he had succeeded. Zoen had stared love in the face and failed to recognize it. She'd been an utter fool.

"Instinct brought you here," Prystian said. "From the moment of your birth, your parents, your teachers, even your friends, honed it until it became a part of you, as unquestionable as the air you breathe or the rock on which you stand.

"Cysgulur created his code to serve the people of Ophigee, but it ultimately enslaved them. It denied human nature. It denied the vagaries of life. It denied even the caprices of Fate. But, worse, it denied the contradictions at its heart. Did you bring contraband to the Whetstone?"

Zoen shook her head.

"You didn't?" Prystian pressed.

Zoen blushed. "No."

"You're unusual. The vast majority do. They break the law in doing so. Yet completing the Ascent absolves them. The law claims to condemn cheating and yet rewards them for their crime because in Ophigeen society, the means don't matter, only the result."

Zoen cleared her throat. "It's better than inheriting your status from your parents."

"And the Diarchs and their heirs—what of them? They are exempt from the Ascent." He waved Zoen silent before she could speak. "Don't bother to recite the myriad reasons this should be so. Those answers are drummed into every child in Ophigee before they think to ask the question. You are taught to see your rulers as cogs in the system, victims even, denied the life you take for granted to be superior, while they live in luxury in their palaces, enjoying the fruits of your labor. When a benefactor dies, their assets go to the state. Who is the state? The Diarchs, of course."

Many times, Zoen's parents had subtly mocked the Diarchs over the breakfast table. Behind their veneer of reverence, they regarded their monarchs as little better than house thralls. "Sometimes, it's hard to know who are the thralls."

"We all are thralls," Prystian said, "thralls to a law as cruel as any demon in Empyrosis. Some of us accept that thralldom, love it as if we chose it, close our eyes and stuff our ears to its injustices. The Whetstone is ample proof of the malady inflicting our society. It is supposed to be where an Ophigeen child enters adulthood, but it has become a place of slaughter. You've seen it for yourself. You were very nearly a victim of it. It certainly murdered your sister."

Zoen bristled. "She might still be alive."

"She's not. You know she's dead."

The truth could no longer be denied. The dam of stubborn hope cracked, and sorrow poured through her. She wailed and burst into tears. Prystian drew her to her feet and hugged her trembling body until her convulsion of grief passed. His embrace comforted her. It took her by surprise when he stepped away.

"The Stedfasters murdered her," she said, wiping her eyes.

"They slew her, but her true killer is the society that bred them. The Stedfasters prefer to turn to cannibalism than throw in their lot with us, because we threaten their dream of becoming benefactors. Ophigee and all its empty promises await them on the far side of the Ouroboric Gate. The Diarchy would welcome them back with open arms and happily forget your sister and the others they slaughtered. I'm sure they'd rise quickly to prominent positions. The ruthless always do."

Zoen's parents were administrants. What cruelties had they committed to secure their election? Perhaps thralldom would have been a mercy. "But what would you put in its place?"

"The abolition of thralldom and the Ascent for native-born Ophigeens. The dissolution of the Diarchy and the establishment of a new republic that serves its citizens, a true meritocracy."

Zoen forced a smirk. "Like Gyre." It, of course, was the epitome of corruption.

"Don't look for your answer in what exists. Forget your preconceptions. Dream of what might be." She thrilled as his hand touched hers. "The best vengeance you can have for your sister is to break the system that destroyed her."

He continued to talk, but the words lost their shape as they poured through her. All she could cling to was a feeling, a certainty that he was right, that Olen must be avenged, that Ophigee must fall. Zoen could have no loftier ambition than overthrowing the Diarchs and the depraved law that shored up their power. She would give her life to cast them down. She wept again for Olen, but also for Govren, and poor Nezon, and Drinith, and Oristan, and all the others sacrificed in the name of Cysgulur's law.

Prystian fell silent.

"I'm sorry." She wiped her eyes.

"Don't be," he murmured. "Tell me all about your journey here. Fisken mentioned a foreigner from Gyre, Drinith, accompanied your group..."

35

———

Drinith and Siga lay face down, their hands tied behind their backs. A boot between Drinith's shoulders pressed her to the floor as the woman, Redanaxan, remonstrated with another Upriser.

"They must be Stedfaster spies, Axalisan!" she roared. "How else would they have Olen's ring?"

"We found it!" Siga growled indignantly.

"How?" Redanaxan demanded. "Where?"

"We found it on her corpse," Drinith said. Could she trust them with the truth? As far as they were concerned, the Stedfasters must have killed Olen. "Before we left the Stedfasters' territory."

"You just happened upon her corpse and took her ring?" Redanaxan growled. "I don't believe you."

Axalisan, blushing beside her, cringed. Evidently, he was her subordinate, but he folded his arms and shook his head. "They could be telling the truth."

"I'll get the truth out of them by one means or another."

Axalisan cleared his throat. "I'm sure they'd admit being Anarchs of Empyrosis if you tortured them enough. But that's not our way. It's not Prystian's. Mistreating these prisoners won't bring Olen back. Or Lesym."

"Lesym's alive!" Drinith cried. "At least he was when we last met at the exit to the Stedfasters' territory. He should be on his way here with the other surviving candidates from our party."

"Then why isn't he here already?" Redanaxan asked. "How can I be sure you're not simply making up a story to save your hide?"

"Let Prystian speak to them," Axalisan urged. "He'll uncover the truth faster than any of us."

Redanaxan flashed a malevolent sneer at Drinith. "I'll talk to Prystian. In the meantime, put them in cells until he is ready to deal with them."

Drinith released a stale breath she had forgotten to exhale as the boot lifted off her. At Redanaxan's command, Uprisers hoisted her and Siga to their feet. Axalisan assigned four other Uprisers to his escort.

"You were playing with fire standing up to her like that," one of them whispered to Axalisan as soon as the party had rounded the corner.

Axalisan sighed. "She's not herself with Lesym missing."

Another Upriser snickered. "I'm sure she'll thank you later."

"I'm sure she will," Axalisan sighed.

The cells were shallow alcoves carved into a prison chamber. The Uprisers sealed the prisoners into them with gnarled lattices of dried roots. Drinith's wrists still burned even after the ropes had been removed.

From the far side of twisted bars, Axalisan appraised her, his arms behind his back. "If you have done nothing wrong, you have nothing to fear, despite the impression Redanaxan might have given." He pursed his lips as he rocked back and forth. "She and Lesym were... close. She's not normally prone to such unreasoned vindictiveness."

"That's good to know," Siga said, his voice brimming with sarcasm. Drinith's jaw tightened with a repressed smile.

Axalisan frowned. "On the other hand, if her suspicion proves to be correct..." He made a sour face. "We may not eat our enemies, but we know how to deal with spies."

Redanaxan, flanked by two Uprisers, entered the chamber and stalked over to Axalisan. "I've spoken to Prystian. I'm to take the boy to him."

"I'm a man, not a boy," Siga groused.

"You're not an adult until you complete the Ascent," Redanaxan said.

"You haven't completed the Ascent either, girl."

Redanaxan's grin scorned him. "That may change soon enough." At her sharp nod, her two escorts dragged him from the cell.

"You two, wait outside with him," she said. "I'll accompany you to Prystian's chambers." She and Axalisan watched them leave. Siga, rubbing his wrists, gave Drinith a final anxious glance as he disappeared through the door.

"I'm sorry about earlier," Axalisan murmured.

Redanaxan shook her head. "Nonsense. It's I who should be sorry. With Lesym missing..."

Axalisan waved his hand. "No need to explain."

"He was alive the last time I saw him," Drinith said.

Redanaxan turned sharply and glared at her, but a brittle composure quickly smothered her anger. "I hope you're telling the truth." She strode out of the cavern. Axalisan's party followed, leaving a single guard. He settled on a rocky outcrop and studied her with unnerving intensity. Drinith lay in the corner of her cell, closed her eyes, and wished him away, but the sound of him clearing his throat intruded on her attempt to sleep. She couldn't relax. The softest sound, real or imagined, jolted her awake.

Excited whispers came from the hall.

"What's happened?" the guard asked through the doorway.

"Lesym's back," an unfamiliar, more distant voice answered. "He's brought friends with him, candidates who escaped the Stedfasters."

If true, he could corroborate Drinith and Siga's story.

Had Siga mentioned the corpses to Prystian? If the Uprisers' leader was involved in their deaths, it would be easy for him to condemn Drinith and Siga as enemies of his revolution. His followers were so devoted, they'd never question him. Drinith could only wait and pray Siga didn't tell him about their discovery at the cascades.

She greeted Siga's return with a sigh of relief. She rushed to the bars across the entrance, grabbing them with both hands. The guard stood; Siga signaled him to relax with a casual wave. Something outside the cavern caught the guard's eye and he sat back down. Siga had strolled in with no escort, a sign he had won the trust of their captors. But something was wrong. Why was he frowning?

"I asked Axalisan to wait outside. I wanted to talk to you alone." He glanced at the guard. "Lesym and the others have just arrived." He fiddled with a metal band on his finger—Olen's ring. They must have given it to him after his release. Noticing her interest, he covered it with his other hand. "I'll make sure Zoen gets it." He struggled for breath as he spoke, as if he choked on pent-up rage. "At least she's a true Ophigeen. To think I had begun to trust you. My first impression had been right all along."

"What you talking about?"

"You're a spy."

Drinith sighed. "We've been through this already. I was wrongly accused."

Siga planted his hands on his hips. "You're a spy all right, but not for Gyre. You serve the Diarchy. In retrospect, it explains so much. Why else would they permit you to take part in the Ascent? Why did the drakers let you climb back up to talk Oristan down? The Diarchy sent you to investigate the dearth of candidates passing through the Ouroboric Gate. They couldn't send an Ophigeen without calling into question the Ascent itself. But you"—he stabbed a finger at her —"you're a foreigner, permitted to take part on a technicality. Your connections to Gyre would make you appear an ideal ally for any rebellion brewing down here. In short, you're perfect bait."

"No no no." Drinith shook her head. "This is madness."

"Of course, you would say that," Siga sneered. "Fortunately, Prystian saw through you." He strode toward the door. "Goodbye, Drinith. I won't waste my time wishing you good luck."

"Siga, wait!" Drinith cried, but he was gone. "Prystian is wrong."

"Prystian is never wrong," the guard said with a smirk. "If he says you're a spy, then you are one."

Drinith seized the bars. "What's going to happen to me?"

The guard shrugged. "You'll get what any traitor deserves, I suppose—an execution. Prystian will decide."

Drinith shook the bars in frustration, but the guard only laughed.

36

———————

The gap kept yawning between Quiescat and his companions. Panic jolted his heart every time they slipped from his sight. He dreaded being left behind.

"Hurry!" Lawster roared yet again. He threw up his hands. "Or I'll leave your worthless hide behind as a snack for the crag wolves."

Quiescat panted too heavily to think of a cutting rejoinder. His lungs burned. His heart quivered high in his chest. His legs and arms felt like useless weights, as if the muscles had turned to wood. If he dropped dead, it would be a mercy. But no, Drinith needed him. He had to keep fighting.

"Tinmar, get back there and help him," Lawster ordered, but the draker ignored his captain. His loyalty evidently didn't extend to risk being a crag wolf's meal. Quiescat might as well be on his own for the help his companions would be if one of the beasts caught him.

The others stopped and exchanged perplexed glances. Quiescat heaved himself up to them, relieved to have a moment to catch his breath.

"What is that?" Tinmar asked.

Lawster slapped Quiescat's shoulder so hard, his legs nearly buckled under the blow. "Perhaps our educated friend knows, because I certainly don't."

Quiescat warily approached the glistening black curve. Why was it so perfectly black? Usually, dreameries were transparent. There should be some hint of the rock on the far side. Something tapped against his chin. A sudden coldness gripped him as the cord of the pouch holding the Tear tugged against the back of his neck. He grabbed the floating pouch, felt the force pulling on the Tear against his sweaty palm. "It's a dreamery. We'll have to find another route."

Lawster's brow crumpled in confusion. "This shardlet is famous for its lack of dreameries."

"Nonetheless, this is one." Quiescat kept the Tear firmly grasped. "It is as solid as the rock that surrounds it—stronger. We will find no way through it. Best to turn around."

They hastened back the way they had come. They had to reach the last junction before—

A howl echoed down the tunnel, then another, and another, overlapping into a bestial crescendo. Quiescat and his companions froze. There could be no escape now.

Chains jangled. Boots trod alongside the patter of canine feet. Ophigeen soldiers accompanied the pack.

"We could surrender, take the green," Nykostar suggested.

Tinmar nodded enthusiastically. Lawster took a step backward, then another. "They mightn't give us the option. Are you sure we can't pass through the dreamery?"

The Fate Healer aided supplicants occasionally, but would she help the Larcener's successor? "I doubt it, but I can't say for sure," Quiescat said.

"That's better than a no," Lawster said, racing back to the dreamery. Quiescat and the others followed.

Clinging to the Tear, Quiescat stood behind the rest as they hammered their fists against the dreamery.

"Let us in!" Lawster demanded as he kicked the dreamery. Quiescat boggled at this outrageous sacrilege. What did the man think he could achieve by slighting Fate?

Nykostar raced down the tunnel toward the oncoming warriors. "I'm a born Ophigeen held against my will! I'll take the green! I'll take the green!"

"And you saved her, Oracle," Lawster muttered. "Guess you'll be rewarded but not in this life." He waved his sword. "I don't know about you two, but I'm not spending the rest of my days as a stinking slave." With Tinmar running alongside him, he charged down the tunnel toward an oncoming flood of Ophigeen warriors, their voices merging in a battle cry.

Fear tightened like a noose around Quiescat's throat. No, not fear—the necklace holding the Tear. In his fright, he had dropped the bauble and now the dreamery drew it, pulling the cord taut as if trying to choke him. He grabbed at it, squeezed his hand around it. The warriors, in reddish-purple and white livery and pointed helmets, kept coming like a torrent of steel, engulfing the two drakers. Quiescat cringed as they closed. He stepped back, toppled. The guards' fierce visages stretched in eye-popping wonder as the tunnel fell away.

And as it did, a wizened face filled Quiescat's vision. A golden earlobe peeped from beneath the great swathes of iridescent hair sweeping down over the woman's naked shoulders. The sneering gash of her mouth displayed rows of interlocking triangles of gold. Her crystal eyes, sparkling and inhuman, stared scornfully at him. It was her, the source of his now dead oracular power, the creature he feared beyond all else—the Fate Healer. Every terrified scintilla of his being urged him to flee, but he couldn't move, trapped in this unyielding amber of Fate. But she could. She moved through it as easily as if it was air.

He felt the icy touch of her golden hand against his throat. Ripping the pouch from his neck, she pried it open. Between a golden finger and thumb, she held the Tear. She molded it as if it was a piece of dough. She stretched it out into a long, gleaming spike. She appraised him a moment as a surgeon might. All Quiescat could do was watch in horror as she lifted it above her head like a dagger. If only his straining heart would burst and save him.

The point of the blade closed on his right eye like slow lightning. He willed his eyelids shut, but they refused to budge even a fraction. His whole body screamed, but no sound came from his mouth. With a final bright explosion, the blade struck. Both of his eyes transformed into two balls of burning pain.

He landed on rough stone, outside the dreamery. Cold white stars littered the black firmament. The noise of grinding wheels drew his attention to a passing cart. Its driver peered down at him and sniffed as if Quiescat was excrement on the street. The cries of hawkers selling their wares rose around him. Quiescat felt damp cobbles as he scrambled to his feet. Passersby eyed him with suspicion as he attempted to rub away the patches of dirt on his clothes. The wetness seeped through, soaking his back.

Beyond the crowds milling along the street loomed familiar temples. The Fate Healer had dumped him back in Gyre, days away by dragon from where Drinith fought for her life.

He leaped toward the sphere and hammered its glassy surface with both fists. "Let me back in! Let me back in!"

"Stop!" someone shouted behind him, but he wouldn't. He would keep pounding on the dreamery until he broke it, or it broke him.

Hands clamped on his arms and dragged him from the crystal sphere. He wriggled uselessly. "Please, have mercy. Let me in."

"That's up to the judge," one of the cordents holding him said.

"Where are you taking me?" Quiescat asked.

"To the jail for being disorderly."

That wasn't the only crime Quiescat had committed in this city. He was not merely a pauper, but a hunted felon. He'd end up a guest in Inkeep for the rest of his miserable days, mourning a princess, dead and forgotten, thousands of leagues away.

37

Zoen's jaw should have hurt from her ear-to-ear grin, but an intoxicating elation numbed any pain. She had never known bliss so perfect, so forceful, so vital. Nothing in her life had prepared her for this euphoria coursing through her. To sit in the presence of Prystian felt sacred.

"After we overthrow the Diarchy," he said, "the Ascent will kill no more Ophigeens like your sister."

Why did he have to mention Olen? A tear of grief and anger dropped into the ocean of bliss, only for its ripples to quickly dissipate across its placid surface.

"I know you've been lonely," Prystian said. "You've grown up a stranger in your own society. Your own parents spurned you. But here, you'll never be alone again. You'll be connected to a greater whole. You won't have to prove your worth every day of your life. You'll be valued for who you are."

She listened with breathless reverence, wallowing in his silken voice. It enveloped her like a blanket, safe and warm. She wondered how he could have such presence given that he must be only slightly older than her, but it was a dim notion, hardly worth retaining. She could have listened to his voice, so soft yet so sonorous, forever.

"You mustn't blame the Stedfasters. They are victims as much as you. Your vengeance must be directed at the system that sent you to the Whetstone. The Diarchy sent you and your sister to your deaths."

Prystian was right, of course. How could she doubt otherwise?

"The Diarchy is a hollow fiction. You've already witnessed the reality of its dogma laid bare in this place. Good people die for nothing here, sacrificed on the altar of manufactured tradition. Others are driven to cannibalism to survive out of misplaced loyalty to an institution that cares naught if they live or die. Death and chaos might run rampant in the Whetstone, but don't think above the Halo Sea is any better. Everyone lives in fear. The violence and cruelty might be more subtle, a veneer of civility might be maintained, but the life of a benefactor is just as fraught with uncertainty as any thrall's. Think back to your parents. Perhaps, behind their bravado, you may have glimpsed that fear from time to time, that gnawing disquiet caused by the precariousness of their status."

His sudden silence jarred her. He strode over to the window and gazed into the bright cyan sea on the far side. He plucked at the surface of the wall of water. Her jaw dropped at the realization there was no glass. If he pierced its skin, the sea would rush inside until the wound healed. "I must speak to your other friend now. As you leave, please tell her to enter. Don't worry. We shall talk again, you and I."

Being dismissed in favor of another stung, but Prystian had asked her to do something and she must do it. She hastened to the chamber where Toskar waited.

"Prystian will see you now." Vexation edged Zoen's voice.

Toskar's eyes widened. "Did everything go all right in there?"

"Everything's fine," Zoen muttered as she strode past her. Toskar's timid stare pierced her foul humor. It must be disconcerting to witness one girl leave in tears and the next angry. She paused, turned. Toskar froze midway between standing and sitting, transfixed by Zoen's stare. "Don't worry. He's really...nice." Her grin at the inadequacy of her description drew a smile from Toskar who proceeded hesitantly to Prystian's chambers. Zoen headed to the kitchen.

Why had she become so angry all of a sudden? Because of Olen. Prystian had steered her away from her natural inclination to take revenge on her sister's murderers. Her chest tightened. *I'm being unreasonable. I shouldn't blame Prystian. I should save my anger for the Diarchy.* It was funny how the heart ruled the head sometimes. She glanced around in case somebody was nearby. As if anyone could overhear her thoughts.

"There you are!" Lesym exclaimed as he appeared from around the corner. "I was coming to collect you. How did your interview with Prystian go?"

She flashed a smile. "He's amazing."

"He certainly is," Lesym said. "I was blessed to be his first follower." He rubbed one hand with the back of the other. "I remember my first encounter with him. I thought him a worthy successor to Cysgulur. My naivety back then makes me feel foolish. There was so much I didn't grasp. Of course, the Lawgiver is but a pebble at the foot of the mountain that is Prystian. He is truly a marvel, so wise beyond his years."

Lesym was right, of course, but why hadn't Zoen heard of this prodigy before? A magnetic personality like his couldn't have gone unnoticed. "He was a member of your group?"

"Believe it or not, I bumped into him in some random tunnel." Lesym's eyes sparkled as he laughed. "But I realized from our first meeting that I had encountered someone special."

As they entered the kitchen, Fisken leaped from her seat and rushed over. Recovering from the shock of her hug, Zoen mechanically reciprocated. Her lack of enthusiasm made her nervous. Shouldn't she be more in tune with Fisken's fervor?

"He's amazing, isn't he?" Fisken cried.

"Yes," Zoen said.

Fisken turned to the other Uprisers sitting on the bench. "I've never witnessed her so bereft of words before." Her voice quavered with laughter.

Zoen added her forced chuckle to the other's raucous guffaws and titters.

Fisken dragged her toward the bench as the other Uprisers urged her to join them.

"I'll see you later," Lesym said with a casual wave. "I have a few jobs to do."

As soon as Zoen sat down, the interrogation began. A bearded youth leaned forward. "You met Prystian. Is he not amazing?"

"What did he say to you?" a girl asked excitedly, eliciting a couple of shushes. "Hey, if Prystian didn't want her to say, he'd have told her so. He didn't, did he?"

"No," Zoen admitted. Perhaps it might have been easier to lie. Even a hint that Prystian might disapprove of their curiosity would silence them. They looked at her with such desperate hunger, their eyes pleading for detail. She shared everything except what he had said about Olen. That was nobody's business but hers.

"I'm really jealous of you," a second boy said. "I've met Prystian many times, of course, but that first time is so special. I remember being quite drunk with joy afterward."

"I was so dazed, I walked into a wall," the girl declared.

As the others around the bench rushed to share similar anecdotes, Zoen felt increasingly lost. Apart from her initial euphoria in Prystian's presence, Zoen's experience diverged strikingly from the declarations of ardor piling on top of her. No anger for them. Their bliss had continued long after their audience. Seizing on the familiar face entering the kitchen, she leaped to her feet. "Siga!"

A wan smile spread beneath his glower. At least he, too, remained detached from the prevailing fervor.

"How did you get here?" she asked.

The scowl deepened. "I came here with Drinith."

"Where is she?" Zoen asked, peering at the entrance behind him.

"The traitor's safely behind bars for now."

Zoen shook her head. "What did you say—?"

"I vouched for her!" he roared, thumping his chest. "Like a fool. Fortunately, Prystian saw through her. She's an agent of the Diarchy."

Zoen swallowed an expletive. "You hated her from the start."

He arched his eyebrows. "Apparently, I should have trusted my first impression."

A hand gently touched Zoen's arm. Fisken looked up at her with a mixture of sadness and pity. "We've only known her a few days." Of course, Prystian's condemnation ended any doubt she might have harbored.

Arguing with her, Siga, or any of the Uprisers was hopeless and liable to place Zoen under suspicion. She sat down and forced a smile. "You're right. Prystian knows best."

The neighboring Upriser patted her shoulder. Others nodded in approval. Siga filled a bowl with root mash and sauntered toward an empty bench, but the group around Zoen made space for him. With obvious reluctance, he joined them. She shied from his jarring glare, so out of place among all the oblivious, happy faces.

"I'm tired," Zoen said, looking for an excuse to escape his presence. "Is there somewhere where I can rest?"

"I'll show you to a dormitory," Siga said. If he noticed a few sly glances cast in his direction, he hid it well. She hesitated. How could she refuse his company without causing offense?

Fisken yawned and stretched. "I'll come with you. I'm wrecked."

"You know the way?" Siga asked.

"I had the tour earlier."

"Then you don't need me. I'll stay here."

"As you wish," Zoen said, doing her best to maintain a veneer of amiability. Thank dragons, she'd be free of that glower.

As they strolled toward the dormitory, Fisken tugged on Zoen's sleeves, drawing her gently to a halt. Zoen shied from her curious gaze.

"I couldn't help but notice you seemed unhappy back there. You know if you need to, you can always talk to me."

But would you understand? Zoen didn't understand herself. She heaved the corners of her mouth upward. "I'm just tired."

"Of course," Fisken said with a sympathetic pat of her shoulder.

"You seem happy here," Zoen observed. Fisken had arrived here at the same time as Zoen, only a few hours ago at most, and yet she behaved as though she had been an enthusiastic Upriser for as long as Lesym.

Fisken nodded, her grin swelling. "I feel at home here. I've found my leader, someone worthy of my loyalty. I feel complete." Her hand strayed to her cheeks, wet with joyful tears.

"I'm glad for you," Zoen said. Why could she not feel the same? Why did her encounter with Prystian stir up only anger? Zoen had never been much of a sister to Olen while she lived. Avenging her offered Zoen her best opportunity to make amends. But Prystian's redirection of her urge for vengeance from Olen's actual killers to the Diarchy felt like a betrayal of her sibling. Hot tears stung Zoen's eyes and crawled down her face.

Misreading Zoen's weeping as mirroring her own joy, Fisken seized her in a hug. Some small quiet part of Zoen yearned to pretend the girl embracing her was Olen, but at the moment of realization, revulsion overcame her. Olen was dead, murdered, eaten. Brushing the wetness from her eyes, Zoen gently extricated herself from Fisken's embrace.

Entering the dormitory was a relief. At last, Zoen might have some time alone to brood. A dozen unfurled bedrolls were arranged into two neat rows in the cavern. A girl busily swept the floor with a crude brush made from bundled roots. "You two must be new."

Before Zoen could introduce herself, excited voices rippled down the tunnel. A boy raced into the room. "We're all to meet Prystian in the kitchen," he gasped. "A Diarchist army is climbing up the Whetstone toward us." He bounded away.

A strange elation gripped Zoen as she followed Fisken out of the dormitory. At last, an opportunity to avenge Olen in some small way might be at hand.

The large crowd already filing into the kitchen stuttered forward with such frustrating slowness, Zoen worried she mightn't even get inside. On finally entering, she was forced to stand at the very back. There must have been fifty or more Uprisers crammed into the room.

Most sat on the floor unless they were lucky enough, like Siga, to secure a seat on a bench. Toskar stood at the far side of the room, evidently infected by the same rapture that gripped Fisken. Prystian's deputies stood with their backs to the fire, facing the crowd. Lesym wore his habitually placid smile, but Redanaxan looked grim, her hands folded into a cradle in front of her. A third deputy, a boy with a bright scar on his forehead, glared at the crowd as if ready to pounce upon the slightest provocation.

The room erupted in cheers and clapping as Prystian sauntered into it. As he moved through the parting crowd, hands reached out to touch him. He neither refused these intimacies nor acknowledged them. Joining his deputies, he exchanged a few words with them before turning to the rest of his followers. He opened his arms as though embracing their acclaim, emboldening them to praise him even louder. He swept his arms across each other and the cheers ceased. An expectant quiet settled over the gathering.

"We knew this day would come," Prystian said. "The Diarchs could not ignore the dearth of candidates reaching the Ouroboric Gate forever. It not only starves their regime of new adherents but ultimately calls into question their right to rule. The seed we sowed here is about to germinate. Soon, it will bear fruit. It is time for us Uprisers to live up to our name and take our rebellion beyond the Ouroboric Gate."

He paused as the crowd broke into a chant. "Prystian! Prystian! Prystian!"

A wave of his hand silenced them. "This will take great sacrifice on our part. Some of us will forfeit our lives."

His nod drew Lesym to step forward. "The approaching guards bring crag wolves with them. Their keen sense of smell may scupper our plans, so Eonusum"—Lesym nodded at the scarred boy—"has already picked a contingent to slow the Diarchists' progress. Another team under my command will fight them here."

Redanaxan paled. She bowed her head and wiped her eyes.

"The rest of us will play their prisoners," Prystian said, "and wait patiently in cells for the Diarchists to capture the camp. It makes no difference whether they let us finish the Ascent or force us to take the green. Either way, we'll finally rejoin Ophigeen society to foment the Diarchy's overthrow."

Gasps rippled through the crowd, only to fade to a dumbfounded silence. Behind him, Redanaxan wept. When Prystian spoke of *us,* he wasn't including Lesym among the survivors. It was plain from Lesym's stern demeanor that he, too, did not expect his contingent to survive their encounter with the Ophigeen soldiers. It must have taken every bit of Redanaxan's devotion to Prystian not to throw herself at his feet and beg for her beloved's life.

Prystian turned to her. As his arms closed about her, she shied from his embrace. They held each other, their heads resting on each other's shoulder, their faces turned inward from the crowd. She emerged from the clasp, still tearful but smiling. Lesym mouthed thanks to Prystian and hugged her.

"The latest arrivals will play prisoners," Prystian said, his gaze falling directly on Zoen, or perhaps she imagined it. "The rest will be assigned according to lot. Good luck, everyone. Remember, I'll be with you."

As he swiftly departed, Lesym picked up a small bowl. "Short roots with me. Long roots to the cells."

Eonusum plowed through the surging throng toward Siga's bench. "New arrivals, please identify yourselves."

Zoen lifted her hand, but Siga had to point her out to Eonusum. The Upriser impatiently beckoned her over.

"Follow me," Eonusum growled once Toskar and Fisken had joined them. He led them into another chamber with cells sealed with dried root meshes.

"This is a different jail to one where I was held before," Siga said. "How many prisons do you need?"

Eonusum sniffed. "This is where you'll be imprisoned until the Ophigeen guards arrive. Remember your story. We held you captive. We wanted you to join us, but you refused. We intended to hold you here until we broke you."

"Do you really think this will work?" Siga asked.

"The benefactors are as arrogant as they are shortsighted. You'll be telling them a story they want to hear. Any of you carrying weapons?"

Everyone handed over their knives except Siga, who was unarmed. Eonusum dispersed them to separate cells.

Zoen's throat tightened as Eonusum braced her door shut. "This plan had better work," she muttered under her breath.

"Good luck," Eonusum said, departing.

"Siga, what are you doing?" Fisken asked. Zoen rushed to the bars and peered out. Siga had used a knife to cut the cords holding the door of his cell shut.

"Siga, you lied to Eonusum and disobeyed his orders. You're going to get us all in trouble," Toskar pleaded.

"If you're happy playing the prisoner, then stay," Siga said. "But I'm leaving." He dashed to Zoen's door. She stepped back, afraid. Why was he bent on entering her cell? She stifled a scream as he flung open the door and barged inside.

"What do you want?" she demanded, her fists raised in a futile threat.

"Your sister's dead," he said.

"Tell me something I don't know," she muttered. "The Stedfasters butchered her. Prystian confirmed it."

"The Stedfasters didn't kill her," he said. "Prystian did it."

"Don't listen to him," Toskar warned. "He's talking rubbish."

"Siga hates you. He hates us all," Fisken said.

"He abandoned us when the cannibals seized us," Toskar said. "His behavior condemns him as an agent of Diarchy."

"Yes, he must be a spy, a traitor!" Fisken yelled.

"Here," Siga said. In his open hand lay a tarnished ring.

Zoen covered her gasp with her hand. "How?" She clutched the ring and studied it. There could be no doubt. It had been Olen's.

"We found it on a corpse at the bottom of a cascade far beyond the Stedfasters' territory. Whoever or whatever murdered her couldn't have been a Stedfaster. We have to rescue Drinith before the Uprisers kill her." He offered his hand. "Will you come with me?"

"Don't do it," Toskar warned.

Fisken shook her bars. "Don't listen to him. Don't believe his lies."

Dazed by Siga's revelation, Zoen let him drag her out of the cell. Toskar and Fisken's shouts followed her out of the chamber, but the ring held tightly in her hand deafened her to their warnings.

"We need to get out of here," Siga said. "It won't take long for their caterwauling to draw the attention of our jailers." Footsteps cut through the shouts. "Then every Upriser will be hunt—" Zoen shunted Siga into the nearest dark nook. "What the hell do you think you're doing?" he hissed as he wrested free of her grip.

"Somebody's coming. Listen."

A half-dozen Uprisers marched down the corridor—Sulgara and his patrol, led by Lesym. Bringing them to a sudden halt with a swiftly raised hand, Lesym turned to them. He looked pale and sickly. He wiped his mouth with a trembling hand. "Last chance to turn back. I know this situation is different from that of Kaliop. She had to be dealt with. She couldn't be trusted. This group, on the other hand, if there was more time..."

He stared at the ground, then looked up. "Remember, we have to do this to protect the rebellion. We are all willing to sacrifice our lives for it." He glanced at the entrance. Toskar and Fisken still yelled for attention. "If they truly believe in the revolution, they are willing to sacrifice their lives for it. If not, they deserve to die." He gave a resolute nod, as if agreeing with someone else's point.

Zoen held her breath. *This can't be happening. I must have misunderstood him.*

At Lesym's signal, the Uprisers drew their knives. Toskar and Fisken greeted their entry with relief.

"What can we do?" Siga begged, choking on the words. "There's too many of them."

The girls' excited babble turned to screams. As one fell silent, the other screeched all the harder.

"There was nothing we could do," Siga whispered to himself. "What could we have done? Nothing."

Zoen yanked him after her as she fled. Olen's ring cut into the fist wrapped around it. They needed to survive if Olen was to be avenged. And Fisken and Toskar. And Drinith, too. The Uprisers must have murdered her already. And countless other lives sacrificed for the sake of this insane rebellion. This madness had to stop. Prystian, the spider at the center of this web, must die.

38

Bound to a pole, Drinith watched Prystian pace the room, stop, smile at her, pace some more.

He paused before the window and peered through it. His tap of its surface sent ripples across it. "This is certainly a little miracle. The same force that holds the Halo Sea around Ophigee prevents the water from pouring inside. Cut it with a knife and it bleeds water for a while, but the wound quickly heals. We live in a strange world. The more you learn about its vagaries, the more you realize how little we know." He turned to her and grinned.

"You killed those unfortunates we found at the cascades," Drinith growled. It was pointless to pretend ignorance. He had already decided she was a threat.

His smile broadened. "You know, sometimes it's nice not to have to pretend to be someone you're not. Manipulating the human mind is a wearisome process. That's why I mostly talk one to one. Speeches to the masses are fine to reinforce messages, but it's so much easier to manipulate desire on an individual basis."

His candor must mean he intended to kill her. "I knew you must practice some sort of mind control," Drinith said. How else could he turn Siga against her so quickly and thoroughly?

He tapped his left temple. "Not mind control." He pointed to his chest. "Heart control. You must till their emotions first before you sow the seeds of thought. It's easy to win them over if they want to be won. Emotion binds them to you better than any argument. It leaves a seamless graft. The logic of emotion is impervious to rationality."

"Why bother to tell me all this?" Drinith asked.

Prystian shrugged. "Loneliness? An urge to brag? Nobody appreciates my artistry, not even my distant master, though I'm sure he is more than happy with its results."

"And he is...?"

"His Imperial and Immortal Majesty, of course."

"Magian."

Prystian nodded, his black eyes aglitter with glee. "Magian the Infinite. That's right."

Drinith's heart sank. *Has my campaign against Magian drawn his agent here?*

"Don't think yourself so important," Prystian sneered. Was it a guess, or could he really peer into her mind? "Magian laid his plans for Ophigee and the other scavengers of Noster long before your arrival. Do you imagine his ambitions could be bound to only one shard? His goal is nothing less than conquest of the Crevast. Ophigee, Gyre, and their rivals are all built on sand. They will all be washed away when the tide of Rhumgadian steel floods their shores."

I was right! Or rather, Quiescat was. Magian is bent on the conquest of Noster and beyond. At least Gyre's blockade has put a crimp on his plans for now.

"Somehow you've found a crumb of comfort in what I said," Prystian said bemusedly.

How did he...? Can he read my mind? Maintaining a blank expression, she seized upon the most ludicrous thought that she could imagine. *I love you.*

He showed no hint of surprise. He couldn't read her thoughts, but what about her emotions?

"You have a question?"

So, he could somehow intuit her feelings even when she did her best to conceal them.

He grinned. "I guess I've answered it for you."

"So this rebellion is nothing but a sham."

Prystian turned toward the window again. "My mission is to sow discord in Ophigee, weaken it, bring it down if I can. The Ascent is Ophigee's weak point. Making it hellish for the candidates causes them to question not only the ritual but also the society that depends upon it. It was quite easy, really. Poison the roots below to create famine conditions, then offer succor to the survivors. Kill those who prove resistant to my influence and turn the rest into willing soldiers against their own people."

"And how does this army marching up the Whetstone fit into your plans?"

He clapped his hands and rubbed them together. "Perfectly. I started preparing for that eventuality from the first day I arrived. I'm actually surprised the Diarchy has been so slow to act. In the little drama I've concocted to deceive the Diarchs' minions, some of my people will play the villains. They'll put up a valiant defense, but in the end, they'll be overwhelmed by their foes' superior numbers. I and the rest of my followers will pretend to be their prisoners and wait patiently in our prison cells for the Diarchists to seize the camp. It makes little difference whether they decide to let us finish the Ascent or force us to take the green. Either as thralls or benefactors, we'll return to Ophigeen society, connecting with other malcontents and fomenting rebellion.

"The very fact that guards had to scour the Whetstone in this manner undermines any pretense of the Ascent's sanctity. I'll make sure that when His Imperial and Immortal Majesty's dragons perch here, they'll be welcomed as liberators. Perpetual governorship of Ophigee will be my reward for my efforts."

A predatory grin spread across his face. "I must eat to sustain myself through the trials of the next couple of days. That's why you're here."

His entire face slackened and peeled back. His false hair dropped to the floor. The hood of skin retracted until it bunched at the back of his head. Drinith stared at the inhuman creature gazing at her with glossy black eyes. A writhing mess of blood-slick worms as thick a thumb covered the rest of its head. Its hideously wide mouth hung open, revealing a fat silver slug lurking within.

This couldn't be real. It had to be a dream. "Wh...what are you?"

The monster smiled. "We have many names, but we prefer to call ourselves cruons. Our home shard is so distant you've doubtless never heard of it. We were almost hunted to extinction there when His Imperial and Immortal Majesty offered us sanctuary. We were little better than animals, but he raised us up. He has collected the hated and the feared from across the Crevast and given them purpose."

How many of these creatures existed? What other horrors had Magian recruited?

It sauntered toward Drinith. "Enough talk. The hunger is upon me. How about a little kiss?" As its mouth fell open again, the worms stretched toward her, each one bearing the circular mouth of a leech.

39

Zoen peered around the corner. The guards outside the entrance to Prystian's quarters had gone, possibly summoned to hunt her and Siga.

"This is madness," Siga whispered. The murder of their friends had left him broken. "We should at least check if Drinith's still in her cell first."

"She's dead," Zoen insisted. "They were going to kill us because we *might* betray their plan. Prystian had already marked her out as a definite enemy. They killed her first."

"They're going to guess we'd come here."

"No, they won't," Zoen whispered back. "The Uprisers will assume we'll try to head toward the approaching Diarchists. They'd never imagine we'd come here." They couldn't guess the violent anger inside her, the hunger for vengeance, so strong it had dragged Siga here despite his reluctance. He still hoped to survive, but Zoen no longer cared about her life as long as she had her revenge.

"We have to get in there," she said. "We have to get in there *now*." *And kill Prystian.*

"It's too dangerous," Siga said. "Survival is our best revenge. If we warn the Diarchy's forces—"

"Prystian will have time to escape."

"He's more likely to pretend to be a prisoner."

Zoen shook her head. "We don't know what he might do. But we know where he is now, so this is the time to strike."

Two Uprisers approached the door, knocked, waited patiently for an answer.

"Well, I'm not willing to throw my life away tackling them," Siga asked. "If you want to take on two guards, be my guest."

She dashed for the entrance. Siga swiped a hand at her, too late to catch her. As she rounded the corner, the two Uprisers turned and stared at her. One rested his hand on the hilt of his sheathed knife.

"You're wanted in the kitchen," she said, bending over and panting. A glance behind her confirmed Siga hadn't followed. She straightened. "Lesym wants you."

The Uprisers exchanged glances, approached her with unnerving caution. Zoen forced a smile as the taller of them looked her up and down. His compatriot sauntered past her. Her hesitant glance over her shoulder met his suspicious stare.

"Why would Lesym send you?" the other guard asked, his eyes narrowing. "You're new, aren't you?"

She hesitated. Should she agree or—? The boy at the rear threw his arms around her, while the other drew his knife.

The boy holding her made a gurgling sound as he fell over, taking her with him. His lifeless corpse took the worst of the blow as they hit the floor. Gushing blood blinded her a moment. Above her, Siga, unarmed, faced the remaining guard. Zoen seized the knife stuck in the dead man's neck, wrenched it free, and stabbed at the other guard's leg. He kicked her hand, sending her weapon skittering across the floor. Siga pounced, grappling with his foe for his blade.

Zoen scrambled to her feet and drove her knife at the Upriser's side. He swung Siga into her path, but the distraction allowed Siga to wrench his knife from his grip. Siga slammed him against the wall, stabbing him until he slumped on the floor, lifeless.

Zoen's heart shriveled as she stared down at her blood-soaked clothes. Was this chill hollowness what vengeance felt like? She took out Olen's ring and stared at it to remind her why she had come here.

A shrill scream from Prystian's chambers snapped her out of her shock. She limped after Siga toward it. As they burst into the inner sanctum, a monster stared at her a moment before its shroud of skin rolled over its features and it became Prystian again.

"Kill it!" Drinith cried. "Before it slaughters us all!"

"Free Drinith," Siga said to Zoen. "I'll take care of it."

Zoen dashed over to Drinith and started to cut through the rope holding her. The drying blood on the hilt of her knife made it tacky. "Stop moving," she growled as the straining rope kept shifting, knocking the blade from its notch.

Drinith stilled. "Hurry up!" But in Zoen's trembling hand the knife could find no purchase. She glanced over at Siga. Why did he stand there, frozen, while Prystian closed? A smile stretched Prystian's face, the same one that had seemed so beatific and warm, now transformed into something monstrous. With a single stab to the throat, he felled Siga.

"Hurry!" Drinith croaked.

Prystian stepped over the gurgling boy. "Zoen, stop. The knife is so heavy and you're so weak and dizzy. Drop the knife."

The voice crept up Zoen's spine and permeated her mind, inducing a terrible wooziness. It had a tangible presence, almost like a scent, sweet and intoxicating. But the biting pain of the ring squeezed in her fist screamed at her not to surrender to the voice's seduction. Nothing must tempt her from pursuing vengeance for Olen and the others. She snarled to drown out Prystian's beguiling timbre as she manically carved the rope.

It snapped, the knife slicing Drinith's arm. The girl yowled in pain but threw herself forward, rolled across the floor and snatched Siga's knife. "His power can't work on both of us at once." With a long screech, she charged at Prystian. Zoen did the same.

Drinith froze, her face slackening with bedazzlement in the onslaught of Prystian's honeyed words. As his face turned toward Zoen, she drove her knife at it. He slapped her arm away and punched her in the gut, knocking her backward. She steadied herself and staggered toward him, gritting her teeth against the sharp jolting pain in her belly with every step. Drinith attacked Prystian, froze mid-step, again falling under the spell of his voice. With knife held ready to strike, he crept toward her, maintaining eye contact, still droning on with his incessant chatter.

Zoen charged at him. With all her might, she drove her knife at him, lodging it deep in the side of his neck. He turned toward her, wresting the weapon from her hand, and stared at her with such surprise, disbelief, and disappointment, she had to laugh. Drinith lunged at him and buried her knife in his back. For a moment, he tottered. The human face peeled back, again revealing the monster beneath. The silver tongue darted out with a plaintive squeal as the creature keeled over and slammed against the ground.

Zoen looked down into those glistening black eyes visible through the mess of dead tendrils, and wondered how such a horror could have ever held such power over her.

Tearing cloth drew her attention to Drinith kneeling beside her and making crude bandages. "We had best get that wound wrapped and then get out of here."

Panic seized Zoen as she stared down at her belly. From a narrow black line, a rivulet of blood poured down her tunic.

"You'll be fine," Drinith assured her. Distant wolfish howls rose up. "We just have to keep moving." She nodded to an opening. "That tunnel leads to the Ouroboric Gate."

"What about Siga?" Zoen asked.

Drinith knelt beside the boy and, checking for signs of life, shook her head. "He's dead." She rummaged under his tunic, pulled out a square piece of red cloth, and tucked it away.

"This is for him." Zoen turned again to Prystian's corpse and spat in the monster's face. Prystian blinked. Somehow, it still lived. Zoen screamed. As the creature tried to rise, Drinith threw herself upon it. She stabbed, stabbed again, and kept stabbing long after the monster had collapsed.

"Uh...think it's dead this time?" Zoen asked.

Panting, Drinith stood over the mutilated body. "I think so." She gave it a swift kick just to be sure; there was nary a flinch. She wiped her blade against a clean patch on her bloody clothes before slipping it into an ill-fitting sheath with difficulty. "We have to go."

Drinith dragged Zoen toward the exit. Every step was like a kick to Zoen's gut. Her foot hurt so badly, she could hardly walk on it. She tried to pull away, reaching for a wall for support. "Leave me."

Drinith's grip tightened. "You can't give up this near to safety. We can't be far from the Ouroboric Gate."

Another wolfish howl rose up—much nearer. Someone in the distance screeched. The Diarchists must have arrived.

"The Uprisers will be here soon to escort their master to the jail," Drinith said. "They won't take kindly to his slaughter. We have to move."

With a nod, Zoen lurched onward, spurred as much by that bestial howl as Drinith's warning.

40

Drinith pulled Zoen along. Zoen's wound was severe. She wouldn't last long without treatment. The girl knew it, too, judging from the way she met Drinith's reassurances with dubious looks.

"If crag wolves catch up with us," Zoen said, "leave me."

Drinith grinned. "You can't really expect me to throw you to the wolves."

"If you're not careful, your lame jokes will kill me before the wound ever does." Zoen's titter disintegrated into wheezing. Her legs buckled. Slipping from Drinith's grasp, she dropped to her knees. She bowed her head. "I can't go on. There's no point in both of us dying."

Drinith lifted her onto a rock. Zoen struggled as Drinith attempted to sling her across her shoulder.

"Stop it!" Drinith snapped. "It's hard enough to figure out how to do this right without you writhing all about the place."

Zoen relented, and Drinith finally secured her comfortably across her back. Thankfully, Zoen proved a light burden. With a last glance behind her, Drinith hurried along the scree-littered tunnel.

Higher and higher she climbed, sweating from the exertion. The heat of Zoen's body made her back hot and sticky. Zoen's dead weight caused her shoulders to ache. Drinith longed to reposition her burden, but she daren't risk dropping Zoen. The smell of blood filled Drinith's nostrils.

Zoen's head dangled limply, her eyes shut. Hopefully, she had simply passed out. No time to check for signs of life. Drinith hadn't the means to heal Zoen, anyway.

They couldn't be far from the Ouroboric Gate. Ophigee's healers could surely treat Zoen's injury. Desperation gave Drinith strength as she carried Zoen up a long incline.

A howl froze the blood in Drinith's veins. The crag wolf that made it must be close. The scent of her blood-daubed clothes and Zoen's wound must be strong enough for it to follow them. Drinith redoubled her pace. The scree shifted beneath her. She had to reach out with her free hand and steady herself. On one stone, a blotch of blood caught her eye. It looked too fresh to have come from her clothes. Zoen must be bleeding. The wetness across Drinith's back was more than sweat. Was that creeping coldness coming from Zoen or Drinith's own fear? Drinith kept moving, praying to the gods that Zoen's people spurned to keep her alive a little longer.

Another howl, closer. As Drinith ran, slipping and sliding on the scree, Zoen bounced on her back.

At last, a long horizontal well stretched before them. A relief of a snake coiled along its length. This had to be the Ouroboric Gate. But from behind them came the sound of something large bounding up the scree. They weren't going to make it. *So close.*

"Drop me," Zoen whispered. "Save yourself."

"No!" Drinith spat between gulps of air.

Distant figures filled the far end of the well.

"Help," Drinith wheezed. The guards didn't answer. Either they didn't hear her or they didn't care.

A menacing growl filled the tunnel. A paw scratched stone, then another paw, and another, gaining pace until they rolled together into a lope.

"Down!" a voice boomed.

Drinith fell to the floor; Zoen rolled off her back. Drinith crawled across the girl and cradled her chill body in her arms as she looked back. A wolf's jaws filled the tunnel. The beast climbed up the side of the well until it was upside down. Its charge shuddered to a halt, and it dropped into a whimpering, trembling ball of hair and horns. A springbow bolt made a dull thunk as it pierced the beast's hide and the creature stilled.

The guards must have killed it, but they didn't come rushing to Drinith's aid. The sound of more wolves bounding up the scree echoed down the tunnel.

"Help us!" she pleaded as she rose to her feet. She hadn't the strength to lift Zoen onto her back, so she dragged the girl along by the arms.

If Zoen dies because of this, I promise you'll all be sorry. Rage gave Drinith strength.

A burly man clad in white snakeskin dashed from the Ouroboric Gate. "Is she still alive?" he demanded. What was the administrant, Syascin doing here?

"Barely, but she'll be dead soon if we don't get her out of here," Drinith rasped.

As Syascin threw Zoen across his back, the crag wolf's corpse shifted. It flopped over as two more crag wolves crawled over it.

Drinith almost buckled under Zoen's weight as Syascin thrust the unconscious girl into her arms. "Get her to safety!" he growled as he readied his springbow. "I'll hold the crag wolves back as long as I can. Tell Zoen, I'm sorry."

Zoen's eyelids fluttered open. She reached out a hand blindly. "Father," she whispered, but Syascin had already turned his back on them. As Drinith dragged her away, he shot the springbow at the rapidly closing wolves. The leading wolf's charge stuttered as the bolts struck, but it kept coming.

Syascin retreated a few steps, reloaded.

Talon guards helped Drinith to pull Zoen through the gate only after she had crossed the threshold.

"Congratulations, Benefactor," one of them said apologetically.

"Help him!" Drinith yelled at the guards and pointed at Syascin. She made to dash toward him, but the guards held her back.

"It's forbidden to cross the Ouroboric Gate from this side," one of them said. "By doing so, Syascin Brave has damned himself."

"The Ouroboric Gate was open only because of the administrant's orders," another muttered. "It's normally kept shut unless a candidate knocks on it. There's no telling how the Diarchs will react to this breach in the law."

Drinith hadn't the strength to pull free from their resolute grasp. As the great metal door began to close, Syascin's bellow echoed along the tunnel. "Is she alive?"

As Drinith desperately looked for any hint of life from the insensate girl lying at her feet, a crag wolf slammed into Syascin. For the briefest moment, it looked as though he might hold his own against the creature, but the wolf swiftly overwhelmed him, its gnashing jaws splashing the tunnel with blood.

"For gods' sake, help him!" she cried, but the circular metal door shut with an irrevocable clang.

The guards' grip eased and Drinith slid to her knees beside Zoen. She pressed a hand against Zoen's lips but couldn't feel a breath.

"We'll take her to healers. They might be able to do something for her," a guard said, unable to mask his skepticism. As he and his colleagues carried Zoen away, Drinith followed, unsure if her friend still lived.

41

As the cordents slammed the cell door shut, Quiescat picked himself off the floor and surveyed the chamber. A pile of straw in one corner might have been intended as a bed, but it hardly sufficed as a pillow. The lidded slops bucket reeked with stale excrement. According to popular rumor, the cells at Inkeep were worse. But Quiescat was broke, so this dank, cramped cesspit of a room was as good as it might ever get for him.

Unless Elca Trajar helped him. His skin crawled at the prospect of meeting her again, but where else could he turn for aid? Surely curiosity would tempt her to visit if she knew of his incarceration.

He pounded the stout door with both fists. "Help! Help!"

"Quit your banging or I'll bang you," a muffled voice eventually roared back.

The threat only made Quiescat redouble his efforts. "I must talk to whoever is in charge urgently. It's a matter of life and death."

"I'm warning you one last time. Don't make me come in there."

But that was precisely what Quiescat wanted. He hammered even harder with raw knuckles and kicked the door.

"Right. I warned you," the jailer groused.

Quiescat stepped back as the bolt on the far side of the door squealed open. Would the jailer, in his rage, even hear his plea? The door swung against the wall and the jailer, a little, pale gray man, stomped inside. His lined face puckered in fury. Above his head, he brandished a wooden club. "Guess I'll have to beat some manners into you."

Terror rooted Quiescat to the urine-slicked floor. He winced in dread as he peered from behind the pathetic shield of his raised arms at the jailer bounding toward him. The man suddenly froze, his eyes rounding with fright. He fled out the door, slamming it shut behind him.

What in the name of Empyrosis had just happened? What could the jailer have seen that so appalled him? To soothe his jitters, Quiescat strode back and forth across the cell. He rubbed his face, trying to get a sense of its shape. Nothing struck him as unusual. Surely the guards who had arrested him would have noticed any deformity. Perhaps some drug or other that the jailer had consumed had made him prone to delusions.

The door opening cut short Quiescat's pacing. The jailer entered again, this time accompanied by two other yellow and black cordents —a female captain and her male subordinate. He might have been one of the pair who originally arrested him. Quiescat couldn't be sure. As the captain's gaze met his, she took a sharp intake of breath. "How did you miss that, Yodray?"

The other cordent shrugged and pulled a face. "I noticed his eyes glistened a bit. He was behaving as if he was drunk. I assumed he was."

The captain gave him an incredulous stare.

Sudden elation gripped Quiescat as he recalled his encounter with the Fate Healer in the dreamery; she had stabbed him in the eye. "Is there something unusual about my eyes?"

"They're like shimmering balls of glass," the captain said.

Had the Fate Healer replanted the Tear? Had she given him back his oracular power? "Bring me a mirror." Quiescat added as an afterthought, "Please."

The jailer and Yodray looked at the captain. She shook her head.

"You'll have to request that from the magistrate in the morning." They didn't trust him, and why should they? Quiescat might be a demon in disguise or some other horror from a distant shard. They would not risk their jobs and possibly their lives doing him favors.

"Then, please, at least let Meritocrat Trajar know I am here."

"I'm not in the habit of bothering meritocrats with such requests," the captain said. "Every second vagrant hauled into a low jail demands an interview with the Ducalion. But in this case..." She shrugged. "I'll see what I can do." Her mouth contracted to a thin, straight line that brooked no further plea or argument.

"Thank you," Quiescat said as his three captors backed out of the cell and shut the door. Suspecting that they wouldn't be back until the morning, Quiescat sat down on the straw bed and waited. He stood and paced the cell again, his eyes drifting often to the barred windows for the first hint of dawn.

The door's bolt squealed. Quiescat made a pathetic effort to brush the dirt off the front of his clothes in case Elca Trajar had come. His mussed condition must make him look like a beggar.

The door opened, and Jarma stepped into the cell.

Quiescat attacked her with his fiercest scowl. "Come to gloat?"

"I've been looking for you for half a red month," she said with ill-concealed exasperation. Impossible, he couldn't have been away for that long. "What did you think you'd achieve by running off like that?"

"Traitor!" Quiescat snapped. "Trajar warned me you'd succumb to Savarel's scheming."

Jarma shook her head. "I've a good mind to let you rot here for the trouble you've caused. I cannot believe you'd give credence to that serpent's slander."

"You weren't exactly rushing to defend me against Savarel's. I heard every word through the door."

"I was buying us time, you fool. I'm sure Savarel has no love for me either. I needed to give her the impression I'd make a pliant ally. I intended to seek your advice on the matter, but you were already making your escape."

"And what about Tazran? Why was she arrested? Why was the Gad Moon Inn raided?"

Jarma shifted guiltily and glanced down, suddenly taking extravagant interest in her shoes. "That was my fault," she said, looking up. "I turned to Cordent General Scylax for help in finding you and things got out of hand. I was even put under house arrest for a brief period while the cordent general investigated your flight. Tazran's free now and the damage done to the Gad Moon Inn has been repaired."

"And Woad?"

"He was captured outside a tenement temple, but escaped on the way to Inkeep. There's been no sign of him since."

"I should have trusted you," Quiescat said.

"You should have," Jarma said.

"I'm sorry."

"Save your apologies for the Widow. Tazran's fit to murder you over Woad."

"I can't blame her," Quiescat admitted. He had caused all this trouble, and for what? He had failed to save Drinith. "I'll talk to her."

"Stay clear of her for now. I'm not joking. She'd beat you to a pulp before you got a word out."

Quiescat nodded.

"What happened to your eyes?" she said. "They're as they were before you...yielded the Tear to Abecedar."

Quiescat's heart leaped. Could he really have regained his power? He smiled despite himself. "The Fate Healer did something to me. I'm not exactly sure what."

"I'll see if I can get you freed," Jarma said. "The cordent general was supposed to meet me here."

"Good morning, Meritorian." Greny Scylax entered, a fleshy, little man with a mean smile. His greeny yellow complexion reminded Quiescat of a corpse, but his watery blue eyes shone like gemstones. The yellow stripe extending down the right shoulder of his black robe identified him as a cordent general. He removed his black conical helmet with its rat king emblem, revealing the sparse gray curls still clinging to a balding pate. "I see you two are getting reacquainted."

"Can you release Quiescat into my custody?" Jarma asked. "I am happy to vouch for him."

Scylax puckered his lips as he rubbed his chin. "Technically, I should hold him until your meritocrat returns, but under the circumstances..." His tight smile stretched a fraction. "I bring you some good news. Drinith has survived the Ascent and plans to return to Gyre as soon as possible."

"Thank the gods!" Quiescat exclaimed. Jarma's face so mirrored his joy, it shamed him for ever doubting her.

"You asked for a mirror?" Scylax produced a looking glass from beneath his robe. Quiescat hesitated to take it from his outstretched hand. "Go on. Have a look."

Quiescat took it and angled it to reflect his face. Two crystal spheres stared back at him. He gasped, his free hand lurching to cover his open mouth. The mirror slipped from his fingers and shattered on the floor. The scattered shards multiplied his reflection across the cell. From the bigger pieces, the two spheres regarded him with detached coolness, but elation transformed the face in which they were set. Quiescat punched the air and whooped. Drinith was safe and the Tear of Fate was truly his again.

42

D rinith paced the reception room. It had been five days since she had passed through the Ouroboric Gate. She hadn't seen any familiar face in that time except Niod Humble, whom the Diarchy had assigned as her liaison. His congratulations had been so grudging, she had laughed in his face.

Her brief meeting with Siga's parents haunted her. It had been quite a bureaucratic struggle to arrange it with their benefactors. The thrall couple's smiles remained so fixed throughout the encounter, Drinith had begun to wonder if they understood their son was dead. Only as his mother took the little square of cloth did her obsequious grin falter. For that moment, she revealed herself as a broken woman, a grieving mother, and then the mask slipped on again.

Niod's entry made Drinith pause. It must hurt to squeeze his face into such a chiseled frown.

"Have you chosen which of the virtues you wish to take as your name?" he asked irritably.

It didn't matter what name she chose. She was going to return to Gyre at the first opportunity and never return. "Patience," she said with a bitter smile.

Niod's eyes popped wide. "Patience," he murmured under his

breath. He snorted. "Patience it is then. I'll inform the Keeper of Virtues. There's usually a celebration to mark it, but you may refuse it if you wish."

As much as she might enjoy going through with it to irritate her prickly liaison, it might delay her departure and she had no desire to stay here longer than she had to. "I will decline so on your advice."

He winced as if stung. "That is entirely your decision."

"Quite."

"The benefactor Zoen Perseverance wishes to visit you."

"Of course. I will meet with her," Drinith said, taken by surprise. Her own attempts to see Zoen had been sternly rebuffed by her physicians on medical grounds while she recuperated. So Zoen had chosen Perseverance. An apt name for her. The girl was a fighter.

"Very well," Niod muttered, stalking out of the room without a goodbye.

Drinith alighted on a chair and enjoyed the sunlight streaming through the window. The Halo Sea gleamed below all the way to the curved horizon.

The door opened. Drinith rose. Zoen hobbled inside. Even her smile looked frail.

"You look well," Drinith said.

Zoen dismissed her flattery with a wave of her hand. "You're too kind. My healers are not as skilled as preservators, and I cannot yet afford the cost of treatment at our Great Preservatory. I'll be many months recuperating." She wobbled dangerously.

"Perhaps we should sit down," Drinith pulled a chair toward her.

Zoen collapsed onto it. "Thank you." Drinith sat across from her and waited patiently while Zoen mopped her face with a handkerchief.

"I just wanted to thank you for your help," Zoen said. "I'd have died like Siga and the others but for you."

"It's a shame we couldn't have saved more," Drinith said. "They didn't deserve to be forsaken down there."

"I saw Nykostar," Zoen said. "In thrall green. I asked if I might buy her in time, but everyone discouraged me. It wouldn't be seemly under the circumstances. She's destined to be the chattel of someone with less of a grudge, if such a person exists. The surviving Uprisers were dealt with as harshly as any traitor or criminal thrall might be. You know…"

She left unsaid the grisly fact they had been tossed into the Crevast to burn in the inner sun. Drinith had been invited to attend the execution but declined.

They sat in awkward silence until Zoen spoke. "My mother has been very supportive since my return."

"I'm so sorry about your father. If I could have done more to save him…"

"I have no doubt of that," Zoen said. "He knew crossing that threshold doomed him. I was wrong about him, about everything. He was a good man despite his faults. From the moment I left for the Stepstone, he had maintained a vigil at the Ouroboric Gate in hope I might reach it. If he hadn't ordered the guards to keep the gate open, if he hadn't rushed to our aid, the crag wolves would have killed us. I plan to make sure his sacrifice isn't in vain."

She drew a circle with her finger on the armrest. "I have been apprenticed to Sabolio Wise. My mother says he'll be promoted to an affluentor very soon. Affluentors aren't allowed to take on apprentices, though they can keep any they had before their promotion. It's quite a coup. I had my pick given you and I are the only new benefactors to pass through the Ouroboric Gate for quite some time."

Drinith blushed. She wasn't a real benefactor, only an interloper who had gained her position through a legal loophole.

"You've heard that the Ascent has restarted?" Zoen asked.

Drinith sucked in a breath. She hadn't. "So soon? The Diarchy is composed of many intelligent men and women. Surely they must realize the Ascent is folly."

Zoen straightened on the chair. "Whatever do you mean?"

"Look at the countless candidates who died in the Whetstone."

Zoen's jaw tightened. "Prystian was responsible for everything that happened—the Uprisers, the Stedfasters, everything."

"But Prystian exploited the Ascent's innate weaknesses."

"I understand improvements have been made. More dragon patrols, for example."

"That's not enough," Drinith said. Surely Zoen must grasp that. She had come so close to dying down there. The Ascent had killed her sister. And her father. "The whole system needs to be overhauled."

"So Prystian claimed," Zoen said icily. "I should warn you not to test my friendship too much. I don't want to have to report such treasonous talk."

The realization slapped Drinith so hard, she lost the ability to speak for a moment. Somehow, they had gotten to Zoen—the Diarchy, her mother, Sabolio Wise, perhaps even her own pride. Now that the system she had despised benefited her, she had let herself be seduced by it. "I see."

"What do you expect of me?" Zoen demanded. "To overthrow centuries of law and tradition that has served Ophigee so well?"

And what of the dead in the Whetstone? How did Cysgulur's law help them? Drinith bit back her retort.

Zoen sat forward. "Tell me, is your homeland, Gyre, the utopia you want Ophigee to become?"

Far from it, but Drinith hesitated to reply.

"Exactly," Zoen said, regarding her coolly as she leaned back in her seat.

Drinith glanced about the room. Perhaps she misread Zoen. She might be afraid to admit her hatred of the Ascent here where someone could be eavesdropping. But her face gave no hint of such furtiveness, only frosty indignation. "You weren't so enthusiastic about Cysgulur's Law when I carried you to the Ouroboric Gate."

"I was delirious and dying," Zoen said. "I owe you my life, which is why we can speak so frankly. All I ask is that frankness doesn't extend to harping on about the faults of Ophigeen society as you perceive them."

In the uncomfortable silence that followed, Drinith struggled for something to say. They had little in common other than their shared experiences on the Ascent, and those were not the sort to inspire happy reminiscences.

"I must go," Zoen declared. "I have an appointment with my physicians."

Drinith helped her to the door. They made their goodbyes with brittle politeness. Drinith watched her hobble some distance down the hall. Closing the door, Drinith leaned against it. She couldn't even persuade Zoen to turn against a system that had come close to murdering her. What hope had she to convince Rhumgadians to risk their lives to overthrow their tyrant emperor?

The sooner Drinith returned to Gyre the better. But would the meritocrats accept an anointed benefactor as one of their own? She was a foreigner to begin with, but now her loyalties were apparently split between Gyre and its bitterest rival. She was Drinith Hax and Drinith Patience. Still, she'd find no help in this place. And Quiescat and the others would be waiting for her back in the Halcyon Republic.

43

The reflection in the mirror taunted Quiescat. His crystal eyes returned to him the appearance of being the Oracle again, but no visions came. Not even dreams leavened his deathly slumbers. He was still as blind to the future as any other mortal. He couldn't guess why the Fate Healer had returned the Tear. Her reasons remained as opaque as the future.

He glanced about his bedchamber. It all looked so solid and real, but Drinith's misadventure on Ophigee had shown how fragile their life in Gyre really was. Quiescat was an intruder here. Drinith and Jarma, as well. They'd be always seen as outsiders, particularly him. He felt like a guest who had overstayed his welcome but had nowhere else to go.

A clearing throat drew his attention to Fenvar. He hadn't heard the butler enter his room. "Yes?"

"There's a report of another dragon from Ophigee approaching. It should perch very soon. I took the liberty of preparing a casquar palanquin."

Quiescat nodded. "Yes, we'll leave at once." He and Jarma had gone through this ritual well over a dozen times since they learned

Drinith would return. At least, on this occasion, it was during the day and he didn't have to climb half-asleep out of bed. It didn't matter when a dragon hailing from Ophigee arrived. He was determined to be at the port waiting for it in case she was a passenger.

Jarma awaited him impatiently downstairs. "You took your time."

Quiescat mumbled an apology as he opened the door and invited her with a wave to lead the way. The palanquin waited at the bottom of the steps. The giant black birds that carried it jerked their heads to glare at their passengers, their bright orange casques forming permanent frowns above their beady red eyes.

"We'd be quicker walking," Jarma grumbled as she climbed into the cab.

"True," Quiescat said as he settled into the seat across from her. "But we need a palanquin for Drinith. She mightn't be in fit state to walk." They went through some variation of this conversation every time they set out for the perches.

The palanquin gently swayed as it moved forward.

"We've had a distinct lack of visitors since Drinith's survival became common knowledge," Jarma observed icily. "Not even your friend, Elca."

"She's no friend of mine!" Quiescat snapped.

"And invitations to feasts and ducal receptions have declined to a grudging trickle."

"I hadn't noticed," Quiescat admitted. He wouldn't be invited to either at the best of times. "Hardly surprising though. The jackals have learned to their chagrin that there's no carcass to pick and moved on."

"I hope you're right. I wonder how Drinith's elevation to an Ophigeen benefactor will impact the meritocrats' trust in her."

"They must know she had no choice."

"Ophigee is Gyre's fiercest rival. Drinith's loyalties were already suspect because of her royal heritage. Now her allegiances straddle an ancient and bitter enmity. We must protect her as best we can from any repercussions, but without an insight into the meritocrats' thinking, we're blind." She sat rigid, her jaw clenched, the dark frustration in her eyes mirroring his own sense of powerlessness.

"If Drinith arrives today, we'll soon learn their intentions." Quiescat meant the comment to be a crumb of comfort, but as it tumbled out, he realized too late it was the opposite. Cordents might arrest her the moment she disembarked.

"Don't be so sure," Jarma said. "The meritocrats are subtle. Look how two of them had sought to divide us."

The wound had been sutured with apologies and promises, but it had not fully healed. A tension remained, an unspoken distance between them.

"I did more to divide us than any meritocrat," Quiescat said bitterly.

"You did." Jarma peeped through the curtain. "But that's behind us now."

Woad waited for them at the perches. Much to Quiescat's relief, he had resurfaced a few days after news of Drinith had percolated through the city. He led them to the dragon's assigned landing spot, still empty, and they settled in to wait. After some time, the dragon, the *Yawning Maw*, swept in. Quiescat held the fluttering hood of his cowl against the fierce gusts from the beast's wings as it slowly descended onto the perch. It had been a humbling sensation to stand before such fierce wind the first couple of times he had done it, but now he was as inured to it as any draker or dockhand. The waiting restarted, this time for the customs party to complete its inspection.

"No sign of any other welcome party," Jarma said as she leaned against a canvas bale. Quiescat sat on a squat barrel, but its hardness quickly became uncomfortable. He straightened as the customs officers climbed the gangplank. Drinith strode up after them. Quiescat waved. She didn't see him at first, but as soon as she spotted him, she waved back. He resisted the urge to run to her as she approached. She halted, her joy turning to confusion. "Your eyes? How?"

He sighed wearily. "It's a long story. And even in telling it, I can't explain the how or the why."

"I've a long story myself," Drinith said, hugging Jarma.

Woad shook her hand. "Welcome back."

Quiescat reflexively scanned the pier. No sign of cordents, thank the gods. Drinith's embrace took him by surprise. Its warmth cheered him despite his awkwardness.

"There's a decent teahouse nearby," Quiescat said. "We can talk there."

The Faithful Brew, nicknamed unfairly by some wagging tongues as the Fatal Brew, was cramped and dingy, but the tea was flavorsome and its cakes, if of limited variety, were surprisingly good. Quiescat and Jarma had fallen into the habit of coming here after previous unsuccessful vigils for Drinith. The four of them took a table by a dirty window. "Tea and cake for four, please," Quiescat called to the owner.

"Which cake?" the scowling woman grunted.

"Whichever. They're all good."

A large pot of tea and bowls landed on the table, followed by chipped plates bearing four raisin buns.

Quiescat readied to tuck into his bun with gusto when he noticed Drinith's disinterest in hers. "The buns here are delicious. You should try them."

"I'm not hungry, thanks," she said. "I had expected to be arrested as soon as I disembarked." She poured a bowl of weak tea and cradled it in her hands, as if drawing comfort from its heat.

"I know the Ophigeen government sent a letter to Gyre confirming you were alive," Quiescat said. "As to the rest of its contents..." He shrugged. "I don't know. Only the meritocrats have that privilege." He chewed a bite of his bun. It lacked flavor for some reason.

"You've put on some weight," she said with no hint of criticism. She paused, adding leadingly, "Among other things."

"The eyes? Yes, that's quite a story."

Drinith sipped her tea. "I'm not going anywhere."

He told her of his journey to Ophigee, carefully editing its sordid beginnings, downplaying the discord between himself and her best friend. He braced for an interruption from Jarma, but she nibbled her bun without comment.

He took much pleasure in the widening of Drinith's eyes as he described his encounter with the Fate Healer and his bizarre return to Gyre.

"You must think I've succumbed to madness," he said.

She shook her head. "I passed through the same dreamery twice, but I didn't meet the Fate Healer." She shared her own story from her arrest to her final meeting with Zoen.

"Don't blame yourself," he said. "We're all trapped by our biases. You asked her to turn against everything she had ever known. You asked too much of her, at least for now."

Jarma scrunched her nose. "Her doubts lasted until they no longer benefited her."

Greny Scylax entered the tearoom, removed his helmet, and gave a sniff, both offended and offensive. "Good lady," he bawled to the owner, "give me a pot of your best tea, red as blood and brewed so thick a spoon could stand in it."

Everyone tensed as he approached their table. "Drinith, it's so wonderful to see you back in Gyre. Mind if I join you?" His tone seemed amiable enough. Nobody had entered with him.

Woad rose from the table. "Have my seat. I've lost my appetite. I'll be outside." He must want to check if any cordents lurked nearby. Quiescat envied his escape from Scylax's boorish company.

Scylax plopped into the seat and cleared away Woad's tea bowl by pushing it toward Jarma. "Go for a walk."

She directed a dumbfounded stare at him.

"That's right, you. I need to talk to your meritocrat and the oracle alone."

Quiescat cringed. The last thing he needed was for this sour meritocrat to reopen his barely healed rift with Jarma by favoring him over her.

She straightened. "I'm a meritorian. You can't talk to me like that."

Quiescat opened his mouth, but nothing came out. He didn't dare overstep his place by interceding on Jarma's behalf.

Scylax grinned. "I'm a cordent general precisely so I can talk to anyone any way I feel like. Go."

"Wait outside," Drinith said. "Hopefully we won't be long."

"I'm sorry you feel you've been insulted," Scylax said with blatant insincerity.

The scowl Jarma flung at the table as she exited the teahouse stung Quiescat. He should have spoken up for her if only to show he was on her side. *Too late now. Damage done.*

The owner planted a pot of tea and a bowl before the cordent general, then left without thanks. A strainer rested across the bowl. Scylax poured some tea through it. Evidently dissatisfied despite its deep red color, he tossed the strained leaves back into the pot and stirred it with one of the knives on the table.

"I'm surprised I didn't receive a summons from Thaxen the moment I disembarked," Drinith said.

Scylax's sly smile did nothing to improve his ugly face. "We thought it best if I met you first." Quiescat and Drinith both knew the cordent general hunted spies and traitors. He might be here to toy with them before he had them arrested. Jarma and Woad might have already been taken into custody outside.

Scylax picked up Woad's half-eaten bun and took a huge bite. He raised a finger. As he chewed, Quiescat held his breath. Scylax swallowed. "Good cake. Quite a find, this place. You two shouldn't look so worried. Drinith only did what she must to survive on Ophigee. The Parliament appreciates that. The Shopkeepers have signed up to the truce and joined the blockade. They're even agitating for a military expedition to Rhumgad to unseat Magian. Quite the conversion." He ate another bite of the bun. "Your mission has been an extraordinary success."

Quiescat and Drinith exhaled in unison. Scylax guffawed as he poured his tea again. He put his fingers in his mouth and whistled. Quiescat gasped, looked to the door, expecting a half-dozen cordents to swarm inside. Thaxen Savarel entered alone, her forbidding scowl sweeping the establishment before she locked her gaze onto the table.

"I'm not a dog to be whistled at!" she thundered as she took Jarma's vacated seat.

"Cake?" Scylax said sweetly, offering her the remains of Woad's bun. She waved it away in disgust. He finished it, washing it down with the contents of his bowl, and slid the remnants of Jarma's in front of him.

Thaxen folded her arms. Hatred burned in her black eyes as they fell upon Quiescat. She took a deep breath. "Drinith, the advice I gave to your meritorian with the best of intentions appears to have ignited some discord in your household. I apologize."

Quiescat sipped his cold tea to soothe a sudden tightness in his throat. *First, Thaxen comes to meet Drinith and not the other way around, and now, a fulsome apology, albeit delivered in a truculent monotone. Thaxen must be acting under duress. She won't forgive being humbled like this. The wise course would be to feign ignorance of her abasement to avoid adding to it and deepening her wrath.*

Drinith pouted. "I warned you, Thaxen, not to meddle in the affairs of my household. I hope this humiliation teaches you to heed my warning in the future."

No no no. What is she thinking?

Savarel slapped the table. "Who do you think you are?"

"A meritocrat and every bit your equal," Drinith said primly.

"You're a foreign upstart! A spit in the eye of our traditions!"

"You forget yourself, Thaxen," Scylax said, clamping a hand on her arm as she attempted to rise. Thaxen ripped free of his grip but sat back down. "I understand this is difficult for you, for both of you, but Gyre's welfare must take precedence over our personal likes and dislikes."

"Of course," Thaxen said, her rage cooling.

"You, Thaxen, have long held your position as Intelligencer General because of your exemplary service to the Halcyon Republic," Scylax said. "Our state has also profited from Drinith's endeavors and, I'm sure, will continue to do so, particularly now that the Oracle has regained his powers."

Quiescat felt like a fist was squeezing his heart. A lie had come close to destroying Drinith and him, and yet now Quiescat must live with another to protect them. He daren't disabuse the meritocrats of their false assumption that he could glimpse the future.

"We all must do our part to protect Gyre," Scylax said. "Are we all agreed on that?"

"Of course," Thaxen said.

Quiescat nodded, as did Drinith.

Thaxen stretched a calloused hand toward Drinith. They glared at each other as they shook hands.

Thaxen rose. "If we're finished here, I have other matters that demand my attention."

"Of course, Thaxen." Chewing on a chunk of bun, Scylax watched her leave. "You've made an enemy, it seems," he said to Drinith. "But you made it long before today. In any case, neither of you need to fear her. No meritocrat, no matter how powerful, would dare to stand against the will of the Meritocracy."

"What of Meritocrat Trajar?" Quiescat blurted, blushing.

Scylax emitted a wheezy chuckle. "Your powers have indeed returned, it seems. As Thaxen's star dims, Elca's brightens. The Meritocracy has made her a second intelligencer general, her remit focusing on our Rhumgadian interests. You'll be working closely with her from now on." He paused. "You look ill, Oracle."

"I'm fine," Quiescat lied as he tried to quell his fright. His crystal eyes would protect him from Elca, from all the meritocrats. He needn't fear them.

Scylax gathered the last bits of cake into a pile and swallowed them. He grinned. "You'll also be working with me." He licked crumbs off his thick fingers. "We know Magian found Ophigee's weak point and tried to use it to topple its government. He has proved to be the consummate strategist. What might his agents be up to now in the Halcyon Republic? They may be planning to destroy us from the inside, exploiting those very things that make Gyre what it is, the glues that hold it together. You two are going to help me find those agents."

Quiescat sipped his lukewarm tea. It appeared that the newfound admiration and gratitude of the Meritocracy would protect him and Drinith from its members' wiles for now. The new alliance with Ophigee brought them a step closer to the overthrow of Magian. They had been lucky so far, but how much longer would their luck last?

A WORD FROM THE AUTHOR

Want to find out what happens next? The best way to learn about future releases in this series and my other works my email list at https://photocosm.org/.

It would mean so much to me if you could leave an honest review wherever you purchased this story.

Feel free to email me at noelcoughlan@photocosm.org to ask any questions or share any comments you have about this book. I love to hear from readers.

Best wishes,

Noel

facebook.com/photocosm

twitter.com/noel_coughlan

goodreads.com/noel_coughlan

amazon.com/author/noelcoughlan

bookbub.com/authors/noel-coughlan

GILDED TREASON

The city state of Gyre once lauded Drinith as a hero. Now, she has become its most notorious fugitive.

Two of Gyre's most powerful oligarchs are murdered the same night, plunging the city into turmoil. Suspicion falls on Drinith. Her home is raided, her friends are arrested, and former allies turn against her.

Betrayal haunts her every step through unforgiving streets and alleyways. Everyone from the most chivalrous courtesar to the lowest sword for hire hunts her. Can she keep ahead of them until she unravels the city's darkest secret and reveal the identity of the killer?

Gilded Treason is the third book in the **Champions of Fate**, an epic fantasy series with fast-paced action and intriguing characters set in an immersive imaginary world.

THE GOLDEN RULE

Elf. Warrior. Saint. Heretic. Monster. Despised by two peoples, this pariah might yet prove to be the savior of both.

AscendantSun serves a dead god no longer. Adopting the religion of his human enemies, he haunts their mountains hoping to make amends for his violence toward them. Now, a figure from his past threatens to restart the ancient conflict he has struggled so long to put behind him.

War is coming again to the mountains, but this time he'll fight the legionaries he once commanded. Prophecy is against him. Numbers, too. But the greatest peril is the distrust of his human allies. Can he forge an effective alliance before the bright power rising in the east destroys them?

A Bright Power Rising and *The Unconquered Sun* compose **The Golden Rule,** a two-part epic fantasy for readers who enjoy unique and intriguing world-building.

SHORT STORIES

Fantasy:

No Escape

A desperate warrior carries a baby girl across a foreign desert. Although truth and honor are tattooed on his face, Tharo has abandoned both virtues in his quest to protect his charge. But it's only a matter of time before he fails her. Another man stalks them, a hunter no prey can escape, the dreaded Souldiviner.

(Prequel to *Fatal Shadow*)

The Parting Gift

Certamen's god is dead. His people, the Ors, are broken and enslaved. He finds consolation in the knowledge that they are safe... But not for much longer. Their masters, facing decimation by disease, are growing desperate. Desperate enough to kill.

(Prequel to *A Bright Power Rising*.)

The Fate Healer

Draston's master, Hamvok the Merciful, craves a royal ancestor or two to legitimize his tyranny. But every avenue of Draston's research has come to a dead end. To save himself from the tyrant's violent displeasure, he commits himself to a path of forgery and sacrilege, risking the wrath of not only the gods, but a far more terrible entity, the dreaded Fate Healer.

Science Fiction:

Alienity

Four short stories about aliens ranging from humorous to deadly somber.

Horror:

The Murder Seat

Dr. Herbert Marriott has a problem that only murder can solve. Luckily for him, the perfect weapon is locked away in his rundown museum, one too incredible for any court to accept. The cursed chair kills all who rest upon it. But will Herbert's victim be so easily drawn to her fate?

Hoard

Laura is Ger's last hope. His hoarding has ruined the lives of his neighbors and now threatens his own. As Laura and her team prepare to clean out his property under the glare of cameras, she is unaware that a sinister secret lies buried beneath the morass of junk, a dark truth waiting to kill her.

ACKNOWLEDGMENTS

I want to thank Pamela Cangioli and Kevin Cook from Proofed To Perfection for their editing work. I also must thank C.B. Moore for proofreading the book.

I also want to thank Nick Lloyd and Tanya Wheeler for beta-reading the novel.

Finally, thanks to the good people at MIBLart for their fantastic cover.

ABOUT NOEL COUGHLAN

Noel lives with his wife and daughter in the West of Ireland. He writes epic fantasy, science fiction and horror.

From a young age, he was always writing a book. Generally, the first page over and over. Sometimes, he even reached the second page before he had shredded an entire copybook. And you couldn't even recycle all that wasted paper back then.

When he finally wrote and published a book, it took him fourteen years. *The Golden Rule* became two books so let us be generous and say he averaged seven years per novel. He has gotten a little faster since then. Honest.

His hobbies include writing, reading, and reading about writing. He has written about reading in the past, and he still writes about writing. He would happily stay at home all day writing, but the family dog, Ruby, insists on taking him for daily walks.

His pet hates include writing his biography and referring to himself in the third person.